A Demon Summer

ALSO BY G. M. MALLIET

Pagan Spring

A Fatal Winter

Wicked Autumn

Death at the Alma Mater

Death and the Lit Chick

Death of a Cozy Winter

A Demon Summer

A MAX TUDOR NOVEL

G. M. MALLIET

MINOTAUR BOOKS

A THOMAS DUNNE BOOK

NEW YORK

A THOMAS DUNNE BOOK FOR MINOTAUR BOOKS.
An imprint of St. Martin's Publishing Group.

A DEMON SUMMER. Copyright © 2014 by G. M. Malliet. All rights reserved. Printed in the United States of America. For information, address St. Martin's Press, 175 Fifth Avenue, New York, N.Y. 10010.

Designed by Omar Chapa

www.thomasdunnebooks.com
www.minotaurbooks.com

The Library of Congress has cataloged the hardcover edition as follows:

Malliet, G. M., 1951–
    A Demon Summer / G. M. Malliet. — First edition.
        p. cm. — (A Max Tudor Mystery ; 4)
    ISBN 978-1-250-02141-0 (hardcover)
    ISBN 978-1-250-02142-7 (e-book)
    1. Police—England—Cambridgeshire—Fiction. 2. Murder—Investigation—Fiction. 3. Mystery fiction. I. Title.
    PS3613.A4535D47 2014
    813'.6—dc23

2014019884

ISBN 978-1-250-06625-1 (trade paperback)

Minotaur books may be purchased for educational, business, or promotional use. For information on bulk purchases, please contact the Macmillan Corporate and Premium Sales Department at 1-800-221-7945, extension 5442, or write to specialmarkets@macmillan.com.

First Minotaur Books Paperback Edition: September 2015

10 9 8 7 6 5 4 3 2 1

This book is dedicated in fond memory of crime writer Robert Barnard (1936–2013).

CONTENTS

ACKNOWLEDGMENTS

My thanks to the historians, guides, and staff of Fountains Abbey, Mount Grace Priory, Rievaulx Abbey, and Whitby Abbey for their vast knowledge, patience, and ability to make the distant past real to visitors from the twenty-first century. Particular thanks to the "sheep farmer's wife" of Mount Grace Priory and to the Rev. Peter Canon at Fountains Abbey for sharing their enthusiasm and knowledge. As always, all mistakes are my own.

Special thanks to all the warmhearted and welcoming people of North Yorkshire, England.

CAST OF CHARACTERS AT MONKBURY ABBEY

MEMBERS OF THE ORDER OF THE HANDMAIDS OF ST. LUCY

ABBESS JUSTINA—the superior of Monkbury Abbey

DAME HEPHZIBAH—the elderly portress of the abbey

DAME TABITHA—the guest-mistress, nicknamed Dame Tabby. A gruff woman with a bouncer's build, she makes sure guests of the abbey toe the line.

DAME INGRID—the kitcheness, affectionately called Dame Fruitcake

DAME OLIVE—sacrist and librarian, she has an encyclopedic knowledge of the abbey's long history

DAME PETRONILLA—the infirmaress, nicknamed Dame Pet. Responsible for the care of the sick and dying at Monkbury Abbey, she is also an expert on plants and herbs.

DAME SIBIL—cellaress of the abbey

DAME MEREDITH—formerly the cellaress, now a patient in the abbey's infirmary

SISTER ROSE—ex-military, now a novice preparing for admission to the order

MARY BENTON—a postulant preparing for the novitiate

ABBESS GENEVIEVE—a visitor from St. Martin's, the order's motherhouse in France

VISITORS TO MONKBURY ABBEY GUESTHOUSE

MAXEN "MAX" TUDOR—a former MI5 agent turned Anglican priest, he is sent by his bishop to investigate certain unusual disturbances at the old abbey.

CLEMENT GOREY AND HIS WIFE OONA GOREY—wealthy American benefactors of the nunnery. They want their souls prayed for and are willing to pay top dollar for the privilege. But where has all the money gone?

XANDA GOREY—their willful and wily teenage daughter

PALOMA GREEN—a flamboyant businesswoman who owns an art gallery in Monkslip-super-Mare, she organized a fund-raiser for the restoration and expansion of the guesthouse at Monkbury Abbey.

PIERS MONTAGUE—Paloma's lover, a photographer and expert on medieval architecture. He helped Paloma raise funds for Monkbury Abbey, donating several of his famous photos. Then the funds began inexplicably to dry up.

DR. LEROY BARNARD—a summer squall forces him to stay overnight at the abbey.

RALPH PERCEVAL, 15TH EARL OF LISLELIVET—Lord Lislelivet's sudden interest in religion seems out of character to everyone, particularly Lady Lislelivet.

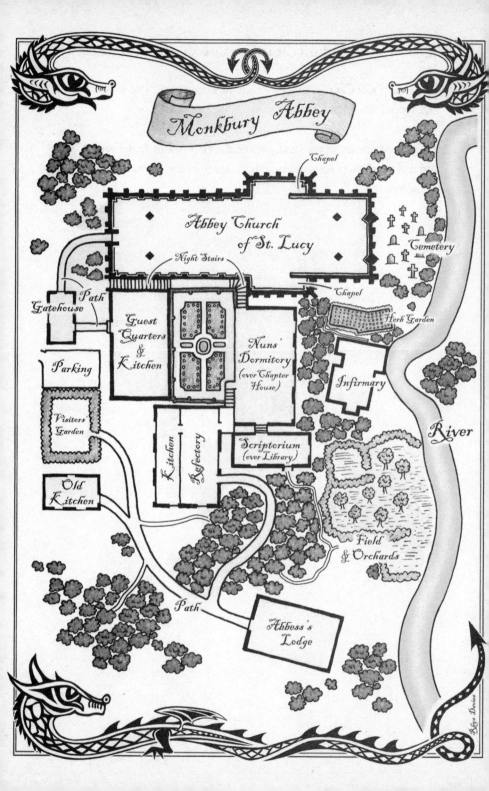

Monkbury Abbey

Chapel

Abbey Church of St. Lucy

Cemetery

Night Stairs

Gatehouse

Path

Guest Quarters & Kitchen

Chapel

Herb Garden

Parking

Nuns' Dormitory (over Chapter House)

Infirmary

Visitors' Garden

River

Kitchen

Refectory

Scriptorium (over Library)

Old Kitchen

Field & Orchards

Path

Abbess's Lodge

They had their lodges in the wilderness,
Or built their cells beside the shadowy sea;
And there they dwelt with angels like a dream.

—*Robert Stephen Hawker, Vicar of Morwenstow*

PROLOGUE

"I have a surprise for you," said Lord Lislelivet to his Lady, as the maid cleared the last course from the vast expanse of their mahogany dinner table. Lady Lislelivet may have imagined it, but wasn't there just the hint of a smile playing about the woman's lips as she hoofed her way back to the kitchen? Such impertinence.

Lady Lislelivet narrowed her eyes, watching Maybel's retreating back. The dog, Scooter, geriatric but game, shambled along in her wake, no doubt hoping for table scraps. Tonight Maybel wore a T-shirt with "Born This Way" scrawled across the back. Well, that explained it. Lady Lislelivet's many attempts to talk the woman out of jeans and T-shirts and into a more suitable maid's ensemble had failed. Still, it was hard enough to get any help these days, let alone good help. One took what one could get.

Lady Lislelivet dabbed at her lips with her napkin, to hide her annoyance both at the maid's constant mutinies and her husband's hints at pleasures to come. Hardened by the grindingly slow passage of the years of her marriage, and skeptical as to her husband's definition of "surprise," she did not look as thrilled by the prospect of a spousal treat as might have been expected. Often, Lord Lislelivet's surprises sprang up, to coin a phrase, when he was between mistresses. Altogether, Lady Lislelivet preferred it when her husband was kept otherwise occupied in London. That way, she could pursue her own surprises, unimpeded.

Her eye caught on the photo decorating the wall nearest her. Her husband was suffering buyer's remorse over it now, as it didn't really suit the grand style of the house. Caught up in the excitement of the auction, and goaded by her and by a few drinks, he had paid too much, never intending to get stuck with a dark, moody photo of Monkbury Abbey. What was really needed for this room was an oil painting of some august ancestor or another astride a horse.

Setting down her wineglass, Lady Lislelivet uttered a cautious, "O-o-oh?" just as Maybel returned with two plates containing lumpen mounds of something that looked like currant-studded coal.

"Yes. You remember the fruitcake? The little gift from the nunnery? I thought it was time to pry open the tin, as it were."

Was that all? Still, he knew how she hated fruitcake. Or he had known at one time. His fleeting concern for what she liked and disliked had gone with the wind, like so much else.

On further reflection, it was jolly difficult to imagine anyone apart from her husband actively liking fruitcake. A holdover from his days of being coddled by a nanny, no doubt. Only the upper classes would think to poison their children with the type of vile nursery puddings they went in for. She wouldn't use rice pudding to plaster the walls of her house in Tuscany. Just for one example.

"It's not Christmas," she said flatly, as Maybel practically threw the plate down before her. Typically, she had forgotten to provide a pudding fork and, on being reminded, plunked down a soup spoon instead. Lady Lislelivet had begun to suspect Maybel saw through m'lady's thin aristo-cratic veneer and was choosing these not-so-subtle ways to show her con-tempt. So much for working-class solidarity.

"It is Christmas wherever you are, m'dear," said Lord Lislelivet.

Gawd. It was hard to say which was worse: the fruitcake or the forced gallantry.

Lady Lislelivet felt a little scruffle of fur against her ankles. Scooter, begging as usual. She handed off a few bites to him when her husband wasn't looking and scooped the rest of the fruity sludge into the napkin on her lap.

Fortunately, as it turned out, the dog ate only a bite or two. Scooter didn't seem to care for the fruitcake, either. So his symptoms were much milder than those of his master.

Lord Lislelivet, wolfing down his fruitcake with carefree, childish pleasure, would be taken very ill, indeed.

PART I

Matins

Chapter 1

ABBESS JUSTINA

The community as a whole shall choose its abbess based on her goodness and not on her rank. May God forbid the community should elect a woman only because she conspires to perpetuate its evil ways.

—The Rule of the Order of the Handmaids of St. Lucy

The bell rang for Matins in the middle of a dream, as it often did. Just as she would enter deep sleep—the scientists had a name for it, she could never recall what—Abbess Justina of Monkbury Abbey would be awakened by the bell. This was seldom a welcome interruption, for Abbess Justina was given to pleasant dreams, more often now dreams of her childhood and young girlhood, dreams in which she would be reunited with her family.

It was just before the hour of four a.m. in June, *millennium Domini* three.

She rose from her narrow bed and dressed by candlelight, first sluicing cold water over her face. Long habit made short work of putting on her habit. It was a costume whose basic design had not changed much over the centuries: atop her sleep shift of unbleached muslin came a black tunic that fell to the tops of her feet, tied at the waist by a cord, and over that was worn a scapular of deep purple—an apron of sorts that draped from the shoulders, front and back, falling to below the knees. The fabric at her wrists was smocked in a pretty diamond design halfway to the elbow, to keep the voluminous sleeves in check. For all its antique quirkiness, it was a practical garment, suitable for work and contemplation, the fabric handwoven on-site of wool from abbey sheep. On ceremonial occasions and in chapter meetings, she would carry her staff of office with its little bell as a symbol of her authority and her right to lead. Otherwise her garb was identical to that of the women in her care.

Nothing in her costume was made of leather, not even her sandals, just as nothing in her diet came from the flesh of four-footed animals. In summer, out of doors, she wore wooden clogs. Meat was forbidden except in cases of illness, when the Rule of the Order of the Handmaids of St. Lucy allowed it for those recuperating.

The abbess still marveled at herself, at times—that she, such a clothes-horse in civilian life, such a devourer of women's style magazines, given to obsessing over the latest hair products and adornments, had adapted so readily to the habit. Coco Chanel would probably have said the classics never go out of style.

Well, it was difficult to say what Coco might have made of the clogs.

Now Abbess Justina's hair was cut straight across the nape; every few months or so she would wield the scissors herself, chopping away without the aid of a mirror. She wrapped her shorn head tightly in a linen coif, pinned at the crown, a bit like Katharine Hepburn's in *A Lion in Winter*. Over that was draped a black veil, held in place by a narrow woven circlet meant to represent a crown of thorns. She tied a linen wimple like a baby's bib around her neck. Pinning the coif and attaching the veil took some minutes, the pins stubborn in her swollen fingers. The headgear was worn back from the forehead to allow half an inch of hair to frame the face, the single concession the order had made to modernity. In medieval times a wide starched headband would have sat atop the coif fitted so tightly around face and neck. Truth be told, in those days the headdress might have been adorned with pearls and gemstones, for the nuns of yore had on occasion had a little trouble keeping to their vows of poverty, not to mention chastity and obedience.

Abbess Iris, who had ruled just before Justina, had been the one to decide on the need for a change of habit, modifying the traditional style. The color of the scapular was the major innovation—the deep blue-purple of the iris, as it happened. Of course it all had to be done with the bishop's approval. The poor man had been absolutely flummoxed at having to pronounce on women's fashion. He was shown several sketches, like a magazine editor being presented with the new fall line, and vaguely pronounced any of them suitable. The deep purple he thought a slightly racy departure from the centuries of black but he did not demur.

Dear Abbess Iris. A flamboyant but wise character. Now long gone and buried in the cemetery of Monkbury Abbey.

Pity, thought Abbess Justina, she'd done away with the style that covered much of the head, for it would have hidden the gray hair and jowly neckline that had come as one of the booby prizes of late middle age. But at least the coif and veil still prevented one from looking like a Persian cat as the gray hair gained its ruthless hold, like kudzu. If they'd had to change anything, she thought they might have shortened the skirt length, for she still had strong, shapely legs, the product of a youth spent climbing the Welsh mountains like a billy goat. Nun or no nun, one liked to present a pleasing and vigorous appearance to the world.

Following timeless ritual, Abbess Justina reverently kissed a large wooden cross before draping it round her neck to lie flat against her chest. Around her shoulders she now buttoned a hooded mantle. In choir she would pull the hood over her head, for warmth, and for privacy. It also was wonderful for hiding the expression. A strategic bend of the neck and tuck of the chin and one could be as private as a turtle pulling in its head. These little things, these momentary escapes into solitude, were what made living in a community possible.

Learning how to put all this on without the use of a mirror was one of the biggest challenges of the life. She had yet to see a novice who didn't need extra time in the morning to get all the bits and bobs attached in the right order.

That and mastering the Great Silence. And learning to loosen family ties. And any other number of things that made people wonder why they bothered, these crazy women who chose to live in the middle of nowhere, working and singing and praying. There was no answer to that, but the single-word answer that could be given was Joy. We do it for Joy.

Sometimes she caught a glimpse of herself in the plate-glass window in the kitchen: she liked taking a turn at kitchen duty now and again, even though she was exempt from chores because of her position. It kept her humble. It also gave her access to the thrum of what was really going on in the convent. Interplays and tensions and little personality conflicts that could grow into internecine warfare if not closely watched. Lately there had been undercurrents, of that she was certain. They seemed to date to the time of the earthquake, she thought, registering the irony. That had been a year ago, almost to the day, and measuring just over five on the Richter scale, it had rocked the abbey from side to side in the most terrifying way. For who in England was used to earthquakes?

But the "emotional" undercurrents seemed to be connected with the appointment of the new cellaress, an unpopular choice in some quarters, she knew. The sisters had formed an attachment to Dame Meredith in that role, but of course there was no question of her being able in her weakened condition to carry on that heavy responsibility. And of course forming attachments of any sort had to be discouraged.

There was also some tension surrounding the new novice, although whether she was the cause or the result wasn't clear. She was not adjusting well to the religious life, which was never a completely easy transition for anyone. Post-traumatic stress disorder they called it now. PTSD. And no wonder, given Sister Rose's history. The new postulant, as well—Abbess Justina had serious reservations about the new postulant, Mary Benton. Vocations were so rare nowadays. She supposed it was possible they had, unwittingly, lowered the standards somewhat, allowing Mary to sneak past.

Still, what was clear was this: There was great change afoot at Monkbury Abbey. What was uncertain in Abbess Justina's mind was whether all that change would prove to be for the good.

PART II
Lauds

Chapter 2
MAX TUDOR

Most willingly and in all humility shall the followers of St. Lucy
heed the voice of authority, avoiding disobedience, which leads
to sloth and chaos.

—*The Rule of the Order of the Handmaids of St. Lucy*

A few weeks after Abbess Justina's reluctant awakening, as the days
stretched lazily toward the time of the summer solstice, Max Tudor, the
vicar of St. Edwold's Church in Nether Monkslip, also woke early. To be
sure it was not nearly so early as the ordained rising time of the abbess
and the other nuns at Monkbury Abbey, but Max was still bleary-eyed
from last night's tryouts and rehearsals for the Christmas ensemble band,
and to him it felt like the crack of dawn. To say the least, the tryouts had
not gone well, becoming an occasion for umbrage, hurt feelings, and the
occasional stifled sniffle. Max knew he had no one to blame but himself—in the bulletin enlisting participants he had, in a moment of typical
good-hearted optimism, specifically stated that all ages and skill levels
were welcome to participate.

The results were predictably appalling, but there had been moments
of a sort of goofy charm, especially for the parents who had invested
heavily in some expensive instrument or other for their offspring. Who
knew there were so many nascent trombone players in the small world of

Nether Monkslip? Or that cymbals were making such a comeback? Die-hard music lovers found excuses to leave early, but Max was duty-bound to stay, an expression of astonished delight pasted onto his face. Even he, being somewhat tone-deaf, grasped intuitively that this was not the sort of music designed to soothe the savage breast.

Still wondering how he might diplomatically break the news that there might not after all be room for everyone who wished to participate in the band, Max dressed quickly, discovering in the process that his best cassock had not come back from the dry cleaner's, leaving him with a choice between a torn cassock and one with yesterday's egg down the front. As he was to learn later, his housekeeper Mrs. Hooser had forgotten to hand in his order when Fred Farnstable came by to collect the dry cleaning. Fortunately the vestments he wore for the service would cover the spillage, but he'd have to return to the vicarage to change into civilian clothes before starting his morning rounds. He had promised to drop in on Mrs. Arthur at the urging of a social worker from the school in Monkslip-super-Mare, who suspected Mr. Arthur had begun using the children's lunch money to finance his rounds at the local pub.

He made toast and carefully boiled an egg in the vicarage's archaic, stone-floored kitchen. After a quick glance at the headlines (a Shiite group calling itself the "League of the Righteous" was operating is Iraq; one had to admire the staggering humility in the choice of a *nom de guerre*), he set off along Church Street to take the early service. The day was warm and sunny, with flowers spilling from window boxes wherever he looked, the weather nicely cooperating to lift his mood.

But the morning was not done with him yet. He and the acolyte looked high and low in the St. Edwold's vestry but could not find the gluten-free wafers. Mrs. Penwhistle was allergic to gluten, and as she was a regular at the early service Max always made this concession for her. Finally, Elka Garth at the Cavalier had to be prevailed upon to provide a small loaf of gluten-free bread for Max to bless.

On his return to the vicarage an hour later, he found a note on his desk in Mrs. Hooser's scrawling hand: "Call your Bishop."

Oh, fine, thought Max. The bishop seldom rang unless he had a bone to pick. In fact, he rarely telephoned at all. Which is what made this sudden directive rather alarming. Max considered asking Mrs. Hooser if she knew what the man wanted but was stopped by the utter futility of the idea. Mrs. Hooser's weakness—her refuge, in fact—was that she lived in a state of blissful unawareness: she simply did not notice much of anything that went on around her.

He put the note aside for the moment, in favor of the even more dreaded task of going over the accounting books for St. Edwold's and the two other churches in his care. There was an unexplained spike in expenditures under the "Misc" column. He saw it was for antibacterial wipes and realized it was for the OCD family group that had started meeting at St. Cuthburga's in Middle Monkslip. There were the normal expenses for facial tissues for the Al-Anon meetings, where a certain amount of tearful sentiment was to be expected. Max had always thought it interesting the AA meetings, by way of contrast, went through far fewer tissues.

This minor sort of expense was meant to be offset by donations from the group members themselves, but times were hard and the donations voluntary, so Max had become adept at shoving money from one fund to another to cover the cost. He also had been known to dip into his own pocket when all else failed. He couldn't allow a few pounds to keep anyone from getting the help they needed.

Having exhausted all diversions, and knowing it couldn't be delayed forever, he reached for his phone to call the Bishop of Monkslip.

A few steps away from the vicarage, Elka Garth worked behind the counter of the Cavalier Tea Room and Garden. Her cotton sweater was smeared with flour and blueberries, and it was buttoned crookedly, possibly because the top button was missing, anyway. She had tied back her hair in a bright paisley scarf to keep it out of her eyes as she worked, and she had made a rare experiment with makeup. With her eyelids dusted with lavender to go with the purples and reds in her scarf, she looked, thought her friend Suzanna, lounging over her second cup of coffee, rather pretty, if in

a hectic sort of way. Almost as if she were planning a night on the tiles—
which was out of the question, if one knew Elka.

It was too bad she led such a difficult life, keeping the shop and her
son alive single-handedly, but the beauty of the woman was that she seldom complained. She just created her glorious pies and biscuits and her
marzipan creatures—the tiny owls and geese and hedgehogs and mice
lovingly crafted and generally sold online, to be shipped off in their little
individual nests of glittery paper—and somehow in this endeavor reality
seemed to get pushed aside, to be dealt with on another day. Her current
passion was for perfecting a shortbread recipe that incorporated dried lavender flowers.

Elka's young assistant Flora was either contributing to or mitigating
the chaos in the kitchen, it was difficult to say. But in any event Flora's
apron, unlike her employer's, always was pristine, devoid of flour or batter.

Elka seemed to have a talent for surrounding herself with young
people who did not like pulling their own weight, thought Miss Agnes
Pitchford, watching the scene with her gimlet-eyed stare. Miss Pitchford,
long retired after terrorizing generations of youth in the village school,
sat near a window of the shop, reading that day's news and maintaining
a running commentary on the inbred foolhardiness of Britain's elected
leaders. Miss Pitchford was an anachronism, a throwback to the era of
the sedan chair—a living testament to a time when elderly spinsters were
borne about in boxes to attend missionary teas and strew their visiting
cards about the village. They might make the occasional brief stop to administer relief to the ungrateful poor of the village, but more often their
aim was to attend a private Bible exposition or violin solo or some similarly gay and carefree pastime. That they did all this dressed head to toe in
draperies and scarves and hats with feathers and netting and hatpins and
other impediments to comfort, regardless of the season, was probably a
testament to their inner and outer fortitude. England was built upon the
steely backbone of such stalwarts as Miss Pitchford and her kind.

Much else in the village had not changed—had refused to change.
The Nether Monkslip Parish Council, in particular, was fearless in stand-

ing in the way of progress. Much of the struggle against modernity was to no avail. But that didn't prevent the villagers from fighting the good fight, at home and in the trenches.

Suzanna Winship, sister of the local doctor, shared a table with Miss Pitchford in surprising peace and equanimity, for two personalities more diametrically opposed would be difficult to imagine. Suzanna, outrageously gorgeous and sexy Suzanna, had been one of Max Tudor's most ardent admirers in the days before Max and Awena had so clearly staked their claims to each other.

Max's arrival in the village some years before had electrified the female population of Nether Monkslip, for Father Max Tudor was everything they could have wished for: kind and decent (basic requirements, of course, for a vicar), handsome and youngish (both huge bonuses), rumored to be a former MI5 agent (so daring and mysterious!), and most of all, unattached and, to all appearances, available. A lamb ripe for sacrifice on the marital altar.

The women got busy, either throwing themselves at his feet or pushing their nieces, daughters, and best friends at his feet. Church attendance skyrocketed, along with volunteerism for the little chores that needed doing around the church—cleaning the brass and silver, preparing the vessels for the Eucharistic services—that might bring them into closer proximity with Max.

But Max remained steadfastly uninterested. Oddly oblivious to the frenzy of self-sacrifice and do-goodery he had unleashed. Perhaps he thought it mere coincidence that the St. Edwold's Altar Guild suddenly had more helpers than it could accommodate, all of them female, and all of them jostling for a slot in the rotation. The church flower rota became a free-for-all, with the altar bouquets growing more grandiose and extravagant with each passing week.

Max remained clueless to all the passionate storms of hope and speculation. And just when the women's bafflement and frustration at his cluelessness reached a fever pitch (particularly in the case of the village's anointed vixen, Suzanna Winship), it was noticed that Max was to be seen more and more often having dinner at the home of Awena Owen, the owner of Goddessspell. Or seen having dinner with her in one of the handful of restaurants in Nether Monkslip. These occasions became so frequent, no branch of the village grapevine could for long accept the "maybe they're just friends" theory that was tentatively bruited about. Finally at Awena's winter solstice party, it became glaringly apparent that Max and Awena could not keep their eyes off each other. When Awena's pregnancy began to show a few months later, it became apparent they could not keep their hands off each other, either.

The village phone wires lit up. It was a *cause célèbre*, of course, and a bit of a scandal, but that it did not become fodder for malicious gossip was a testament to the high esteem in which both parties were held. The villagers loved both Max and Awena (by now dubbed "Maxena") and could only wish them well. The villagers even managed to conduct a rare conspiracy of silence, for Max's bishop had so far been spared the news that his most charismatic priest was in a now-permanent relationship with the village's only neo-pagan. What the bishop might have done had he known, no one could guess, but no one, not even the scandalized Miss Pitchford, was going to help the man out with a "thought-you-should-know" telephone call. Adopting an atypical transcendent detachment, the villagers decided as one to let the fates handle it.

Elka Garth of the Cavalier Tea Room and Garden had been much surprised at Suzanna's easy capitulation to the situation. It was not as if the High Street of Nether Monkslip was littered with highly eligible bachelors.

"It's nice of you to be so gracious about it," Elka had said after Awena's winter solstice party, when the attraction between Max and Awena had been evident to the most obtuse observer.

"Why are you surprised?" Suzanna had demanded. "I can be gracious. I can out-gracious the Queen when I feel like it. Goddammit."

Alrighty, then. A little more work on the self-awareness front and Suzanna might be good to go, thought Elka. But she did seem to have recovered from the "loss" of Max, whom she had never in fact stood a chance of winning over. The arrival of Umberto Grimaldi in the village to open the White Bean restaurant with his brother had created a much-needed diversion. Fortunately Suzanna's interest in Umberto seemed to be reciprocated, even though the late hours he necessarily kept at the restaurant were a frequent source of complaint.

Miss Pitchford had at this point in her reading reached the lines describing the less-than-altruistic activities of a peer known frequently—too frequently, it was felt—to darken the doorway of the House of Lords.

"Lord Lislelivet," she said, "certainly is a mover and a shaker; I'll say that much for him. I knew his mother. Lovely woman. Breeding tells. I am not certain *he* is all that he could be in the scrupulousness department, however." Her voice trilled the vowels in "scrupulousness," like an opera singer going for the high notes. "But that I suppose is too much to ask these days. The noble families are all going to rot. Why, in my day . . ."

But no one paid her any mind. The name Lislelivet only had meaning for people like Miss Pitchford, who read her Debrett's the way she read her Bible. "How do you say 'jackass' in French?" Suzanna was asking Adam Birch, owner of The Onlie Begetter bookshop, who sat beside her. They had been talking of a recent resident of Nether Monkslip, a man with a flawless French accent, now sadly deceased, although whether sadness was called for in this particular man's case remained a point of debate.

"I'm not sure," said Adam, turning to Mme Lucie Cuthbert, who squared the table where they sat. "*Comment dit-on* 'jackass' *en français?*"

"I think it's just 'jackass,' but you should wave your hands about as you say it, holding a Gitane."

"Ah."

Elka, from behind the counter, paused long enough in her trek to and from the kitchen to ask, "Has anyone seen Awena today? I wanted to ask her about food for the ceremony."

"I saw her working in her garden on my way over here," said Suzanna. "She said she'd probably join us for elevenses."

"You're talking about the . . ." Miss Pitchford stopped on a deep breath, finding it difficult to go on. "The public union of Max Tudor and

Awena Owen, of course?" She was not at all certain how she felt about these loosey-goosey, New Agey goings-on, and would in fact have roundly condemned them as a travesty had she not been as fond of both Max and Awena as she was. The whole situation was a scandal that would not have been tolerated in her day. A travesty up with which no self-respecting Anglican bishop should put. But it was, she had to concede, a new day.

Elka nodded, smiling as she dried her hands on a linen dishtowel worn through to near transparency. "The handfasting ceremony. I wouldn't miss being there for the world."

"People will come from miles around," Suzanna agreed. "Umberto is taking me—I managed to get him to agree to one day away from the restaurant. Besides, he's donating some of the food."

Miss Pitchford sniffed loudly and went back to her reading. The duke of York was rumored to be getting remarried, and the duchess was at long last to be given the old heave-ho from the marital home. As a scandal, The Situation between Max and Awena simply paled by comparison.

"I thought you had decided never to trust a man with beachy waves in his hair," said Elka. Suzanna had expressed certain doubts over whether Umberto really was spending all his free time in the White Bean.

"I came to realize that was natural. Can he really help it if he has better hair than I do? Besides, that was all just a misunderstanding."

"I am so glad to have lived to see the day," said Adam. "Max and Awena. Such a perfect couple. And with a baby on the way!"

A sound between a sniff and a snort erupted from Miss Pitchford. This situation with the baby was too much for her, and she looked sternly over the top of her newspaper to indicate that a change of topic would be *quite* in order.

"At least there is one thing we can be sure of: she's not after his money. Vicars don't make any money," said Suzanna.

"I shouldn't think that was the primary consideration on either side," said Elka. "It's obviously a true love match." And she sighed, releasing a little cloud of organic coconut flour into the air.

Five minutes later, they looked up as one as Awena Owen came gliding in. She did not waddle, noted Suzanna, the way most women in the advanced stages of pregnancy would waddle. Due in September, now mere weeks away, she moved like a train on a track, her long skirts hiding her locution. Or like a tugboat pulling an invisible ship into harbor. That she managed to look both womanly and, yes, sexy in this inflated condition was completely galling to Suzanna, who admitted no competition in the sexy department.

Still, it was Awena, and even Suzanna found it hard to hold a grudge where the much-beloved neo-pagan was concerned.

"May I have a glass of kale juice, Elka—if it's not too much trouble?"

Elka had begun offering fresh-squeezed juices like kale, cucumber, spinach, celery, and carrot. After some initial reluctance ("I don't eat anything green that doesn't come with dressing," Suzanna had said, speaking for many), most of the villagers had been won over. While Elka's pastries would never be resistible, the sales of healthier choices were gaining ground. Elka herself had lost a stone, most of it around her middle. Just the week before she had introduced shots of fresh ginger, wheat grass, and acai juices. Awena was her best customer in the wholesome juices department.

Nothing about her delicate condition had slowed Awena down—in fact, she was busier than ever, sought after by the BBC and by publishers wanting her to write a tie-in cookbook. But Awena, rather than reading the contracts on offer, had spent much of the past several days harvesting chamomile flowers and raspberries to dry for the tea she shared with Max and sold in her shop.

She'd spent the evening before blessing and packing a collection of oils and botanical bath salts, the blessing meant to revive any plant spirits dampened during processing. Nothing shipped out of Goddessspell without an earnest Goddess-speed from its owner. It was rather as if she cracked open a bottle of organic champagne against the side of all her offerings to the public.

In May, Awena had held a special candlelight "Pray for Peace" ceremony in the room at the back of her shop, an observance in honor of

Vesak, more commonly known as Buddha's Birthday. Awena had on several occasions lured a young Buddhist monk to make the journey to Nether Monkslip to lead a meditation class. In the beginning, he had caused a genteel commotion on the steam engine train from Staincross Minster in his orange robes, his demeanor unruffled as he was transported in silent dignity, his eyes closed, but now the regular passengers were used to him and asked after him to the conductor if he didn't make an appearance on a given Saturday.

Recently, Awena had been helping Tara Raine prepare for a weekend of rest and rejuvenation at the meditation retreat being hosted by Goddessspell at a nearby seaside resort. They would be offering heart-centered yoga asanas, deep relaxation via yoga nidra or "yogi sleep," blissful harmony of One-Being using the chants of nada yoga, peaceful integration of the soul through guided imagery, healthful walks along the sunlit shore in honor of the goddess Shakti Vahini, and wholesome balanced meals. "A regular Tie-Died Hippie Granola Bliss-out," as Suzanna had described it to her brother. A feature at the retreat would be a healing session using the techniques of energy medicine of the Peruvian Andes, along with a session of rune healing as practiced by the ancient Norse people.

Suzanna felt this was rather a scattershot approach to healing: If you threw enough runes at a problem something was bound to stick. But she had come to a grudging acceptance of the power of spirituality that seemed to permeate Nether Monkslip via the medium of Awena. And, as Suzanna often said, she was willing to try anything once. She was always rather hoping Awena would offer Tantric sessions at Goddessspell, but so far no luck.

While loudly maintaining her complete indifference and skepticism, Suzanna had been among the first to sign up for the weekend. Knowing that absence made the heart grow fonder, she thought it was time to put a little distance between herself and Grimaldi the Elder and his beachy waves.

But as she told her brother, "If I should return home wearing a knitted headband, a cockleshell bracelet, bells on my toes, butterflies in my hair, and bleating about my Spirit Master, please know that you have my advance permission to have me committed."

At least it was all grist for the mill of Suzanna's new position as magazine editor of the *St. Edwold's Parish News,* which she had renamed the *St. Edwold's Herald,* insisting that it gave the enterprise a more global reach. It was a position of enormous power but one she was determined, she said, not to exploit.

"There will be no phone tapping on my watch," she had solemnly assured Max.

Max hesitated. After all, this was Suzanna. Suzanna who had bribed four-year-old Matt Nathall to vote for her entry in the St. Edwold's Crumpet Bakeoff.

"You do realize," Max had said, "it is a simple matter of announcing local weddings and baptisms and the church flower rota and times for services. There's nothing global about it, Suzanna."

"Oh, but it can be so much more," Suzanna had replied, eyes aglow with the spirit of tattling pioneers like Pulitzer and Hearst. Her background in journalism made Suzanna a natural for the job, and she looked forward to shining a light on village doings.

Max, fearing an outbreak of yellow journalism of the worst sort, had emphasized that the position was temporary. It was, in fact, a task he enjoyed doing himself when time permitted, but his other duties continued to encroach. Not to mention his continually being drawn into murder investigations. Not to mention the approaching demands of fatherhood.

Fortunately for everyone noteworthy in the village, Suzanna, also head of the Women's Institute, had additional fish to fry. Her planning for the Christmas Fayre was already well underway, spawning deadly strife typical of preparations for the Harvest Fayre, although with nothing to match the lethal animosity of previous years. Unlike her predecessor in the role, Suzanna ruled with a firm but benevolent hand.

She was just putting the finishing touches to an org chart when Tara Raine went by the Cavalier on her bicycle, headed to teach a class at

Goddessspell, a yoga mat tilted at a rakish angle in the bike's basket. She rang the bike bell as she passed.

"I should get back," said Awena, declining Adam's offer of a chair. "I've spent the morning gathering plants from near the Sacred Spring on Hawk Crest. Next to the monastery, it's the most peaceful spot in the village. I left an offering for Sul."

"Okay, I'll bite," said Suzanna. "Sul?"

"She's a goddess of fertility and healing. The Celts worshipped her."

Suzanna eyed Awena's stomach.

"It certainly seems to be working. I'll stay well clear, thanks for the warning."

Awena smiled. "Just don't drink too much of the spring water. It's very rich in minerals and needs to be diluted with ordinary water."

"No worries."

Chapter 3

MAX AND THE BISHOP

No one should repeat to those outside the abbey the business of
the abbey. Nor should anyone sent to conduct the business of the
abbey return with idle tales of what she saw or heard while outside the gates, because that causes the greatest harm to all.

—*The Rule of the Order of the Handmaids of St. Lucy*

Max had been summoned to the presence of his bishop. It was getting to
be a regular routine. Only this time, it appeared, he was not to be probed
with uncomfortable questions about either his private life or the little
bursts of publicity that had erupted around the various recent murder
cases he had helped the police solve. The bishop wanted something from
Max, as he had made clear on the telephone. It was a situation so rare as
to be both flattering and alarming.

So Max showered and quickly changed back into his cassock—the one
with the egg on it, the lesser of the two evils on offer to him that day. He
threw the Land Rover into high gear and set off for Monkslip Cathedral,
the seat of Max's spiritual and temporal leader, the Bishop of Monkslip.
Along the way he left the torn cassock for repairs at the Stitch in Time.

"I think you might have some food on your cassock," observed the Right
Reverend Bishop Nigel St. Stephen.

"Yes, I do apologize," said Max. "I tried to wash it off, but I'm afraid I made things rather worse. It was the only one I had available . . ."

"Your housekeeper . . . my secretary did mention she seemed a bit vague on the phone."

"Mrs. Hooser gets rather overwhelmed," said Max. In fact she was unsatisfactory in every conceivable way as a housekeeper, but even worse as a mother to two small children. It was for Tom and Tildy Ann's sake that Max was willing to put up with quite a lot from Mrs. Hooser. The vicarage gave them somewhere to go and be reasonably well-supervised when they were let out of school.

Max looked around at the spacious headquarters office of the Bishop of Monkslip. The bishop's office was like a Shangri-la to Max, with all its spiffy new computer equipment twinkling in the sunlight admitted by ancient mullioned windows. The bishop's screen saver rotated a series of photos of Monkslip Cathedral as it appeared in all seasons. The credenza where slumbered a high-speed printer also held a photo of the bishop's wife and four daughters, but it was an updated version from the one Max had seen before. In this image, the eldest daughter, her gamine face peering as through a forest of curly auburn hair, looked to be of an age to go to university. Max commented on it.

"She is going into the theater," the bishop informed him, "and has applied to the RADA in London. I find it all rather disquieting. I don't know where she gets this show-biz gene from."

Max started to point out that the church with its pomp and circumstance, not to mention its costumes, was not without a theatrical element, but thought better of it.

"I was hoping she would choose a more stable profession," the bishop went on. "The thing of it is, she has real talent. If you'd seen her in *Troilus and Cressida* you'd have been amazed. My little girl! I just don't want to see her go into a profession where rejection is so much a part of the game."

"The urge to protect her must be overwhelming," said Max. He was thinking of his and Awena's unborn child, due in mid-September, an event he anticipated with equal parts stark alarm and unbridled happiness. What would he do to protect his child? What wouldn't he do?

"It is a constant battle between wanting to let her fight her own bat-
tles and wanting to send her off to a nunnery where she might be safe.
Might being the operative word. Which brings me to the reason I asked
you here, Max. Thank you for being willing to drop everything at a moment's notice."

"Your secretary indicated it was important."

"It is. Whether it is urgent, I'm not certain. I hope not."

"Financial shenanigans?" said Max. "In a nunnery?"

Five minutes later, the bishop was still filling Max in on why he'd
been summoned to Monkslip Cathedral. He'd begun with an introduc-
tion to what he thought were the key pieces in an emerging puzzle.

"I'm afraid so," said the bishop. "At least, the appearance is of financial shenanigans. Money that was fund-raised to expand and refurbish
the Monkbury Abbey Guesthouse has largely disappeared. It is too early
to say if or how the money was misappropriated. I'm rather hoping it just
got, you know, misfiled somehow. Put into Column A when it should
have gone under Column B."

Max, reflecting on the books for Nether Monkslip and his other two
churches, rather doubted this was possible, but then the nunnery probably
had many more revenue streams to account for than his tiny parishes and
bigger weekly expenses than facial tissue and antibacterial wipes.

"And for a nunnery," the bishop was saying, "just the appearance of
such a thing is alarming. If it turns out to be true . . . well, I don't have to
point out the implications for you. It would tarnish the image not just of
Monkbury Abbey but of the entire monastic tradition, which, as you also
know, has had a lot of scandal to live down in the past."

A dodgy nunnery? Not unheard of historically, as the bishop had
said, but surely nowadays . . .

Max's imaginings were gleaned from hazy school lectures, in which
out-of-control monks and nuns of the Middle Ages had gone from wealth
to decadence, as often happens when power goes unsupervised.

"I don't really know a lot about the order," said Max.

"You are not alone," said the bishop. "They are members of the Order of the Handmaids of St. Lucy of the Light, which is an offshoot of the Benedictine tradition. A far-reaching tendril, I might add. They are following many of the precepts of the sixth-century *Rule of St. Benedict*, but for obvious reasons they have had to make some modifications over the centuries. Corporeal punishment, just to mention one thing, is not so much in vogue as once it was. The Lucians used to be considered a bit of a fringe group, actually, but those days are long past."

"Yes, now that you refresh my memory, the name sounds familiar," Max said. "The Lucians. Still, I've only just heard of the order."

"I am not surprised. They are quite a small group: thirty-one in number, down from hundreds of members in their glory days. Although lately they have established a bit of a presence in the world. I understand recruitment inquiries are up."

"It's quite an ancient order, isn't it?"

"Yes. The original Lucians were founded as a double order in the eleventh century by people wanting a simple and secluded way of life. Like many such, they were reactionaries—in revolt against the wealth and worldliness of other orders of the time."

"Until corruption crept in again."

"Quite. Not all nuns and monks were corrupt, as you know, but Henry the Eighth was nothing if not thorough in putting his own ideas in place. Monkbury Abbey was spared the worst excesses of the Reformation because it was so remote—even dismantling the buildings to repurpose the bricks and stones for other uses, as commonly happened elsewhere, wasn't all that practical. So large parts of its structures were preserved even though Mother Nature soon took over: the place eventually became overgrown and ramshackle in appearance, the haunt of ghosts, hobgoblins, and the occasional passing hippie."

The bishop hesitated, peering at Max. The handsome priest, gregarious in many ways, was strangely reticent in others. He so seldom spoke of his past. The bishop supposed that was part of his MI5 training, but the reluctance to talk of his experiences clearly ran deep. Not surprising, that. Spying was a dangerous and dirty business.

"You have a relative in the religious life, am I right?" asked the bishop.

"Yes," said Max. "An aunt. My father's sister. I can't say I know her at all well: her convent is cloistered. For obvious reasons, she wasn't a big part of my childhood. When we'd visit, we could only see her face through a grille. I remember being frightened of that when I was small, even though she was of course very sweet and kind and made a big fuss over me. It was the situation that worried me: it isn't natural for an aunt not to be able to hold her own nephew."

Max thought how like his father she had seemed. That same ascetic quality as his father's, given full range. The same reserve and stoicism. An otherworldly cast that he suspected would not have thrived outside the gray walls behind which she continued to live out her days.

He had been negligent in not having visited her for months, an oversight he vowed to correct soon.

Bishop St. Stephen studied the priest before him. He hoped he was doing the right thing in taking Max away from his expected duties in Nether Monkslip and sending him off on a mission to, essentially, spy on a religious order. But was there anyone he could think of more readymade for the task? Not a soul. Being MI5 called for a man with chameleon qualities: he not only could tell no one what he did for a living, but he had to make certain what he *said* he did for a living sounded as boring and ordinary as possible. Even the bishop wasn't sure what Max had really got up to during those MI5 years. It was undoubtedly better not to know the details. What mattered was the man before him now, whose integrity he never doubted.

Max prompted conversationally, never dreaming it all would have anything to do with him: "You say there are thirty-one of the sisters? That is a sizable group these days. What do you know of their backgrounds before they came to Monkbury Abbey?" He added, "Please don't tell me one of them was an accountant."

"Actually, one was, but they all share jobs routinely and the nun with a background in accounting doesn't seem to have been solely in charge of the funds. The job-sharing scheme is meant to keep them both humble and cross-trained, you see. There are a few key positions that remain stationary—the abbess, for one; the cellaress, for another. They mostly came to the religious life after a full exploration of the outside world. When we think of nuns we think of a convent full of virgins singing in the choir and scrubbing stone floors. Even those of us who have been called to religion ourselves—those who should know better. The Order of the Handmaids of St. Lucy admits widows and always has, and today it boasts a few of those—several with children living. There are women from the business world, from academia, from all walks of life, really. Abbess Justina, to name one, was quite a London presence in her day."

The best leaders of establishments such as Monkbury Abbey, Max knew, combined a generosity of spirit with a steely practicality and a gift for diplomacy. "I would think some experience of the outside world would be a bonus to the nunnery," he said.

"Absolutely, it is. And they are not interested in recruiting naïfs who see the nunnery as a place to hide. It is a life to be embraced with joy and in full knowledge of what the postulant is leaving behind."

Stopping to adjust the collar at his neck, which looked too tight for such a warm day, the bishop went on: "They lean toward the Anglo-Catholic tradition, but they seem to be more interested in preserving the monastic traditions and rituals of the Middle Ages than in modern religious debate. They emphasize a return to the devotions of old and a wish to abandon the distractions of modern life. Who can blame them? Their main argument is that the earliest members of the C of E had no quarrel with their practices, so why should we?"

"So I gather there has been some discussion about . . . let's say, *policy* . . . with the abbess?"

"Oh, on many occasions. The situation bears watching, but they seem to me to be earnest and devout, avoiding the excesses of the medieval church."

"No hair shirts either, then," said Max. "That's a relief."

"No, no. I should quickly put a stop to any hint of that sort of thing."
He straightened an already immaculate pile of pages on this desk and
leaned over to arrange a pencil that leaned lopsidedly in a cup on his desk.
"In the past, as now, where monasteries or nunneries got into trouble was
usually with the financial situation, which bred envy, which bred . . . oh,
all sorts of ills. Rich benefactors willed them money, wanting special
prayers said for their souls. They often ear-marked their bequests for certain parts of the nunnery, such as the infirmary or the guesthouse. Back
in the day, the infirmaress, for example, might have control over a sheep
farm left to subsidize her part of the operation. You can see where this
could lead: perhaps a woman with no experience of sheep was suddenly
responsible for their welfare and the milk and cheese they produced. Her
duties as estate manager might take her away from the nunnery for days
or even weeks at a time. The fact that she controlled a large portion of the
nunnery's income might create internal conflict and might also lead to
serious debt."

"No audits?"

"Finally, yes, that is exactly what had to happen. Annual audits. It is
a tradition—a rule, in fact—that is strictly upheld to this day, although I
have tried to steer clear of micromanagement. I don't interfere and I make
it a point not to. I have never felt a need to. Not until now, perhaps. Better
to delegate authority wherever possible. I see no harm in what they are
doing."

Max was not certain that religion should follow the latest business
management fads. Both as an MI5 agent and as a priest he had seen the
theory of delegation of authority deployed with disastrous results. Too
often managers had no real idea of the psychological limitations of the
young, untried subordinates they were entrusting with other peoples' lives
and welfare.

"The Abbess Justina," the bishop was saying, as if tracking Max's
thoughts, "is a sound woman. A good manager who commands respect.
She is perhaps a bit vain, I think—she is a tall, handsome woman. The
day-to-day operations are in the hands of the cellaress, as is usual, the

abbess being the big-picture person. She steps in only when there is something the cellaress can't sort out herself, which is seldom."

Max was still left thinking of cases in his own history where upper management remained clueless while the lunatics one rung below ran the asylum. He had every faith in the bishop's good judgment, but how often did he see these women?

"Anyway, Abbess Justina: she offers what I have always regarded as a Ronald Reagan style of leadership. Not unintelligent—far from it—but ten minutes after speaking with her you are not certain exactly what it was she said. Still you feel somehow that everything is going to turn out all right."

"She is charming, then."

"Oh, yes. She is possessed of quite a natural charm. Loads of charm."

"How long has she been the abbess?"

"Not long. Her predecessor was elected in the 1980s, I believe, and was reelected in 2000. She died a few years ago."

"And what did Abbess Justina do in—let's call it her civilian life?"

"She was a financial consultant."

"You're not serious."

"Oh, yes. She was quite a successful one. Made *mucho dinero* in the City. Then one day, she just packed it in. Not unlike yourself, Max. You came to us rather out of nowhere, it seemed."

Max nodded, acknowledging the comparison and avoiding the possible invitation to elaborate on his past. "It takes a person like that sometimes—a vocation, I mean. Although I didn't have all that much *dinero* to give up."

"Men such as yourself are not motivated by money."

"Thank you," murmured Max, pleased and flattered by the comment. "There is no prioress?" he asked. The norm in this sort of outfit was that there be a second-in-command—the real power behind the abbess, who was often more of a figurehead.

The bishop shook his head.

"The cellaress of Monkbury is in charge of the physical running of the place. She is the prioress in all but name, but they've had to mothball that title."

"You did indicate it was a thriving operation," said Max. "That should negate the 'need' for any financial chicanery."

"You would think so, wouldn't you? Yes, the nuns are extremely enterprising. They grow all manner of fruits and vegetables and sell their leftover crops. They are also very much into drying herbs and making preserves and so on, which they sell with great success. They have a little gift shop connected to the guesthouse, and they also sell products online; they have quite a professional-looking Web site: MonkburyAbbey.com. It's a natural fit—the online store allows them to maintain their isolation and independence while bringing in a steady revenue stream for repairs and ongoing expenses. They also loom rugs and throw pots and things, and as I recall they make a significant living from their embroidery, making vestments, christening robes, things like that. But by far their biggest success is their fruitcake."

"The fruitcake." *Okay.* This did not strike Max as a money-making proposition any more than selling plum preserves, but he was willing to be surprised.

"You'll see," said the Bishop. "My wife ordered several last Christmas as gifts. It was a Christmas we'll not soon forget. It packs an astonishingly high alcohol content. I can see how the alcohol might mask the flavor of anything that should not be in there."

"I'm sorry. Did you say, 'should not be in there'?"

"Yes. I'll get to that in a minute. They recently teamed up with the National Trust to sell some of their goods via the trust's stores. Quite an astute financial move—I gather the cellaress was the moving force behind this plan. The partnership has been a runaway success and the nuns could name their price but are charging basically what the goods cost to make. I gather the abbess insisted on that. The pottery pieces have become collector's items, in particular the terra-cotta crèche scenes."

"The fruitcake?" Max asked, desperately trying to get the bishop to the point, even though he suspected he was not going to like it once they arrived there. "There was a problem with the fruitcake?"

But the bishop breezed on. "Dame Potter they call one of them—she runs that show. Louise Dietz was her name in civilian life. She also does some work in stained glass that to my mind is of museum quality. By the way, my secretary can provide you a file with names and some background on all the sisters." Before Max had time to wonder why he should need such a thing, the bishop swept on: "Dame Potter makes things like garlic pots, wassail mugs, bowls, and salt pigs—I had to ask the wife. You keep salt in it. I don't know why. This is the sort of useful thing you'll learn when you're married, Max."

But Max was not quite ready to cross that river. He had news for the bishop with regard to his marital arrangements that, for the life of him, he could not see how to introduce into the conversation. An announcement that a child was on the way would, as sure as rain comes from storm clouds, be followed by joyful inquiries about when Max had gotten married, and by hurt feelings at not having been invited to the wedding, and by the need for explanations that might make matters worse. Max was rather hoping that the problem would resolve itself in a few weeks' time with the bishop never knowing there was an "issue." Instead Max said, his voice carrying a high note of optimism, "Fruitcake?"

The bishop sighed. "Fruitcake, yes. I am afraid accusations have been made. Wild, unsubstantiated rumors. Someone—someone rather well known, alas—is claiming he became ill from eating some fruitcake he brought back from a visit to Monkbury Abbey. He went on a religious retreat there, you see."

"Who is this person, if I may ask?"

"Lord Lislelivet."

"Lord Lisle*livet*?" Max repeated, not even bothering to keep the scoff of skepticism from his voice.

"Yes, I know," said the bishop. "My reaction was much the same as yours."

"Lord Lislelivet has no known connection to Monkbury Abbey, has he?"

"Actually he does. Like you, he has an aunt in the religious life. But it's been many years since he visited her. I gather he has shown a sudden interest in going on retreat."

"That's totally out of character," said Max flatly. He knew Lislelivet by reputation and his appearance at a nunnery retreat was a laughable concept, barring miraculous conversions. Which, Max reminded himself, always remained in the realm of possibility. Max was a dealer in miracles himself—miracles were his stock in trade, it could be said. And so he had to hold out the wild hope that even such as Lord Lislelivet might be brought into the fold. Still . . .

"You do see the problem," said the bishop. "It's a criminal matter or it soon will be if Lord Lislelivet cannot be calmed down. There has to be an innocuous explanation. They are *nuns*, for heaven's sake. They don't go around poisoning people."

"When did this happen?" Max asked. "I mean, when did he come to—obtain—the fruitcake in question?" Max struggled hard to maintain a professional demeanor, but really. This was just the limit.

"It was last fall—months ago. Perhaps there was a batch of bad fruit- cake from that time—they are still trying to sort out what may have hap- pened."

"The accusation is that the cake was poisoned?"

The bishop nodded, a look of such misery on his face Max immedi- ately felt sorry for the man, his instinct to help kicking in. His mind turned over the possibilities and surrounding questions. Why poison? Was someone trying to create scandal? Why? Was it a plan by one of the nuns to keep visitors away? Revenge by someone with a grudge against the church? An accident?

The question as to why Lord Lislelivet had been the target of foul play took Max down quite a different path. Max had never met the man and knew of him only from newspaper accounts, but nothing spoke to his being a well-loved and cherished member of the nobility, or even an ad- mired if feared one. In a privileged category bound to inspire envy and resentment, Lord Lislelivet stood out from the rest—a leader, as it were, in arousing class warfare.

"What," Max asked, "does the abbess have to say about this? You've spoken with her?"

"Yes, yes, by satellite phone. I spoke with her right away. She has no theory as to what happened and is as baffled as anyone."

"My first thoughts are that this poisoning, if such it was, was an attempt to create bad publicity for Monkbury Abbey. It might almost be a personal vendetta, even one against the abbess herself. A strong leader is not by definition popular in all quarters."

"Yes, of course that is a possibility. An abbess is the linchpin holding a nunnery together, for she wields near-total power, appointing all subordinates. Even though in theory decisions are made democratically, she always makes the final decision."

"There is perhaps some bad feeling about some of her choices?"

"That is possible," the bishop acknowledged. "That would need to be ferreted out."

Max suddenly was feeling decidedly ferrety. Surely the bishop didn't intend him to—

"I want you to go there and find out what you can, Max. All you can."

Well, this was a new one. In all his days with MI5, he had never been sent to spy on nuns. Not even once. He said as much.

"The scandal must be stopped in its tracks," replied the bishop. "I've asked the police for discretion while we launch an internal investigation. It is at least on the surface a criminal matter but one taking place months ago, so I gather it is not a priority with them. No one died, you see, and all these months later it will be jolly hard to sort out."

With a sigh, the bishop put his hands on top of his desk, the fingers spread, as if he might be trying to cause the desk to levitate. The gold of his very large episcopal ring caught the sunlight. His hands were surprisingly rough and reddened; Max knew the bishop was a keen gardener, and visitors to the beautiful cathedral grounds were unaware that the man with a hoe in overalls turning over the soil in the flowerbeds might be the bishop himself, dressed in mufti to escape detection.

"You can see how the scandal would ruin them overnight," the bishop continued. "And it puts me in rather an awkward position. I have given them almost complete free rein and autonomy. In return they've been self-sustaining—not once have they called on the church for financial help, even during the lean years, and they did have a few of those. The abbess before Abbess Justina was a bit of a spendthrift and given to what I'd call ornamental changes—but even there I just let her go, as it didn't seem to be anything requiring my attention. So what once would have been lauded as benign management might now be . . ."

"Might be regarded as dangerous neglect," Max finished for him. "Even active neglect. I do understand."

"So if you were to look into it and find that the nuns are blameless in all this . . . you do see, Max?"

Max did see. The bishop was hoping against hope that a theory of an "outside agency" would hold and that Max would uncover evidence in support of that theory.

"Yes," said Max. "But, Bishop, whatever I may discover, if it is the truth—well, then it is the truth of what happened. I won't be able to alter or undo what I find, as awkward as it may prove to be for the church."

"Of course not. I wouldn't expect you to. I just hope . . . and pray . . ."

"Quite," said Max. "That it's not an inside job. When did you last talk with Abbess Justina in person?"

"I visited there only last year. It was a formal visitation, you know, to see that all was well."

Max nodded. Part of the creaking machinery of the church in post-Reformation Europe had been increased vigilance over the goings-on in convents and monasteries.

"And was it?"

"No. No it wasn't. And that is of course what is bothering me now. That I should have heeded my instincts. Asked more questions. And now there's what might be a case of attempted murder. Could I have prevented it somehow? That will haunt me."

"What did you sense was wrong—the finances only? Or something more?"

"No, no. Finances looked all in order then, on paper at least. I'm no forensic accountant but the bottom line looked sound. Business was booming, in fact. It was when I talked with each nun in turn. Something that was *not* being said was what I heard, if you follow."

"What?"

"I don't want to prejudice you by telling you specifics in advance of your visit. You can't investigate something like this from a distance. I've made arrangements with—what's his name? That DCI who was involved in the affair at Chedrow Castle."

"DCI Cotton," Max supplied for him. DCI Cotton operated out of Monkslip-super-Mare and generally investigated homicides and other major crimes. It spoke volumes that he was involved already; things had to have crossed a certain threshold for Cotton and his team to be poised to run about, notebooks blazing. Lord Lislelivet must have complained loudly.

"Yes. Yes, that was it," said the bishop. "DCI Cotton."

"You can't fill me in a bit more?"

The bishop studied the ornately carved ceiling of his office as he searched his memory. "They were jumpy, some of them, when last I saw them. Decidedly jumpy. It was most un-nun-like behavior. Nuns should be serene. They should just glide along, cool, calm, and collected. But I could get nothing out of them. I did ask. However, I didn't press when I was assured all was well. Again, one doesn't want to micromanage, and the abbess is a completely competent sort of woman."

"Did you get a sense of an ongoing feud, personality conflicts, anything like that?"

"They had the usual petty squabbles—you can't shut people up together in such isolated circumstances and expect otherwise. But *this*? Attempted murder in order to discredit the place? No.

"Max, I'll speak plainly. I want you to go out there. I want you involved. If anyone can get to the bottom of this, you can. There have been other complaints, you see, one from an individual well placed to make trouble."

Max was in the midst of his usual dilemma when confronted by a crime. The investigator part of his nature was champing at the bit to get

started. The priest in him was dismayed at all the projects in Nether
Monkslip that would be left in abeyance for his return, the Christmas
ensemble band being the least of his worries. And now to leave Awena's
side for even a day . . . Monkbury Abbey was only a few hours from
Nether Monkslip, but even so . . .

"One can't ignore the fact that money talks," the bishop was saying.

Max dragged his mind back to the conversation. "Anyone I would
have heard of?"

"Clement Gorey and his wife, Oona. They've been major benefactors
of Monkbury Abbey over the years."

Max whistled softly. Nearly everyone knew the eccentric American
by name and reputation. "I suppose a financier of Clement's caliber would
be particularly incensed at being played for a fool financially."

Again a look of despair enveloped the face of the ginger-haired prel-
ate. He must have been working in the garden recently, thought Max, for
his complexion was a red several shades darker than normal.

"And now Lord Lislelivet and his wife are hopping up and down
about poisoned fruitcake. Just imagine the headlines—no! It doesn't bear
thinking about. Both the men and their wives are quite concerned—
naturally. The situation must be contained."

A bell had sounded in the far reaches of Max's brain, the part where
cold cases were filed.

"Wasn't there an earlier scandal involving the Lislelivet family? A
kidnapping?"

"Lord Lislelivet's brother disappeared. Yes. An appalling tragedy,
that. So you see, this coming on top of everything is bound to attract
attention—too much and of the wrong sort."

Max, despite himself, was intrigued. "I'll of course see what I can do.
But I can't hold out a lot of hope. What is probably needed with regard to
the missing funds is some sort of forensic accountant. I can barely get the
books of St. Edwold's to balance each month. I—"

"No, of course, your bailiwick is murder most foul, not fiscal shenanigans and pranks—just do your best. I must say, the whole fruitcake

thing strikes me as a lark designed to harm the reputation of Monkbury Abbey. Not something, well, more serious."

"Not attempted murder."

"We shall soon know more. There was fruitcake remaining in Lord Lislelivet's larder—there always is; fruitcake does linger so—and it was sent to the police lab for testing. But I think diplomacy might be what is needed right now, more than business savvy or analytical skills. Whatever is going on, we need to keep Mr. Gorey satisfied that we are conducting an open and thorough inquiry. Calm him down until we know what is what. The same goes, of course, for Lord Lislelivet. In his case, I rather get the impression he is weighing whether news of an attempted attack against his person would ruin or enhance his reputation. While he is deciding, there is still time."

Max smothered a laugh. Lord Lislelivet was known for waffling on every issue under the sun, from the care of children to that of old-age pensioners. He voted not with his heart, God knew, and not with his pocketbook, but with the flair of the born politician looking for whichever angle would ensure his survival. If he was up against Abbess Justina and she was as smooth an operator as the bishop said, he may have met his match.

The bishop, catching and misreading the smile playing at Max's lips, said, "Good. So you'll do it. I admire your can-do attitude, Max. Always have. That's set then. Just be sure someone covers your duties at St. Edwold's for a few days. See if Father Arthnot is available. Good-bye and keep me posted."

"Erm . . ." Max knew he should be used by now to these sudden dismissals, but somehow the bishop always caught him flat-footed.

"Oh, by the way," the bishop turned from his computer, where an incoming e-mail had caught his eye. "Try to get there before nine tonight."

Tonight? Who had said anything about tonight? "Why is that?" Max asked.

"They keep the Great Silence after Compline, which is at nine p.m. You won't get a word out of them until after Lauds the next morning.

This is a *such* conservative group." The bishop seemed to feel that fact could not be emphasized enough. "Oh, I've had chats with them here and there over the years, little pep talks, trying to egg them further into the twenty-first century. I could grant special dispensation to let them talk to you, but under the circumstances I think it best that you see them as they are and not ruffle any feathers by throwing them off their usual schedule."

If a possible attempted murder by poisoning hadn't done that already, Max didn't know what would, but he saw the bishop's point. Better to cause the least disruption possible on first arrival.

"I could celebrate the Eucharist for them while I'm there," he offered.

"A sort of special guest appearance! Yes, yes—that's a good idea. I'll see that Father Riley is notified—he is their usual celebrant. Some of the nuns, the highly, *highly* traditional ones, still prefer a male priest. Which is odd when you think about it. Anyway, I'm sure they would welcome the little change in routine."

"I'll do what I can, but—"

"You can be there tonight, can't you?" The bishop reached for the immaculate pile of paper printouts stacked at one side of his desk.

Max said, "Not for at least a day, Bishop, I shouldn't think. Loose ends to tie up at St. Edwold's before I go, you know the sort of thing."

"Oh." The bishop did a poor job of hiding his disappointment. "Well, that will probably be all right. Lord Lislelivet has said—quite loudly—he will be on his guard while he's there."

"While he's *there*?"

"Oh, didn't I say? Yes, he is there this week. I don't know for how long. I'm surprised he hasn't hired a food taster, but what he means of course by being 'on his guard' is that he won't eat anything that isn't offered to the community at large. He's probably travelling with a large supply of energy bars and such."

"I can't imagine why he's there at all, frankly. It seems quite a mad thing for him to do."

"Me, either. Surely it would be wiser to stay away until this mess is cleared up. He claims to have had a religious experience when he was there before."

"A what?"

"I don't understand it either," the bishop said impatiently, with a pointed look at the pages now spread before him on his desk. "Nor do I believe him. I rely on you to get to the bottom of it, Max." He looked up. "Oh, I suppose I should mention: all the people currently on retreat at the guesthouse were there some time in the fall, just not all at same time. And the fall is when Lord Lislelivet picked up the fruitcake in question."

"That is an odd coincidence, surely," said Max.

"DCI Cotton says they are all there again."

"What? That seems beyond coincidence."

A latent interest in crime was showing on the bishop's face, mixed with genuine concern. He's become an eager participant in all of this, thought Max.

"Not when you think about it. The whole thing is coming to a head out there. You'll see. Well, good-bye and Godspeed, Max. Toodle-oo. I'm really frightfully late for my next appointment."

And Max, seeing no option, rose, made a deferential bow, and left the office.

The Right Reverend Bishop Nigel St. Stephen stopped shuffling his papers and punching his computer keys long enough to watch him go. The bishop thought of himself as a patient man, a big-picture sort of bloke. In his mind, the two things went together. A benign philosophical stance combined with the patience to watch and wait as the Creator made all things clear. But the incidents at Monkbury Abbey had shaken him from this Siddhartha-like pose.

Something had to be done about the situation at the abbey, and something had to be done ASAP, before all hell broke loose.

But ASAP would not be soon enough.

When Max reached the vicarage later that same evening, he found two urgent messages waiting for him in Mrs. Hooser's hieroglyphic scrawl.

One was from Bishop St. Stephen, and one was from DCI Cotton of the Monkslip Constabulary. Somehow, Max knew even before he picked up the heavy Bakelite phone to begin dialing that the two messages were connected.

PART III
Terce

Chapter 4

MONKBURY ABBEY

But let us ask the Lord: Who will find rest upon your holy mountain?

—*The Rule of the Order of the Handmaids of St. Lucy*

Monkbury Abbey lay almost directly to the north of Nether Monkslip, past Monkslip Cathedral, a few miles past Muckleford Piddle and a few further miles east of the roundabout at Temple Monkslip. Max made record time the next day in light traffic, stopping once for petrol at a motorist convenience stop. He decided against the "healthy" option on the menu there, opting for a quick pub meal in Temple Monkslip.

Afterwards he entered rolling countryside that in ages past had been as flat and sodden as a rice paddy. Spotting the nunnery in the distance, he pulled into a lay-by to take in the full postcard-worthy view. A marvel of medieval construction surrounded by a wide river, Monkbury Abbey clung to the craggy, steep mountainside like a walled castle of the Languedoc, to which it may well have owed its inspiration. It was difficult to tell what was rock and what was building.

An evening mist rose from the river at the mountain's base, enveloping the bottom, so that the abbey seemed to float suspended against a turquoise sky shot through with copper. Greenery grew nearly to the summit of the walled precinct; a narrow road could be glimpsed winding to the top like a swirl of soft ice cream. A cruciform church with Norman tower was the crowning glory; from there the abbey buildings tumbled higgledy-piggledy down the hill, clinging to the sides until they came to a stone wall. This plunged straight into the river like the long train of a lady's skirt.

Max thought, smiling to himself, that the only possible word for the nunnery was "impregnable."

He had consulted a drawing and photographs on the Internet before setting out and knew the steepest wall comprised one side of the infirmary. The buildings where the nuns slept, ate, and worked surrounded the eastern and southern sides of the cloister garth. To the west, set slightly apart, was the guesthouse.

Animals, specks of white and brown, could be seen grazing on fields surrounding the complex. The place looked utterly self-contained—mysterious, forbidding, and inexpressibly beautiful.

And despite its splendor, Max did not want to be there. He did not want to be anywhere Awena was not.

He put the Land Rover into gear and set off up the hill.

His phone conversation of the previous night with DCI Cotton had lasted half an hour. The DCI had confirmed the lab results were back on the fruitcake retrieved from the country home of Lord and Lady Lisle-livet. The cake had definitely been tampered with.

"But whether deliberately or accidentally, of course they can't say," Cotton told him. "To some people—me, for example—good-for-you berries look exactly the same as bad-for-you berries. That's why I avoid the great outdoors at all costs. As far as I'm concerned they invented the supermarket to keep me out of forest glens. But the experts suggest it may not have been an attempt to kill outright, but to make someone decidedly uncomfortable. Who, after all, in their right mind would eat more than a few bites of fruitcake?"

"It was something in the nature of a cruel prank, you mean. But why would anyone go to the trouble?" Max wondered.

"It's an unorthodox situation, to say the least—if you will pardon the expression. When all this first came up, the Bishop of Monkslip himself called the station, asking to speak with me. Once the switchboard determined it was not a hoax they put him through to my flat, where I sat blamelessly watching a *Downton Abbey* rerun. The bishop is desperate to have us approach the matter with all diplomatic caution. I gather he has already asked you to look into a few things at the abbey. I've had a brief look-see myself but I didn't have a lot of time to devote to it."

"Yes, he asked me to take a look around," said Max. "He said that beside the berry incident, there might be some financial irregularities. Perhaps he was hoping against hope the berries would prove to be harmless—the lesser of two evils. It is not impossible that Lord Lislelivet would raise a big stink over a minor matter for publicity purposes."

"Ah, you know him."

"I know enough of him," Max replied. "So. Whether we are talking of a prank or attempted murder, this ninny apparently has taken himself off to the abbey to be right in the thick of things."

"Apparently. It's set to blow sky-high once Lord Lislelivet hears someone's tampered with his food in a meaningful way. I would agree with your bishop that it all needs to be contained—cleared up as quickly as possible. Quietly, if it can be. If the situation called for discretion before, it now calls for the highest diplomatic finessing we can bring to bear."

"The press—"

"The press and media have not been informed," Cotton told him. "Yet. Of course they'll learn of it in time, but right now they've no idea. Even Lord Lislelivet seems not to have told them. If he had, it would be all over the news by now."

"Oh, but surely . . ." Max trailed off, tried again. "You must—"

"Surely nothing. Must nothing. There is no clause in my oath of office that requires me to broadcast every detail of every case to the media immediately I become aware of it—or before I'm even certain there is a case. Quite the opposite. I spend more of my time than I care to fending off people with notebooks and microphones so they don't bugger up every investigation, for me and for whoever might be a suspect. The media find out about things in the usual ways, using their usual methods—some of them, like bribery or wiretapping, not particularly attractive methods. But so far we've got a window of opportunity before they come swooping in, shirttails untucked, ties untied, swearing to high heaven and trailing cigarette ash all over the place. And that's just the women."

"The women are much better behaved," objected Max. "As a rule."

"Generally smarter, too. They run rings around the men."

"All the more reason, you'll have to play it straight with any reporters. If and when they find out you kept this quiet they'll have your guts for garters."

"Of course I'll be straight with them. It's just a question of when I'll get around to it."

Max, after taking a brief survey of his conscience, found he wasn't overly concerned about the ethics of keeping details from the media. There were centuries of precedent, after all. As a theological conundrum, he thought it was in the category of wondering how many angels could dance on the head of a pin. If justice or reputation were at stake, certainly then concealment would be out of the question. But delaying media inquiries into the investigation? A gray area. Dark gray, but gray. He mostly wondered how on earth Cotton thought he would get away with it for longer than a few hours. A day at best. A week? Never.

As if reading his mind, Cotton said, "We won't get away with it for long, of course. But Monkbury Abbey is its own little world, isolated from the outside, undisturbed by modern inconveniences. And therefore completely unable to withstand any sort of media onslaught. I shudder to think of it, Max—when it happens, and it is bound to, it's going to be awful. Simply a bloodbath. As always, the innocent will suffer along with whoever is responsible. And these women—these nuns—are true innocents."

"Except perhaps for one of them."

"Well, yes. It doesn't bear thinking about."

"What makes you think the BBC isn't at this very moment rolling up to the front gate of the abbey in one of its vans?"

"The abbess has told no one but the bishop about what's happened. And Lord Lislelivet is being the soul of discretion. Totally unlike his usual self."

"But the financial irregularities . . . surely there is a connection?"

"That is why I need you, Max. I have to say I don't see the connection."

"The bishop said much the same cast of characters as were at the abbey in the fall with Lord Lislelivet are there now."

Max heard the rattle of a sheet of paper being unfolded.

"We have a family group: Clement Gorey, Oona Gorey, and their daughter, Xanda Gorey. The Goreys have donated a king's ransom to Monkbury Abbey over the years. An amount nicely calculated to ensure they are remembered in perpetuity. Clement seems to be the ringleader in this financial investigation.

"Then we have Paloma Green. She owns an art gallery and was apparently responsible for holding a big fund-raiser for the abbey at her gallery. You know the sort of thing, where people who know nothing about art show up and eat little canapé things wrapped in bacon and drink white wine until they've bid an insane amount on some photo or painting that's captured their fancy because blue is their favorite color. Anyway, this shindig raised a lot of money to expand and improve the existing abbey guesthouse. To blend the medieval with something that can be heated in winter. Paloma's boyfriend, Piers Montague, is with her at the abbey now, although he was not among the guests when Lord Lislelivet carried off the tainted fruitcake. The boyfriend is a photographer specializing in gloomy portraits of ruined monasteries."

"Is there any other kind?" asked Max.

"No, I see your point. Not in England, at any rate. They always look so depressing, don't they, those images? But in a beautiful way.

"And then there is himself, Ralph Perceval, the Fifteenth Earl of Lislelivet. A walking advertisement for the sound thinking behind the French Revolution, if you ask me, however much we may despair of their extreme methods. He does not appear to have the same investment of money or reputation in the situation as do the others. What reputation? I hear you ask. But still, what his wife thinks is that he is there on a treasure hunt."

"Come again?"

"A treasure hunt. It has been rumored that something is buried in the abbey precincts, something of incalculable value. Something Holy Grailish. There's some book just come out that's sparked a renewed interest. The nuns will have their hands full as it is, dealing with the fortune hunters flocking to their gates. Combine that with poisoned fruitcake and missing charitable donations, and they've got a perfect storm of trouble."

"Holy Grail?" Max repeated. "You are kidding me, right?" It was so—what? So feudal, so archaic. Max could almost feel the centuries begin to dissolve around him. The electric candles in the vicarage seemed to shape-shift into rushlights as he stood incongruously clutching a telephone, his spare modern garb transformed into the long folds of a cleric of the middle ages.

Cotton had the grace to keep silent while Max turned everything over in his mind. Or perhaps Cotton was busy reading a report on his computer. He was the ultimate multitasker.

Finally Cotton said, "So, when can you get there? Time really is of the essence, Max."

Max Tudor sighed. He supposed the peace and quiet of the abbey might at least give him an idea for his sermon.

"As soon as I can pack a few things and find someone to cover for me here. I really do need to work on my sermon. More importantly, there's someone I must visit in hospital. It can't be put off."

His parishioner Chrissa Baker, who had resisted all sane advice and stayed with her abusive husband, had finally fulfilled one of the predictions as to her likely fate and landed in hospital with a broken jaw. Injuries suffered at her husband's hands, of course. Max was going to bring all his persuasiveness to bear to get her to leave him. He'd already arranged a flat for her to stay for a month and was working on finding her a job in Staincross Minster.

"All right," said Cotton. "Bring enough clothing for about three days.

You can leave the laptop behind, assuming you have one. This lot is strictly of the parchment-and-quill school of sermon writing."

As the "Zed" key on the vicarage computer was currently stuck, Max thought there might be compensations. The malfunction had played havoc with last week's sermon, which in keeping with the Law of Sod had been about the prophets Ezekiel and Zechariah.

"Oh, and Max?"

"Hmm?"

"Thanks. I owe you a beer."

"You owe me a hefty donation to the widows-and-orphans fund."

"Done. Gladly. I'll write a cheque tonight." This was what Cotton liked about Max. He wasn't above a dab of genteel extortion in a good cause.

"And you could come to Morning Prayer once in a while. It wouldn't kill you."

"It might, when the roof of St. Edwold's caved in on me," said Cotton.

Chapter 5

THE PORTRESS

The portress should be a wise old woman not given to roaming about.

—The Rule of the Order of the Handmaids of St. Lucy

At the top of the hill, his headlamps picked out painted wooden signs that politely directed him to the abbey gatehouse and firmly away from the restricted area of the nun's cloister.

Max parked and walked over to a wooden door set deep within the stone wall of the gatehouse. He lifted the large brass knocker, shaped like a cross, and pounded it against the massive studded door of a type most often found guarding the entries to ancient Oxbridge colleges. After waiting what seemed an unreasonable amount of time he knocked and waited again. Well, there must be someone at home, he thought. It's not as if the sisters would have taken it into their heads to go see a movie together. Just as he was lifting the knocker to try again, an eye appeared at the peephole. "Thanks be to God!" warbled a thin, high voice from inside. Sounds of an almighty struggle reached his ears. A scraping and clanging of metal and a creaking of wood as the door opened inward, inch by slow inch. Tempted as Max was to help, he feared he might frighten whoever it was on the other side if he started pushing against the wood. Instead he waited.

And waited. To be greeted at last by a nun of prodigious, Old

Testament-like age—an ancient woman, shriveled by weather and time, with a pointed nose and large, compassionate eyes, a bit like Dobby the Elf in *Harry Potter*. If she had Dobby's ears, too, that fact was hidden by her white coif and black veil surmounted by a woven circlet.

Calling on all her remaining resources, the woman gave the door a final tug and then, to Max's amazement, stood on tiptoe to kiss him, once on each cheek. She looked as delighted to see him as if he were a long-lost relative—the good sort of mislaid relative one does hope to see again. She seemed to take his arrival in her stride—probably the abbey had been alerted by someone on the bishop's staff. But Max sensed there was more to it than that: it was as if she saw his visit as somehow inevitable. It was only fanciful thinking on his part, he knew that, but it really was as if she'd waited a lifetime for Max Tudor to appear.

She had lost a few teeth with the passing years but still she could offer a good and welcoming smile, the soft folds of her face settling comfortably around her eyes and mouth. Her grip on his hands was firm. Indeed it could be said she clung fiercely to him in her struggle to remain upright. Now she inched back and peered up into his face, making a study of him. She smelled of soap—lavender and another flowery scent he could only guess at—and of sunlight and starch. There was also the pleasant but faint odor of honey that he decided came from the beeswax candles that were dotted around the room behind her to the right. A hand-lettered wooden sign identified it as the portress's lodge.

Max bore the scrutiny patiently, without flinching. It was her job, after all, to assure the safety and security of the abbey by not allowing in random strangers, although he began to think her age and various evident infirmities might make her the worst possible candidate for the job. Indeed, he thought he detected behind the thick lenses of her glasses a film over the eyes that might be the beginning of cataracts.

Finally she seemed satisfied by what she could make out of his appearance. "You'll be wanting the guest-mistress," she shouted. "I'll go and fetch her, presently." Slowly she turned, as good as her word, and began a measured shuffle toward her desk in the lodge's reception area, behind which some sort of primitive call system anchored her to the rest of the building. Max, who had followed her through the large wooden door, shutting it behind him and slotting all the barriers back in place, watched her wobble slowly to behind the counter where she apparently spent much of her day reading and praying, for surely there were few visitors to occupy her time up here. A little prayer book lay open at the page where Max by his appearance had interrupted her contemplations.

As she continued the long walk back to her station, Max assayed a friendly greeting and a trial question or two, and it soon became apparent she was quite deaf, replying in a nonsensical way to anything Max said. He did manage to establish that her name was Dame Hephzibah. When he asked her how long she had been at Monkbury Abbey, she replied that she felt fine and thanked him kindly for asking. "And God willing, I'll live to be a hundred," she added. He imagined that inability to hear might come in handy during the Great Silence, but right now it only added a wrinkle to his investigation. Finally, pulling out the notebook he always carried with him, Max wrote down in large block letters his most pressing question.

HAS DCI COTTON LEFT A MESSAGE FOR ME—
FATHER MAX TUDOR?

The DCI had promised to keep Max updated with anything breaking in the case. What Max most wished to hear was that it was solved and he could return home to Awena.

She took the notebook from him and holding it up to her eyes, studied it closely. Finally she removed her glasses and looked closer still. The glasses caught on the edges of her coif, complicating their removal.

"Good heavens, no!" she yelled at him. Like many people who were hard of hearing, Dame Hephzibah compensated for the loss by shouting. Max felt his pulse quicken slightly as her response reverberated off the stone walls. For an elderly, small woman she had tremendous vocal power.

"And to have a detective inspector need to call here at all," she added. "Bless my soul, I never thought to live to see the like!"

Turning away, she continued her penguin-like progress, and Max at last realized her destination.

There was a bell pull hanging from the ceiling, and much like Lady Grantham in Downton Abbey, Dame Hephzibah apparently used it to communicate that she needed assistance. Grabbing the rope, she clung swaying to it for dear life, much as she had clung to Max, and by using her meager body weight as a force of gravity, managed to yank the bell three times as three times her feet left the ground. The three-bell ring probably was a sort of code for "Visitor at the Gate." Max walked further inside the lodge and stood with his arms held slightly out from his body in order to catch and break her fall if need be. It was a very near thing that she might not be able to return to earth and could sway up there forever like a woman ascending a rope version of Jacob's ladder.

But at last she landed safely on her tiny orthopedic shoes, releasing the rope with the expert timing born of years of practice.

And smiling happily, she said, "Dame Tabitha, our guest-mistress, will be with you shortly. She will show you your lodgings in the guest-house.

"Would you like some tea while you wait, Father?"

Chapter 6

THE RULE

All are to follow without questioning the teachings of the Rule as set forth herein. Let no one dare to deviate from these instructions.

—The Rule of the Order of the Handmaids of St. Lucy

Max followed the portress's directions to park his "motorcar," taking a dirt road that ran around the outer wall of the guesthouse to the gated visitor's area. The gate was equipped with a solar-powered keypad for which he had been given the passcode.

A nun waited for him at the door to the guesthouse. He assumed this was the guest-mistress, Dame Tabitha. Dame Hephzibah had confided that her nickname among the nuns was Dame Tabby, but, "Best you not call her that unless she gives you permission."

Dame Tabitha was an immensely large woman with a bouncer's build. She had Dame Hephzibah's kind eyes, but hers were younger eyes, and they sat rather far apart in a wide face.

"You'll be Father Maxen Tudor," she said, consulting her clipboard with brisk efficiency. She made as if to relieve him of the small valise he carried, but he demurred.

"Please call me Father Max," he said. "Everyone does."

She showed him to a small entryway and down a long hallway, pointing out as she went the guest kitchen and the bath facilities.

Max was well aware of the dictum of St. Benedict that guests of a monastery were to be welcomed as Christ himself. This open-door policy was sacred to monk or nun, down to the present day. Max had to wonder how often this utopian innocence had been repaid with thievery and worse.

At one time, monasteries had been duty-bound to provide sanctuary for criminals on the run. Once inside the walls, no sheriff could touch them, whether they be murderers or pickpockets.

Or embezzlers.

Or poisoners.

Which rather brought Max to the point for his visit.

"I gather," said Max to Dame Tabitha, "that many of the people here this week are repeat visitors."

"I think they all are," she said vaguely. "Their gathering here—I believe—has something to do with the plans for the new guesthouse." She massaged the knuckles of her large hands like a prizefighter contemplating a rematch.

"You are not pleased to have a new guesthouse?" he hazarded.

"Oh, it's not that. It's that, well." She was clearly wondering if this were idle gossip. She seemed to decide it was mere opinion and thus okay. "From the architectural plans I've seen, it looks like an asylum, and I don't mean as in 'sanctuary.' It looks like a home for the insane, but with big windows. Very modern, you know."

"Ah," said Max neutrally.

"Still, it is not my place to comment," she added virtuously.

"They were all here in the fall?" Max prompted. "Everyone connected with these plans in some way?"

She paused. "It was in the fall when the plans for the guesthouse expansion were being finalized. An architect was here to talk with the abbess and the cellaress. And Lord Lislelivet was here." A dark shadow seemed to cross her face at the name. "That's all I remember for certain. The Americans weren't here for long—that I do recall. Mr. Gorey is a hearty eater, and keeping his plate filled is always a challenge. And he is a meat eater. We do not serve meat except to those who are ailing. It is against the Rule."

"I see."

"He and his wife have always been most generous to the abbey," she added sternly, as if Max had suggested otherwise.

"Very kind of them, I'm sure," he murmured.

In a former life Dame Tabitha might have worked in a pub, keeping the hooligans at bay. Max was guessing at her background and would continue to do so until he had had time to study the potted histories provided by the bishop's office, but she gave every impression of being worldly-wise and gruff almost to the point of rudeness.

Max again tested the waters.

"There are other visitors now?" he asked, knowing the answer full well from talking with Cotton.

"A pair from Monkslip-super-Mare. I don't gather they are married. Even if they were they'd get separate rooms."

Max beamed his approval at this chaste arrangement. This seemed to soften her, just one degree. The massive shoulders relaxed. "I was forgetting the girl: Xanda is her name. The Goreys' daughter. A bit of a handful. No harm in her, I don't think. But pink hair and blue fingernail polish? I mean, really."

"It all comes out in the wash," commented Max.

"*Hmph*. At least," said Dame Tabitha, "you have good weather for your visit. This past spring was a trial. We thought the lambs would wash away the minute they were born."

"It's peaceful here," observed Max. He had become aware of an almost eerie absence of sound. Probably something to do with the thickness of the abbey walls. "It almost takes some getting used to. I can see why people are drawn to the abbey."

"People nowadays are seeking something. Most of them don't know what."

He'd been following her down a secondary, narrow hallway lined with doors. Finally she came to a stop before a plain wooden door at the far end. It was painted blue and bore a small brass plate that labeled the room MATT. 9.

She turned to throw open the door, which was unlocked.

"More private for you here," she said, flipping on a light switch. This was answered by the feeble illumination of a low-wattage, energy-saving bulb.

"I see." That was nice, although Max wasn't sure privacy was what was wanted in an investigation. Being in the thick of the action was more like it. Still he nodded, indicating his pleasure with a smile—a smile that was not returned. In fact, Dame Tabitha seemed unwilling to meet his eyes. Perhaps it was their proximity in the small room. She stood awkwardly, her large frame blocking the door once he had entered—blocking him in.

She cleared her throat.

"Here's the drill," she said, and launched into what was undoubtedly a much-rehearsed speech: "Matins, or Dawn Prayer, is at four a.m. Lauds is at six, Terce at nine, Sext at noon, None at three, Vespers at six, and Compline, or Night Prayer, at nine p.m. Got that? The Great Silence follows immediately after Compline. Matins at four means rising at three forty-five a.m., when our sisters assigned to the night vigil come to wake us. You may join us at any service you choose."

Pausing in her narrative, Dame Tabitha peered at him from her wide-set, tilted eyes. Like a cat's eyes, they were, and suddenly Max saw how she got her Tabby nickname, with her small chin and wide cheekbones enhancing the illusion. The litany she had just recited was a test, Max felt, of his devotion: Would he embrace this military-style regime? She did add, with a tiny access of compassion, "When you get to be my age, Father, you're generally wide awake at four a.m. anyway, so it's not the hardship it once was. I have learned to welcome the sound of the wake-up call to prayer—even in the dead of winter, when it is very hard to force these bones out of bed. Apart from fireplaces, the convent is heated by generators and solar power—and the hydroelectric generator we installed in the river last year has been a Godsend."

Max acknowledged this by a nod of his head. At just the thought of Monkbury Abbey in the middle of an English winter he could feel his temperature drop a notch. The advantage of the old stone walls in summer would be that, outside the sun's direct rays, one would be comfortably cool. There was of course no air-conditioning.

"After Matins, we have some quiet time to ourselves, she continued. "After Lauds comes the end of the Great Silence, then breakfast."

Max reflected that, for many people, that would be a full day put in already, and time for a nap. But they were only getting started.

"Guests join us for our midday meal and for supper. For breakfast, you are on your own in the guest kitchen, where cold cereal and fruit and so on are provided."

She paused. Was he taking all this in? He nodded.

"We work after the midday meal and after three p.m. prayer we have a light tea. Afterward is private time for those who choose, but for postulants and novices, there are readings and reflections that are a part of their training. We have one of each at the moment—Sister Rose and the postulant named Mary Benton." She sighed. "Things are not as they were in my day, when we would easily have had a dozen of each, like hens running underfoot."

"Time marches on," Max murmured sympathetically.

"Lights out at ten p.m. sharp. I cannot emphasize enough that the time of the Great Silence is sacred and can only be broken with permission from the abbess or in an emergency."

Again she peered closely at him, as if gauging him for tendencies toward late-night carousing and general debauchery.

"The door that links to the abbey proper is kept locked at all times," she said with, he thought, unnecessarily pointed emphasis.

"So if a sister were to enter the guesthouse on an errand, she would lock the door behind her?"

If she found this question strange she gave no sign of it. "At all times," she said.

"Even if she were going to be here only a moment or so?"

"All times." She was starting to economize on syllables, so Max didn't see that he could get much further with this line of inquiry. If

Dame Tabitha were to be believed, and he didn't doubt her for a minute, there was no access to the off-limits cloistered area from the guesthouse.

Dame Tabitha was looking at him as if to be certain he quite understood everything that was expected of him, behavior-wise.

He smiled, hoping he looked sufficiently innocent of plans to break uninvited into the nun's dormitory.

"Do you have any further questions, Father?"

"Why, yes, if you wouldn't mind."

Her expression suggested that had she been wearing a watch, she would pointedly have consulted it. But she waited, again massaging her giant's knuckles.

"Do you get many visitors?" Max asked.

She shrugged and allowed herself a small smile. Was it his imagination, or was she relieved at the general nature of his question? "We've a full house most weekends," she told him. "During the week, it's mostly retired and unemployed folk. They are wise, I think, to use their free time to contemplate their next move. For the unemployed, we don't charge. We ask them to make a donation when they are better equipped to do so."

"That is really most kind of you."

She blushed, as if it were all her own idea.

"It used to be the policy never to ask for a specific sum but after we had entertained several dubious guests we had to begin suggesting a minimal amount. One person stole the light bulbs, if you can believe it. But after we mentioned what it cost us to keep the guesthouse running, guests generally exceeded the suggested amount, sometimes by hundreds of pounds. There is no accounting for people."

"No, indeed. You must be kept very busy."

"My, yes. I'm kept busy, praise God. But not as much as the guest-mistresses of the past. Monkbury Abbey has had its share of queens and duchesses and their entourages come to lodge with us. They seem to have been nothing but trouble.

"I do not wish to boast," she added, "but we have always been famous for our hospitality. And for our cooking. And for our choir."

"Everyone is welcome at all the services?"

"Absolutely. We also invite people to lend a helping hand with whatever needs doing. Male visitors are invited to help chop wood and do the heavy lifting." She looked meaningfully at her latest male visitor, assessing his potential for manual labor. Max resisted the impulse to flex his biceps.

"Oh, of course," he told her. "I'd be delighted to help where I can." If nothing else it would give him an excuse to mingle with whoever was about.

"We have trouble taking in the deliveries sometimes, you see," she said. "The bags of flour and whatnot for the fruitcake. Ah, I see you've heard of our fruitcake? Yes. And of course there is the garden. I heard Dame Petronilla say the other day she was getting behind with the vegetable garden. She's coming down with a cold."

"Just let me know. I would welcome the chance to be out of doors."

"Many of our visitors seem to feel the same way. Some are in search of the 'simple life.'" There was just the merest hint of scorn on the last phrase, but she went on to say, "We've never had anyone refuse to help in the garden, for example, although we have had visitors whose help has been on somewhat of a sliding scale. I can't say our resident artist has been of much help." Her voice dripped irony on the word "artist."

"I wasn't aware you had an artist in residence," he said, knowing from Cotton's brief descriptions she must mean Piers Montague, the photographer, and friend of Paloma Green.

"My, yes," she said. "You'll come to hear of him, I'm sure. He's already been asked several times not to photograph the sisters; we are not on display."

She had edged away from the doorway and now stood in the corridor, illuminated by a single electric bulb augmented by sconces between each door.

"It's all quite atmospheric," said Max, and indeed this was an understatement. It was dark enough he felt he'd have trouble finding the door in an emergency. "Haunting."

"The guesthouse was at one time a lazar house," she told him. "A leper hospital. Twelfth century. It was the sort of place nuns were sent to serve as a penance for, erm, moral incontinence and other serious lapses. The hard cases who never seemed to learn anything. Of course, there were always the truly devout nuns who asked to serve in this way—they saw it as a privilege, you see."

"Remarkable," said Max. And of course with no hope of a cure, and no real understanding of the disease, it was for many of the nurses a terrible and almost guaranteed death sentence.

"There also was a leper chapel at one time—sadly, it's gone now," she told him.

"That is too bad," said Max. "Except I'm glad there's less need of it now."

"Normally we don't mention the origins of the place to the guests," Dame Tabitha confided. She lowered her booming voice to a rumble, like a helicopter on a strafing run. "It puts some of them off. Even though it was centuries ago, the images it conjures up are . . . not so restful. Just think—people used to believe God visited terrible diseases like leprosy only on sinners."

"We haven't traveled so very far from that sort of superstition," observed Max.

"I really must fly," she announced. "Full instructions and a map are on the desk. You've missed your dinner. Shall I bring you a tray?"

Max shook his head. "Thank you, no. I had a pub meal on the way here. A place called the Running Knight and Pilgrim."

"Ah! Well, I've heard they do a decent fry-up. But it wouldn't have been organic and fresh like the food we serve. Dame Ingrid, our kitcheness—she is a marvel. You'll see. But for breakfast you are on your own, as I've said. The guest kitchen's cabinets and drawers are all labeled as to contents."

He nodded. "Thank you. I'm sure I'll get everything sorted."

"Good night, Father. Feel free to join us for Compline."

She bustled away, skirts billowing behind her like a black sail.

Max closed the door and looked around the room. It was small, with a large picture window at one end. Nearest the window and against one wall was a desk; over it hung a matted and framed photo of the cloister gardens, presumably an offering from a prior guest with artistic leanings. It may even have been a Piers Montague, although it was unsigned. Near the desk was a washbasin with mirror—that mirror would be forbidden in the nuns' cells, he suspected—and behind that a tall, shallow row of shelves with stacks of fresh towels and linens. Behind the shelves was a built-in open cupboard with assorted clothing pegs and hangers. Flat against the other wall was a single bed, at the foot of which was an end table with a reading lamp. Next to that a cushioned armchair completed the basic décor.

The room was nicely heated, and when he tested the hot water tap it ran lukewarm, nearly hot. He wondered if the nuns enjoyed the same amenities as the guests. He suspected their water, if they had running water, would run cold.

Max picked up from the desk a sheaf of paper, mimeographed and stapled together. It was headed "Rules for Our Guesthouse Visitors," and it contained a map and a number of admonitions designed to preserve the quiet and safety of the place. Smoking was of course prohibited, as was alcohol. Tape recorders were permitted so long as they were used with earphones, but musical instruments were not allowed. Mobile phones were not mentioned, but he imagined such things had not been discovered when the rules were being drawn up. Or perhaps it was known that they were miles out of tower range.

Reading material "of an uplifting nature" was provided in the guesthouse library as well as in the guesthouse living room, and retreatants were encouraged to attend daily services so long as they confined themselves to the visitors' seating area in the nave of the church. A schedule of psalms and readings was attached. Guests also were welcome to use the small chapel attached to the guesthouse for private prayer and contemplation.

Finally, it was pointed out that while the abbey generated its own electricity, each guest room was provided with a battery-powered lantern for use in case of emergency; this item could be found in the room's cup-board. The bishop had already advised him to bring a torch.

"But you won't be needing an alarm clock," the bishop had added. Had there been a twinkle in his eye when he said that?

It was delicately suggested at the end of this long list of warnings and admonitions that donations were in no way obligatory, but that the cost to operate the guesthouse was fifty pounds per person, per night. Three daily meals and snacks were included in the stay. It seemed an eminently fair request to Max. He wondered if anyone had ever had the temerity to stiff the good sisters.

Awena, if she had been there, would have said such a thing would absolutely guarantee bad karma for the future, probably forever.

Surely she would have been right.

And how devoutly he wished Awena were there. Closing his eyes he sent up a prayer, which as always included Awena and the child she car-ried, a prayer cloaked in anxiety—*please please please* let them be all right—and in wonder:

He was going to be a father.

He. Max Tudor. A father.

The idea would not take hold, no matter how often he repeated the words. He had always loved children, but this was a new frontier.

He sat and took a few deep breaths.

Breathe in for a count of six. Hold for a count of six. Release for a count of six.

It was a calming technique he had learned from Awena, the most serene person he had ever met.

It helped a bit to quell the panic that lately simmered at the edge of his consciousness. Most of her ideas did help. He wondered if he should pant as they'd been shown in the birthing classes they'd been attending but decided against it.

After a few minutes he collected his sponge bag and plunged into the semi-darkness outside his door, feeling his way toward the men's shower room.

PART IV
Sext

Chapter 7

THE VISITORS: I

All visitors to the abbey shall be made welcome, as we recall in
Matthew: "I was a stranger, and ye took me in."

—*The Rule of the Order of the Handmaids of St. Lucy*

The next morning, Max was wakened by the early bells—the very early
bells calling the nuns to prayer. He gave a fleeting thought to joining
them but turned over and went back to sleep.

An hour later he entered the kitchen to find a central wooden table
with eight mismatched chairs slotted round it. In the middle of the table
were a bowl of fruit, another of fresh brown eggs, and a tray of eating uten-
sils individually wrapped in cloth napkins. Ranged along the walls were
cupboards; a large, old-fashioned sink; a stove (ditto); and a small refrigerator—no microwave. One small window, facing east, overlooked the magnificent cloister garden and was framed by a tied-back muslin curtain.

It was, as Dame Tabby had explained, strictly a serve-yourself setup
and, although basic, seemed designed to accommodate almost every
breakfast preference a guest could wish for. The refrigerator revealed a tub
of what looked like freshly churned butter and a cloth-covered plate of
farm cheeses. There also were a colorful variety of preserved fruits—blue,
red, and a pale golden color. Max started to reach for one of the jars—it
looked like it might contain blueberry preserves—and then thought

better of it. He saw a jar of honey on a nearby shelf and chose that instead. Why, he asked himself, ask for trouble?

He found a fresh loaf of brown bread, clearly homemade with seeds and nuts, and rooted around in several drawers for a bread knife. He cut three thick slices off one end of the loaf, realizing how hungry he was—the pub meal of "bubble and squeak" of the day before had been filling but it seemed an age since he'd left the Running Knight and Pilgrim.

He heard the door open behind him. The man who entered the room could only be, from DCI Cotton's pithy description, Piers Montague.

The photographer, conceding nothing to the season, wore the standard-issue artsy uniform of black turtleneck and black slacks, accessorized with an expensive belt and Italian loafers of a buttery soft black leather. Piers's dark hair would have been the envy of any woman, let alone man, and it fell with silky precision across his tanned face from a deep, gleaming side part. Max was to learn that Piers frequently tossed his head to one side as he spoke, and, as if to display the skill of his barber, his hair obediently flicked back in place each time. Max, with his own tousled mane, felt he might look like a windswept poodle by comparison. Piers had dark eyes of a brooding melancholic cast that probably went down a treat with the ladies, who would want to help him unburden his soul, and indeed he had the breezy, offhand confidence of a man whose conquests probably were legion. Max disliked him on sight, fighting back the groundless, instant prejudice as unworthy of someone of his religious calling. Somehow he suspected it would be a long fight with many hostages taken on both sides. Everything about Piers Montague, beginning with his name, just rubbed Max the wrong way.

"Hello," Max said. He extended a hand in friendly greeting and was repaid with a bone-crushing grasp. He resisted the urge to crush back, and in no way let his face betray that his fingers were left in crumpled pain by the encounter. *What a jackass.*

"Oh, Paloma, darling. There you are," said Piers, turning as a dark-haired woman of middle years entered the room. "I was just getting ready to set out with my camera. It's a nice day for moody outdoor shots. Lots of shadows. Then I thought I'd stop into the church once the nuns have done praying." He turned to Max. "I love these old buildings. I studied to be an architect at one time. Today's designs can't hold a candle."

"Well, *hul*-lo," the woman said to Max. This had to be Paloma Green, whom Cotton had described as "artistic—runs a shop selling high-priced paintings and things for the upscale sitting room." Paloma gave her caterpillar-like lashes a slow, preliminary bat in Max's direction. The impression was of an extra effort involved in opening and shutting the weighty trim of fur around her eyes, but more likely it was part of a practiced vampy act she trotted out whenever a good-looking man crossed her path. The too-tight leopard-print pants, the plunging neckline of her short-sleeved jumper, the jangly "gypsy" jewelry at her neck and wrists all spoke of a woman clinging as hard to youth as the elderly Dame Hephzibah clung to her bell rope.

For some reason, Paloma Green looked familiar to him, but Max could not think how he had come to cross paths with such an exotic creature. Certainly it hadn't been in recent years. She was much more the sort of person he might have dealt with in his MI5 days in London; this va-va-voomy persona was not associated in his mind with placid Nether Monkslip. He'd have noticed her long before now, if only as serious competition for Suzanna Winship, the official village vixen.

Paloma shook Max's hand. She said, "Piers a-*dores* architecture and goes around taking snaps of everything. And of course this place just *oozes* atmosphere. It's haunted. Naturally, it would be," she said, matter-of-factly. Before Max could question her basis for this claim, she added, "Piers has done a lot of restoration work and he specializes in pictures of scenic old ruins."

"Not including you, my dear," Piers said laughingly to Paloma. But she did not share the laughter. Max had the impression it was a very old and very tired joke between them. Piers clearly was ten years younger than Paloma, at least. Although her shoulder-length hair was curled in the chocolate-y brown swirls popularized by the duchess of Cambridge, Paloma probably had a fifteen- or twenty-year head start on the princess.

The curls were held back from her face by a patterned strip of scarf that just missed clashing with the rest of her ensemble. She wore a great deal of makeup, and even Max could tell the eyelashes were fake. A blind man, he corrected himself, could see that they were fake.

He had the idea it was her makeup he was remembering, more so than the woman herself.

"I mean to say, architecture, particularly medieval architecture, is my passion," said Piers. "Given half a chance, I might have become an expert. But my parents were *so* working-class and they didn't believe in the sort of university education that sort of career would require, and once photography began paying the bills . . ." He shrugged. "I was stuck." A whiny note had entered his voice as he sang the refrain of the undernourished genius. It was not an attractive sound.

Max thought of the ongoing renovations at St. Edwold's, which seemed to be a permanent fact of the economic life of his parish, along with purchases for facial tissue. "I do feel I know rather a lot about building renovation and restoration, one way and another."

Neither of them invited Max to elaborate on his expertise. Paloma was still looking a bit miffy, and Piers was clearly eager to get away before she took it into her head to follow him. Max had the impression of a relationship under some stress. Was this in any way related to the mysterious financial doings at the nunnery?

Sensing at last that his joke about Paloma's age had fallen flat, Piers said after a few stiffly awkward moments, "Well, I'll be off now."

"Actually, I'd appreciate it if you'd stick around a moment," said Max. "I have a few questions I'd like to ask if you wouldn't mind."

"Of us?" They exchanged glances. Piers said, "*W-a-a-l-l-l* . . . I don't think I—"

"You are staying at the abbey as a sort of spiritual retreat?" Max asked, smiling ingenuously, keeping the skepticism from his voice. All were welcome to seek renewal among the nuns—people from all walks of life and background. But these two were as out of place as Viking raiders at a car boot sale.

Paloma confirmed this impression by saying, "Well, hardly. I mean, jeez. No, we're here in more of a . . . supervisory capacity. Or, investigative. Wouldn't you say, Piers?"

"*W-a-a-l-l-l* . . . sort of," he agreed, but judiciously. "Paloma helped raise funds for the abbey's new guesthouse, you see. And I donated several of my best photos. Sort of a goodwill gesture—you know. For the publicity. We thought it would be a lark to spend a weekend in the country and see how our good deeds were being put to use."

"*If* they were," he added.

"If?" asked Max.

"I don't see any signs of construction or groundbreaking, do you? Still, it's not completely a waste of time. As I've said, I am enamored of old ruins." Wisely, this time he did not even glance in Paloma's direction. "But it's . . . rather quiet here."

"Ah," said Max neutrally.

"It's not what we'd expected, to be sure," Paloma offered.

And you were expecting—what? Max wondered. *Cirque du Soleil?*

"But you've been here before?" Max asked.

"I have," said Paloma. "But how did you—?"

"It's *really* quiet here," Piers elaborated, yawning. "I have just returned from a two-week trip driving alone around Leeds, on commission, looking at sites some building magnate wanted photographed. That was a lawless riot by comparison."

Paloma had apparently forgotten her question to Max. Again batting her eyes, she said, "If things don't pick up, we'll probably leave tomorrow. I can't even get a signal on my mobile out here. I left my gallery in the charge of an imbecile, and it's the busy season."

"Uhm," said Max. "Well, each to his own. Personally, I'm looking forward to a little down time away from the World Wide Web." He added politely, "Where is your gallery?"

"In Monkslip-super-Mare." She mentioned the name of an art gallery on the High Street in the popular seaside resort. It was one of many galleries, but one serving the upper end of the tourist trade.

The penny dropped. Max knew where he must have seen her before.

"You carry Coombebridge's work!" he exclaimed. Lucas Coombe-bridge was an artist living in secluded Monkslip Curry who had nonethe-less achieved a global renown for his seascapes. Max owned several of his smaller works, bought at a time when they were still within reach of the salary of a country parson. Max happened to know the woman before him had been granted exclusive rights by the artist to display and sell his works. Max also knew, as it was an open secret, that she was one of many former lovers of the infamous painter.

"Yes," she said, pleased at the recognition.

"I've bought several paintings from you," Max told her, "but that was long ago. And I'm sorry to say that while you look familiar somehow I don't think I remember you from the gallery." The more he thought about it, the more he was sure he'd not met her in person. "I'm certain I would have remembered," he added gallantly.

She expanded visibly. The over-the-top costuming surely was in-tended to make the biggest impression possible, and she was pleased it had succeeded. "I'm not often there," she said. "You probably saw my photo in the promotional literature for the gallery. Coombebridge was a right—ahem . . . he was a right stinker, but his commissions set me up so well I soon didn't have to be in the shop much. I travel abroad a lot." She held out one arm and jangled the attached bracelets, as if to show what could be bought if one went abroad.

"His work is *so* overrated," scoffed Piers.

"Not a match for *your* work," she exclaimed loyally. But the wink, not meant to be seen by Piers, was aimed at Max.

"Well, it's been a pleasure, I'm sure, Mr. . . . ?" Piers began. Max re-membered he was not wearing his collar. He'd thrown on a jumper and jeans and trainers, not really expecting to meet anyone this early.

"It's Father Max Tudor, actually."

"Ah!" They both looked taken aback, as though a priest were the last thing they'd expect to meet in a nunnery.

"Well, I guess *you're* here on retreat," said Paloma.

Max smiled. "Sort of," he said. He thought he might quiz them some more later on their reasons for being there, not that he expected to hear the truth.

But for right now, he was hungry.

Chapter 8

THE VISITORS: II

Be tolerant of the young and the old.

—*The Rule of the Order of the Handmaids of St. Lucy*

Once Paloma and Piers had left, she trailing scarves and he creeping after, a model without a runway, Max resumed assembling his breakfast.

He was just slicing peaches for his granola when the door swung open to admit a young woman of indeterminate years—she could have been sixteen or thirty, but her costume, like that of a child playing dress up, suggested the lower end of the age scale. She wore a black leather jacket over a full skirt of tie-died fabric, and beneath it showed several layers of petticoats, also of rainbow hues. Her black boots matched the jacket; purple-and-black striped socks, worn over white lace stockings, peeped from the tops of the boots. Her hair was a thatch of white-blond, randomly tipped in pink at the ends. Max saw that her fingertips were indeed painted blue, as had been reported by Dame Tabitha. He took a wild guess that this was Xanda, daughter of the American family, the Goreys. She was short and slightly pear-shaped, and with the hair she looked like a baby chick that had come out the worse for wear in an Easter egg decorating competition. On entering the room she had the preoccupied look of adolescence, but on seeing him she switched on a cheery smile: *Here, at last—something new!* She had a gap between her front teeth that added to her charm.

"Don't tell me you're in with this bunch," is what she actually said, looking him up and down. She had a high-pitched, girlish voice with what he recognized as an American Valley girl accent. "You don't look like a religious maniac." Then she hesitated. "Wait. You're the priest sent to look into all the, like, stuff going on here, aren't you?" She waggled her blue-tipped fingers on the word "stuff" to indicate the fluidity of the situation. Max wondered how she had deduced his calling, a question she answered by saying: "My mom said there was '*such* a nice-looking priest' sent to sort things out."

This place must rival Nether Monkslip for jungle-drum communiques, thought Max. Her mother must have seen him arrive last night, when he was wearing his collar, but how she had known his mission . . .

"And if mom notices," Xanda went on gaily, "it must be one hot-looking dude. You don't mind my saying that, do you? You are hot, you know, for an old guy. It's not like you're a *priest*-priest, with vows of celebrity and all." Max nodded his agreement, biting back a smile at her gaffe. "Anyway, there's no one else here who fits the bill. I mean, that cop Cotton is good-looking, but I know who he is—he grilled me for simply *hours*, you know; it was wonderful! So much like *Law and Order*—do you get that here? Yes? And God knows Piers thinks he's a gift sent to women from above. But for sure I know what Piers looks like. That's 'Piers Montague, Artist.' Everyone always refers to him this way, you will notice. 'Piers Montague Comma Artist.' What a berk. If you hear a lot of commotion at night around here, it's probably him, meeting up with Paloma Green. Who they think they're kidding, I do not know. And anyone can hear the bolt to the women's side of the guesthouse open—it's like Grand Central. Now, that DCI Cotton is a different story. Hubba, as they say, hubba."

"I've been wondering exactly why he's here," said Max. "Piers." He looked hopefully at his new source of information. She was hardly a reluctant witness, although how unbiased a one he couldn't be sure. She seemed to share his withering assessment of Piers, which moved her up several notches in Max's estimation.

"'Piers Montague, Artist,' you mean? He was part of the fund-raising effort. The idea was that famous *artistes* would be invited to donate paintings and photographs they'd made of the abbey and religious stuff like that. He's also studying some paintings in the church—he says. He's a restor . . . restorative . . ."

"Restorer," finished Max for her.

"Yah," she agreed. "But me, I wonder what qualifies you to be sorting things out at the abbey? I mean," she added, "no offense, but this can't be in your usual line of work. Shouldn't you be baptizing babies or healing the sick or something?"

"DCI Cotton asked me to be here," Max said mildly. It seemed best to leave it at that. She struck him as the sort of precocious woman-child who would pepper him with questions given half a chance. He decided to turn the tables.

"You must be Xanda," he said. "What an unusual name. Very pretty."

"They had to name me something to balance out the last name Gorey. Always makes me think of a horror flick about an alien creature from the planet Zicon or something. And it is not short for Alexandra. For once in their turgid, stuck-in-the-mud lives, my parents anticipated a trend. You know: *Buffy the Vampire Slayer*."

"It's a very pretty name," he insisted, thinking her parents couldn't be all that stodgy or they surely would have put a clamp on her hair and costume choices. Although, when did parents have any real say in those departments? "You are here with your parents, I take it?"

"As if I had a choice. You don't seriously think I'd be here without them, do you? It's summer vacation time back home. I just finished my freshman year in college. I'm studying medieval literature. Not my choice, believe me. Some days I could just die. *Die!* I'm trying to talk the folks into letting me switch. My mother says he who pays the piper names the tune. But I don't even know what they're talking about in class most days. Complete waste of money. I threatened to drop out. They practically commanded me to come on this trip with them. They think it will change my mind. My father especially is a real Anglephile." Whatever they were teaching her in college, it was not vocabulary. "My parents both love everything about England, beginning with the Queen and that naff son of hers. I could just *gag* I'm so bored. Harry looks like he could be fun, though." Max assumed she was talking about HRH Prince Harry. Max still had connections in SO14 who reported that guarding Harry was an exercise in burlesque comedy intermixed with moments of sheer terror. Xanda twirled the end of one blond-pink lock, evaluating Max's own potential for livening things up.

"When do you leave?" he asked.

"Whenever my father's convinced himself he isn't being ripped off," she replied. "Or when he's satisfied he has been and decides what to do about it. What 'legal recourse' he has, as he puts it. But he's taking his sweet time about it. I mean, they're nuns, after all. It's a bit hard to go around accusing them without a lot of evidence, wouldn't you say?"

"Ripped off?" Max asked casually, pouring a cup of coffee for himself and offering her one.

"Yeah. It's something to do with money," she said, lowering her voice and leaning in confidingly. "Money that should have gone into replacing electricity and plumbing and things here in the guesthouse can't be accounted for. There was supposed to be an addition to the building, too, and there's no sign of it." She examined one blue nail and began smoothing back the cuticle with her thumb. "My father is furious and 'demands an accounting.' I think he brought Piers Montague, Artist, and that art gallery owner woman on board to back up his protest. That's just a guess, but my father is good at getting people in his corner."

Turning away, she started rooting around in various cupboards, opening the small fridge to pull out a milk bottle. She proceeded to pour half the contents into a large glass and took a sip, eyeing him over the top.

"You didn't know all this?" she asked. "I would bet you did."

"I know there is some question in your father's mind, and presumably in your mother's, about the dispersal of various funds he's provided the abbey."

"Big question, yep. Mucho problemo with the missing dinero, yessiree. He's rich, you know, my father. He actually believes God wants him to be rich, which probably helps, don't you think?"

"I suppose it does, rather," said Max.

"He's an investor. Meaning, he invests other people's money. In what, I don't know. Just stocks and stuff like that. But he's pretty good at guessing how the market will move. And just because he's rich doesn't mean he is okay with being ripped off. He hasn't half been torqued since we got here. 'Where are the earth-movers?' he wants to know. She lowered her voice to a basso boom, in what Max was to learn was a fair imitation of her father. "'Men with shovels? Pitchforks? *Some*thing?'"

"He came here to investigate, did he?" Max prodded. "To determine whether his money was in good hands?"

"Yah. But he and my mom come here at least every summer, anyway. Have for years. It's their idea of fun, this sort of religious fandango. Just imagine. Well, I guess you can imagine, but. . . . They used to leave me with my aunt in Boston, thinking that was safer somehow. They had no idea—my aunt is forty but she *rocks*. I mean really—she sings in a band. But this year, as I say, my father decided it was time to 'expand my horizons.' Ugh. *Shrink* them, is more like it. No computer, no cell phone, no television. *Jesus*. Oops, sorry, Father. No disrespect intended. But I am just about reaching my limit, you know? The animals are not as much fun as I was led to believe."

"Animals?"

"Sure. It's a working farm. They have goats, and the nuns make cheese and things. The goats creep me out. Those *eyes!*" Hunching her shoulders around her ears, she shivered with distaste. "Even the little ones."

Max was sympathetic. It had not been all that long since he himself had been a teenager. He could imagine that Monkbury Abbey held little scope for someone her age.

"*And* they barely have electricity," she went on. "The lights went out the other night. The hamster or whatever turns the wheels that make the generator go must have escaped."

"They are somewhat off the grid out here," agreed Max.

"Are you going into the village soon?" she asked.

"Erm. I just got here," said Max.

"I don't suppose I could . . ."

"Borrow my car?" Max laughed. "No. But if I go into the village you'll be the first to know. You can come with me, but with your parents' permission, of course."

"I'm eighteen," she insisted.

"Still," he said. Better to keep the peace with the Goreys, whom he had not even met, than disturb the peace in anticipation. Her father didn't sound like the type of man to approve a joyride for his daughter, particularly in a foreign country with a strange man.

A big sigh at this from Xanda. Apparently this Max person was going to be as tedious about everything as her parents were.

Clearly playing her trump card, she said: "I don't know how much more I can take, you know. They communicate with these elaborate hand signals at meals on Sundays—the nuns, I mean. The only sound you can hear is a spoon striking the bottom of a bowl, or the occasional crunch of a raw carrot or a stick of celery, or the clacking of someone's dentures. It's too horrible for words. *Ghastly*, as the English say. But worse than the silence is the readings the nuns do at dinnertime. Stuff from the scriptures, and 'uplifting' advice from martyrs and hermits and the utterly clueless, all delivered in this, like, *mono*tune. *God!*"

"Monotone," corrected Max automatically. "I'm sure it's a bit boring. But there is the fresh air and the little sheep, right? And perhaps fishing if you're so inclined . . . I suppose . . . ?"

He trailed off. She looked at him as if he had taken leave of his senses.

"I hope you're joking. Do I look like a fisherman to you?"

"I just meant, there must be compensations. The peace and quiet. Those are hard things to come by, day by day. Perhaps it's something you'll appreciate more as you get older."

"Not I," she said flatly. "I never want to get old, not like this bunch. Even the postulant—she's not much older than me, and *what* a drip she is. She doesn't even know who Eminem is. I want to live my life in, like, the fast lane—you know? If I ever get out of here alive, I mean. At least the attempted murder livened things up."

"Who told you it was attempted murder?" he asked her, rather sharply. Then more gently, he added, "I mean, what makes you think that?"

"Dunno." She twirled one of the pink-tipped strands at the side of her head. "Stands to reason. I mean, have you met him?"

She would not be drawn further on what exactly stood to reason. After a few delicately phrased attempts at pinning her down, Max returned his attention to his granola.

"My father is always on about the mandolin," she said conversationally after a while. She began picking through the bowl of fruit on the table. "He collects things, my dad."

Max imagined he could afford to.

"That's an interesting hobby," he said.

"I guess. He likes religious art. You should see our house. It's like living in a cathedral."

She had sat down across the table from him, and using the knife he'd left lying there, began trying to peel an apple without breaking the skin. She got about halfway through.

"Rats," she said.

Max, still puzzling over what on earth she was talking about, finally put it together.

"You mean Mandylion," he said.

"Yeah, that's it. My dad's obsessed with the mandolin. He's not the only one."

"A Mandylion," Max repeated. "It is thought to be an image of the living Christ. There are several versions, none that can be authenticated." He thought of the reappearing image back in his own church of St. Ed-wold's, which stubbornly reemerged on the wall despite his best attempts to eradicate it with paint and plaster. As little Tom Hooser loudly and repeatedly insisted, it bore a strong resemblance to the face on the Shroud of Turin.

"Of course," Max added, "it is all the purest speculation. Wishful thinking at its most intense. Everyone wants to know exactly what Christ looked like when he walked the earth. And there is no one who can know."

"Didn't the apostles or somebody leave a description in the Bible? Didn't anyone make a sketch or something?"

Max smiled. A child of the Internet age, she would find it hard to grasp that describing the physical Christ would not have occurred to anyone. Also that he didn't leave written words or autographs.

That photography had not yet been invented.

That, in any event, much that was recorded in the scriptures had been recorded long after the fact.

Max merely shook his head. "No such luck," he said. "So I am to take it you are not religious yourself?"

"No. I leave all that to the people who go in for this sort of thing." With a wave, Xanda indicated the other inmates of the abbey. Realizing what she'd just said might have sounded rude, considering her audience, she added, with the urgent gaucheness of youth, "I didn't mean you, of course. It's your job, like, and I'm sure you're really good at it. But my parents . . . I've just had it up to here with being told what Jesus said and what Jesus thought and how I'm breaking the rules all the time. And my hair! Why do adults always make such a thing of hair? Besides, you should have seen it before. Curly, but not in an interesting way. More like escaped-lunatic curly."

"They're very devout, your parents?"

"What a nice way of putting it. They're crazy, actually. Our house also looks like a gift shop in Lourdes. They dragged me there when I was ten. Let me tell you, there is no plastic left in France that hasn't been melted down into a statue. I don't know why my parents don't just convert over to the Catholic side. They're so—what do you call it here? High Church? Yeah, so High Church it practically makes no difference."

There was a movement outside the window overlooking the cloister. Xanda pointed and said, "There they are. Meet the parents. If you dare."

Max stepped over to the window and saw the couple walking in the cloister, near the north alley that ran beside the church. The cloister was actually a large square garden with fruit trees and flowers, now coaxed into bloom by the summer heat. The U.K. as a whole had endured a rainy spring, but now the Monkbury Abbey garden seemed to be reaping the full and glorious benefit. The cloister was surrounded in traditional style by a roofed arcade on all sides, with the nunnery buildings opening off of it. There was what appeared to be a stone well in the center of the garden. Max remembered reading somewhere the waters of that well had miraculous healing powers.

The couple were near enough Max could see them clearly over the top of the muslin curtain. Clement was a large, tuna-headed man with a shiny bald pate and round wireless spectacles perched precariously on the bridge of a fleshy nose. He had small teeth like rows of baby corn kernels, misshapen but gleaming white. He wore what Max thought of as the uniform of the travelling, well-off tourist, genus American: khaki pants with large pockets on the legs, and a short-sleeved polo shirt unbuttoned at the neck to reveal a clean white T-shirt. He had on expensive white trainers with a tread fit for an all-terrain vehicle.

Mrs. Gorey—Oona—was, like Piers Montague, dressed in black, but in some drapey fabric that hung loosely from her shoulders to cover what looked to be a substantial frame. Somehow Max didn't think this was an arty choice on her part, as it was in the case of Piers. She may have thought of it as proper nunnery-visiting garb, but, although black was all the rage these days, this clothing was funereal rather than stylish. Her hair was like a balled-up fist, the blond curls tightly corkscrewed to her head. She had a pretty little face but it wore a mean, pinched-in expression.

Max was reminded of one of those grand ladies whose effigies could be seen carved on medieval tombs, her husband lying beside her and perhaps a little dog curled at her feet. Her expression stern and forbidding, just *know*ing she was on her way to meet God in person at last. Judging by her strong visage and the sturdy walk of this living example of grit and fortitude, Max imagined Oona Gorey could easily hold her own against her powerful husband.

He turned back to Xanda.

"The fun couple," she said. "As I told you, they adore this place, which gives you some idea of the limits to their definition of a fun vacation."

"Perhaps you could learn a craft while you're here. The sisters are famous for their skills at pottery, just for one example."

"Oh, yeah. I suppose. I was helping Dame Potter the other day. But that is *so* not me."

"What is you?" asked Max gently.

For that she had a ready answer, surprising Max somewhat. Generally, at her age, the answer was more about what she did *not* want to do. "I want to study fashion design. In New York, at the Fashion Institute. My father 'won't hear of it.'"

"Ah," said Max. "I suppose he holds the purse strings and decides what you study, and where."

"You got it."

"Is there any chance of a scholarship?"

"Not when you're rich, no."

"I meant a merit scholarship. You know, based on your talent."

"I dunno." It didn't seem to have occurred to her, strangely enough. The rich really are different, thought Max. A glimmer of something like hope crept into her eyes.

"Why don't you look into it?" said Max. "You're not a minor any longer. Once your father sees you making your own way, he may come around." Remembering his own father, Max added: "If slowly."

"The minute I'm near an Internet connection again, which can't be a moment too soon, I will look into it. Thanks."

A rather loud, throat-clearing *harrumph* could be heard from the hallway, along with the sound of a rather heavy footfall.

"That would be the lord," said Xanda. "Lord Lislelivet. Sorry to do this to you, Father, but I am *so* out of here."

Chapter 9

THERE WAS A
CROOKED MAN

The sisters should remain vigilant to each other's needs as they
eat and drink, so that no one at table need ask for anything.

—The Rule of the Order of the Handmaids of St. Lucy

Max actually welcomed the intrusion, for here was a chance to meet the
devil in the flesh.

Lord Lislelivet was much smaller than he appeared on the telly,
where Max had seen him in various ceremonial appearances in the House
of Lords, dressed head to toe on high occasion in feathers and swords and
other inherited bling. As one of the few remaining members sitting by
virtue of a hereditary peerage, Lord Lislelivet was a vanishing breed. Perhaps the glittery accoutrements added inches to his height, for in person
he was a small man, one who might have been mistaken for any man on
the street except for the certain glow of privilege that exuded from every
pore.

Today he was dressed casually in a linen sport jacket on top of an
open-collared shirt and cotton chinos. If he added a tie, he'd be ready to
take a last-minute business meeting at his club. Dark-haired and olive-
complexioned, he had that special polish that came with having loads of
money and access to the best bespoke tailors, that sheen of hair and skin
as if he had been spray-painted with fairy dust. Prince Charles had the

same patrician look of hair blown into place by royal hairdressers and of shoes polished to a deep gleam by royal shoeblacks.

Like many men of his breed he also wore an invisible cloak of entitlement. Max had dealt with many such in his career, as he had often been called in by MI5 when the have-nots showed signs of wanting to exterminate the haves, as happened routinely. The haves sat in their resplendent drawing rooms and sipped their single malts, these winners of the inheritance lottery, as they poured out their distress at being targeted yet again. Most of these men were charming, if oblivious. Lord Lislelivet struck Max as leaning heavily toward the oblivious side, not feeling an overarching need to waste his limited resources of charm.

As Max pondered how much to tell Lord Lislelivet of the reason for his being there, the Lord stole the initiative.

"I am glad," he said, "the bishop is taking this seriously. You have been sent by the bishop from Monkslip Cathedral, have you not?"

"In fact, I am the vicar of Nether Monkslip," Max replied. Feeling that he towered over the man, he stood back an inch or two to try to even the eye level. "Father Maxen Tudor. But yes, I am here at the behest of the bishop. Obviously, the situation concerns him mightily."

"The *vicar*?" Lord Lislelivet repeated, obviously taken back by Max's low station in life. "Of—what was it—Nether Monkslip? And where on earth is Nether Monkslip?"

"Not far from the Channel," Max answered vaguely. "A few miles from Monkslip-super-Mare."

"So you're not officially attached to the bishopric? You're not part of the bishop's official investigative team?"

"So far as I'm aware, the bishop does not maintain an investigative team." Max struggled to keep the exasperation from his voice, although the image of the bishop trailed by a bodyguard of MI5 agents did raise a smile. "It's not the Vatican, you know. Just one smallish diocese of the Church of England."

"Well," said Lord Lislelivet. If he'd added, "I suppose you'll do," Max might have turned heel and left the room. Instead the man unbent enough to say, "The bishop is a sound man. An Etonian, you know. I suppose he knows what he's doing. What exactly are your qualifications for this investigation?"

Every bone in Max's body resisted the impulse to provide Lord Lislelivet with a summary of his C.V., although he was fully aware that a mention of his MI5 background would instantly have placated the man. There was about it too much of a tone of pandering to live up to Lord Lislelivet's inflated sense of his own worth—of a need for all the forces in the kingdom to be brought to bear on this fruitcake problem of his. "I simply have an inquiring mind," said Max evenly, "as well as a desire to arrive at the truth of what happened to you. The bishop has found my involvement in . . . similar cases . . . useful in the past."

There. That sounded sufficiently James Bond-ish, thought Max. Cue the *Goldfinger* theme. He arranged the muscles of his face in a suitably inscrutable mask, like an avenging samurai sent by the shogun from the court of the emperor. It seemed to do the trick, for Lord Lislelivet said no more, but regarded him warily, a new respect in his eyes.

"I would appreciate it if you would fill me in," said Max, looking to seal his advantage. "The bishop was rather sketchy as to detail. You were here at the abbey last fall, I gather?"

"Yes. I came on a religious retreat. Fresh air and quiet, you know. A chance to reflect and restore the soul, what? And a chance to see my aunt. She lives here, you see, and she has not been at all well."

"Um hmm. This would have been during the summer recess of the House of Lords?"

"Yes. As I recall, the return of the house wasn't until October 8 last year."

"And how did you come to have this offending fruitcake in your possession? Did you buy it from the gift shop here at the abbey?"

"No, as a matter of fact. Although I intended to buy one there, which is the odd thing. A gift for the little woman, you know. The fruitcake they make here has become world-renowned."

"This was your first visit to the abbey, was it?"

"By no means, but it was my first visit in quite a while, sad to say. I would be the first to admit I've neglected my aunt shamefully over the years. We were never close. The way of life she chose precluded that. And once my mother died, years ago now . . . I'm afraid my visits fell off completely. It was my mother who felt duty bound to come and visit, you see. I was—well, I was a young man and I found the whole setup rather off-putting, if you follow."

Max did follow, as it happened, and would have used precisely the same terms. All these women shut away from the world. He had always found it hard to understand and his own visits to his aunt were too few and far between.

"So, how did you come by the fruitcake?" Max asked him again. By this point, Lord Lislelivet was attempting to master the industrial-size toaster that dominated one counter of the kitchen. The trick, Max knew, was to slot the bread on the grill and let it slip inside the conveyor, without forcing it. The way Lord Lislelivet was going about things, there was sure to be a logjam followed by the smell of burning toast. Max was familiar with the more recalcitrant type of machine from his time at university, but perhaps Lord Lislelivet had had his own scout to prepare breakfast for him. Max took over, setting dials and pushing buttons with a flourish, disproportionately proud at the opportunity to demonstrate his competence in this culinary matter. His time spent with Mrs. Hooser had not been in vain; in self-defense he had been forced to learn a few basic survival skills.

Lord Lislelivet began struggling with a jar of currant preserves. Max took it from him and gave the lid a whack with the dull side of a knife to loosen it. Lord Lislelivet looked suitably impressed, almost as if he thought Max could survive for months alone in the arctic circle with just a harpoon and a spool of thread. Surely this would translate into more confidence in Max's sleuthing abilities, although Max was not entirely sure why this was so. But Lord Lislelivet seemed easily fooled, and Max was enjoying himself.

"So," he repeated, handing back the opened jar.

"On second thought," said Lord Lislelivet doubtfully, "perhaps I won't have anything to eat with fruit in it."

Max nodded. "Right, I see. An egg might be better. Now, the provenance of the fruitcake?"

"Well, that is what should have alerted me that the situation was perhaps unusual. I found it in my room here at the guesthouse before I left. You have noticed how none of the doors have locks? So anyone could have come along and slipped it inside my room."

"Was it packaged or labeled in any way?"

"It was wrapped in cloth—some homespun sort of thing—and it had a note attached, saying, 'With the compliments of Monkbury Abbey,' or words to that effect."

"You didn't save the note?"

The man shook his head. Now he held an egg in one hand and a pan in the other. He seemed to have arrived at a basic understanding that both items were needed in order to produce a boiled egg. But it was clear he did not know how to set about doing it.

Max took the pan from him and, filling it with cold water, set it on the stove to boil.

"So, the note was unsigned," Max said after Lord Lislelivet's egg was under way.

"That's right."

"I don't suppose you saved the wrapping, either?"

He shook his head. "All long gone, I'm afraid—thrown in the fire when I got home." He laughed. His laugh was a dry little *heh heh*, devoid of humor.

It was a shame, thought Max, that key pieces of evidence had been destroyed. "It was handwritten, the note?"

"Yes, but in block letters. I suppose that should have made me wonder. But it's a nunnery, for God's sake. I assumed it was a nice little parting gift they gave to all the guests."

"I see." Using a slotted spoon, Max dropped the egg into the water before it could reach a roiling boil, and turned down the heat.

"And when did you realize there was something off about it?"

"It was several weeks later. Months, actually. A fruitcake is not something one dives into right away, you know. It sits there for a while, making one feel guilty until one eats it. It could actually have sat around for years, but one night I had it for a pudding when I didn't want the fresh fruit my wife had planned. She's always on some slimming regime, and I wanted something more substantial, you see."

"Yes. So you had some fruitcake and . . . there were symptoms. How soon after you ingested it?"

"About two hours after we finished supper. I was taken quite ill. My wife and I had the identical meal, you see, except for the pudding. She later admitted she hadn't touched the fruitcake, but gave some to the dog. The dog was taken ill, too. That's how I knew the problem was with the fruitcake."

"And immediately you got on the horn to the bishop's office?"

"Not right away," said Lord Lislelivet. "I didn't quite know what to do, to be honest. It was rather unprecedented, apart from a spot of food poisoning once when I was in Delhi on business. But finally my wife convinced me I had to tell someone. It could have been a bad batch of fruitcake going out around the world, you see." What his wife actually had said was that she was sick of hearing him complain about that stupid fruitcake, so why didn't he do something about it? But Lord Lislelivet didn't feel compelled to repeat their marital conversation verbatim. So much of what transpired between him and his wife, once he came to think of it, was unrepeatable in polite society.

"I never doubted it was a mistake or accident," he concluded. "Now I'm not so certain."

Max removed the egg from the water, having nicely judged the timing by his wristwatch. If Lord Lislelivet had not asked for a two-minute egg, Max might have been tempted to show off by cracking an egg open with one hand, a trick he'd learned by watching Awena work in the kitchen. He was absurdly pleased to have mastered this new skill. Now he found an egg cup on one of the open shelves and deposited the egg inside, just as the toast was emerging from the toaster. He set this meal on the table before Lord Lislelivet, who thanked him with a nod, and proceeded to tap around the edges of the egg, breaking the shell. Max noticed he cut his toast into soldiers for dipping, the way a child would do.

"I have to ask, Lord Lislelivet," began Max. "It's a bit delicate. But is there anyone here who would wish you harm?"

"No! Not at all. The very idea is preposterous." He seemed genuinely astonished at the question. But that could be because he had no ene-mies—an impossibility, in Max's experience. Every man had enemies, whether earned innocently or deliberately—or because he believed him-self to be so greatly loved that the thought of enemies was impossible for his mind to entertain. From what Max knew of Lord Lislelivet's charac-ter, the second alternative was much the more likely: Lord Lislelivet's ego would protect him from the reality of how he was perceived and regarded. His mind simply could not take in the fact that someone would deliber-ately want to harm him.

In fairness, thought Max, how many of us could live with that truth?

Chapter 10

THE EVIL OF AVARICE

In offering for sale the products of the nunnery, beware the evil of avarice. The nunnery must always be known for fair dealing.

—*The Rule of the Order of the Handmaids of St. Lucy*

Max left Lord Lislelivet ten minutes later, none the wiser as to who might have wanted to poison the man—except in a general sort of way—and why. Lord Lislelivet may have been no one's idea of a man to spend a lazy summer day with, but he did not rise to the category of killable villain, so far as Max could see.

Max was drawn to visit the medieval church, officially the Abbey Church of St. Lucy. The nuns would have finished their morning prayers by now and would be in the chapter house, confessing their faults to their sisters and receiving their penances, and being assigned their daily chores.

Max took the outer walkway to the main door of the church, which remained open to all visitors. There would be another door near the altar that led into the chapter house and further inside to the cloistered area, and this by tradition and necessity would be barred to outsiders.

He moved reverently down a side aisle toward the small Lady Chapel, with its sanctuary lamp indicating the presence of the sacrament. He knelt briefly at a *prie-dieu*, then took a seat on a wooden chair, letting the peace settle round him. Half an hour passed without his being aware of it, his thoughts retracing the path his life had taken and peering toward his future with Awena and their child. It was utterly still and quiet; Nether Monkslip was a noisy and bustling hub by comparison. Here the silence was complete without even the thrum of electricity running in the background, the hidden buzz of modern day life that permeated everything.

He was entirely alone except, he imagined, for the ghosts of those who had come before, making their pilgrimage to this holy place. For in centuries past the church would have been the repository of sacred bones and books and embalmed bits and bobs of long-dead saints, artifacts to which people would pray for a cure for themselves or a loved one. The prayers must have been answered, at least some of the time, for the abbey church had enjoyed centuries of renown, drawing rich and poor to come and pray within its walls, and many a benefactor had left money in his or her will for the nuns to continue their lives of prayer and work.

Benefactors not unlike Clement Gorey and his wife. Did a hard-headed man of business really believe he could buy his way into heaven, wondered Max?

It was time to orient himself to as much of the place as was open to him. He couldn't wander without invitation into the obviously closed-off areas, outlined in red on the map provided in his room, but the fields and glens dotting the area around the nunnery were open to all. And the abbey kitchen, the nucleus of his investigation, was set apart from the strictly cloistered area, as were the infirmary and the abbess's lodge.

Max left the church by the main door, following the signs for the gift shop. It was empty except for the elderly portress who had greeted him the night before, Dame Hephzibah. Stepping inside, he saw that behind her was a window overlooking the entrance to the convent. In this way she could do double duty—keep an eye out for visitors and mind the store. He imagined there were not that many customers on a given day. She smiled at him, giving him the full benefit of her toothy grin.

"Goodness, Dame Hephzibah. They certainly get a day's work out of you," he said.

"I begin each day asking the Lord to use me up," she said. "It looks like he's not done with me yet."

"I should think not. You are far too valuable here with us."

Max looked at the goods on display, attractively arranged on wooden shelves and tables. Many were wrapped in oilcloth or paper and tied with ribbon rather than sealed with the ubiquitous plastic. Everything seemed to be of a very high quality as well as reasonably priced. He thought if there were time and opportunity before he left the abbey he would load up on presents for Awena. And for the baby—his eye caught on a small frilly dress of exquisite workmanship, fit only for a newborn. He could see it was all hand-stitched, the cloth embroidered, white-on-white on nearly every inch. A christening gown, perhaps. It was one of the many topics he and Awena had not decided on, the baptism of the baby. His church taught that it was necessary. Awena held that the child could decide for itself when the time came.

But first things first. He and Awena still had the marriage ceremony to navigate. And by careful willingness to accept and adapt to one another's beliefs and sensibilities, they had arrived at a solution to that first impediment.

In one of the history books he collected, there was a photo of a whalebone casket from the eighth century, decorated in both Christian and pagan images. It was a blending that apparently had bothered no one at the time, and it seemed to him he and Awena could arrive at a similar give-and-take balance in their union. Given one day at a time.

"Do you have children, Father?" Dame Hephzibah asked.

"The first is on the way," he told her. "Due mid-September."

"Oh!" She beamed. "How nice for you and your wife."

How to explain? How to begin to explain his tangled yet wondrous situation to this dear old heart? Max smiled at her and replaced the little gown on the shelf, carefully refolding its tiny lacy sleeves. His fingers were too clumsy for the task and Dame Hephzibah kindly took over for him.

In one corner a Christmas tree made of twigs and burlap displayed handmade wooden ornaments painted bright colors. There were all the animals of Noah's ark and stars and flowers and snowflakes. At the foot of the little tree, which stood about three feet tall, was a primitive crèche scene of exquisite workmanship, the figures—Mary, Joseph, and the baby Jesus; a shepherd and a wise man; the ox and the lamb—made of painted terra-cotta. He couldn't help but smile looking at Joseph's concerned expression as he stared awestruck at the child put into his care. Max looked at the price tag on the crèche scene and could not believe his eyes. It belonged in a museum and they wanted only a few pounds for it.

He walked on. From a branch artfully stuck in a pottery jar hung several dozen rosaries of variously colored beads, positioned to reflect the light. Shelf after shelf along one wall was stacked with jars of honey of every conceivable flavor, like almond or raspberry. The label on the jar of creamed honey told him it had been crystallized into a butter-like spread and was recommended for use on toast or hotcakes. He had just finished breakfast but could not wait to try this delicacy. Surely hotcakes were no challenge to a man who had now mastered the egg?

There were bundles of herbs hanging from the rafters, as in Awena's Goddessspell shop. "Herbs from the Physic Garden of Monkbury Abbey," read their labels. Shelves of books nearby held, in addition to the expected devotional tomes, several rows of books and tracts on cooking with herbs and the medicinal uses of herbs and the use of herbs in the pickling process. To Max, this was all close to necromancy.

"Our infirmaress is an expert botanist," Dame Petronilla informed him. "She has written several of those pickling pamphlets. And of course Dame Fruitcake—Dame Ingrid—has some wonderful recipes. Those little booklets are nearly as popular as her fruitcake. Although I am quite convinced, between us, that she keeps her really special secret ingredients to herself."

Did she realize what she was saying, Max wondered? For hopefully, none of Dame Ingrid's special secret ingredients involved poison.

There were jars of hand creams, and candles, and jams and preserves made of all varieties of fruit. Including, of course, the ubiquitous berries. The labels informed him that the berries were hand-picked on the premises. That, he told himself, might soon no longer be considered a selling point. There also were sweet biscuits of every variety, lumpy with seeds and nuts and—yes—berries again. The orange marmalade containing whiskey looked tempting, and looking at the contents label, he wondered if whiskey on toast in the morning might be a slippery slope. Some of the goods, he noted, like the wines, were imported from St. Martin's, the order's motherhouse in France. Dame Hephzibah saw him reading the wine label and said, "We are thinking of expanding into beer production one day, but for wines we still have to depend on the motherhouse. Abbess Genevieve Lacroix is here again to discuss with Abbess Justina ways to strengthen the bonds between our two houses. The French have such a way about them, don't they?" she added wistfully. "Some of the cosmetics we have on sale are theirs. I gather from our visitors that the face lotions work wonders on wrinkles. For people who worry about such things I am certain that comes as a blessing." Her face exploded in a smile as she said this, wrinkles radiating in every direction. "But such an enterprise as making beer and wine would mean more involvement with outside vendors. People who sells grapes and suchlike."

She shook her head.

"There is some resistance to the idea?" Max asked her.

"We like to keep the world at bay, Father. It's why we came here. Why *most* of us came here. Although . . . I have to say it is gratifying to meet the needs of others with our products."

Max waited for her to elaborate, but judging by the thin line into which she had drawn her mouth she had said all she had to say on that subject. "However, we may soon open a little restaurant for visitors," she added, "serving coffee and a cream tea for those who come to visit our church. That sort of hospitality would be more in keeping with the Rule."

He came upon a small, hand-lettered sign that declared that the proceeds of sales from the shop went to fund a Christian missionary and orphanage in Africa and to sustain various other good causes, including a rape crisis center. All of this seemed to Max added inducement to help empty the shelves if it would help the good sisters in their work.

And what a shame if that work were interrupted by some terrible rumor that their goods were tainted.

Max could understand the demand being created for the nuns' produce in the outside world, a world with its reborn interest in the natural, the pure, the homemade. Was it somehow an opening for the return to the corruption and vice of religious houses of the past? How much, wondered Max, did the abbey rake in in a year, selling its humble goodstuffs? Surely not all that much. There were too few nuns to work the fields, ply the needles, and stir the pots for homemade jams and jellies. Not to mention, get the famous fruitcake into production.

But there now were also the Internet sales, which Max gathered were gathering quite a head of steam. He wondered how they managed that, living off the grid as they did, and made a mental note to ask Xanda, who looked like she would be clued into all things Internetty, as opposed to Dame Hephzibah, who did not.

The sisters were of course most famous for their Boozy Fruitcake, as it had come to be called (Forever Fruitcake as a marketing concept having failed). Max had remembered that an article about this particular abbey product had appeared in the *Monkslip-Super-Mare Globe and Bugle* and had been picked up by one of the London dailies, and he had searched out and reread the article before setting out for the abbey. An enterprising reporter had given it the boozy name, which had stuck, sending sales rocketing heavenward. St. Lucy's Boozy Fruitcake was a confection of honey, sherry, and brandy, and unlike the usual regifted doorstop cakes, these were actively sought out by devotees. Demand crashed the convent's Web site for a time, but the nuns quickly rallied, offering ten percent off and special prayers for those who had been inconvenienced.

Now they shipped many hundreds of loaves a year, this in addition to their honeys and jams and illustrated pamphlets and the exquisitely embroidered babywear. Famous London babies, he gathered, would not think of being christened in anything but a linen gown from Monkbury Abbey, and having now seen a sample for himself, he could understand why. Even once the nuns realized they could charge the earth for these goods, they kept prices strictly in line with actual costs, allowing only a modest profit, for this was the law as laid down in the Rule of St. Lucy, which governed their lives.

They also made beeswax candles, offering beekeeping classes on oc-casion. They had even managed to breed a special type of bee that was less aggressive but more efficient.

Max thought how fascinated Awena would be by all of this. She claimed her bees were gentle because she talked to them. He had asked her once, half in jest, what she talked to the bees about. She had replied in all seriousness that they seemed to like hearing the weather forecast. He had learned not to challenge her on this sort of thing, for her knowl-edge seemed sure, born not of whimsy but of unsentimental experience.

But what, wondered Max, would Miss Pitchford of Nether Monkslip make of the competition for her own infamous—and some said, lethal—fruitcake?

Reminded of his mission, he asked Dame Hephzibah to point him in the direction of the abbey kitchen. It was time for a talk with Dame Fruitcake.

PART V

None

Chapter 11

IN THE CHAPTER HOUSE

When serious matters confront the nunnery, the abbess shall call the whole community together to take its advice. She shall listen to all, particularly the young, for God often reveals more to them. But the final decision is the abbess's to make, and all shall obey.

—The Rule of the Order of the Handmaids of St. Lucy

Half an hour before Max's tour of the gift shop, five women had sat huddled by a small fire in the chapter house, for despite the heat of the day, the ancient walls could hold a morning chill like a damp woolen cloak. The chapter house was not in any case designed for coziness. Situated at the east side of the cloister in the conclave area forbidden to visitors, it was the corporate heart of the abbey, if corporations could be said to have a heart, its narrow, low-reaching windows like the floor-to-ceiling vistas over a modern-day New York skyline. The room was an elaborate gothic chamber ringed by stone-hewn benches, with rib vaults springing from round pillars, a majestic meeting space meant to humble those who gathered there, meant to tame and subdue.

The room's vast size was now a rueful reminder of how many nuns the space once had been able to accommodate. Someone had once proposed to move the chapter meetings into the more comfortable warming room, an idea that had quickly been voted down. The cellaress in particular had been adamant that the room would one day again be filled to overflowing if they waited patiently for the void to be filled. It was a somewhat New Age, "if we build it they will come" brand of thinking to which not all subscribed, but Tradition, they all agreed, was Tradition. And Tradition was what mattered.

The abbess generally sat on a raised seat, but in deference to the informality of this occasion she sat on one of the stone benches, flanked by the others. The nuns' feet rested somewhat irreverently on the grave of one of the monastery's medieval greats, Abbess Junella. Her resting place, outlined by an elaborate tomb marker, was a special tribute to a long and peaceful reign and to the wealth of the family from which she had sprung, for generally abbesses were buried in row upon row of sarcophagi in the crypt that ran beneath the church.

For centuries the serious business of the nunnery had been conducted in the chapter house. Momentous decisions discussed and voted on. Sometimes, voices were raised, and an abbess's diplomatic skills tested to the limits.

Here the nuns met daily for a reading of a chapter from the Rule that framed their days. Often, the abbess would expound on that day's chapter, particularly if it were one of the more problematic rules, difficult to obey and enforce. Infractions against talking during forbidden times were common. Little lapses of behavior, like a show of un-Christian irritation at a sister who was slow or doltish or just always *there* were common.

Of course, part of the routine of chapter meetings was for the sisters to confess their faults to one another. The rather devilish part of this routine was that those who failed to acknowledge fault might be publicly accused. There was, in other words, no escape—no rest for the wicked. Unless, of course, one were lucky enough to have been unobserved in a transgression of the rules. Most tended to hope their misdeeds, large or small, would go unnoticed by anyone but God.

The meeting today was very different, however. Abbess Justina had asked a select few of her nuns to stay behind: the cellaress, the librarian, the cook, and the infirmaress. It was nearly an unprecedented request, and privately they speculated on the occasion for this hush-hush meeting. Especially since the Rule of St. Lucy decried the exclusion of others from important decisions.

It's like a cabal, thought Dame Olive, the librarian, mystified. They sat quietly, as they had been trained to do, their faces impassive and their eyes downcast. But their excitement betrayed itself in the rustle of skirts as they wriggled for purchase on the uncomfortable stone bench or in the soft click of prayer beads being sifted through restless hands. Dame Olive knew she wasn't at the gathering to take notes, her usual role—that was for certain. The abbess had expressly requested that no record be kept of this meeting and that it not be talked about outside these walls. Dame Olive pushed her heavy lenses up the narrow bridge of her nose in consternation. It was all most baffling.

The cook's natural humility left her even more mystified than Dame Olive. What, wondered Dame Ingrid, could she possibly have to contribute? Such a small and select group indicated the topic might be financial, and Dame Ingrid would be the first to claim ignorance. The joy of her life was that she had given up daily concerns, like balancing a chequebook, and could devote herself to cooking, which she considered to be a pious offering to God. In part of her mind she struggled against a nagging sense of flattery to have been included in this august company. Then she wondered if that were a fault of pride she'd have to confess later. Probably it was. Bother.

Unless . . . *unless* . . . She had just had a horrible thought. Unless all this had something to do with the fruitcake? Her famous fruitcake, and that . . . that little man, with his shocking accusations? The beads dropped into her lap as the train of thought tunneled through her mind, toppling the calming litany of her prayer. Her leg began to throb. Normally, she welcomed this reminder of her sin and just punishment, but today it just plain hurt. It hurt like the devil . . .

Meanwhile, the cellaress was thinking, too, about their "special" visitor. Dame Sibil would of course be civil to him but she planned to avoid the pompous little upstart if at all possible. Her forehead beneath her pronounced widow's peak crinkled into a frown of displeasure. She was a product of the class wars in Britain, the daughter of a mining family that could rightly claim to have gotten the shaft by various British governments. No matter what Lord Lislelivet did, and no matter how long he lived, the fact of his aristocracy damned him forever to a fiery perdition in Dame Sibil's book. Her own dear father had been a martyr to the cause, dying from pneumonia after a protest fast he was in no condition to undertake. So, a pox on Lord Lislelivet and all his houses, was all Dame Sibil had to say on the matter. *If* this special meeting were to do with him, and it was difficult to see how it could be. She trained her alert stare on the abbess and waited.

The cellaress looked like an owl waiting for her night's prey to emerge, thought the infirmaress. Dame Petronilla, for her part, had a patient to see to and wanted no part in whatever this meeting was about. It was nothing to do with her, she was sure. She had left the postulant in charge, for lack of a better choice, but the girl was such a goose. Dame Petronilla cradled her wide jaw in one hand, a worried expression creasing her narrow forehead. Just as she was about to ask permission to be excused for urgent business, the abbess began to speak.

And when she spoke it was not about Lord Lislelivet or fruitcakes, although she touched on those topics in passing. Rather, it was about the much-delayed expansion of the new Monkbury Abbey Guesthouse, and the reasons behind the delay.

First swearing them all to silence, she spoke for twenty minutes without pause. And when she was finished, she made each in turn state aloud their promise. Only the cellaress dared register a protest.

"I won't lie," she said stubbornly. "Especially since I think what is called for here is the opposite of secrecy."

"I'm not asking you to *lie*," said Abbess Justina, thoroughly affronted. "But if anyone comes to you with questions that make you . . . uncomfortable, send them to me."

And might that someone be the dark and handsome vicar, wondered Dame Olive, who already had caught a passing glimpse of Max Tudor. For even a nunnery dedicated to the Almighty operated on a grapevine of ruth-less efficiency, and the arrival of Max with his movie-star looks was news, however one looked at it. And sent by the bishop, no less! The postulant had speculated aloud that Max might be here scouting locations "for some religious movie. You know, like *Ben Hur*." It was uncharitable of her even to think it, Dame Olive knew, but the postulant Mary always struck her as being a few peas short of a casserole.

"Just . . . say nothing," said the abbess. "For now. On top of the whole business with the fruitcake, we can't have this come out. Not *now*. You do see that. We must stay ahead—what is the phrase, Dame Cellaress?" And she turned to Dame Sibil as to one with vast years of experience of corpo-rations and spin doctors, hoping the flattery might work. It did seem to thaw her, just a notch.

"You mean that one must stay ahead of the story," supplied Dame Sibil.

"That's precisely it!" exclaimed the abbess.

They all exchanged glances, but it was Dame Petronilla who readily agreed. The abbess was right: they could only cope with one catastrophe at a time. One, or two.

"It's been a secret for so long," she said. "What do a few months matter?"

Chapter 12

THE KITCHENESS

The kitcheness shall consult with the cellaress over the wise provisioning of the abbey but the cellaress shall have the final word on the amounts and types of food provided to the kitchen.

—The Rule of the Order of the Handmaids of St. Lucy

Dame Tabitha the guest-mistress had greeted Max with a dutiful bow, Dame Hephzibah with a dry little kiss, but Dame Ingrid grabbed his hand fervently in both of hers, pumping it enthusiastically. She looked as though she wanted to clasp him to her ample bosom but thought better of it. She contented herself with a joyous cry of "Thank heaven you're here!"

"I am most happy to be here," Max said politely. But it was only partly true and he did not feel particularly heaven sent.

"Welcome to the fruitcake factory, Father Max."

"I had read of your fruitcakes before I ever came here," said Max. "You have achieved quite a following. Congratulations."

Dame Ingrid's complexion exploded bright red at the compliment, and she dipped her head in bashful acknowledgement. "I'm sure I do my best," she murmured. She had a constellation of freckles across her nose and cheeks; red hair coiled at her temples. "And of course, I couldn't do anything without my sisters. Without the support of the abbey. Without, needless to say, God's help. I—"

As this was turning into an Oscar acceptance speech, Max cut in.

"Would you mind if I asked you a few questions about your work?"

"Of course not, Father." Her hazel eyes shone at the prospect. She was a tall woman, so tall that Max could meet her eye to eye. Her rounded features gave her a wholesome, milk-maidish appearance, as if she might at any moment break into a yodel. "We often have visitors—people at the guesthouse are generally curious to see the famous cakes being made. Of course, it's a process of months, so at any given time you will only see one stage of the process. This is how we keep the recipe secret—oh, yes! You need not look so surprised, Father. Industrial espionage comes with the territory when you have a product as popular as ours."

Max briefly closed his eyes, nodding in solemn understanding. "My lips are sealed," he said.

"We once had a man come to a weekend retreat only pretending to be here for spiritual refreshment," she leaned in to confide. "He was from a major biscuit manufacturer and it was obvious from his questions and his general demeanor . . . well. The Rule tells us we must welcome all who come to our door, but it does not say that we have to reveal our secrets to any passerby of ill intent. Right." She picked up a wooden spoon and waved it like a baton. "So now, I'm simply assembling the batter. We deal in large vats now, rather than bowls. We had to step up the process to meet demand."

Her face glowed with pleasure as she warmed to her topic. This was clearly a performance she had starred in many times.

"Now, fruitcake has been around since the time of the Egyptians." She looked at him expectantly, anticipating the punch line.

"That explains the fruitcake one of my aunts kept sending us," he said. "Perhaps my mother simply mailed it back every year. Our family version of the curse of the Pharaohs."

"Ha!" said Dame Ingrid, delighted. Max was playing right into her hands. "That is where fruitcake got its bad name—those dried up, amateur attempts. With all due respect to your aunt. Now, *my* fruitcake—I mean, *our* fruitcake—succeeds because it is baked at a very low oven temperature for just the right amount of time." First looking over her shoulder, she lowered her voice. "Shall I tell you the secret ingredient?"

Max nodded solemnly. The ingredient he was interested in was poison, but he guessed that was not what she meant.

"Pineapple," she said, and Max struggled to look astonished. She placed one finger against the side of her nose, and nodded. "Chunks of pineapple soaked in rum—I won't tell you for how long, no use asking me! I'll never tell. But that makes the difference you can taste. None of this drizzling rum over the top of the cake—that's the lazy woman's way. Too late by then to save it."

"The word 'pineapple' will never pass my lips," Max assured her.

"I can tell if a man is trustworthy, Father. I knew a thing or two before I came to the convent. I came here later in life, later than most of the others."

"Have you always been a cook?"

"Yes, I cooked professionally. For many years."

He waited, but she seemed reluctant to say more. He watched as the blood again rose in her already hectic complexion. Her high color may have come from the heat of the stove, of course. The room was nicely warm, as the day was just getting started. By noon with all the ovens going it might be deeply unpleasant to have to work here.

"Here, let me show you something." She turned with an awkward movement, grasping the table edge to steady herself. One of her legs appeared to be shorter than the other or may have been injured, for she walked with a noticeable hitch, and without the gliding locomotion of her sisters. Indeed, she had the sort of rolling gait one might associate with someone who'd spent her life aboard a whaling ship. Now she made her way to a door at one side of the kitchen proper and motioned him to follow her into another room.

"See, here is the oven," she said, finally rolling to a stop. "And over there," she pointed to rows of shelves lining two walls, "over there are the resting fruitcakes. The beauty of the fruitcake is in its need to sit and mellow for several months—there is a lesson for us all in that, do you not think, Father? 'Consider the lilies of the field . . . they toil not, neither do they spin.' Neither does my fruitcake. All will be well," she added, surveying the rows of fruitcake either resting or being readied for baking, "so long as the generator doesn't break down."

She went on to explain that over six hundred cakes could be made at a time in the specially built oven. The cakes would be left to sit, patiently awaiting their weekly lashings with more liquor. Max, reminded of Miss Pitchford's Deadly Fruitcake (so-called by the villagers), imagined the old schoolmistress's envy at the sight of so many loaves being produced on such a vast scale.

"And you manage all this yourself?"

"Good heavens, no. We all take turns in the kitchen. I have lots of help. Some help is more helpful than others, if you follow. The new postulant and the novice will take time to train—we all needed time when we first got here. How easy it is to forget that! In the old days, we would have had a frateress to help—someone who saw to the crockery and such. We all have to be a bit more flexible in our duties these days."

So they all just shoved along together and somehow it all got done, without friction, without animosity, hidden or otherwise, thought Max. Was any human organization ever so free of strife as this one appeared to be? Well, the attempted poisoning of Lord Lislelivet, or whatever it was, strongly suggested otherwise.

"The oven was built to my specifications." She pulled open one of the oven doors and turned to him, her face beaming with pride. "See? See how each pan has its own little shelf? 'Special-built' cost the moon but after many months our prayers were answered."

Max took a guess.

"The Goreys?"

She nodded. "Mr. and Mrs. Gorey have been most generous to the abbey over the years. We thank God for them every day. Of course, we thank the Goreys, too, but it is God working through them."

"How long have they been coming here on retreat?"

She stopped to think, chin resting against her thumb.

"Forever," she said at last. "The daughter, though—this is her first visit. Poor thing doesn't seem to quite know what to do with herself. It takes some people awhile to adjust to the quiet."

"I think that is a particular challenge of this day and age, for all of us."

"Too right," she agreed.

"Could you tell me something of your background, Dame Ingrid? What you did before you came here to the abbey? You indicated you were a professional chef."

"Well . . . I guess that would be all right." Shutting the door to the oven, she steered him back into the kitchen proper. She took a simmering kettle off the hearth and asked, "Some tea while we talk, Father?"

Max nodded, and when she had got them both sorted with cups and saucers and spoons, she sat across from him at the wide wooden work table.

"Yes, I was a cook before I came here," she said. "Only then I called myself a chef." She laughed. "That was just me putting on airs. A cook is someone with a loving heart, wanting to keep his or her loved ones well nourished. A chef, though—a chef is something else. In my case, a showoff."

"You worked in restaurants?" Max asked.

"A few, when I first finished my training. I was born in Sweden, in Stockholm, and I went to Le Cordon Bleu in Paris."

Max, impressed, made a whistling sound.

"Yes," she said. "I was *awfully* proud of myself. Shockingly ambitious, I was. The competition is unbelievable, Father. Who can make the best soufflé in the world—it becomes a matter of life and death. Ridiculous. And the tempers you see in a restaurant kitchen, the chef exploding all over everyone, causing accidents. I once saw a man badly burned when a soup kettle overturned during a scuffle. It is the opposite of a peaceful and nourishing occupation. And the language could scorch the paint off the walls."

"So you gave it up, to come here?"

"Not right away. I went to work as a private chef—that word again. A private 'chef.' For a novelist and her family, in Hampstead." And she named a famous thriller writer, the sort of author whose fame and flair with the art of storytelling kept airport bookstalls thriving.

Max, despite himself, was intrigued. "Really?" he asked. "What is she like?"

"Well," said Dame Ingrid. "She was nice. The photos make her look awfully mean, you know. That's because of the sort of blood-and-guts stories she writes—maybe her publicist thinks she should look forbidding, to match her books. I never understood it, myself. She was divorced, and her kids were a handful. I acted as their nanny half the time, since their mother always had her head in the clouds. But she was generous about paid leave and things."

She was quiet for a moment, stirring her cup. Max prompted: "So why did you leave?"

"It's difficult to explain. . . . One day I came here on a retreat. I wasn't Anglican at the time—you know how we Swedes are, Father. Lutheran at birth, even if we never set foot in a church."

"Your parents weren't religious?"

"My parents were content to leave my spiritual growth to chance. It is such a different culture there, Father. Anyway, I came here thinking I'd enjoy the quiet, read a bit, get away from the children, who were a full-time job when they got to be teenagers, let me tell you."

"How did you come to hear of the abbey?"

"I think I saw an article about the place—their arts and crafts were already beginning to attract attention. Anyway, once I saw the abbey . . . well, that was the first step on a long road. I didn't really mean to attend the services, that wasn't part of the plan, but the beauty of the nuns' voices singing, the surroundings, the cloister garden, the clean air—well. Something happened to me that weekend; it is so difficult to put into words. I didn't just want to convert, you see. I wanted to live here. To dedicate my life to that peace and beauty. To God and serenity. I knew that right away. Isn't it odd? I knew I would live here one day.

"But I couldn't just up and leave my employer. Because she drank, you see, while her kids ran wild. I don't know when she got any writing done, to be honest, but somehow she produced a book a year. You know the sort of thing that can happen when a single mother, even one you'd think had lots of resources, is overwhelmed. I used to think if she wrote nicer stories it would help—not focus all day on horrible murders and tortures and such. A nice Agatha Christie type of story, you know? A *nice* sort of murder. But I suppose she wrote what paid the bills for her and for the kids. She had let her husband run off without paying child support on the condition he never came near her or the kids again. And he didn't.

"Anyway, I was her personal chef for about three years. She liked me to cook healthy foods, which she would wash down with a quart of scotch a day. Go figure. I stayed until the children left for university, and then I left, too. I suppose that sounds heartless?" she asked. "I often think about it . . . about her . . ."

This time the rush of blood to her face definitely was not from the heat of the room, but from a memory that still seemed to pain her, no matter how many times she may have talked of it or thought it over. And Max had the idea she often thought of it and wanted finally to hear that the voice in her mind saying she had behaved selfishly was wrong.

Max shook his head. "I don't see how your staying would have made any difference. If she one day decides she's had enough, that day will not arrive because you or anyone scolded her into it or protected her from the inevitable day of reckoning." A vision of his parishioner Chrissa Baker crossed his mind just then. "It is too bad for the children, though. It was kind of you to stay for their sake, until they were launched."

The relief on her face, and her wobbly smile, told him how long she had worried over what she surely saw as her defection from the household.

"That is true: if you are determined on destruction, no one can protect you."

"Do you ever see the children?"

"Oh, yes. They come to visit me here sometimes—not often. I suppose in my heart I adopted them as my own and I do miss them. One can't help it."

Max hesitated, wondering how to bring the subject round to the main purpose of his visit to Dame Fruitcake in her abbey kitchen.

"The recent events . . ." he began. "Lord Lislelivet . . ."

Again the flush of color. He felt he could monitor her blood pressure if only he had a detailed color chart. She was just saved from plainness, he realized, by that high coloring and by the attractive hazel spark in her eyes. He could see her in another life, away from here, sitting before her own hearth and surrounded by very tall children and grandchildren, perhaps getting ready to prepare a meal for her own family. Again he marveled at the sacrifices so willingly made by these women.

For her part, Dame Ingrid was thinking: Were we not supposed to notice how handsome Father Tudor was? Well, we might be the sisters of St. Lucy, patroness of the blind, but we aren't blind. She smiled in a flustered way and said, "You'll be wondering about those berries. Believe me, I have wondered, too."

"Where did they normally come from? Were they imported from elsewhere?" That might be too much to hope for, but he thought it was worth a shot.

"As much as possible, we harvest them ourselves. But the demand has been so great, we've had to augment our supplies. The cellaress orders the quantities I tell her I need. We recently took in a shipment from the motherhouse in France."

"You say everyone helps out in the kitchen?"

"Oh, yes. They all take turns. Everyone except the abbess is required to help, according to the Rule. But Abbess Justina does not excuse herself. She likes to pitch in, now and again."

"It is hard to imagine her having the time."

"It is harder to imagine the cellaress having the time. But the abbess very wisely insists we all be treated the same, as much as is humanly possible."

"I can see why that would be necessary. The emphasis on fairness."

She stirred her tea, spooning in more syrup from a little white jar labeled AGAVE in neat cursive script.

She said, "St. Benedict was so wise about the ways of humans. He understood anger, and envy, and ego. He understood that danger could come as easily from within a community as without. He understood above all that we can't choose where we love: that seems somehow preordained. Some may call it heresy but I've always thought it to be true. We don't choose in these matters, which is why we so often see these oddly matched couples out there in the world: beauty hand in hand with beast; genius conquered by the pure of heart. It makes no sense—probably not even to the couples themselves."

Max smiled, thinking life would be so much easier and, at the same time, so not worth living were he facing a future with a woman more "suitable," more "mainstream," than the endlessly fascinating Awena.

"Anyway," continued Dame Ingrid, "the abbess is no different from any other human being. She is bound to have her favorites. But it is fatal to the community to let those favorites be known. The trust is gone once you show that sort of fallibility."

"It's lonely at the top then," said Max.

"If it's not, it should be," she asserted, and Max was struck again by the savvy of this otherwise humble and unworldly woman. "Anyway, in the old days, the cellaress would have been in charge of the kitcheness, and I would have reported to her. But when it is Dame Sibil's turn to help out in here, things are the other way round, and she is to be guided by me."

"Oh?" Max had picked up a certain wry note in her tone, noticing the topic of favoritism had led her directly to comment on the cellaress. "And how does that work out?"

She smiled. "Not all that well. Dame Cellaress—that is, Dame Sibil—is used to being in charge. Old habits die hard. No pun intended."

Max returned the smile.

"What did she do in her life before the nunnery?"

"I'll tattle no tales, Father," she said. "Really, I don't know the specifics. I gather she was a big noise in the City, but we don't reminisce about such things here."

"Even though you've lived together for years, some of you? Known each other for years?"

She nodded. "We simply don't talk about personal things. We certainly don't talk much about the past—that is forbidden by the Rule. Talking to you as I have done is a different thing, but even there—it doesn't do to wallow, even under the guise of unburdening one's soul to a priest. But maintaining privacy about the past is the only way we can shuffle along together in peace in such a small community.

"We had an American postulant here once who tended to 'overshare'—her term. And then she would thank us for sharing, almost regardless of what we said to her. 'Pass the butter' or whatever. And the questions! Why this, and why that. She was a lovely girl with a big heart and a true vocation to serve, but she didn't last long here—she did not understand it when no one reciprocated her rather gushy fervor by baring their souls in return. It was partly British reserve, I suppose, but partly the psychology of being packed in together like commuters on a crowded train. We know that the only way we survive here is by erecting a privacy fence around ourselves. Anyway, she left us finally, and I heard she went on to become a missionary with another order, out in Africa somewhere, which work I think would suit such an outgoing type very well. Our more shuttered way of life requires that we maintain our own boundaries.

"Christ alone," she concluded, "knows the secrets of our hearts. More tea, Father?"

Chapter 13

THE LIBRARIAN

Books are to the soul what food is to the body. Let the sister in charge of the scriptorium be alive to the rare sanctity of her duty.

—*The Rule of the Order of the Handmaids of St. Lucy*

Max left Dame Ingrid soon afterwards. He knew she had limited time for chitchat, much as she had seemed to be enjoying herself. He first asked about the nunnery's archivist, knowing they must have one.

"You'll be wanting Dame Olive, our librarian," she told him. "She's forgotten more about the place than most of us will ever know." And finding a small scrap of paper in the pocket of her work apron, she drew a map to guide him to the library and scriptorium.

"I'll send word ahead that you're on the way," she said.

Dame Olive's face, a pale oval swathed in white linen, floated toward him out of the darkness of the library stacks.

It was a delicate face, the perfect egg shape of the head emphasized by the cruelly taut wrapping of the coif under her chin. Heavy dark-framed glasses overwhelmed her small features; Max could see the red marks on her nose where the frame weighed too heavily. Her hands as they constantly adjusted the frames were as small, precise, and tidy as a dormouse's. The coif seemed to bother her, and her fingers slipped often beneath the fabric to hold it away from her skin. Max wondered if she might have been allergic either to the fabric or to the detergent used to wash it. If so, it would be like wearing a hair shirt. Did she need to wear it quite so tightly wound?

Like Dame Ingrid, Dame Olive greeted Max with an enthusiastic if more demure, "Thank heaven you're here!"

Max felt his fame as a sleuth had somehow preceded him. Flattering as it was, he hope the nuns weren't overestimating his ability to get to the bottom of their public-relations crisis.

She stood back and gestured him to a seat across from her oak desk. The cavernous stone room was lined floor to ceiling with books, most of them leather-bound and creaky with antiquity. Library ladders ran on rails the length and depth of the wood-paneled room.

Dame Olive herself looked comfortable in her domain, as if she had somehow always been there, a guardian at the fount of knowledge. They exchanged the usual pleasantries, and Max said, "What an impressive collection you have here."

"We have a small assortment of books that can be borrowed, but the archives date back centuries, and they of course cannot be removed," she told him, as if forestalling any plans he might have to run amok in the stacks. He saw that many of the older volumes were chained in place, a holdover from centuries past when hand-copied books were worth their weight in gold.

He commented on the chains, saying: "I would imagine much that is here is valuable?"

"It's all valuable to me," she replied. "But thieves, then as now, have always been drawn by the notorious riches of Monkbury Abbey. The gold and silver plate, as well as the books."

"Thieves?" asked Max.

"Oh, I didn't have anyone specific in mind. No indeed. I was talking of the past." She adjusted the heavy glasses against her nose. "At Monkbury Abbey, much of the income once was generated by providing access to relics and objects of veneration—that was the case in religious houses everywhere. There was—usually—nothing cynical in this. We had our own miraculous relic in the church—a femur said to belong to St. Lucy, as well as part of her shin bone—but the casket and most of its contents were destroyed by King Henry's men."

"So the visiting throngs of pilgrims vanished overnight," he said. "It's a shame, really." He was thinking more of the casket, no doubt a work of art made of gold and silver and inlaid with jewels. Whether its contents had ever had anything to do with St. Lucy was doubtful. Relics were a dime a dozen in the medieval church, and many were of uncertain provenance. But simply counted as a loss to the historical record, the devastation was sad to witness at places like Rievaulx and Whitby. For Dame Olive, no doubt an historian at heart, the damage must be particularly galling.

"Not just the religious relics—the saints' bones and bits of cloth from their cowls and so on—but many of the books of the time were destroyed," she said. "And not all of them religious tomes. There came a point where the destruction was indiscriminate. But someone managed to preserve some Anglo-Saxon poetry that is really quite . . . erm . . . *earth*y. No one knows how it came to be at the abbey." She smiled. She had a big wide smile, almost too wide for the small features, so tightly wrapped. With her smile, the linen seemed to cut into the skin.

"But are they valuable, the poems? Or is anything else in the archives?" he asked. He was thinking of Piers, with his shiny Regency tresses and his interest in things ancient, and of Lord Lislelivet, with his beady eyes and his sudden interest in things monastic.

And of the Goreys, who for all their generosity had an evident interest in things financial.

"That depends on whom you ask, Father. As Stephen King has said, 'Books are a uniquely portable magic.' And as I've indicated, value is in the eye of the beholder." Max muffled his surprise that she would quote the master of horror tales.

"What is your own favorite reading?" he asked. Not *Carrie*, surely.

She sat back, unused to such questions. "We aren't exactly encouraged to read for pleasure, Father. Nor do we have scads of leisure time. But I would have to say I have a fondness for poetry, a fondness which has never left me."

"Ah. Who is your favorite poet?"

"Oh, I have too many favorites to name just one. I'm reading Leonard Cohen at the moment."

Max smiled. Cohen was a poet and songwriter who'd written extensively about religion, having been ordained a Buddhist monk while retaining his ties to his own Jewish faith. He'd also had a lot to say about women and sex, which mysteries seemed to confound him.

"Surely," he said, "the Rule of St. Lucy would allow for a little poetry in your lives."

"It would, in balance and moderation," she replied. "St. Benedict was big on balance and moderation." She hesitated, adding, "But even so, his own monks tried to poison him."

"I've never quite understood why they did that. They could have just asked him to leave."

She smoothed the fine light wool of her voluminous skirt. "I suppose they felt he would not listen. Saints are like that."

Did he imagine it, or was she hinting at something? For the reference to poison seemed deliberate. No doubt it was a subject uppermost in all their minds. But try as he might, Max could not see parallels between a sixth-century religious reformer, annoyingly righteous as he may have been, and a twenty-first-century British lord with a reputation for fast cars, fancy women, and underhanded dealing. And yet both had survived attempted poisonings by people they had in some way provoked.

He looked around at the surrounding walls of books. "I'd like to look through the archives, with your permission."

She had a habit of peering over the tops of her glasses in classic librarian style, as if to read the fine print, or to assess the character of the person before her. She was probably just trying to compensate for the near-sightedness that was surely an occupational hazard.

"How long do you have?" Her small hands fluttered from the desk to adjust her glasses. "Really, Father, you've no idea how much accumulates in a nunnery over time. But of course you may browse to your heart's content. I just hope you're not allergic to dust. *I'm* not allergic, but I do have a well-developed sense of smell and being in the stacks can be a torment."

"I may just need an hour or two," said Max, with no real idea how long he needed, since he had no clue what he was looking for. It was too much to hope he'd stumble across a treasure map hidden within the endpapers of an old volume.

In line with his thoughts, she said, "Research expands beyond the time allotted. Always. When I update our Web site I lose hours if I get distracted by researching other sites. And the use of bandwidth is prohibitive for us."

He'd seen the Monkbury Abbey Web site. It was impressive. It not only provided information about the abbey, it had a shopping cart where people could buy the goods the nuns produced. They also took prayer requests online.

"Where did you learn Web design?" he asked.

"I taught myself through trial and error." As with the cook, Dame Ingrid, there was an unmistakable note of pride in her voice. "The site was the cellaress's idea—she is a great champion of progress. If a nun from the eleventh century were to see the shopping cart, I wonder what she'd make of it."

"I had forgotten the abbey went back that far."

"Oh, yes. The original abbey was founded by Princess Aethmurtha of sacred memory. We're lucky to have retained much of the original fabric of the place. When the nunnery was abandoned following the dissolution, villagers in Temple Monkslip came to pilfer the stone and lead. But whatever was built with the stolen material collapsed or burned to the ground. In the end the villagers decided it was better to leave it alone, and the monastery was left to tumble down of its own accord. Thank God, because that is what saved it."

"Superstition," said Max.

"Would you call it superstition, Father? I would call it justice."

She took off the heavy glasses and polished the frames against the fabric of her gown. Her face without the glasses looked strangely blank, the eyes hollow and unfocused. "We survived so much. Even before King Henry, we had the Black Death. And for a while in the fourteen hundreds the nunnery was in the care of an Oxford College. Those were dark days, indeed." She said this without a shred of humor. "But then . . . the centuries passed. It's always been one thing after another. We will survive."

Yes, there was some comfort if one took the centuries-long view. Max looked around him. "It's a sizable library," he said, trying to read the faded bindings on some of the books in the row above her. "I suppose many of the nuns were high born and thus able to read."

She nodded. "Many also could write beautifully. Our scriptorium was a going concern for many years—it's the room on top of this one, above the library. We now use it as a reading room." She replaced the glasses. "Alas, the fire destroyed so much."

"The fire?"

"Yes. Fifteen hundred, or thereabouts. We lost many things of value." She shook her head, a mournful expression on her pretty face. "There are gaps in the archives to this day. We lost nearly everything—the parchments and scrolls, the records. You'll see."

Max, as his eyes skimmed over the shelves filled with beautifully preserved texts, recalled that in *The Name of the Rose* the abbey library had caught fire, destroying everything—the books and then the abbey itself. The killer in that book had wanted to prevent the spread of "dangerous" knowledge. The killer alone, of course, got to decide what was dangerous.

He noticed the "we." "We lost many things of value." It was as if it were yesterday, part of their recent history, and as if the loss still rankled. What had happened to the convent's nuns long dead was the same as what happened to nuns present.

"How free," Max asked, "was the abbey of the charges of corruption made by Henry and his men?"

"Not very," she replied smoothly. She adjusted the frames to peer at him. "Some of the abbesses in the past went in for spending in a big way and found ingenious ways to pay for what they wanted. The cellarist and the sacrist in particular had many opportunities for cooking the books. There are veiled references to these things in the archives—if you will excuse the pun."

"I'm sorry?"

"Nuns? Veils?"

"Ah," he said. "Of course."

"The nunneries were no different from any other place where human beings gathered. The women often wanted autonomy from their bishop, you see—to avoid visitation and inspection and oversight."

"It may have been a matter of wanting to be let alone," said Max. "Some bishops are more interfering than others."

"Of course. Luckily, our bishop is quite a reasonable man, as you know. And the . . . well, *other* sort of corruption is well in the past."

"Other?"

"We were a double monastery once, you know. That leads to its own particular temptations."

"Ah."

"Of course, we being British, things never got as bad here as at the motherhouse in France. Heloise and Abelard—that was not a unique situation in the history of monasticism."

"Ah," he said again. The doomed lovers. Although in their case the relationship ended rather than began in the monastic life. "It's a wonder the system worked as well as it did, for as long as it did."

"There was often disagreement. The abbess is supposed to ask everyone for counsel in making important decisions, although the final decision as to whom she chooses as cellaress—just using one example—is up to her. But if it is felt her request for 'input,' as the younger nuns would have it, was somewhat lacking in . . . how shall I say it . . ."

"In sincerity?" prompted Max.

"Sincerity, yes. It can lead to difficulties."

"Are you speaking of the present situation?" Max asked. For it seemed to him she had a particular event in mind.

"I'm sure I couldn't say," demurred Dame Olive. But it was clear to him she was longing to do just that. Max waited as she waged this mental struggle, but in the end she returned to an earlier theme. "Yes, if it's scandal you're after, there was no shortage of that."

Max wasn't at all sure scandal was what he was after, but he let her have free rein.

"There is even a prison in the cellar of the abbess's lodge, did you know? Sometimes people just lost it, I suppose. They'd try to run away but were brought back. The space is used now for storage."

"I suppose they had to make and keep their own laws, as isolated as they were out here," said Max. "A bit like the Wild West, with the abbess acting as sheriff."

She nodded. "At times they overcorrected, with an emphasis on strict enclosure—no men allowed except to administer the final sacraments to a dying sister. The priest offering the mass was hidden by a screen, and a turntable was used so the nuns could receive communion."

"Rather sad, that."

"In a way, but it all meant their autonomy increased. They controlled their own money, you see. Always the first step. No one had ever told them what to do before, these aristocrats, and they weren't going to start letting men, in particular, take their freedom now. Better to operate in secret."

"They played the system to their advantage."

"Played it brilliantly," she agreed.

And were they still playing, wondered Max?

"St. Lucy's, at least for a while, was extremely wealthy, and that, as you know, Father, brings its own problems. The place was better off once it fell back into its forgotten and somewhat neglected state."

"It doesn't look neglected now."

"No. People have been most kind."

"The Goreys?"

"Yes."

"Lord Lislelivet?"

"Not so much."

And as much as Max may have wished it, it was clear she was not going to elaborate. He tried a change of topic.

"You have always been assigned to work in the library?" he asked.

"In recent years," she said. "But I have helpers, and they alternate. That way, no one person thinks she knows it all. And in case of illness, someone else can take over. Poor Dame Meredith, when she fell ill . . . that was terrible on many levels. She was the cellaress, you know. A key position."

"Perhaps I could visit her while I'm here," said Max.

"Oh, I am sure she would like that. It is good of you to suggest it. She doesn't get many visitors and it would cheer her. I'll mention it to Dame Infirmaress."

"No need. I plan to talk with her later today. Dame Olive, how long have you been at Monkbury?"

"Since I was eighteen," she said.

So young. "Did your parents approve of your decision?"

She laughed. "My parents were appalled by my decision. They just didn't get it. They still don't. They show up quarterly for visitation days. My mother, you can tell, wants to drag me out by the scruff like a way-ward cat." She paused, her expression a strange mixture of longing and confusion. "I don't know why I'm telling you this. You have a kind face." She paused, visibly pulling herself together. She stood to let him know the interview was over. "Now, I will leave you to what research you will. Was there a particular time in our history that interests you, Father?" she asked.

"All of it, I suppose. Perhaps I'll start with the Reformation."

"Over there," she pointed. "All that section. It starts with Luther and continues on.

"I'll be here for the next hour if you should have any questions, Father."

Chapter 14

THE INFIRMARESS

A separate building shall be maintained for the ill, and an infirmaress known for patience, piety, and competence shall be appointed to oversee their care.

—*The Rule of the Order of the Handmaids of St. Lucy*

Max spent over an hour in the archives. It was all fascinating in its way, and a test for his limited Latin, but nothing suggested to him a reason for poisoning Lord Lislelivet. Fantastical tales of treasures and miracles abounded, but if Max or anyone had been hoping for a treasure map, they were out of luck.

Returning a volume to its shelf, he wondered if he might be wandering too far from his mandate. Since it was poison that brought him here, his time might be better spent talking to someone with medical knowledge.

He asked Dame Olive for directions to the infirmary. "If it is Dame Petronilla you're wanting, she'll likely be in the garden with her herbs and plants on such a warm day. Try the grounds past the cemetery."

She gave him detailed instructions on how to get there.

"She'll have left the novice in charge of patients while she tends her plants. Well, the one patient of the moment: Dame Meredith. You will remember to go and talk with her, Father? It's the cancer, you know.

Right now she'll be recovering from her latest hospital visit, so perhaps tomorrow afternoon would be a better time. It is in the afternoons that time hangs heavy for her, and she becomes prey to worry. Nighttime is even worse."

Max assured her he would visit the next afternoon, and thanked her again for allowing him the run of the place. He put from his mind for the moment the idea that she had opened up the archives to him as a way to keep him off the subject of recent abbey history.

The library opened onto a wooded area, and a gravel path took him past the abbess's lodge, which he could glimpse through the trees, and on past the infirmary, which at the moment housed only Dame Meredith and the novice keeping watch over her. As he breached a small hill beyond the cemetery, the gardens came into view, a splendid green Technicolor against which a nun in white wielded a hoe. The narrow woven circlet sitting atop her veil made her look from a distance like an Arab sheik. The white was probably in homage to her nursing duties, but he thought it probably was welcome under the hot sun.

She looked up to welcome him, her face with its wide jaw and narrow forehead emerging from the enveloping fabric. The coif was slightly askew and he could see the tan line where sun never reached the sides of her face.

"You may call me Dame Pet, Father, if you like. Everyone does."

But the informality didn't suit her, somehow. Behind the friendly smile, he sensed a well of reserve. Of course, his mission was to spy, which, if she knew it, hardly made him a welcome addition to her daily routine.

He said, indicating the rows of healthy plants and blooming flowers: "This is amazing, the variety you have here."

She looked with pleasure over her work. "I like to grow not just 'useful' things like herbs but things of beauty. St. Francis said there should always be space set aside for flowers, particularly sweet-smelling ones, to remind people of the sweetness of the Lord. Have you seen the cloister garden yet?" Max nodded. "It is my pride."

She removed her gardening gloves, and dabbed at her face with a clean white handkerchief. "St. Francis used to preach to the flowers, too."

Max smiled at this. Some of his parishioners in their pews were like potted plants during his sermons, now he came to think of it. "G. K. Chesterton thought St. Francis did not *want* to see the wood for the trees," he told her. "I have always thought that was rather a perfect line."

"Chesterton. Of course—he wrote the Father Brown mysteries. I read all of those when I was a girl. I trained as a nurse, you know, and during the long night watches I read mysteries to stay awake. We all did."

They had fallen into step on a grassy verge around one of the planted beds. She stopped to pull a weed that had dared encroach.

"I imagine you keep a doctor on call?" Max asked her.

"Of course. Dr. Barnard. But we bring him in only if someone falls seriously ill or if they present with symptoms that stump me."

"Ah," said Max. "But you are formally trained in medicine?"

Dame Petronilla nodded. "And I've taught myself a lot about herbal and holistic medicine since I came to Monkbury. Still, I wouldn't presume to make medical decisions outside my scope. We have one sister who is quite ill, and of course we take her to hospital for treatment. The best we can do for her here is offer palliative care."

"I wonder that you didn't choose a nursing order. That didn't appeal?"

She shrugged, her eyes surveying a distant past. "I think, Father, that what interested me most was the cure rather than the patient. I mean that the healing properties of plants are so fascinating, and so miraculous, I felt I could study them endlessly. And of course, plants don't complain. They die, alas, as patients do—I had a hard time with losing patients." She paused, and again Max had that sense of something held in reserve. "A very hard time."

He decided not to press her. Instead he said, "Dame Hephzibah told me you know a great deal about botany—I saw some of your pamphlets in the gift shop. I suppose you know that I am here at the bishop's request to find out what I can about this—well, about this fruitcake situation."

"Yes, we all know. The abbess told us in chapter." Dame Petronilla, tucking her gardening shears in her basket with her gloves and her collection of herbs, said, "I wonder why they used tutsan. That is very odd."

Really, the grapevine here was a match for Miss Pitchford's in Nether Monkslip. "How did you—?"

"The abbess told us."

Max assumed the abbess's information came from the bishop via DCI Cotton. "Why do you say it's an odd choice?" he asked her.

She massaged her wide jaw with one hand, thinking. He was reminded of the actress Minnie Driver, with her triangular face. Finally Dame Petronilla said, "Tutsan is not an *efficient* choice. Not at all what I would have chosen to do away with someone—may God forbid I should ever wish to do such a thing."

"I'm certain you never would think of it. But why do you say that—about the inefficiency, I mean?"

"Because if someone were bent on killing, something like black bryony would be a lot more effective than tutsan for their purposes. Or yew berries for that matter—absolutely deadly. And of course, we have yew trees growing in abundance in the cemetery—nothing could be easier to find anywhere in England. Whoever it was chose to use a berry that was not necessarily going to kill anyone, not unless they ate a lot of it, or were susceptible in some way to it. One might almost say . . ."

"Yes?"

"One might almost say the wish was to *sicken*, not to injure seriously."

She stopped to run the handkerchief beneath the edges of her coif, pulling the fabric from her face as she did so. The sky they stood beneath was slightly overcast but it had turned into a sultry, too-hot day for gardening. Her enveloping garments couldn't have helped much.

"What is tutsan, anyway?" He knew the answer, as he'd looked it up at the vicarage on the Internet, but he suspected Dame Petronilla had a knowledge of such things more encyclopedic and accurate than any search engine's.

"It's a member of the St. John's wort family," she told him. "Its proper name is *Hypericum androsaemum*. It grows in the woods near here; it's a sort of shrub. It's also called sweet amber—it's quite a pretty plant when in bloom. We use the leaves as an herbal medicine, but it is meant to be applied topically—to treat wounds, you understand. It is not meant to be eaten like an ordinary berry. Certainly no one in their right mind would put the berries in a fruitcake. And that is what this inquiry is about, is it not?" She observed him shrewdly. "Whether we are dealing with someone in their right mind? And whether they might not, in true G. K. Chesterton fashion, strike again?"

Max turned his head, ignoring the sudden blaze of interest from her canny blue eyes.

"When does tutsan come into season?" he asked.

"It blooms from June to August, and then its berries appear. They start out green, and turn red. When fully ripe they are a deep purple color."

So, thought Max. The berries involved in the fruitcake poisoning were likely harvested in the fall of last year. That fit the timing of Lord Lislelivet's visit to Monkbury Abbey. Whoever did this would not have had access to the berries before then, unless of course the berries came from the previous fall, which seemed unlikely. As it was, the fruitcake sat around untouched for a long time, as fruitcake is wont to do—if tightly packaged it could last on the shelf for years. Max sighed. No one would ever be able to figure out who was responsible for the poisoning, since all of this had been set in motion so long ago. It was in its little way the perfect crime.

"Now," she said, "the yew, or *Taxus baccata*—if that had been used we'd have a different story. The red berries of the yew are, as I say, pure poison. To be specific, the inner seed of the berry is poisonous. Every child has been warned since ancient times not to eat the berries."

Max knew the yew was poisonous and certainly felt he had always known this, although he couldn't credit a particular adult with passing along that tidbit. His parents were the last sort of people to possess folkloric knowledge of this nature, neither his charmingly ethereal mother nor his intellectual father. Perhaps whoever did this just didn't know enough to commit an effective poisoning.

He was not sure he himself would recognize black bryony unless it wore a sign, and the same went for tutsan. But the odds of Dame Ingrid the kitchener not knowing her berries? A million to one against, he would wager. Having produced so many fruitcakes in her day using her super-secret pineapple formula, could she help but notice that one of her staple ingredients had changed its size, shape, smell, or color, if even slightly? But that hadn't happened. She had noticed nothing and reported nothing unusual.

"There is one possibility," Dame Petronilla was saying. "Someone may have mistaken the tutsan for belladonna—for deadly nightshade, that is. Both are plants that produce black or very dark berries—at least at their final stages of growth, the tutsan berries are dark, and although their shapes are different, someone without my knowledge . . . well, they might mix them up. When they are in flower, now, that is a different thing. Tutsan and belladonna are quite different and only someone with no knowledge whatsoever could mistake one for the other."

She added gloomily, surveying the perfection of her garden: "As few as two berries of belladonna can kill. If that is what they thought they were dealing with, Father—well, that is quite a different matter."

"What would be the symptoms of belladonna poisoning?" he asked.

She returned her gaze to him. "Visual distortion, rapid heart rate. Women used to use it to enhance their looks—it dilates the pupils, you see. Makes them big and dark, like doll's eyes. Why that would be thought to be attractive to men I cannot say. Women silly and vain enough to use it cosmetically over a period of time were running the risk of blindness."

A bee buzzed between them, and Max became aware of a row of hives a short distance away. Dame Petronilla, unperturbed, watched the bee going about its propagating business.

"We grow the berries near the beehives to ensure a good harvest— the bees do all the work. Shall I show you?" She motioned him nearer a forested area, where bushes and shrubs of berries were being cultivated.

He recognized plump blackberries being trained upwards in a shaded area. She gestured to a sunny spot several yards away, where a post-and-wire system supported raspberries, and pointed out currants growing on bushes, without the need of support.

"We use a natural insecticide made from dried chrysanthemum," she told him. "Everything we grow is as natural as we can make it. Raspberry beetle can be a plague."

He did not fail to take in her familiarity with poisons. Still, what would kill a beetle might not harm a man.

"So you see, Father, we grow all sorts of berries—edible ones, that is. Raspberries and blackberries. Also red, black, and white currants. For jams and jellies. And, of course, for the fruitcakes," she added. "We have to hire outside help for the picking and pruning, but we do as much as we can ourselves.

"It's a miraculous system," she added. "The way the bees and berries support one another, I mean. Nature is genius."

Max, who had never much enjoyed the company of bees, nodded his agreement, while gently coaxing another one off his sleeve.

"They only sting if agitated," she warned him.

"Yes, I—*ouch*." He looked at his hand. Bees were like cats, he decided. They always knew where they were least welcome.

"I have a salve for that in the infirmary," Dame Petronilla said. "I'll have some delivered to your room. It's made from lavender oil. You can also rub some honey on the sting. No one understands why, but it seems to neutralize the pain."

Max thanked her, adding absently, "It seems to me most of the berries here are deliberately planted. So it's unlikely someone could accidentally harvest anything . . . untoward, like tutsan."

"Precisely. We use wildberries too, of course, in a lot of the baked goods and preserves that come out of the abbey kitchen. But tutsan? No one would knowingly grow tutsan with a view to harvesting it. Those berries that sickened Lord Lislelivet grew wild. I can show you where they— Oops! I guess I'm a suspect now."

"No one has ruled out accident, Dame Petronilla."

"Dame Pet. Please."

Had someone deliberately tried to poison Lord Lislelivet? It seemed to Max the answer hinged on how well acquainted the poisoner was with the different berries growing on the property.

He looked past Dame Petronilla to a far grove. "I see you're growing apples, too. There is a woman in my village who sells apple cider in her shop—all different ciders made from specific apple varieties, like using different grapes for different wines."

"What a delightful idea. Maybe one day . . . we just don't have enough people to take on any more ambitious projects right now. Producing cheese is stretching our limits at the moment. So many things require a fulltime commitment."

"That seems to be a recurring theme. That there is a battle between bringing income to the abbey and having enough people to handle the workflow."

"It's more than that, Father, although 'battle' may be too strong a word. 'Conflict,' perhaps. We are conflicted. Every project that takes time away from prayer and contemplation is at odds with our true mission."

"Yes, yes, I see how that could happen."

Chapter 15

THE ABBESS

The abbess shall be set above all, and above all others shall she be wise, fair, and loving, tempering her sound judgment with mercy. . . . The abbess should gladly welcome guests and travelers to her table.

—*The Rule of the Order of the Handmaids of St. Lucy*

He returned to his room via the guesthouse kitchen, where he stopped to apply a spot of honey to the bee sting. He was not surprised that it helped.

At the small desk in his room, he took out his notebook and began jotting down his impressions so far. An hour later, the notes covered less than two pages but showed him two patterns. One pattern had to do with wealth. It was clear that although the nuns were stretched as to resources, they were doing very well in terms of sales to the outside world.

The other pattern, a mere suggestion so far, indicated that not everyone was as thrilled by this success as they might have been. Dame Hephzibah was content in her little showroom of a gift shop, and Dame Ingrid was happy in her kitchen. Dame Sibil, the cellaress, was all in favor of progress and was a champion of the Internet, or so he gathered. But Dame Olive, the librarian, had indicated oh-so-delicately that there was some friction between what Max thought of as the traditionalists versus the go-getters. Dame Petronilla, the infirmaress, had mentioned this as well.

He had the idea they all might have wanted to say more but were held back by vows that prohibited them from breaking rank or discussing outright the business of the nunnery. Indulging in idle gossip was also forbidden, and he supposed all of this might fall into that category. Priest he might be, but he was an outsider who would, with any luck, go away soon and leave them to get on with it.

He became aware of a slight movement outside his door, and as he watched, an envelope appeared, slipped over the sill. He sat a moment, expecting a knock or other communication to accompany the delivery. None came, and whoever left the note had crept silently away by the time he opened the door. He saw just the hem of a skirt disappearing around the corner.

He opened the thick envelope, embossed on the flap with the abbey's ancient seal. This depicted a woman wearing a heavenly crown, presumably the Virgin Mary or perhaps St. Lucy herself. The envelope contained an invitation to dinner from the abbess of Monkbury Abbey. It was hand-written in blue-black ink with a thick-nibbed pen.

DEAR FATHER TUDOR: PLEASE COME TO DINE WITH ME
THIS EVENING AT SEVEN P.M. I LOOK FORWARD TO
MEETING YOU. YOURS IN CHRIST, ABBESS JUSTINA

Max rubbed a hand across his chin and decided he needed a shave, because of course he would obey the polite summons. Gathering up his kit and a change of clothing, he made his way down the chilly hallway of the men's section of the guesthouse, following the signs to the bath fa-cilities. As he had already discovered, these were spotless and seemed newly spruced up—indeed, they still smelled of paint, and one sink still had the manufacturer's warranty and instructions attached to its pipes by a plastic string. The water in the shower, a built-in modular affair, was as scalding as he chose to make it, so the various "green" devices the nuns had installed for generating electricity and heating seemed to be working. He toweled off with a white towel, thinned by repeated washings, and prepared to meet the abbess of Monkbury.

•   •   •

Of necessity the abbey cloister did not tidily enclose a traditional flat
square: the grounds stepped down or rose up or even halted abruptly to fit
the space allotted on the mountain perch. The design owed much to the
Roman country villa plan, being built with covered walkways around a
central plaza-like area designed for quiet comfort, for reading and reflection, with benches and nooks under shaded trees. Traces of the Roman-
esque could be seen in the fantastical carvings of animals and demonic
creatures on the cloister arcades and the central wellhead.

Max skirted the edge of the cloister garth, heading toward the abbess's lodgings in the southeast corner of the compound. He could hear
the River Easewinter below, rumbling its way to the sea. It would branch
off into the smaller River Pudmill on the way, the river that ran beneath
the jagged brow of Hawk Crest in Nether Monkslip. If he'd had a boat he
could have jumped in and been home with Awena in a few hours. She'd
be cooking her evening meal right about now, something wholesome and
cruelty free, and saying over her food a prayer of thanks to the universe
for sharing its abundance. Max sent up a similar prayer with the wish to
rejoin her soon.

He reached the door to the abbess's lodge and pounded on the knocker
with strength sufficient to reach the further edges of the building. The
lodge was a massive structure that gave every outward appearance of
being full of byways and nooks and crannies, and he doubted very much
if the abbess had a full staff to run the place. But he waited no more than
a minute before the door was opened by a young woman in her twenties,
wearing the plain white band with black veil of the postulant. Her dress
fell to below her lisle-stockinged knees, and was gathered unattractively
into a bunch of fabric at her waist by a rope, precisely like a sack of pota-
toes. Still, she had a fresh young face with a fading tan, and a pleasing
expression with a sweet and welcoming smile. Circling at her feet, to
Max's surprise, was a small white dog.

"Praise be to God," she said. Then she added, "Stop it."

"Hmm?"

"Not you, Father. The dog. He is the abbess's pet and thinks he runs the place. He pays me no mind whatsoever, because she spoils him rotten. Please come in. The abbess has asked me to seat you. She will be with you shortly."

"And you are?"

"I am Mary Benton," she replied. She bestowed on him her wide, sunny smile. "I am a postulant here. I'll be taking my first vows as a novice in two months. If God wills it."

The part about God seemed an afterthought; she hadn't yet mastered the drill. "Have you been here long, Mary?"

"A few months. I . . . I suffered a personal loss, you see. My husband. I had just finished an art history course last winter in Italy and planned to continue in that career. God had other plans."

"So you took a holiday, wanting to think?"

She had been in the process of stifling a yawn. She stopped to look at him, startled. "Excuse me: I am still getting used to the interrupted sleep. How did you know that, about the holiday?"

"I did the same thing. My life was turned upside down and I went on an aimless holiday, to Egypt. That is when I 'got the call,' as they say. Besides, I don't think you got that tan from hanging about an English garden in winter."

"Ah, I see. You're very observant." She ushered him down a long drafty hallway and into a grand room, its large wooden table set for two people near one of two large fireplaces. It was a room designed for entertaining queens and potentates. Painted heraldic shields hung against dark-paneled walls, and tapestries so old they looked as if they would disintegrate at a touch crowded the walls. There were no portrait paintings, which befitted a monastic place, he supposed. It was vainglory to have one's portrait done or one's photograph taken, even if one had risen to the high rank of abbess of a famous nunnery such as Monkbury. Especially if one had.

Mary Benton asked him to sit in one of the throne-like chairs, promising again that the abbess would join him in a few moments. She walked away, her sandals looking several sizes too big for her feet, and closed the door behind her. Max was left in splendid isolation to try to decipher the faded tapestries and the various shields. He imagined the shields had something to do with the various nobles who had left their riches to the abbey, with the hope that someone would remember to pray for their souls. The abbey shield itself, depicting the woman in her heavenly crown, took pride of place over the fireplace nearest him.

The door opened and in glided Abbess Justina.

Max rose to greet her. He was struck first by her Renoir coloring—pink cheeks, blue eyes, flawless fair skin showing not a trace of her age, although from the files provided him by the bishop's secretary he knew Abbess Justina Berry was in her early fifties. The hair peeking from the edges of her coif was dark and only lightly streaked with white.

She wore the same clod-hopperish sandals as the postulant, but the lack of proportion to the rest of her body was muted by the long purple skirts falling nearly to the stone floor. The little white dog who had greeted him at the door emerged from beneath her hem.

Max in his boyhood had spent a brief and unproductive period in an Anglican school while his parents were posted overseas. The nuns who taught him had worn a starched headdress that stood out from their foreheads in elaborate origami folds, the elegant structure topped by a veil of soft white linen. Abbess Justina and the other handmaids of St. Lucy wore a more relaxed affair, although remembering Dame Olive's evident discomfort in the library he still wished for them a less constricting coif, particularly in summer.

"Good evening, Father," said the abbess. "How good of you to join me."

"How good of you to invite me."

"Goodness had less to do with it than curiosity," she said, smiling. "The situation that brings you here is alarming and, well, curious. In addition, your fame precedes you—oh, no false modesty, please Father Tudor. 'The Chedrow Castle Affair,' as the press calls it, was extraordinary. But let's have our meal, and over some of the lovely French wine from our motherhouse we'll talk of what your theories are of the matter. I know you have spoken today with Dames Ingrid, our cook, Olive, our librarian, and Petronilla, our infirmaress. Perhaps you have gleaned some ideas. But—"

Judging by the distant, loud clatter of crockery against cutlery and glassware, the postulant had dropped a tray. Abbess Justina heaved an enormous, patient sigh that rippled the snowy drapery of her wimple like a slow-moving avalanche.

"Mary is a dear young woman, but . . ." Her voice drifted off. "She has a lot to manage."

"They all do," said Max.

"Yes," she agreed. "We've a dwindling number of applicants, so we're spread thin. Just for one example, Monkbury Abbey had a chantress at one time to manage the church services, lead the prayers, and train the novices to sing. What a luxury that seems—one wonders what she did with all the free time. Dame Olive does all that now. And the cellaress does double duty as almoness—making sure whatever we produce in excess gets distributed to the poor. Lately there has been a great deal of excess, praise God."

Max wondered if all that abundance presented any sort of temptation to the cellaress or to anyone, really, with access to the abbey coffers. Including, as he supposed he must, the abbess. It would not be the first time that an abbey found itself vulnerable to fraud and graft or, at best, accusations of same. The bishop had his system of checks and balances, but as Max well knew, any system devised by man could be circumvented by man. Or woman.

The postulant appeared with a bowl of salad and a basket of bread. These she set before them in rather an unsteady fashion and retreated backwards, bowing awkwardly. She did not seem to have a gift for waiting at table. She did not speak, and Max gathered she was not allowed to. She disappeared back through the door, which presumably led to the lodge's private kitchen.

"The rest of the appointed jobs we've had to let slide or share," the abbess continued, offering him the bread. "The sisters all take a turn watching out for our one postulant and our one novice, training them up and testing their suitability for the life."

"But you seem to be prospering," observed Max.

"We've been extraordinarily lucky in making our own way and in attracting benefactors. But there are limited hours to the day, and the Rule of St. Lucy requires that devotions be balanced with work. So we do what we can with what we have. It doesn't help that we have such an aging population."

Her right hand fell to her side, and Max realized she was feeding the dog a piece of the bread from her plate.

"His name is Rotterdam," she informed Max.

Max took a wild guess.

"As in Erasmus of Rotterdam?"

"Yes, however did you know?"

Oh how he enjoyed a good insider reformist joke. He wondered that she kept a pet, which surely fell into the category of forbidden personal possessions, but then wondered who would begrudge her the company.

"He was my mother's," she said, answering his unasked question. "When she died, there was no one to look after him. He's a spoiled nuisance with an exaggerated sense of his own importance, but we're inseparable now."

"It is not a life for everyone," Max offered neutrally.

"You don't mean the dog's life? No, of course you don't. We are not contemplatives, but still we all have times of loneliness and doubt."

"I understand," said Max. "That could happen all too easily."

There was a silence, and he said, "There must be occasions when help from outside is needed. How do you manage in case of sudden illness or accident?"

She paused in buttering a piece of bread, her fingers swollen with what looked like arthritis. "I struggle to remember the last time anything like that happened. I suppose it was when Dame Edith fell off the hay loft, and that was years ago. We have had to ring the vet on occasion when one of the sheep or goats is ailing, but otherwise we are able to manage on our own. Dame Infirmaress has learned enough about dentistry to perform routine cleanings, but the sisters go into Temple Monkslip for anything major. The same goes for any serious medical condition, of course. Otherwise permission to leave is limited. It has been some time since any of us have had our eyes examined, and we are all overdue. Dr. Barnard was reminding me of that last week. He is a trained optician as well as a G.P."

"You seem to be almost entirely self-sustaining. May I?" he asked, his hand returning to the bread basket. The bread, difficult to resist, was homemade, fresh and warm from the oven.

"Please," she said. "I've had all I want." Another piece of bread disappeared over the side of the table, presumably into the waiting dog. "For the most part, we grow or make what we need. Certain sisters will go into the village for dry goods and such. Sometimes—very rarely—a sister will need to travel outside for, say, educational purposes. We weren't all born knowing how to raise sheep or cut back certain plants and trees for the winter, for example, and there are times we need to expand our knowledge."

"Your own background is not agricultural?" he asked, knowing the answer.

"Good heavens, no. I am city born and bred, and I didn't know a turnip from a turnstile when I first came here."

"How would you get help, if you needed it?" He'd seen no landline phones on the premises.

"We have a satellite phone to ring the emergency services from Temple Monkslip," she told him, "Or Dr. Barnard. Guests are not permitted to use the phone, but we can relay messages to them if need be." She turned, pausing as the postulant brought in two plates heaped with pasta and tomato sauce. The abbess probably felt, as did Max, that the postulant should be allowed to focus all her energies on not letting the pasta with its red sauce slide right off the plate into their laps.

"Xanda Gorey," the abbess continued when Mary had successfully offloaded the plates onto the table, "seems to have a gentleman friend on the outside who is most anxious to reach her—we soon put a stop to that. The phone is not for amorous chitchat."

"Of course not," Max murmured loyally.

"Of course, her parents have been most generous. Mr. and Mrs. Gorey would like to be laid to rest here, you know. One hopes he would not insist on wearing his baseball cap for the effigy. Have you met him yet?"

Max shook his head.

"He is a brilliant man," she said, but did not offer evidence for this. "Yes, of course in an emergency, such as may yet happen with poor Dame Meredith, we can ring the outside world. There is even a mobile telephone that in rare instances we allow to be used by a sister traveling on business for the abbey. As I say, I can barely recall when we had a situation we couldn't cope with ourselves."

She smiled beatifically, in the manner of one who was sure heaven would provide, no matter the occasion.

A world without e-mail, video, television—all the things that cry out for our attention every day, thought Max. How restful, on the one hand. And how frustrating, on the other—particularly for families who might wish to connect more often with their relatives here at the abbey.

The abbess picked up a fork and spoon, spooling her pasta. He marveled at her willingness to tackle tomato sauce, with the snowy white linen of her wimple at her neck and enveloping her chest and shoulders. It was asking for trouble, like washing the car when rain is in the forecast.

"We augment our electricity with candlelight, as you have seen," she continued. "For a long time we only had enough electricity to power a few kitchen appliances and low-voltage lamps so we could see our way around. Running a cable out here was out of the question and probably will be until technology catches up to our remote needs. Our priority right now is to expand the photovoltaic system—this is part of the guesthouse renovation project."

"So that is still in the works?"

"Oh, yes," she replied smoothly. "Just slightly delayed. We need larger batteries to store energy when we have cloudy days. The guesthouse once was lighted by kerosene lamps and heated with wood stoves. But now fire insurance is difficult to obtain unless we modernize. So woodstoves in the guest rooms have been replaced by gas heaters. Electricity is available in all the cloister buildings, although we still rely on candles in the church. For other areas we have rechargeable battery-powered lamps, like the one provided in your room. We can't have guests falling off the mountainside. Although we strongly urge guests to stay in the areas assigned to them—restricted areas are clearly marked."

"Of course," said Max. "It is after all a cloister."

"But we don't want people to misunderstand—it is part of our life's purpose to welcome guests—to provide a place of peace where they can collect themselves."

"The guesthouse," Max began. "The bishop has said there may be a question . . ." How to put this? wondered Max. "A question of the funds being siphoned off" sounded a bit harsh, if accurate.

"Dame Cellaress can answer all your questions," Abbess Justina said blithely, resuming her hospitality narrative as she twirled her pasta. Her brook-no-interference tone was unmistakable, and Max did not persist, knowing it would push her into a corner from which she might never emerge. She began to speak of daily life in the abbey; he had the idea her descriptions, like the guest-mistress's, might be part of a well-rehearsed lecture for visitors. "On Sundays," she was saying, "there is no work period except for the cook and her helpers. It's a time for recreational pursuits—the aim is to do something relaxing and not related to work or study. Many of the sisters who enjoy reading or fishing take this time as their opportunity. I often go walking or hiking, especially in summer. I like to collect wildflowers. And of course Rotterdam loves it, don't you, my sweet? " She turned her head, apparently addressing the floor, before returning her attention to Max. "On feast days, we decorate every corner of the refectory with wildflowers."

"And this is when relatives might visit?" he asked. "You don't miss just being able to telephone when you feel like it?"

"That is where things get difficult," she replied. Her expression changed fleetingly to one of regret. "Not so much for us—it is a choice we made, after all, even if I would argue that it was God who called us and we simply answered. No, the families have a hard time letting go. They will send gifts that are meant for their daughter alone, or try to 'game' the system—is that the phrase? Game the system so that there is some family emergency every other week that requires the sister's attention. Once we catch on to this, it is firmly put a stop to. We must be cruel to be kind. They do break my heart sometimes, the parents."

Mary Benton reentered just then with bread to replenish the basket. This time, several slices fell to the floor. "Leave it for now," said the abbess sharply. The young woman seemed to be surrounded by chaos the way the cartoon character Pig-Pen was surrounded by dust. Max felt a tug of nostalgia for his own catastrophic housekeeper, that herald of the coming Apocalypse, Mrs. Hooser.

Once she had left them, the abbess confided. "She was recently widowed. We are watching very closely to ensure her vocation is a true one. Many times, people reacting to a tragedy don't know what they want. They cut off old friends, even family, wanting a fresh start, having been reminded of the brevity of life. Mary had thought her vocation was art history, but she came here instead. I'm sure you've seen that for yourself, Father, in the course of your pastoral duties."

"Many times," said Max. "It may just be that Mary is not cut out to wait tables."

The abbess let out a hoot of laughter, startling the dog into an answering bark.

"You are right about that," she said, lifting him into her lap. "All the postulants have to take turns serving at my table, so I can size them up at first hand. Mary is the definition of a butterfingers, but I'm certain God has plans for her that don't involve breakable items. Her biggest struggle with the Rule, as it is for many, is that she forgets to keep the Great Silence after Compline and is constantly having to be corrected for it. The silence is to be maintained throughout the night. She forgets, and will go bustling about, gossiping and blithering about trivialities and asking if anyone has toothpaste she can borrow. I think she's lonely, poor soul." She sighed. "And there, I've committed the fault of gossiping myself."

"'How do you solve a problem like Maria?'" said Max.

"Precisely," said the abbess.

The postulant came in just then with a newly opened bottle of wine. Max recognized the label of St. Martin's from the wines being sold in the gift shop. On the label was a smiling nun framed in silhouette against a vast, sunny vineyard. It was an excellent wine. With an eye on the postulant as she left, the abbess told him, "Not one of us is ever sure of our vocation. As many years as I've been here, I've seen the doubts, and I've felt them myself. But I believe, Father, that we do much good, even hidden away from the world as we are up here. That is why I persist. With or without miracles to reassure me."

"Miracles?"

"We attracted pilgrims to our church and our holy well from the start, and when we were a Catholic house the pope would grant get-out-of-hell-free cards, as my father called them, to people who made the journey here to pray. Many came in search of a cure. Many *were* cured. It was the source of our wealth but not a complete fraud. You do see."

She might have been talking about events from yesterday. In this atmosphere, surrounded by smoke-darkened wood and stones, Max could see how yesterday blended into hundreds of years ago, and hundreds more hence.

"We've also survived all manner of natural disasters," the abbess said. "We even had an earthquake a year or so ago measuring just over five on the Richter scale. Not big by the world's standards, but big enough I watched my own empty shoes march across the floor. I'd never seen such a thing outside of a cartoon."

"Was there much damage?" asked Max.

She shook her head. "No. *That* was a miracle, really. We had to make some structural repairs to the church. The guesthouse plans had to be put on hold for a while. Perhaps you've met Piers Montague? Yes, I see that you have. Anyway, one old wall in particular came tumbling down. How he loved photographing that wall: we were constantly having to shoo him away. Piers reminds me of someone from my youth." Absently, she stroked the head of her little lap dog. From her expression, she might have been thinking, "Someone best forgotten."

"So, Father. I gather you've talked with a few of my sisters already. But I would suggest a talk with our cellaress if you really want to put your finger on the pulse of things here. She manages the day-to-day, you know."

"Yes, thank you. Everyone has been most helpful. I had planned to talk with—is it Dame Sibil?—tomorrow."

"The cellaress, yes."

"I am hoping she can tell me a bit more about your . . . your various enterprises."

"You mean our sources of income," she said candidly, disarmingly. "The inflow and outflow. No need to beat about the bush. I can help you with the big picture, Father. She, of course, knows the details. Much of our income has come from our ties to the local villagers."

Max, savoring the tomato sauce, which was nearly a match for Awena's, recalled the bishop's saying the abbess had a Reaganesque quality about her: an easy and likable geniality, an air of open honesty. He had known such a person when he belonged to a drinking and dining club at Oxford. Hugh Barclay-Watson was the person everyone wanted to be with and be seen to be with—the man who exerted not a single ounce of effort to win the constant devotion of his legions of followers. Who seemed genuinely unaware that he *had* followers. It was Max's first real encounter with charisma on such a scale. The man's murder had come as a shock to everyone in the club, but Max realized in retrospect it should not have done. That kind of effortless power earned one enemies, and if one was spoiled like Hugh by the gifts of charm, one never saw it coming.

Was the abbess similarly blinded?

"What we strive to accomplish every day," she was saying, "and of course fail to achieve, is the transformation of our old selves. We fail, but we keep trying."

Failure, he thought. How badly had a nun failed if she had tried to poison one of the guests?

The abbess might have read his mind. "You are here at the bishop's request to investigate an event that could bring dishonor to this house. A scandal unprecedented in recent history. In fact, to match this, we'd have to look back to the fourteen hundreds, when one of our sisters starved to death in the crypt."

"Good heaven," said Max.

The abbess nodded complacently, gratified by his reaction. "She was an anchoress—you know, a recluse—a mystic. In those days extremes of penance and fasting were allowed, even encouraged among ascetics, the sort inclined to extravagant self-denial. The abbey attracted a few of those. Probably she would disappear for a week or more, eating little, doing penance. Then she died and I suppose no one realized . . . it's not as if she were expected for supper. Her body was left where they finally found it in the crypt—they simply sealed off the area rather than disturb her remains. We know of her only that, due to her great piety, she acted as the sacrist, entrusted to look after the plate and ornaments, the vessels and ornaments and relics.

"I suppose," the abbess added musingly, "I suppose it was a natural job for her, to guard the most sacred objects, since she never wandered far from them."

"I guess thievery was a commonplace."

"It was always a problem," she agreed. "You would think the abbey's reputation for holiness would inhibit people, but it doesn't seem to work that way. It would be difficult to overstate the wealth and power of the abbey. Which is, of course, what led the church in those days into all manner of folly. Would you like more salad, Father?"

Max nodded, and the postulant, Mary, materialized from the shadows to serve him. He reached for the salad bowl but the abbess stilled him with a raised hand.

"Let her," she said. "It is our privilege to serve, and it is also how Mary learns. Isn't it, my dear?"

Chapter 16
THE NOVICE

The novice should be warned in advance of all the hurdles on the path to God.

—*The Rule of the Order of the Handmaids of St. Lucy*

Max slept well that night, attributing his rest to the abbess's excellent wine and to the calming silence that surrounded the abbey. Waking early the next day, he joined the nuns for Lauds, spent some time adding to his notes on the case, then decided on a walk to acquaint himself with the grounds and simply bask in the purity of the bright gold morning air.

Sunshine fell like fingers of light through the trees, making patterns on the grass in dark and pale greens, and there was the slight suggestion of a breeze that he tried to will into stronger action. The nunnery was so high up he felt he was walking on Olympus, quite alone. The only sound was the bleating of sheep in the distance, which now he became aware of it was a constant, a simmer of discontent carried on the transparent, gentle wind.

Beware, he thought idly, *of those who come to you in sheep's clothing*.

Walking slowly, passing the abbess's lodge and the infirmary and the back of the nuns' dormitory, he came to the cemetery with its yew trees. Time had obliterated most of the information on the headstones, although a recent entry to the presumed company of saints was the abbess who had been succeeded by Abbess Justina. A line of Thomas Gray's came into his mind, and he stopped for a moment in reflection: "Beneath those rugged elms, that yew tree's shade . . . each in his narrow cell forever laid."

He tried to avoid walking on the graves themselves, an avoidance he saw more as a courtesy to the dead than a superstitious dread of waking them, even though whatever lay under these old stones had long since turned to dust. This avoidance was not so easy to do, as the stones were scattered willy-nilly, time and geologic upheaval presumably having moved them out of alignment. He did a sort of jitterbug across the area and, shaking off the melancholy of the sad old place, plunged through brush and bushes, heading toward the cliff edge of the grounds. Finally he emerged from a grove of trees beyond the cemetery into a sunlit meadow where goats and the unhappy sheep were grazing. In the water far below, two men went by in a boat. It was a motorboat but they were paddling, their silence probably in deference to the nuns. Max waved, but they didn't see him, intent as they were on navigating the choppy water.

Max walked to the mountain's edge and looked down and along the stone wall that rose straight from the river running beneath the abbess's lodge and the infirmary. A small black door flanked by mooring rings was set into the wall. Presumably it was used for offloading goods or even for catching swans, back in the day when they were prized as much for food as for their beauty.

Max squinted into the sun, peering across the rolling vastness like some ancient mariner, taking in the woodlands and heathlands of the fertile area, imagining that as far as the eye could see was abbey land. He knew Glastonbury Tor sat in the misty distance behind him, pulsing with all the tie-died colors of the rainbow, a sort of small, bare Twin Peak to the wooded tor on which he stood. Archeologists were convinced there was some connection between the two sites but could only guess at what the link might have been.

He came nearer to the grazing animals. Watching the black-and-white-spotted sheep, Max recalled a documentary where a ewe had been tricked into thinking she had given birth twice, so she could be given another ewe's lamb to nurse.

The sheep ignored him, continuing their preoccupied bleating, but the goats stared, an audience awaiting its speaker. There was something, Max had always thought, rather uncanny about goats, something knowing and otherworldly and very ancient in their gaze. He agreed with Xanda that they were ever-so-slightly creepy. They watched him closely as he passed, a human-like grin on their bearded, whiskery faces and amusement in their pale eyes—eyes with those strange, horizontal pupils. It was little wonder pagans had adopted them as symbols of wickedness; Christians associated the goat with the Devil himself.

Max thought of the herd mentality, wondering if the nuns, living in such close proximity, could anymore see and think as individuals. Did they all just look to the abbess for guidance, a practice that had become automatic with the years? She exuded a certain comforting presence, an assurance that all would be well. Max had felt it himself the night before at her dinner table.

The more he thought of it, the more it was difficult to see any of them operating independently. But surely committing a crime like attempted murder required a certain gift for autonomy, a certain willingness to step outside the herd, a turning away from convention and toward chaos.

Hearing the sound of feet softly disturbing the grass, he turned.

The novice, as he could see she was by the abbreviated skirt and white veil of her habit, walked over to him. Her name, as he knew from the information provided him by the bishop's office, was Sister Rose. Watching her approach—she had a steady marching stride, as if she were on parade—he searched his mind for her last name and came up with Rose Tocketts. She had not yet taken vows, at which point she would adopt her religious name, the name under which she would live the rest of her life, the name that would appear on her gravestone when she came at last to be buried under the yews in Monkbury Abbey cemetery. The "Tocketts" would disappear.

"You have a long day," Max greeted her. "I didn't expect to see anyone for a while."

"Do we?" she asked, brushing some dirt off of her hands and then peering up at him, shading her dark eyes against the sunlight. She had a square face with broad, flat cheekbones. Max thought she might be of Eurasian heritage.

"I don't really notice it anymore. One day is much like the last, and one gets used to waking up early. In fact, I have come to like that feeling we have of being quite alone in the world in the early hours. In the Army I often worked the midnight shift, so it feels familiar."

"You never take a break?"

She nodded. "We do. In the summer, if it is very warm, we are allowed to take a little nap in the afternoon. So far this year we've been spared the flooding of last year, but have been given a bit too much heat instead. I can only hope St. Swithin will come through for us in moderation this time."

She was referring to the belief that if it rains on St. Swithin's day, July 15, it will rain for forty days afterwards.

In the county of Monkslip, rain would be most welcome. They had had sun—too much sun. The sort of unrelenting, moist, beating-down heat that made people wonder why, oh why, was nothing being done about global warming?

"I wonder what it is like here in winter," he said.

"I have only spent one winter here. It was harsh."

"But not harsh enough to deter you."

She lifted her shoulders in a shrug, and flipped one end of her veil back over her shoulder. "They give you a lot of time to decide whether you are really cut out for this life. I think I am. But it is easy to delude oneself. The others are an inspiration. They are all so different, from such different backgrounds. And yet they have that serenity . . ." Her voice trailed off wistfully, as though that were an unheard-of gift she was waiting to have bestowed.

"I've noticed it too," he said. "They seem to carry that certain belief that God always has your back."

She turned to him with a start. "The last time someone said that to me, I was shot at the next day. I was spared, obviously, but it turned out not to be true for my brothers in arms. God didn't have their backs."

He'd often seen that reaction among soldiers come back from Iraq—the instant return to the moment when life hung by a thread, as if no time at all had passed. She was right back there.

He noticed she carried a gardening basket and shears. To divert her from her melancholy, he pointed and said, "Roses instead of guns, now. Much better."

"A thousand times better. It's my turn at arranging flowers for the refectory table," she said, positioning the stems. "Another thing I'm not particularly good at—give me an engine to take apart any day, and I'm happy." She walked toward the edge of the field, where a colorful wave of summer wildflowers had made their bright appearance. A hare crossing the field stopped in its tracks.

"Is it all that you expected?" Max asked, following her. "The religious life?"

"No," she said, without hesitation. "You think you know, you think you're ready. But every day I seem to fu—I mean, mess! *Mess* up. I seem to mess something new up. I think what comes hardest for me is the isolation—being the new girl, apart from Mary. That and the stillness."

"And maybe the language?" he asked, teasing her, for he sometimes still had the same problem, matching his vocabulary to fit his new station in life.

She laughed, piercing the air with a great shout. The sheep, startled, turned small faces as one in her direction. Nothing seemed to upset the goats, who continued their disinterested assessment of her and Max.

"Thank you for understanding that," she said. "In the Army everybody just blew off steam with the foulest language imaginable. I wasn't one of the worst offenders, but I'm afraid some of it rubbed off. I've had to really watch myself since I've been here. Bad habits die hard, you should forgive the pun. Anyway, the stillness, when you're used to being rousted at all hours and sent running about shouting, generally to no purpose—well, it is just takes getting used to."

"It's a sea change, yes." Thinking of his MI5 days, he said, "I think I can relate."

"We are given many opportunities for quiet reflection," she went on, "and a part of me says, 'Oh, *no*! Not quiet reflection again! Let me weed the garden or milk the sheep or even scrub floors or something, but not *that*.'"

Max smiled. "I can imagine it all takes getting used to. The cycling down when you're used to being on alert all the time. So tell me: what is your typical day like here?"

"Well . . . it starts early, as you know. But the day doesn't really get going for me until we assemble in the chapter house in the morning, after prayer. The abbess presides, and that is where we get our marching orders for the day. We take turns reading a chapter from the Rule, and the abbess will give a little talk on the meaning of that particular rule. Then the practical matters are discussed—the status of the various projects we have going, how sales are going, which items are being discontinued. It is very like a sales meeting in the outer world, I would imagine—not something I know a lot about. In chapter is also when we confess our shortcomings. That takes quite a while in my case—the breaches of the Rule. And we're given a penance."

"Do the sisters ever report each other for breaking the rules?" Max knew in some orders that was required by custom. It had always struck him as a recipe for disaster.

"You mean, rat someone out?" she asked. "Yes, in theory, chapter would be the place to bring up little lapses they may have witnessed in others. But it's like casting the first stone, isn't it? I've never known it to happen, not since I've been here. We all confess our own lapses—mind our own business."

It had been, thought Max, rather a long shot, that one of them might have seen or heard something untoward and brought it up during the confession period of the chapter meeting.

"Besides," she said, "for anything that happened that was really out of line, we can talk with the abbess about it, in private. That seems infinitely preferable to ratting each other out in public."

They looked out over the enclosure where the sheep were grazing. He asked her what breed they were. "I'm city bred," he apologized. "I can still tell you where to get the best table in London at the last minute and how much to tip the maître d', but I've no clue when it comes to sheep."

"Those ones over there are Friesians," she told him. "I didn't know that either, when I first came here. They use their milk to make soap. They've also started a little trade in farmhouse cheese."

"They," not "we," he noted—she had slipped back into the "they." He wondered how long it would take for her to feel at home enough to start talking automatically of "we," like Dame Olive.

"Don't they have the most wonderful faces?" she asked him. "You wish they could speak. I suspect they talk about us behind our backs." One of the sheep walked over to the fence. She stretched out a hand, which it nuzzled.

"And those in the further pasture are Jacob sheep," she said. "We breed them for their fleece—it's so soft, like nothing you've ever felt. We sell it to hand spinners."

"You never breed them for food, then?"

"Heavens, no. I couldn't bear the idea, really, once I got to know them all."

Max thought of Lily Iverson back in Nether Monkslip—Lily who bred her sheep for their silky wool, which she knitted into award-winning sweaters and rugs. Lily would entirely have understood Sister Rose.

He asked her if it were true that a ewe could be tricked into accepting the offspring of another sheep as her own.

"I've heard of it. I guess sheep are the dumb blondes of the animal kingdom. Very sweet, not awfully bright. The lambs bleat when their mothers are taken away to be shorn—as you can hear. They have to be weaned, the lambs, but they keep the bleating up all day. They'll bleat until their little voices give out, some of them. The mothers cry as well, but not all. Some don't seem to care. If the mum is shorn sometimes her lamb doesn't recognize her when she's brought back. As I say, they're not very bright, poor things. But very dear, they are."

Sister Rose, under the competent exterior, struck him as a bit of a softy, at least when it came to animals. She confirmed his impression by telling him, "This one I've named Ethel. We never slaughter them, absolutely not ever," she assured him again.

"After chapter, what comes next for you?" he prompted.

"We have a time where we can work or study until the bell rings for Sext at midday. In the old days, the abbey employed servants to do the heavy lifting—I don't think I'd have enjoyed it here so much then. There were a lot of grand ladies swanning about, who seemed to treat the place like a spa or a great library. Those who could read and write were probably very happy with the solitude and the relative freedom. They were sent here by their families if for some reason or other a husband couldn't be found for them. And not all of them, I'm sure, saw that as such a bad tradeoff. When you stop to survey the field of what passed for an eligible male back in the middle ages—I mean, please. Women just didn't have a whole lot of choice in those days, or control over their own lives. The nunnery gave them, especially the high-born ones, a ticket out."

Her white skirt caught on a bramble as they walked. She stopped to extricate herself, and went on to say: "Between the noon meal and evening Vespers, there is more time for work and study, although of course we pause for prayer in mid-afternoon, as well."

"For None," he supplied.

"Yes. All that takes getting used to, including just getting the names for things right."

They came to a fence, over which an elderly horse had poked his head. She stopped to rub the blaze of white on his forehead, as if for good luck. He nuzzled her hand, looking for a carrot, which she produced like a conjurer from a hidden pocket.

"Domino," she said. "We keep him for a neighbor when he travels. Domino is a gentle old soul. The neighbor's little girl rides him."

Max indicated the pasture and farmland beyond the river surging below the monastery walls.

"All that is yours, too?" There were largish black and brown lumps gathered under a tree in the distance that he figured must be cows, although at this distance it was hard to tell.

"Since time out of mind," she told him. "It's a fraction of the holdings Monkbury used to call its own."

"And the river . . ."

"Sometimes I just stand here watching it flow, and before I know it twenty minutes have passed. I suppose that is another infraction of the Rule."

"Somehow I doubt it," said Max. "Not of the *spirit* of the Rule."

"It wasn't always like this," she told him. "Until not all that long ago, they routinely dumped waste into the river. Abbey infirmaries traditionally were built near the river so the worst things you can imagine could be dropped straight into the water. It's a wonder they didn't all die of some dread disease. Come to think of it, many of them did."

Turning from the fence, she returned to the topic that seemed to preoccupy her.

"The most common offense we tell on ourselves in chapter is that of not stopping what we are doing when the bell calls us to prayer. It seems I just get rolling with something I'm working on and I'm called away. Half the time, I seem to tune out the sound."

"I would think that was impossible," said Max.

"I know, it is a very loud sound, but when you're focused on something else. . . . Anyway, that is definitely my weak spot. One of many. The others also forget to pull their hoods over their heads when they enter the church."

"I'm sure it will come in time," said Max. "You seem a very determined person to me." He meant it as a compliment, but even as he spoke recalled the havoc determined people could cause if they kept only their own goals in mind.

She acknowledged the remark with a short nod of her head. "Anyway, we take the main meal after Vespers. I gather they used to alter mealtimes according to the season, but not any longer. Artificial light, even the feeble variety available at Monkbury, changed the need. There is a ritual washing of hands before the meal, and we take turns reading aloud. We can't speak during the readings. I am not certain I would survive a nunnery where talking was forbidden altogether."

This silence, Max supposed, was what made the life of the sardine possible, all of them packed together the day long, the modern concept of privacy banished.

"The Great Silence after Compline is easy enough—I'm asleep before my head hits the pillow most nights. The last thing I want to do is stay up and chat. This week I have light duty, though. In the evenings, I merely sit and keep watch on Dame Meredith."

"As I said, it's a long day for you."

"But I love the life," she said simply. "It is hard, but I do love it. I will adjust eventually. Look at that. It seems we're going to get some rain after all."

Indeed white clouds were now scudding against a darkening sky, which held an eerie promise of a summer squall. He decided to return to his room to wash up before lunch and collect a weatherproof jacket, just in case. After lunch he needed to keep his promise of a bedside visit to Dame Meredith in the infirmary.

"Funny, but the cows always know when it's going to rain," said Sister Rose, pointing. "See them in the farthest pasture? They're sitting down. That's always a sure sign."

Good to know, thought Max. Animals, if not people, could be relied on for useful information.

Chapter 17

THE INFIRMARY

*The sick are not to make excessive demands on those who care
for them, but should offer up their sufferings.*

—*The Rule of the Order of the Handmaids of St. Lucy*

"Did you never see *The Nun's Story*?" demanded Dame Petronilla. The postulant, Mary Benton, was sorely trying her patience. The infirmary needed
reliable helpers. Dame Petronilla was more and more convinced Mary
belonged in the kitchen or garden or somewhere she could do less damage
than in what was, in effect, a hospital ward.

"With Audrey Hepburn? Wasn't she lovely in her nun's habit? Those
cheekbones! Yes, of course I did; I loved that movie. I learned all I know
about the religious life from watching that movie. Why?"

Well, that explained so much. Dame Petronilla, busy with tweezers,
plucking the thread from an old pillowcase she was restitching, reminded
herself to be charitable. Mary was a young widow and was still probably
adjusting to that status. Had she been admitted to the order too soon?
Dame Petronilla thought so. But any more, any reasonably able-bodied
young woman who did not appear to be completely insane was being admitted. That explained the high dropout rate, too, she was certain. The
vetting process was not what it once had been.

She looked sternly at her charge, as if she could frighten some sense into her. Mary, like Audrey, had thick, beautifully arched eyebrows over hooded, dark eyes that belied her tardiness and other drawbacks by blazing with intelligence. There the resemblance stopped: Her small white teeth protruded ever so slightly, marring her otherwise good looks. She flashed the teeth now in a tentative, hopeful smile.

"It's the same principle at work here," Dame Petronilla explained patiently, or as patiently as she could, having been reduced to movie metaphors to make her point. "Audrey as Sister Luke kept getting into trouble for wanting to finish what she was doing and ignoring the bell pulling her away. Obedience to God is what matters. It is all that matters. And stop that yawning."

"Sorry, sister. I just can't get used to the long hours yet. But surely, in the case of a nurse who is tending the ill . . ."

"The seriously ill—yes, of course, exception would be made for that. If someone were having a stroke or some sort of fit no one would expect a nurse to stop what she was doing and attend to the Holy Office. But the fact is, once you decide you know better than the Rule, that you are going to think for yourself, you become a disruptive force not only to the nunnery but to yourself and your own vocation. Obedience for all of us is the most difficult thing, because as human beings, we are always convinced we know everything."

"Yes, Dame Pet—Petronilla. Of course you're right."

"I will expect you to mention this when the abbess tells us to name our faults."

"Yes, Dame Petronilla." Oh, bother, thought Mary. I will never get the hang of this effing obedience thing. I *mean*, this blessed obedience thing.

May God grant her a long life so she has time to improve, Dame Petronilla was thinking. It was different in the old days. The infirmaress would in effect be a hospital administrator, with dozens of helpers in her charge. Now here she was, alone with one hopeless postulant to help. Still Mary was adequate to attend to Dame Meredith, who was little trouble. And Dame Petronilla counted herself lucky that there were never many ill nuns. The diet and hard work and peace of their lives saw to that. The fact that they were all aging and liable to give out at once—well, she'd cross that bridge when she came to it.

Dame Petronilla was about to resume her lecture of the postulant when Father Max appeared at the open door.

She sent Mary to make sure Dame Meredith was ready to receive visitors. Then Dame Petronilla herself went to admit the priest to the premises.

"It is difficult to describe, Father Max. The horizon changes here. The more so when you know you are approaching the end at last."

He was at the bedside of Dame Meredith née Fitzwilliam in the infirmary of Monkbury Abbey. In one corner of the room sat the postulant, Mary Benton, acting rather as a *duena* to chaperone the encounter, he supposed. She was darning a sock—rather badly, he thought. In these days of disposable everything, he wasn't sure when he'd last seen anyone, man or woman, darn a sock. Certainly he'd never seen his rather impractical mother do anything of the sort.

"I have reached," Dame Meredith said on a whisper, "the end of my journey."

Journey. When, wondered Max, had everyone started talking about their journeys? Only Awena, the most spiritual of people in his experience, could use the phrase without sounding like a daft hippie. But this nun, clearly, as she said, nearing the end of her time on earth, touched his heart with the phrase. Gently, he squeezed her hand.

"We believe and hope it's the beginning," he said.

Max looked at the pale, drawn face of the aristocratic-looking woman lying before him in the hospital-style bed, with its metal side rails designed to catch a fall. She looked familiar, resembling the portraits of an aging Queen Elizabeth I—a fading Gloriana. Her skin stretched over the high-bridged nose had the gray-bluish tinge of someone who wasn't getting enough oxygen to her blood, and the thinning of her hair, no doubt from the cancer treatment, was evident, all of this giving her likeness to a newly hatched and highly vulnerable chick. Because of her condition, she had been allowed to wear a modified version of the habit, with an old-fashioned nightcap and nightdress in place of the more elaborate headdress and layers of cloth. Her usual habit was on a chair at the side of the bed, folded with military, ritualistic precision, her sandals tucked beneath the chair.

At one side of the room was a folding white examination screen of the type found in hospitals, and beside that was a tall window that allowed a view onto the orchard trees fronting the abbess's lodge. It was as peaceful a place of healing as could be imagined, but with gleaming stainless steel everywhere reflecting the afternoon light.

Dame Meredith opened her eyes suddenly and caught Max staring at her.

"I don't blame you for staring," she said. "I am sure I look as if I lost a fight, which I guess in a way I have. It's a blessing not to be allowed mirrors. We have only the haziest idea what we look like. You would be surprised how freeing that is. Especially now. Losing my hair to chemo, as little as there was of it, was as upsetting for me as I imagine it is for most people with long flowing locks."

At Max's stricken look, her face softened. "Forgive me. I indulge in a lot of gallows humor. It passes the time and it seems to be how I cope with things. Anyway, at Monkbury, we concentrate on the interior—on what's under the hood, so to speak."

He guided the conversation with questions about convent life in general—of the choices she had made, and of how, nearing the end, she had come to regard these choices. Was there regret? She claimed not, or very little.

Max was aware that given the impending birth of his and Awena's child, he was perhaps not in the best position to appreciate the choice these women had made, to forgo family life in the traditional sense. Calling another woman "sister" was a poor substitute for having a flesh-and-blood sister, was it not?

And less than that, the simple pleasures of watching television or taking in a movie were forbidden to them. He had seen no television set anywhere on the guest premises, but a daily newspaper had been delivered, rather late, to the gatehouse. He asked Dame Meredith now about this.

She told him, "One of the villagers brought us a television set when the planes flew into the Twin Towers. We couldn't bear to watch the images. After a day or two the abbess asked that it be removed. There is the Internet, of course, but the longer you are here the more you grieve for the world anyway and don't need the reminders.

"Sometimes the abbess selects passages in the news to be read aloud to us in chapter—generally news of an uplifting nature. A royal birth, for example. We were very excited by the news Prince William and his bride—Kate, is that her name?—were having a baby. That is very rare, however."

Dame Meredith had not elaborated on whether good news was rare or just the reading aloud of it. Max imagined that both things came into play. So even their knowledge of outside events was censored, if such a harsh word could be used. They were sheltered from all that was wicked in the world, so that they could concentrate on the world's healing. He saw the logic but wondered if he wouldn't himself chafe at never being allowed to decide for himself what was important to read and know.

"I suppose I should care less about these things—you would think it would seem irrelevant. But the more the world draws away from one the more interest one takes. I want to know everything, especially the happy and intriguing things. If I have regrets it is really only that I am running out of time and there is so much out there to see."

"What did you mean when you said the world draws away?"

"Haven't you noticed, Father? When you have a disease—any disease—people assume you're contagious. They should give me a bell. A leper coming upon a village in the Middle Ages had to ring a bell to warn people of his approach. I need a bell."

His heart fell at the image. "Mostly, I've found people just don't know what to say and are terrified of saying the wrong thing."

"I live in a place that, when you get right down to it, welcomes death—lives with it, understands it, embraces it. But my sisters are human beings first of all, and no one would welcome reminders of such a sentence as this one. I've told them: no more treatment. I'm done. If I'm going to be cured, God will cure me."

Max looked at her doubtfully. Clearly, the inclination was to pray over the matter some more. God worked in mysterious ways but God also worked through us, thought Max. But according to all he knew of her condition, man's best efforts had already failed her.

"But I know," she told him earnestly, "God is with us even in suffering. God doesn't watch from a distance, but I believe is right here, with me now. He doesn't shoot us full of arrows and then turn away. Who could live believing in a God capable of that?"

Max had no answers for her. His strength as a priest lay not in offering bromides but in listening as people tried to come to terms with unthinkable realities.

He looked again at the tidy room, white and gleaming steel, with some sort of lighted apparatus blinking softly in one corner. Everything was as immaculate as would be expected, and on the way in he had passed some impressively modern if small-scaled equipment. He was reminded of a hospital on a cruise ship—small and compact and able to handle most crises, but at the end of the day extremely limited. A day out at sea and they were out of the reach of helicopters and other ships, and had to trust to what the ship's doctor could manage without the resources of a proper hospital and equipment. Remote Monkbury Abbey was just like being at sea, he supposed, when it came to any real emergency.

He said something of this aloud, adding: "I am impressed at how smoothly the abbey is managed, however. It seems you could go for months here without really needing anyone's help from outside."

She followed his gaze and said, "Dame Infirmaress manages very well. She even makes sure Dame Hephzibah is fed on time."

"I was wondering today how the portress gets her meals, since she always seems to be on duty somewhere."

"Lately Dame Pet has been taking meals out to her, or sends her assistant to do so. It saves Dame Hephzibah having to walk as much."

"Her assistant being Sister Rose?"

"Yes, the novice. Sister Rose. She learned first aid in the Army—actually, she was a full-fledged medic. She's been a real boon to us. Anyway, after the portress is taken care of, Sister Rose fetches her own meal, and sometimes Dame Petronilla's, and takes her meal in private in the infirmary. There's a little microwave and things for making coffee down the hall, in the kitchenette."

His eye caught on the rosary beads on the table beside her bed. Something prompted him to ask, "Do you get many visitors?"

The question seemed to sadden her, but she rallied quickly. "Oh, yes. Abbess Genevieve—she's from the motherhouse in France—she comes to visit daily. Any of them would, if I asked for them, but I especially enjoy her company. I miss being part of the community, you know. I don't have the stamina to get through the daily offices. I imagine I can hear the chanting from here, very faintly, when the wind is right."

She did not mention family visitors, he noticed. The abbey probably had come to be her family after so many years.

"Their voices are indeed beautiful. I suppose the perfect harmony comes from long practice."

"Saint Augustine said that singing is 'praying twice.' Chanting has medical benefits, you know. Scientists have found it alters the brain waves. Haven't you ever noticed how long-lived people in monastic life tend to be? Present company excluded, of course."

Max gave her hand a squeeze. If Dame Hephzibah was any guide, they would all outlive him. He had himself experienced the calming effect of chant early on, as he had sat listening to the King's College Choir singing Gregorian chant or just listening to his Trio Mediaeval CDs.

He looked at Dame Meredith, at the face that belied her years, despite her suffering. He knew she was in her sixties. There must be something to this life they led in granting them that serene composure.

She was saying, "Saints live closer to the divine than we mere mortals can. Not since Abbess Iris passed have we had a true mystic in our midst. She walked with a glow surrounding her. Light seemed to shine out of her pores. You won't believe me, but it's true."

"A bit different from Abbess Justina, then," he said. It was not a question.

"Chalk and cheese," she replied. "Don't misunderstand, but Abbess Justina is a . . . a *figurehead* merely. Charismatic, inspiring, and everything you could want in a leader. But Abbess Iris was—I don't know. Perhaps not of this earth. I'd have done whatever she said, because I felt she was speaking from a higher authority. Even when she insisted on changing the design of our habit. A little thing like that, and no one questioned that it needed to be done, and immediately."

"Because she said so," Max nodded, adding: "Some people have a heightened ability to tune out the world—artists and creators and inventors. And saints. It sounds as if your Abbess Iris was one of them."

"But now—here you are, investigating poison," she said. "Impossible to think of such a thing happening in her day, really. What has happened? What has gone wrong?"

"I hope to find out. What can you tell me?" He glanced back at the postulant-*duena*, but she seemed absorbed in her task. Indeed, at that moment, she let out a muffled yelp of exasperation as she stabbed herself with the needle. There might have been a mild swear word, too.

Dame Meredith shook her head against the pillow in frustration. "I don't," said Dame Meredith, "under*stand* this whole thing about the poisoning. We had a bout of food poisoning not long ago. Nothing too serious, although Dame Hephzibah was taken quite ill and at her age that sort of thing can be dangerous."

"What was the source of the poisoning?"

"We were never certain. We thought something might have crept into the mushroom soup that shouldn't have been there. Some strains of mushrooms are of course not edible—it happens all the time that someone will innocently pick something out of their garden that is better left alone. I'm sure this business with the berries was a similar mistake. Otherwise, you have to believe someone here—at Monkbury Abbey!—has come completely unhinged. It doesn't bear thinking about in such a small, tight community as this."

Max sat back, thinking about that, about the search for perfection that had brought so many of them here. The taming of the spirit and body by denial. The monastic life was built upon the famous words reported by Matthew, in which Christ told a rich man, "If thou wilt be perfect, go and sell that thou hast, and give to the poor, and thou shalt have treasure in heaven: and come and follow me." Could this striving for perfection have turned into a literally poisonous pursuit, a vile intoxication? At what point might seeking to deny every normal human impulse toward desire and self-interest, twenty-four hours a day, tip over into madness?

"Anyway," Dame Meredith was saying, "if you're here to prevent a murder—and that is why you're here, isn't it, Father?—you can be sure I'm not the target. Surely seeing one's enemy die of this horrid disease would be revenge enough to satisfy anyone—assuming someone is after revenge. It is also difficult to see how any of the sisters here could provoke anyone to murder. I would look to the guesthouse for potential victims if I were you."

The postulant Mary was definitely eavesdropping, thought Max, and had pricked up her ears on the word "murder." Naturally enough, he supposed. It was one of the most loaded words in the English language. But Max thought a change of subject was in order, so he led Dame Meredith away from the topic of likely targets.

"How did you come to be here?" he asked her. "To discover you had a vocation?"

Again, the weary look came into her eyes, and Max asked if he were tiring her.

"Not at all," she said. "This is more novelty than I've had in an age. The doctor is due any minute, though. He comes to check up on me—a complete waste of time. He's a good man, though. Devoted to Dame Pet. Anyway, you ask about my vocation. It was more that a vocation seemed unavoidable in the end. I was raised Roman Catholic, in the stream of theology that held that pretty much anything enjoyable was punishable. My parents were *so* strict. I sometimes wondered why they had children, since my brother and I seemed to be nothing but obstacles to their salvation.

"By the time I left home and school I was in search of a place where I was welcome—not a place where I was judged and found wanting, but a place that welcomed me, as a woman, as a human being. And one Sunday when I was feeling down, I went to an Anglican service where the priest said that all were welcome to partake. That got to me. There was no one excluded, and I thought to myself that Christ would have said exactly that. All are welcome to sit at his table. From there it wasn't a far distance to feeling at home here at Monkbury. I came here on a retreat, and I kept coming back."

The same as Dame Fruitcake, thought Max.

"I took to the life, to the order and to the love. The ready forgiveness of transgressions—I think Mary here can tell you how that comes in handy, every single day."

Mary looked up from her work, a white cloth dotted with red spots that surely were blood, and lifted her eyebrows in sardonic acknowledgement.

"Never mind," Dame Meredith told her. "Everything washes out." To Max, she said, "Anyway, before long I was elected cellaress. And I loved it. Every moment. I think sometimes that is why I stayed, even when the dawn awakenings were killing me. I had a job I loved, and people around me who seemed to love and need and appreciate me. We didn't have all this buying and selling to the outside world back then. The Internet! The cellaress we have now, Dame Sibil, is . . . But there, I must not carry tales nor stand in the way of progress as I do it."

"Oh, go ahead," said Max. "Just this once."

That made her laugh. "I thought you were supposed to be a good influence, Father. Anyway, I was only going to say that Dame Cellaress now plans to open up the abbey to the world, more and more, in the spirit of capitalism. That is *not* what we religious are about. It is in fact the very thing that got monasteries into trouble, when they became too worldly. Oh, I shouldn't say anything, but what is freeing about this ruddy disease is one feels one can do and say what one wants, at long last."

Was there professional jealousy behind her words? From what he had seen, the abbey was a great commercial success, putting them on a solid

financial footing, enabling rebuilding and recruitment efforts. But she was
dying of a disease that was slowly eradicating anything that marked her
out as unique and gifted, death being the great equalizer. Perhaps her op-
posing stance in this one area gave her something she could call her legacy.

There was a knock on the outer door, and Mary Benton put aside her
work to answer.

"That'll be Dr. Barnard. You'll be all right, Dame Meredith? I'll be
right back."

"And I am just leaving," said Max. In truth, he wanted a word with the
doctor just to be able to tick that box and say that he had interviewed everyone with even a passing attachment to the nunnery.

Dame Meredith nodded. As the door closed behind Mary, she told
Max: "She won't make it. She's too secular, too attached to the world, and
too quick to anger over small things. If you see your life here as nothing
but a series of sacrifices, if you think only of what you've given up to be
here, you won't make it. Those of us who chose this life don't see anything
but the joy. We're given a glimpse of heaven just often enough that thoughts
of the past are uninteresting, if not positively unappealing."

She added, surprising him, "We get many treasure seekers, you
know. A rather silly book was published about the place by a local fellow
who needs his head examined. It's brought day-trippers and a surge in
applications to stay in the guesthouse. Those who pretend to be here for
spiritual solace—hah! There is treasure in the church, but not of the kind
they mean."

Her fingers plucked at the bedclothes. It was the first sign of agita-
tion she'd shown, and Max wondered if she had a particular solace-seeker
in mind. But she had closed her eyes, as if exhausted, her chest barely
lifting with each breath.

Max said a quiet prayer over her. Then without a good-bye he slipped
out into the corridor.

He waylaid the doctor as he was about to enter Dame Meredith's room,
gesturing him toward the small infirmary kitchen.

"I'd have been here earlier," the doctor told Max, "but five miles out the weather has broken loose. I was soaked to the skin just getting into the car. I thought I'd have a quick shower in the guesthouse to warm up. One of the good sisters is bringing me some hot soup and bread to eat. God bless all their hearts, although I suppose they've already got that covered."

Dr. Barnard was in his mid-forties, running a bit too fat at the waist but otherwise fit and hardy. He had all the brisk and competent demeanor one would hope for in a physician. His dark hair was slicked back in a rather old-fashioned cut, parted in the middle. It was a style that cried out for a handlebar moustache, but Dr. Barnard was clean shaven. His brown eyes brimmed with good health and intelligence. Max was reminded of Bruce Winship, the village doctor of Nether Monkslip. Competent, questing, with a healthy or unhealthy interest in the workings of the mind of a murderer—Max was never sure which. This doctor was, for one thing, older than Bruce Winship and, for another, gave off a certain Harley Street air that Bruce for all his competence lacked. Like a prize hunter, Dr. Barnard was burnished with the polish of breeding and pedigree, and he exuded a confidence in his own abilities that must have gone down well with his wealthy patients. He carried about him an assurance that any bodily invasion of virus or tumor could be routed and excised with minimal effort if only the sufferer would hand himself over to Dr. Barnard unquestioningly. Those wealthy patients probably came to his house for little cocktail parties and belonged to the same clubs, rode to the same hounds, dined at the same grand tables, which would groan under the weight of fatted calves and forbidden fruits.

Max pulled himself out of this culinary reverie to say, "I'm afraid I've upset Dame Meredith a bit. My role was really just to listen, but once we got onto the topic of the church—something about treasure and treasure hunters ruining the place. She is longing for the good old days— you know the sort of thing."

"Oh!" Dr. Barnard laughed. "Many of the nuns feel the same. You'd have to have seen what a backwater Monkbury Abbey was, even a year ago. Dame Meredith ran the show then, you know. She was second in command, as cellaress. You wouldn't believe it now, poor thing."

"There's no hope?" asked Max. "I have seen miracles, in some cases."

"I never discount miracles," said the doctor, "for I've seen them, too. And I never discount the power of mind over matter. Not ever. In this case, however—no."

"How long does she have?"

He shrugged in a "who-knows?" gesture. "Weeks. Days."

"You've been attending her how long?"

"Forever, in a manner of speaking. I am formally attached to the nunnery, as was my father before me. I am called in for anything serious that they can't handle themselves, which almost never happens with this lot. Dame Meredith of course is being treated at a nearby hospital. They and she have agreed, though, that enough is enough."

"So she told me."

"I am just here to see that she doesn't suffer unduly. It's such a shame. She seems a thoroughly nice woman, and she doesn't seem to have anyone in the world. Well, the one nephew who visits on occasion, if you can count him."

"That would be Lord Lislelivet?"

"Yes. A self-serving little jer . . . erm. A self-serving little man if ever there was one. Whatever brings him here, it's not devotion to his aunt, I can tell you that. More likely he's one of the thrill-seeking hordes hoping after treasure.

"Now, if you'll excuse me, Father? She's expecting me."

Chapter 18

THE ABBESS GENEVIEVE

Speak ill of no one.

—*The Rule of the Order of the Handmaids of St. Lucy*

Upon leaving the infirmary, Max came across a bit of a vision—a throw-back to the days when religion reigned supreme, and many heads of religious orders lived as potentates. This could only be Abbess Genevieve Lacroix, a conclusion he reached as much from her regal bearing as from her ornate pectoral cross and the perfect drape of her voluminous habit.

"Good afternoon, Abbess Genevieve," he greeted her.

A majestic nod of the head.

"Father."

"Father Max Tudor, at your service." Without thinking, he had slipped into the courtier role that she seemed to expect, this woman from another time. Almost another planet, an impression she reinforced with her next words.

"I am come from the Mother Ship, St. Martin's. I conduct business with the Abbess Justina. We are selling her convent's goods and vice versa. They have had great success with our face cream."

"Ah," said Max. She meant of course the motherhouse, but her impish expression hinted at the joke. She was perhaps fifty, perhaps eighty—like most of the sisters, who with the exception of Dame Hephzibah appeared to be ironed free of wrinkles, he had a difficult time telling. He could have sworn Abbess Genevieve was wearing a light scent, or perhaps had used a perfumed soap. Surely that was an infraction of the Rule? Or did she have her own rules? It was an idea she seemed to confirm with her next words.

"Never underestimate the reviving and healing power of a nice fragrance," she said. "And of a little pampering with handmade products. I bring this for Dame Meredith." She held up for his inspection a small package, exquisitely wrapped in linen and lace and decorated with a sprig of lavender. "So much better than things produced in enormous factories."

"I congratulate you on your successful alliance with Monkbury."

She nodded, modestly accepting the tribute as hers alone.

Max noted that French women even managed to wear a wimple and veil with a certain style and—dare it be said?—sex appeal. It must be some manual the women over there were issued at birth. Her habit was different from that of the other nuns, so apparently the satellite abbey here in England was free to do as it wished with regard to fashion statements. It was of a dark blue, almost black, and while her manner was a model of correct austerity she managed to comport herself with a certain élan that was missing in the other nuns. She stared directly into Max's eyes, taking his measure. Apparently liking what she saw, she answered, "Thanks to God. We have a most successful partnership now. All the rancor of the past, it is forgotten."

"And may I ask how long you have been here?"

"Not long enough to be of value to you in your investigation," she said quickly. "I only arrived last week."

Certainly, word of his mission had spread—not, Max supposed, that it had been any secret.

"So you weren't here last fall, when the unpleasantness seems to have originated?"

"No. I would have put a stop to it."

"How so?"

"*Mon Dieu*. I would not have allowed that horrid man such access to the nunnery for more than a day. Yes, we are to welcome all, but the maker of trouble? *C'est un homme pas sympathique.* Some exceptions even to Christian charity must be made for the spirit who brings nothing but disturbance. Do we welcome the devil? *Non.* Such a man I fear is this nettlesome sprig of the aristocracy. But I see you do not agree with me, Father."

Max studied her, without seeming to stare, taking in that serene visage, that calm, competent expression that seemed to admit of no trouble, no turmoil. A more sane and rational-looking person would be hard to imagine. Granted, one first had to look past the medieval costume in which she had shrouded herself head to foot. Look past the choice of a lifestyle that rejected much of what was deemed pleasurable or "normal" to the outsider. She had willingly chosen celibacy, poverty, obedience to the Rule—obedience to the call of the bells that told her where to be and when. She had chosen not to have a family, apart from the "sisterhood" that surrounded her. Surely as with any other family, there were members here she would not have chosen to associate with on the outside, but here was forced to get along with day by day, unto death.

She had even chosen to forego the little pleasures most women would allow themselves: a new dress, a new hairstyle, gossip with girlfriends over a cuppa. The scented lotion or whatever she was wearing was surely the limit to the rebellion she permitted herself.

Was this normal?

What was normal? Max in his job sometimes had to distinguish true piety from mental illness, a surprisingly challenging task. One man's vision, as one of his Oxford dons had liked to say, was another man's brain tumor.

"Is there a particular reason for your visit, Abbess Genevieve? I mean, at this particular time?"

"Am I a suspect, then? How very thrilling. I can't wait to get back to France and tell my nuns."

"If you wouldn't mind answering the question?" Max asked deferentially.

He was well aware she'd be within her rights to refuse to talk to him, but she said: "*Absolutement*. It is rather a coincidence, a bit of bad timing on my part. Although I would not have missed this excitement for anything."

"Did you have a chance to meet Lord Lislelivet while you were here? Talk with him at any length, I mean?"

She answered obliquely.

"He is God's child. I remind myself of this constantly."

"You didn't like him."

"I don't suppose God really likes all his children. *Loves* them, yes. But only He knows and sees and forgives all. We humans can only struggle against our dislikes."

"How true. So I gather he is not a favorite. But again, you are here now because . . . ?"

"We talk business," she said. "Abbess to abbess. The church is in great crisis, as you know. Falling vocations. Declining revenue. If we are to keep these grand old places going, or even keep them from falling into disrepair, it will take business ingenuity. We are nearly the last generation that can save all of this." The rosary at her waist rattled as she swept out an arm to embrace the material beauty of their surroundings. The beads were of polished stone, possibly ebony.

"Is Abbess Justina in agreement with you on that?"

"In theory, yes. I think she does not like the . . . how you say . . . the vulgarity of the whole thing. The grubbing after money. To her it is a vulgarity epitomized by the American, Clement Gorey. But I say to you that it will take his sort of know-how to keep this fine old house a religious establishment. Otherwise, they may as well sign the deed over to the National Trust tomorrow.

"And that would be a catastrophe."

Chapter 19

AT THE ALTAR

A sister should never forget that she is always seen by God in heaven, and that her actions are reported by angels at every hour.

—*The Rule of the Order of the Handmaids of St. Lucy*

Max left Abbess Genevieve waiting for the doctor to finish his ministrations to Dame Meredith. Max was sure the French abbess was right about the reviving effects of her small thoughtful present, even if it was too much to hope a bit of pampering could stave off eternity.

Prompted by this thought, he was drawn to the church with its inviting stillness. It was three-thirty. The nuns would have finished the mid-afternoon prayer, None, and dispersed again to their various chores or to quiet reflection on their own. The church would likely be empty until Vespers—evening prayer—at six.

Going by way of the guesthouse and the gate feebly guarded by Dame Hephzibah, he reached the outer door to the church, the door by which visitors were permitted entry to the nave. Just inside, steps to his left led up to the bell tower, which was located at the front of the church rather than atop the cross passage further in. From the entry he again took in the grandeur of the place, the wooden vaults darkened by age soaring over his head. It was easy to imagine heaven was somewhere just beyond the interlaced beams. He spotted the occasional grotesque, too, peering down on him—the puckish, carved faces of inhuman creatures meant to warn or entertain the wandering eye of the faithful below. Max subscribed to the theory that the grotesques were often extreme caricatures of those who had offended the artist in some way. The bulbous eyes and nose, the comically exaggerated leer, the lolling tongue. Surely that was a master who had failed to pay wages on time?

Max walked down the nave, studying the occasional worn inscription underfoot. His internal compass told him the altar faced not directly east as was customary but slightly toward the north. The rocky landscape must have dictated to the early architects what was possible. There was also a chance that a seismic event had shifted the whole thing like building blocks tumbling on sand.

Like many abbey churches, this one had probably started small and been added on to as the nunnery prospered. This would have been not so much a matter of showing off but a practical matter as well, to accommodate and flatter rich patrons who wanted masses said for their souls—patrons like Clement and Oona Gorey. In the beginning the building would have been a simple rectangle; the bell tower may have come later. Special chapels would have been added north and south of the nave and presbytery for the lucrative practice of saying prayers for the dead.

Max crossed the area where the public were permitted and walked up the steps to the choir stalls where the nuns prayed throughout the day. He looked over the stalls with their elaborately carved canopies, designed for beauty as well as to protect the nuns from the cold in winter.

Just then a voice halloed softly across the aisle.

It was Dame Olive, the abbey librarian, in her role as sacrist or keeper of all that was holy or valuable in the church. She had entered from the cloistered area, her footsteps making the merest whisper of sound.

"Don't mind me. I've just brought fresh flowers for the altar." If she was put out that he was in fact in her territory she gave no sign. He stood respectfully back and watched as she adjusted the arrangement, a perfect offering of phlox and marigolds and other summer blooms. His untrained eye spotted peonies and violets and roses, from all of which a heady odor wafted around the altar area and into the choir stalls, mingling with the spicy scent of incense.

Finally satisfied that every bud was perfect, every leaf perfectly unfurled, she stepped back and made a quick obeisance toward the altar.

She turned to Max, saying, "You should see the church decorated for the holy days—for Christmas and Easter and Pentecost. Candles are everywhere, hundreds of candles. And a great fir tree stands behind the altar. We are woken from our beds by the pealing of the bells—*all* of them at once. It is the most glorious racket imaginable. And we have a wonderful meal at midday and at supper."

"With fruitcake for the pudding?" he said lightly.

She returned a sardonic smile. "It would be a shame to stop the custom now, wouldn't it?"

His gaze went to the altar with its finely fashioned altar cloth, the product no doubt of months of eye-straining labor by the nuns. "I'd like to have a look around, if you don't mind. At some of the artwork and carvings. There's no need for you to linger. I know you have things to do."

She hesitated—just a fraction, but Max noticed it. Had she been sent to keep an eye on him? Surely not. She gave him a slow, thoughtful once-over and then seemed to make up her mind.

"Of course, Father," she said. And then added, as if to cover for her prior hesitation, "You may have questions. If so, you can always come and see me. Or Dame Hephzibah—she knows a lot of the history of the acquisitions. Most were donations, of course, or came to the convent as a dowry with the postulants. Some of our work is quite priceless, you know. Oh, and feel free to go up in the belfry. The view is fantastic. One of the bells has a crack in it that is rather worrying—you'll see."

Max nodded. Still seeming to fetch about in her mind for something more to delay her leaving, she finally gave him a short bow and withdrew in the direction of the chapter house with the remaining flowers in her basket. He heard a door into the cloister open and shut behind her.

Max began his survey of the artwork—an exercise in art appreciation that was a pretext for assessing what might be the draw for the unscrupulous visitor. There were various fantastic scenes from the Book of Revelation, designed to induce nightmares. One painting, part of a triptych, depicted the Whore of Babylon. She looked faded, rather as if centuries ago someone had taken a scrub brush to her and her seven-headed beast.

He continued down the aisle. Mary Magdalene washed the feet of Christ, drying them with her red hair. The Apostles looking astonished, not terribly bright—their usual role, as Jesus tried over and again to explain his mission. There was a charming, rather rustic depiction of the Nativity, displayed in an elaborately carved and gilded frame, and it was matched by a painting of the flight into Egypt, with Mary on a donkey, holding the Christ child as Joseph and angels led the way. The artist had had difficulty with profiles, so everyone, including the donkey, looked like the artwork found inside an Egyptian tomb.

Max walked on, smiling, the images doing their job of inspiring and diverting. And of educating a populace that didn't necessarily know how to read. In a niche between two paintings was a beautifully executed statue depicting Christ healing the blind man. Across the centuries, the astonished gratitude of the man could be imagined, even in his carved stone eyes. Max remembered reading that some of the grand early monasteries in England had imported stonemasons and glassmakers from Gaul. The English had learned their lessons well.

The works of art appeared to have been collected over many centuries. Some might even have survived the Vikings, never feted as art connoisseurs. Monasticism had been restored to England only after decades of systematic pillaging. Someone probably had hidden these works for safety, before the marauders arrived.

He turned, taking in the solemn beauty of the nave. Unlike in the pews of his own St. Edwold's, here there were no colorful needlepoint kneelers of vines and crosses and flowers, provided by a long-ago altar guild. He imagined "chapel knees" were not a big concern of the nuns. Visitors were invited to kneel as the nuns did in their choir, on plain wood. The nuns used the 1662 Book of Common Prayer with its poetic and haunting language—a book written by a committee of fifty vicars and academics, each one more obscure than the last. That these men had managed to produce some of the most stirring prose in the English language was still a source of wonder. The nuns would pray the Collect for the Queen, a Queen they never would set eyes on again in their long lives, even on the telly. The whole place was positively creaky with old-world beauty, the twenty-first century having made few encroachments.

He came upon a side altar containing a statue of St. Lucy, the nuns' patroness. The legend, as Max recalled it, was that St. Lucy, a young woman from a wealthy Italian family, had begun her career as a miracle worker around the year 1200 by curing a blind man, a talent for which she would forever after be famous. It was the age of unshakeable belief in God and miracles and wonder. The order must at some point have been renamed in her honor.

Hard now to separate myth from wishful thinking from fact.

Max paused before the statue: Lucy was holding a cloth that she used to cover a man's eyes. He was a bad guy, according to legend, but he was cured anyway. Beside the altar was another carved effigy of the saint, but there was no case or casket displaying relics of her body, as would have been common in the Middle Ages. Max during his time in Italy had been brought up short more than once to realize what he had been staring at was some ghastly relict—some bit of saint's bone or tooth—still venerated by the faithful.

Dame Olive had said the convent had been a popular site of pilgrimage; at one time there probably had been lots of bones and things credited with healing powers. Churches claiming to have relicts associated with the life of Christ were of course at the top of the list of most-visited spots—on the medieval pilgrim's list of "places to see before you die."

His steps took him again to the stunning choir, divided into individual stalls for the nuns. Now he noticed that the head of each stall was carved with scenes from the life of St. Lucy, a bit like a cartoon strip.

Max looked closer at the carvings. From these charming illustrations he came to understand that St. Lucy had categorically rejected the lover chosen for her by her parents or guardians. No doubt he had been a man of pagan beliefs or perhaps he had been a man given to only sporadic per-

sonal grooming, and lacking in compensating charms. One scene showed
Lucy with both hands held out before her, in a classic silent-movie gesture of repulsion. In another illustration, a winged angel appeared in a
vision to a sleeping Lucy. And here some sort of soldier, a man at any rate
dressed for warfare, held a knife to her throat. What a life. Although the
carvings were necessarily worn with age, Max looked in vain for a depiction of the legend most closely associated with Lucy—that she had sacri-
ficed her eyesight rather than her honor. That gruesome bit may have been
a later embellishment to her life story. At least, Max hoped so.

He thought of the anchoress the abbess had told him about over dinner. Perhaps her existence was just hearsay, recorded in some dusty old
tome now guarded by Dame Olive. Or perhaps it had been the poor
woman's job to guard some ghastly token of St. Lucy's brief life, a life
she had strived to make into a perfect offering to God.

Max, now standing at the main altar, found that a train of thought
about offerings led him to Leonard Cohen, one of Dame Olive's favorites.
He'd written that we should forget about perfect offerings, for there can
be no such thing. The lyrics, sung in Cohen's raspy voice, began to sound
inside Max's head.

> *"Ring the bells that still can ring,*
> *Forget your perfect offering."*

Max turned from the altar and walked purposefully down the nave
toward the back of the church. In the porch, he opened a door leading up
the wooden stairs of the belfry. He walked up, scarcely seeing the fine old
masonry, the careful layering of stone on stone, meant to last forever. At
the top, among the four bells, he took in a commanding 360-degree view
of the countryside from each of eight windows: of the river that ran
nearby, and of cows and sheep in distant pastures, of farmland and hills
in the great distance. One of the bells had a crack in it, as Dame Olive
had said. That would need to be seen to. Surely with the sort of money
donated by the Goreys and through fund-raising activities there was no

shortage of cash, although he knew from experience that would be a costly repair.

But nothing else revealed itself, so after a few minutes, feeling a bit like Quasimodo, he lumbered back down the narrow stairs. Although the steps had been kept in good-ish repair, they were designed for smaller feet than his, forcing him into a rolling gait as he descended, alternating with a sideways tiptoe move. He was opening the door to leave the stairwell when he noticed a trapdoor, its old slabs of wood thick and splintering with age. Light showed faintly through the cracks. It had to be an entry into the old crypt. But why would there be a light in there? Even as he watched, the light changed, moving and flickering. Candlelight, or a torch.

Max stepped back, thinking, mapping what must be the layout of the old church in his mind, assuming it ran true to type.

"How the light gets in"—the words ended the Cohen stanza. He recalled it was the title of a recent popular book.

Max saw there was dust coating the top of the trapdoor and then he noticed a padlock, rusting. He knew there must be another way in; if the crypt ran under the nave, as this one seemed to do, it might even stretch as far as the choir and transept. Another entrance might be outside somewhere, although it seemed unlikely. There would, however, be an entrance near the passageway to the chapter house, possibly as a continuation of the night stairs, used by the nuns for direct access to the church.

He was faced with a choice. There was no way that old trapdoor was going to open without a protesting creak, alerting whoever it was to his presence, even if he *could* open it. Apart from the padlock, it was probably frozen shut with age.

And some instinct told him it might be best not to let on. Someone might be down there on some perfectly legitimate business, but still . . . it was the only unexplained happening during his time at the abbey, and he didn't want the chance of its meaning something to the case to slip through his fingers.

He returned to the church proper, closing the double doors behind him loudly, to announce he was leaving.

Chapter 20

DARKNESS FALLS

> It is in the dark of night that we can best hear the beating of our souls. So on leaving Compline, there is to be no speech except in extraordinary conditions or as needed to attend to the needs of guests.
>
> —*The Rule of the Order of the Handmaids of St. Lucy*

Dinner that night was a quiet affair, in keeping with the traditions of Monkbury Abbey. The visitors ate in the refectory with the community, but at their own table, off to one side.

The Gorey family was there, Xanda looking distraught and preoccupied, like someone being held hostage. She would have faded entirely into the darkness but for the candlelight that occasionally glinted off the sparkles in her hair. Paloma Green, likewise making no concession to the austerity of her surroundings, wore a bright chartreuse gown that draped over one shoulder Roman-style and was gathered at the waist by a diamante belt. Her companion Piers Montague sat across from her, also looking out of place and absurdly louche, like a man posing for the cover of a Harlequin romance. Dr. Barnard, who had been attending Dame Meredith, had long departed the premises, or so Max assumed.

And of course, clearly chafing at the imposed restriction on speech, Lord Lislelivet was there. He sat across the table from Max, who thus had full opportunity to witness the shifting in his seat and the eye rolling as one of the nuns read a chapter from the life of St. Lucy. The nuns communicated with hand signals for water or for different items of food they might require. Indeed they seemed able to read one another's minds. Only Mary Benton, the postulant, forgot herself, asking someone to please pass the bread and being silenced by horrified looks from her companions.

The food was plain, as locally sourced as the nearest garden, and delicious. Dessert was a selection of cheeses and homemade bread.

A final prayer of thanks and they were released to attend Vespers. Max opted for a walk around the grounds while it was still light and stepped off in the direction of the ridge overlooking the river. The heat of the day now rose from the grounds in a fine mist; soon the nuns' voices reached him as they warbled the notes of their age-old chant. He imagined he could single out Dame Fruitcake's voice, soaring above the rest. It was a beautiful sound, of mystery and of longing and of giving thanks to a Creator whose existence was never in doubt. He let the beauty of their disembodied voices wash over him and fill him with peace.

Then silence fell. A flash of light, perhaps from the dying rays of the sun, came flickering from the windows of the nun's dormitory. The church service had ended and the nuns had returned to their cloister.

By the time Max returned to the guesthouse, the nearly full moon had nestled like an opal into a deep indigo sky. The summer solstice approached, a holy day in Awena's book. He could imagine the cooking and preparation in anticipation, for Awena's gift was her awareness that everything was sacred, every great and small moment of the days and passing of the seasons worth marking and observing.

No less than the Handmaids of St. Lucy, he supposed, did Awena hallow the sanctity of days.

Some time later, the bells for Compline rang out over Monkbury Abbey, and the place fell into even deeper stillness than before, like an enchanted castle in a fairy tale. It was soon the time of the Great Silence, and Max,

reading in bed, had drifted toward a dreaming sleep. He dreamt he saw
the nuns walking down the church nave in a candlelight procession, their
faces shrouded by their cowls, each of them carrying a small jeweled casket. The sleeping Max, sitting in a pew in the middle of the church,
counted them as they passed. *Counting sheep*, thought his dream self.
Twenty-nine, thirty, thirty-one.

Thirty-two.

Wait. There should only be thirty-one.

The last figure to pass turned back to him and smiled. Max saw
through a shock of icy fear it was not the gentle face of any of the Monkbury nuns he had come to know, but the hideously decayed face that
haunted his nightmares. The face of the man who had killed his friend,
his MI5 colleague Paul, although this face was unrecognizable as anything human. It was, the dreaming Max realized, a stone gargoyle come
to life, blood dripping from its mouth. And now in the way of dreams he
noticed that the face beneath the cowl wore the ridiculous sunglasses with
their white frames and blue lenses, the sunglasses Max had seen the killer
wear the day Paul died.

Lights from an automobile flashed briefly into Max's room, startling
him awake. At first he thought it was part of his dream, or a flash of light-
ning, for in the distance he could now hear the thunder of a summer storm.

It was a late arrival. Very late by monastery standards. Dame Hephzibah would be inconvenienced. The light interrupted Max's sleep but
momentarily, for he had walked a long time that day in the rarified air of
the abbey grounds, and was tired. He started to drift back to sleep, but
the anxious, edgy feeling prompted by the nightmare clung to him. It was
as if he had walked into a cobweb. Max rubbed at his face.

And then a heart-rending scream jolted him fully awake. The book
Max had fallen asleep reading flew from his hands and landed with a
great thud on the floor.

And at that moment the monastery's generator gave out, and the
small light in Max's room was extinguished.

That doesn't sound like any Great Silence to me, thought Max, jumping from the bed. Looking for his clothing by the moonlight streaming into his room, he finally found his jacket and threw it on over his pajama bottoms. He pulled his phone from the jacket pocket and located the torch app. The thing might be useless out here as a phone, but the app helped him navigate the room and find the larger electric torch.

Max set off in the direction of the cloister, for his senses told him the sound had come from that open area. The light now was better; votive lights had been set on small stone projections jutting at precise intervals along the hallway, probably in anticipation of the routine unreliability of the generator. The effect was rather like a landing strip. It was the sort of setting designed for ripples of ghoulish, maniacal laughter echoing down the corridor rather than for the drifting notes of religious chant.

He started toward the kitchen where there was a door into the cloister, then remembered that there was no entry to the cloister directly from the guesthouse, particularly at this time of night. He went to the gatehouse, where Dame Hephzibah was stirring, bewildered, clearly startled awake and wondering whether it was safe to leave her post.

"You heard it, too?" he asked. "Could you tell where the cry came from?"

Shaking her head, Dame Hephzibah pressed both her hands against her mouth in a monkey-speak-no-evil gesture. She pulled a pen and paper from her pocket and wrote down her dilemma. Max read the page she turned to him. Her crabbed handwriting was nearly illegible, but after a bit of thought he managed to translate what looked like, "I need persimmons to spark with you during the Solstice" to its more likely cousin: "I need permission to speak with you during the Silence."

Max nodded in understanding. Had ever, he thought, an investigation been more hampered from the outset than this one, by witnesses who were not even *allowed* to speak except at certain times?

But right now, the immediate problem was that otherworldly scream.

"Dame Hephzibah," he said. "I will square it with the abbess. It's all right for you to talk with me. Just this once. A human life may be at stake."

She nodded, eyes wide and dark with confusion. She was trained to obey, and clearly an ordained Anglican priest trumped an abbess in the pecking order of her small, enclosed little world.

"It came from the cloister," she said. "Near the center—the well, I think." Struggling with a mass of old iron keys, she unlocked the door leading into the cloistered part of the nunnery.

"You go," she said. "I'll fetch the doctor."

Max turned at that.

"Doctor?"

"He drove up just now—you must have seen his car. He asked for a room for the night so he could see Dame Meredith first thing tomorrow. "She's taken a bad turn. He's worried about her."

The moonlight helped, as did the torch. The darkness was otherwise near total. Just avoiding tripping at an unexpected dip in the terrain, he reminded himself that the cloister was not a flat, smooth plot of land, but that it fell in cascading ridges, following the natural lines of its setting. The silence remained absolute. It was a time for goblins and witches and for the ghosts of nuns long dead to be prowling the area, saying their beads. He shooed away the superstitious thought—really, it was impossible in this setting not to have such ideas. He hurried toward the well.

And aiming the torch down into its center, he saw what should not have been there. The soles of the highly polished, Italian leather shoes of Lord Lislelivet, far below. Still wearing the shoes was the lord, his eyes open and reflecting the light, like an animal's captured by headlamps. But from the expression, an expression of outrage and surprise, it was clear he was dead.

Max shone the torch around the area, training his dark gray eyes on the ground. The grass outside the wellhead was undisturbed except for what might have been drag marks of the sort left by the heels of highly polished, Italian leather shoes.

Uttering a mild curse, he went to rouse the nunnery, and to call for needed help to travel the long uphill road to Monkbury Abbey.

．　　　．　　　．

"There was plenty of money to fix that generator," Clement Gorey was saying. "That's why I want to know where the money really went."

Max had rounded up all the inmates of the guesthouse, commanding them to gather in the guesthouse kitchen, for there had been a murder, that was almost certain, and Max wanted a clear head count. From the kitchen he could keep watch over the well in the cloister and see that it remained undisturbed. He had instructed the abbess, roused from her sleep, to similarly command her charges: Nothing must be touched.

The guests were all accounted for: the three Goreys, Paloma Green and Piers Montague. The one new addition was the doctor, Barnard, who had arrived only moments before Max heard the hellish scream—probably the last sound Lord Lislelivet made on earth.

"I think we might want to focus a bit on the murder that took place around the time the generator went out," said Max.

Clement Gorey looked abashed, but only for a second. He rebounded quickly.

"Don't you see? There may be a connection? Where—I say *where*—did the money go? Lord Lislelivet had the same questions about the finances around here that I did."

The same thought had of course occurred to Max, but he merely said, "It is too soon to speculate, Mr. Gorey."

"If not now, when?" he demanded.

Max wondered if the man realized he was quoting Rabbi Hillel. Somehow he doubted it.

"Now, actually. Just not *us*. Meaning, rampant speculation won't get us very far. I've got a call in to the police. They will do whatever speculating is required. We don't want to be in their way."

In fact, Max fully intended to speculate and get in the way wherever he felt it might be necessary, but he did not relish the prospect of having Clement Gorey play Watson to his own investigation.

"I will most certainly be having a word with whatever detective guy they send out here—you can be sure of that."

"I would imagine we all will."

And what a mess that will be. The silence and peace of the cloister ruined by the *clomp clomp clomping* of DCI Cotton and his team. Something had to be done to get the entire matter cleared up as soon as possible, or Monkbury Abbey might not survive.

And he wondered if that possibility had occurred to the murderer.

If in fact that had been the aim all along.

PART VI

Vespers

Chapter 21

NIGHTHAWKS

Each sister shall take a turn keeping the night watch, and in awakening her sisters in time for Dawn Prayer. Only the abbess and the cellaress are exempt from this duty. It is better that the night watch be kept in pairs.

—*The Rule of the Order of the Handmaids of St. Lucy*

An hour had passed. They were essentially just waiting for the arrival of the police and all the specialists in the art of murder most foul. Any chance Lord Lislelivet had simply fallen into the well on some random nighttime stroll about the monastery grounds was out of the question, at least as far as Max was concerned. For one thing, it had to be explained how he had gotten into the middle of the cloister at night—the very heart of the nunnery, really, from which sprang the cloistered parts of the abbey, including the nun's private cells. Someone had to have admitted him to the area.

Xanda had volunteered to make coffee to keep them awake while they waited, and the room had immediately split into British versus U.S.A. factions. The British all wanted their cuppa, and Paloma rose competently to the challenge of putting a kettle on the boil for a proper British brew, while Xanda found filters and drip coffee. The debate over the pros and cons of the caffeinated beverages seemed to divert them from thoughts of murder, if only momentarily. Finally, once they all had their drinks and a plate of chocolate biscuits had been passed around, Max, who had been watching all of them closely, said, "What do any of you know about the system of bell ringing that goes on all day here? Is there one person in charge?"

"What? Is there a point to this question?" demanded Clement Gorey.

"Daddy . . ." said his daughter, warningly.

"I won't know until someone answers me," said Max amicably. "I suppose that to be put in charge of waking everyone for the early morning services you have to be very low on the totem pole. It strikes me as the sort of job for the postulant—the job nobody wants. But it may not be important."

"I think they all take turns," said Oona Gorey. "Sort of spreading the misery around."

"Ah. I'm sure you're right," said Max. Turning to Dr. Barnard, he said, "I was surprised to see you here. I thought you had left yesterday after seeing Dame Meredith."

"I did leave," the doctor replied, stirring sugar into his coffee. "But I was worried about her as I drove away and I realized, frankly, that something was wrong. She seemed agitated, despite the rather heavy dose of drugs I've been prescribing, trying to make her comfortable. So I thought I should return, to be here in the morning and make sure she was all right. Besides, there looked to be a storm brewing, and the roads can be hazardous in the best weather.

"Anyway, maybe it was just time to change her prescription, but I wanted to talk with her again before I went to keep my appointments in Temple Monkslip for the day. I often do that—stay in the guesthouse. They keep a spare room for the last-minute traveler, even when the guesthouse is otherwise full up. Always that one room is kept back. In case the solitary traveler is Christ himself, you know—instant transport to heaven if it does turn out to be Christ, I suppose. Proper honor must be shown to all—particularly to anyone who looks down and out and basically unwashed and hungry. I don't usually fit that description, but it's one of their nicer philosophies, don't you think?"

"I see," said Max. "It was just as you were pulling in that I heard the scream—the cry for help, cry of alarm or panic or pain, whatever it was. Did you hear it?"

The doctor shook his head. "It wouldn't have carried to where I was, just getting my bag out of the car in the parking lot."

"I heard it," declared Xanda. "All the way in my room."

"Was your impression that it was a man or woman crying out?"

"Well, a man, I suppose. It had to have been Lord Lislelivet, didn't it?"

Max turned again to the doctor. "You had a bag with you?"

"Always," he said "I keep a spare bag packed. The byroads in this part of the world are unreliable—last summer half of them washed away. I never know what to expect when I'm out on a call. So I'm always as prepared as I can be."

Max turned to the others. "Did any of you hear anything?"

They all solemnly shook their heads.

"See anything?"

"I did see Dr. Barnard arrive." This from Clement Gorey, and said in a way that implied a major concession. "He came out of the gatehouse, walking toward the guesthouse."

"This was just before all the hubbub?" asked Max.

"It was during."

"I saw him, too," volunteered Piers Montague. Incredibly, Piers was wearing a smoking jacket of the sort made popular by Nick and Nora Charles movies. He needed pomade and a cigarette holder to complete the look. Clement Gorey wore an enormous gray T-shirt bearing a Harvard logo. His wife had stayed true to her all-black wardrobe, and had a black chenille number knotted tightly at the waist. Paloma Green wore something suitable for a performance of Madame Butterfly; Xanda wore gray sweatpants topped with a "Pierce the Veil" T-shirt. Max gathered that was some sort of rock band. Nice. The excitement seemed to be making the spiky hair on her head stand even straighter; yesterday's makeup pooled darkly beneath her eyes. She took a slurp of her coffee under the disapproving eye of her mother.

"Sorry," said Xanda. "Can we go back to bed now?'

"Not just yet," said Max. "The police will be here any min—"

A crunch of gravel outside announced that several police cars, whirl-igig lights no doubt ablaze, were in the parking lot. The sanctuary and peace of Monkbury Abbey had been breached.

The only question was how long before the nuns could return to the relative serenity of the eleventh century. The answer: perhaps never.

Max had earlier phoned DCI Cotton, using the satellite phone in the cel-laress's office. All this activity had involved raising the alarm all over the nunnery, of course. But many seemed to have been awoken by Lord Lisle-livet's dying cry. The habit of sleeping lightly must have become ingrained in most of them.

Max briefly explained the situation to the constable on the desk in Monkslip-super-Mare, and then waited for Cotton's return call. It was not long in coming.

Cotton explained that his men would set up headquarters in Temple Monkslip for the duration but that he, Cotton, would join Max right away.

"But be my ears on the ground until I get there, Max. We're already looking into histories and backgrounds, although some things will have to wait for daylight hours. The abbey doesn't lend itself to this sort of of-ficial raid, nor does it have anything like the connectivity we need to run a full-scale investigation. Besides, I think we'll learn a lot more with the softly, softly approach. I want you to stay on in your quasi-official capacity."

"All right," said Max. He was chafing to get home, but in all good conscience, what else could he do but see it through now? Lord Lislelivet had been killed on his watch.

Cotton sighed. "I suppose I didn't take the poisoning thing seriously enough. It seemed so ludicrous somehow."

"Don't blame yourself," said Max, who was busy blaming himself. "Lord Lislelivet has a reputation for creating a tempest in a teapot. And if

he'd had any sense at all, he'd have stayed a mile away from the place."
Max paused. "I wonder very much why he ran the risk."

"I did advise him that staying away was the best course."

"I suppose I should have tried to talk some sense into the man. But in
fact I barely spoke with him. I thought there would be time . . ."

"Every jam and jelly and berry in the place will all be analyzed now,"
Cotton told him. "Along with all the fruitcake that predates the lord's
visit last fall."

"That wasn't done before?" Max asked.

"Would you really expect us to have the manpower for that?" Cotton
asked. "It wasn't murder before."

"Of course you're right. I'm not sure even now you'll find it feasible.
There are berries and things strewn about all over the place, including in
the guesthouse kitchen." Max paused, considering. "All of that inventory
will have to be destroyed."

"I know. Even though that's not how he was murdered, that is where
the whole thing started."

"It would be quite an effective way to wreck the place financially,
wouldn't you say?" Max asked.

"Yes, I'll be looking at that as a motive. It seems insane—that a group
of nuns could arouse such animosity."

"Not the nuns themselves, perhaps, but what they represent. Religious fanaticism comes disguised in all sorts of ways. And unfortunately
their very innocence makes them a tempting target for a certain type of
person who sees such purity and wants to destroy it."

"The lord's wife has been informed and is raising hell—Lady Lislelivet. From her point of view, it must not be death from natural causes, to
benefit her to the utmost."

"You mean, for insurance purposes."

"Right," said Cotton. "She's not saying, but that's my guess. It needs
to be accidental death. Murder would also pay out, but if she looks like a
suspect, and the spouse always does, then she really wants this thing investigated and solved pronto."

"It is a point in her favor, anyway, said Max. "That she is calling for investigation."

"That is precisely what I would do in her shoes—if I were guilty. I would get on my high horse and pretend to rally the forces of law and order. And alert the media."

"What a stirringly cinematic image," said Max. "Well, I do see what you mean. Although unless she has an accomplice on the inside here, I don't see Lady Lislelivet as having a direct hand in this. For one thing, you'd have to have all the mountain-climbing ability of a billy goat. I'm assuming we're talking about the possibility of a break-in from outside."

Cotton shook his head. "Unlikely. Given good weather, maybe. Given the storm of last night, no. You'd be risking your neck, that is certain. Those rocks would be slippery, and you'd be looking at a nearly vertical climb in some spots."

"I need you here soon," said Max. "I'll try to contain the little crowd of visitors, but I've no authority."

"I'd say you operate under the highest authority, Max. But I do see what you mean. We'll be there ASAP."

Chapter 22

DCI COTTON

If a serious sin be hidden in the conscience of one of the sisters, she shall reveal it only to the abbess or to one of the spiritual elders of the nunnery.

—*The Rule of the Order of the Handmaids of St. Lucy*

"I thought you were supposed to be keeping an eye on things," said DCI Cotton, as if picking up where their phone conversation had left off.

"I know. I know," said Max. "I feel bad enough already, but thanks for bringing it up."

They had agreed to meet in Max's Spartan guest room once Cotton had surveyed the situation and set his team in motion. It promised a modicum of privacy; the other male guests of the nunnery were several doors away and engaged in dressing for the day. Daylight had begun to penetrate the room but hesitantly, as if not sure of its welcome on such a dolorous occasion.

Cotton had pulled up to the nunnery in a squad car, looking immaculate as if he had been ready and waiting for the middle-of-the-night call that brought him here. Not for the first time, Max was driven to speculate on Cotton's private life. He did not particularly seem to have one. Given the finicky perfection of his wardrobe, Max thought he might spend a lot of time laying out his clothes, even starching his shirts and ironing them. It was an absurd speculation. The man was far too busy for such self-indulgent homesteading behavior. Wasn't he?

Right now he was worrying a thread on his jacket that threatened to come loose. Cotton had a precise and orderly mind if one not as intuitive as his friend Max's. While Cotton did not tip over into Mr. Monk–like habits, still he took an inordinate amount of pleasure in, for example, going through his spice rack and discarding tins that had passed their expiration date. Generally he would do this as he thought through a crime scene in his mind. A policeman's life did not allow much time for home cooking, regrettably, for Cotton was a good cook who could be an excellent one, given time to practice.

"Just to get the parish notices out of the way," said Cotton, "why don't you fill me in on your impressions since you got here?"

"I'm not sure any clear impressions have formed," said Max. "Only questions. And the biggest question I have—other, of course, than why Lord Lislelivet was murdered—is why he was here to begin with."

"You mean since, according to him at least, his last visit nearly killed him."

"Precisely. What would make him dare attempt a return engagement? It must have been something important. Unless you buy his story of a sudden and overwhelming interest in religion, which I don't."

"Neither does his wife. I had a brief word with her. She's following this investigation with bated breath, in between appointments with her manicurist."

Cotton summarized the essence of Lady Lislelivet's statements and beliefs.

"It doesn't sound like she liked her husband very much," said Max. "So I wonder why she's pushing now for an investigation into his death—apart from the reasons we discussed."

"I had it verified," said Cotton. "His life insurance policy has a double indemnity clause. I am not sure she wanted it to be murder—although I gained the definite impression she wouldn't mind—but she did want it to be an accident. Death from natural clauses is worth half as much. So she's already started calling round her husband's fellow nobs to put pressure to bear on the right people. Said she just couldn't sleep until she knew the truth, etcetera, etcetera. Cry me a river. I don't think anyone believed her, but finally to get rid of her they agreed to put pressure on the right places in their turn.

"She is *completely* hung up on the value of his insurance policy, and not troubling overmuch to hide the fact. So, yes, let me go out on a limb and say there is no love lost there. For now, if you could just give me a rundown on the main characters here. Not excluding the nuns, I'm sorry to say. We can't pretend they are too above the fray to contemplate murder."

"No, I don't suppose we can," said Max. He proceeded to summarize what he knew or suspected about the guests of the abbey and then gave Cotton a short rundown on the sisters to whom he had spoken. Beginning with Abbess Justina Berry, the superior of Monkbury Abbey, with her Renoir-pink appearance and her natural leader's gaze on the far horizon. He then talked about Dame Hephzibah Laffer, the elderly portress of the abbey—surely, Max added, far too feeble to engage in such a crime.

"Early days, yet," said Cotton. "Let's discount no one for the moment."

Max went on to describe Dame Tabitha Hoppringle—the guest-mistress, nicknamed Dame Tabby, with her mysterious catlike visage and imposing build. Cotton perked up at this.

"Just what we need for this case. Someone able to heft that body in the well. He was a small man in every way, but still. . . . There's little question he was dead when he went in. They're confirming that. Rather helpful that his watch was broken, pinpointing the time as just after nine."

"I think you'll agree that sort of helpfulness is most suspicious."

Max was thinking: for thousands of years the site of the well had been revered as a healing center by pagans and Christians alike. There was something blasphemous in stuffing Lord Lislelivet down that same well to which the sick had come to pray for a miracle cure, carried on litters by desperate families; where the blind had been led to wash their eyes, where women had come to pray for safe delivery in childbirth. Did the murderer know the sacred history of the place? Or was it just a convenient dumping spot, a failed, hasty attempt to hide the body?

Max told Cotton about Dame Ingrid Castle, known as Dame Fruit-cake, she of the red face, hazel eyes, and red hair, her round features scattered with freckles. He spoke of Dame Olive Chandler, the petite sacrist and librarian with her vast knowledge of the abbey. He spoke of Dame Petronilla "Pet" Falcon—the infirmaress, responsible for the care of the sick and dying at Monkbury Abbey, with her expert knowledge of plants and herbs.

"We'll be looking closely at that," said Cotton.

There was Dame Sibil Papelwyk to tell about, the cellaress of the abbey, with her innate ability to keep untangled the many threads of the abbey's money-making schemes.

"But I've not yet had a chance to talk with her," Max told him. "I had planned to see her today. I guess it's a bit late now."

"It's never too late," said Cotton. "We have to solve this before all hell breaks loose, close the door on speculation."

Max next spoke of the dying Dame Meredith Fitzwilliam—formerly the cellaress, now a patient in the abbey's infirmary. Of Sister Rose Tocketts, with her ex-military background, now a novice preparing for admission to the order. Of Mary Benton—a postulant preparing for the novitiate.

"No one seems to have high hopes that she will make it," Max added.

"Dame Meredith?"

"No. I meant the postulant. She is having trouble getting the hang of how things are done here."

Finally Max told Cotton about Abbess Genevieve Lacroix—a visitor from St. Martin's, the motherhouse in France.

"Those are the main players on the cloistered side. There are others, of course. Enough to keep your team busy for a long time."

"On it," said Cotton. "I've had a word with the abbess already. She has promised full cooperation."

"Hmm." Max viewed that promise with skepticism. For one thing, during his time with the abbess, he had been reminded of nothing so much as Lady Baynard of Chedrow Castle, that aristocratic lady so proud of her lineage. The abbess, Max suspected, would cooperate insofar as it kept scandal away from her nunnery. She would pretend at cooperation so well no one would notice the wool being pulled over their eyes.

Furthermore, the nuns might all hang together in an us-versus-them mentality. In fact, everything in their training and mind-set would be to deny the desires of the individual in favor of meeting the needs of the group. Of protecting that group. He had become familiar with this sort of thinking in his work with Chinese spies run by the Ministry of State Security. While the motives of spies for other countries were usually money or ego, in the case of spies for the Chinese, as a general rule, pure loyalty or idealism came into play. No one had to pay them or massage their egos. They did it, for lack of a better word, for love.

Cotton, for his part, was remembering his initial meeting with the abbess. He had held out his warrant card in its case, and she had taken it from him, almost as if she meant to keep it. She'd pulled a glasses case from within the folds of her skirt and carefully threaded reading glasses onto her ears, jabbing beneath that thing they wore wrapped around their heads. She had studied his photo with all the care of an Eastern bloc border guard confronted with a suspected drug smuggler—eyes moving from his photo to his face and back again—before handing the card back to him with a disarming smile.

"I guess we first have to tease out what Lord Lislelivet was really up to," said Cotton. "I know he came here with concerns about money—"

"That was more the concern of the Goreys and the rest. But yes, I'd say all the 'civilians,' shall we call them, were showing a keener-than-average interest in the wealth of the place."

"I thought nunneries were supposed to be poor," said Cotton.

"In fact they are, if you confine yourself to looking at their personal, individual worth. The nuns aren't allowed to own anything much beyond what they wear on their backs."

"Those odd purple frocks," said Cotton.

"Habits," Max corrected him. "Quite. But the order itself is quite wealthy."

"So collectively they are rich."

Max shook his head. "No. Not at all. Think of it as a large corporation, one without an employee-owned philosophy. Or a commune would
perhaps be a better example. All work equally, all share equally. Everything is provided them out of the common bank. But they own nothing of
their own. Monkbury Abbey owns it."

"No wonder the abbey became so wealthy."

"Once the religious orders began to settle down in one place, they
became wealthy. If they had stuck to begging and the mendicant way of
life, I suppose history would have been rewritten."

"I don't follow."

"The early Franciscans were hunter-gatherers. The Benedictines were
settlers. Once they acquired land, there was no stopping them."

Cotton suddenly turned his head toward the window. "What *is* that
sound?"

"It's the sheep," replied Max. "They want their mothers. Or maybe
it's the mothers wanting their lambs."

"Oh." Cotton looked rather crestfallen to hear it.

"Sometimes," said Max, newly up in his sheep husbandry, "it's just
that the mothers have been taken away to be shorn. They'll all be reunited
later."

"Oh! That's good."

Max decided against telling Cotton the bit about how sometimes the
mothers just didn't care about these reunions. Given his untidy upbring-
ing, that might come a bit too close to home for Cotton. Max, wondering
if he could work the reunited sheep theme into a sermon, watched as Cotton took his mobile phone from his pocket, studying the display for signs
of a signal. He actually gave the gadget a little shake, as if stirring the
ingredients inside would help.

"Unbelievable," Cotton said at last. "What century are we in? Anyway, there is one thing to be grateful for. If these women own nothing of
their own to speak of, it makes searching their rooms a breeze."

"Their cells, yes. This," and Max swept one arm round the spare little
room, "this is a palace by comparison."

Cotton, a minimalist to his fingertips, could only admire and approve this philosophy. But the thought of being unable to update his wardrobe at will with a new shirt or tie was chilling.

"By the way," said Max, "I'm sure it will not be news to you that this whole thing will be a massive violation of their privacy. How you're going to get around the sort of objections you are bound to face I'm not sure. It might be as well to bring the bishop's office in on this."

"Abbess Justina used those very words. 'Violation of privacy.'"

"It seems a shame, but there's not a lot of choice."

"I've just had what might be considered rather a Lucifer moment," said Cotton, "but I don't really see why God would ask anyone to give up so much and do without so much. I mean, what sort of God would ask that level of sacrifice?"

"Most people feel that way. But every tax time I am reminded that I really need to simplify my own life."

"In the dead of winter," observed Cotton, "I'd be spending a lot of time looking for a thermostat—that I can tell you. And in this heat I'd bet the habits are deuced hot to wear. I won't bother to ask if they have air-conditioning."

"No," said Max. "Perhaps in the infirmary. Heaters and air conditioners are just one more thing to maintain and repair."

"'Here be dragons,'" quoted Cotton. "This whole setup is so medieval, I expect to encounter some mythical creature at every turn in one of the corridors. And it's so *dark*."

"I think that is intended less for atmosphere than for conserving energy."

"Of course. They're probably living off the power grid."

"There's that, and also it is just part of their philosophy. Not wasting anything."

Cotton, who had taken a notebook from his ever-present briefcase, scribbled a new heading with his biro and said, "I gather that the drill is: drawbridges up after . . ." He began shuffling through his previous notes, presumably from his conversation with the abbess.

"After Compline would be usual," said Max.

"That's right. That's what she told me—the very, *very* old nun who seems to serve as the meet-and-greet person."

"Dame Hephzibah."

"The portress. Right. It's a wonder they haven't been robbed blind over the years. The poor thing can hardly see nor hear, can she? If they were worried about security, they might have chosen someone a little less, well, ancient."

Max smiled at him. "Somehow, I think that, all things being equal, Dame Hephzibah doesn't miss a whole lot of real importance."

"Right," Cotton said again. "She claims she saw a yellow monk last night."

"Where?"

"What does it matter where? She was hallucinating. Imagining things." Off his look, Cotton elaborated: "She claims she saw a yellow monk walking about the cloister garden."

"That's interesting," said Max.

"*And* a white nun. Max, she probably sees angels, too."

"That wouldn't surprise me, either. Anyway, the portress is supposed to be someone of mature years. Someone who doesn't roam about the place when he or she gets restless or bored, the way a younger person might."

"Well, she certainly fits the bill. She looks like she's been planted here since the first Crusade."

"I don't think they were worried about security. At least, not until recently."

"From her vantage point at the gate house, could she see much of the cloister?"

"She could," said Max. "But in truth, the question would be, was she awake to see anything? I myself was asleep and didn't wake until the doctor's headlights woke me. Maybe it was the same with her."

"Just so I'm clear on this," said Cotton. "After the service they call Compline, the Great Silence descended on the place."

"Like a shroud," said Max. "The silence is total."

"And the nuns were locked in for the night."

"That's one way of putting it. I'd say the world was locked out. The door wouldn't open until morning, except for a late-arriving guest in need of refuge, like the doctor."

"So just when everyone was snug in their beds, there was a cry? A shout?"

"Hard to describe," said Max. "I was just coming round from sleep, myself, but it was sort of a shriek."

"Male or female?"

"Ah," said Max. "That's an astute question. There was nothing to say it was Lord Lislelivet crying out."

"The autopsy should tell us more about his condition when he went into the well."

"Lifting dead weight would be a problem," said Max. "For some of the nuns, anyway. But this way of life has kept most of them hale and hearty. Even Dame Meredith could just about tackle a small man like Lord Lislelivet if she surprised him."

"And I suppose being attacked by a nun would come as a surprise to most men."

"Indeed it would."

Chapter 23

SUSPICION...

Evil speech and idle gossip must be curbed lest they become an occasion of mortal sin.

—*The Rule of the Order of the Handmaids of St. Lucy*

As the policeman and the priest surveyed their investigative options and plotted their strategy, Abbess Justina was indulging in a rare second cup of morning coffee, sitting alone at her large refectory table. This was a day if ever there were one for the synapses in her brain to be given all the help they needed.

She'd sent the postulant, Mary, away on a made-up assignment. The beauty of being in her position, Abbess Justina reflected, was that she could act as drill sergeant if she chose, making up pointless tasks and putting it all under the umbrella of discipline. Heady stuff, that. And it was a jolly good thing she was not, Abbess Justina reflected, the type to let power go to her head. Humility was more necessary for someone in her position.

She stood, shaking out her voluminous skirt, where a crumb or two from her breakfast scone had landed in the folds. Rotterdam, ignoring the crumbs as beneath him, wandered off to curl up in his bed in a corner of the room.

Dame Justina wanted very much to go outdoors and walk about to clear her head, but she was worried she'd run into DCI Cotton or, worse,

Father Max Tudor. Why was it that Father Max always seemed to know more about what she was thinking than even *she* knew?

It was nonsense, she told herself. Just a feeling. The man couldn't read minds, after all. No one could. No one but God could do that. But Father Max had been sent here on a mission to flush out the truth, and it had to be said, Abbess Justina had done a few things for which she had no ready answer, if pressed. Explained to people the right way, they would understand, she was sure of it. A new guesthouse was not the most important thing in the world.

Arching her back—the long hours of prayer made her feel her age—she stared up at the abbey's coat of arms over the fireplace. Monkbury Abbey had been founded so very long ago. The responsibility of keeping it going weighed heavily. She didn't want to be the abbess in charge when it all came unstuck.

The abbey, then and now, was blessed in attracting more than its share of rich and grateful benefactors, men and women who wanted the nuns to pray for their departed souls and were willing to pay up front for the privilege of really first-rate heavenly intercession. The nuns had buried many of these pious nobs—their bodies now were interred beneath the floors of the chapels, or they were given a showy tomb with a marble likeness on top, often with feet resting against a little dog like Rotterdam. The fame of those interred at Monkbury was one reason why, when Henry VIII began his destructive, toddler-like rampage against the monasteries and nunneries, the abbey was largely spared.

Monkbury had been left to be overgrown by thorns and weeds and to have its cellars cracked open by the invading roots of nearby trees.

She had often thought it strange and wonderful that when stones had been hauled away to Temple Monkslip to be reused for building, quite often the people in those buildings came to grief. Their businesses and crops failed, or the very buildings themselves collapsed. Word got round that the nuns had placed a curse on anyone disturbing their stones. And of course people of a superstitious age believed it. The place was left to go to rack and ruin on its own.

Until one day the nuns returned and rebuilt their abbey. Not the same nuns, of course, but alike in spirit. They adopted the old customs and adjusted the old rules, reattached their veils to their headdresses, and slipped back into the timeless rhythms of chanting, working, and keeping sacred the holy monastic hours.

Abbess Justina had been at Monkbury for most of her adult life—for longer than she'd been a civilian. After reading history at Cambridge she'd spent a decade in the City, moving by day between a starkly modern office building to a large but Dickensian flat and seeing a married man in his—never her—spare time. She would dress up for him, dress to please him, in clothing and jewelry that did not suit her, that had nothing to do with who she was. And sometimes she would wait, all dressed up and made up, hoping he would call. Shaming it was now, to think of it. She still had no idea why she had done it. It was like another woman had once inhabited her body and mind.

In truth, the habit she wore now was the only clothing that had ever suited her.

His wife had been blameless, a homemaker raising two children, oblivious, and probably when all was said and done worth ten dozen of her faithless husband. She, now Abbess Justina of Monkbury Abbey, had been the home wrecker.

She would not shrink from the fact she had reveled in the role of mistress, had savored the power she perceived it gave her. It was pathetic to remember how important it had been to her, to be desirable, to have that allure—to entice him away from his wife. What Freud would have made of it did not really matter. It was silly, despicable, self-serving behavior. It had taken her ages to realize that any fool could have done the same, that anyone could catch his eye. He was an untrustworthy man and anyone could have filled the role she had played.

She had realized for some time that Lord Lislelivet reminded her of him. Not in looks, God knew, but in that bland shiftiness of character. That sense of entitlement.

The same man, in disguise.

Her lover, like predators everywhere, knew in what low esteem she held herself. All without knowing anything about her lonely childhood and her distant parents, who noticed her only long enough to criticize whatever she did or wore or attempted. He had sensed it immediately. He had played on it. But tempting as it was to blame him, she had been a willing participant in this folly, so hurtful to his wife, so hurtful to her own self.

Both her old occupations, she realized now, were escapes, daylight busyness and nighttime drama, and when both came crashing down at once—the collapse of both the corporation and her personal life—she had taken her buyout and headed to the south of France. Intending to do what, she didn't know. Perhaps it just sounded good. Those postcards sent from Provence, she supposed, were just a continuation of her career, of the upbeat forecasts sent to investors: Everything (on the surface) is wonderful; my life (on the surface) is wonderful. *Perfect*. Was she fooling anyone? Probably not. And finally, she realized how far in contempt she held anyone who fell for her act. So one day in that sublimely rich land of Renaissance vistas, wine, and ancient ruins, she had climbed off the hamster wheel and set herself on a course of atonement to the many faceless people she had wronged. The only atonement she could make to the wronged wife, who had never found out the truth, was to stay far away, forever.

Was her dramatic life change an overreaction? She never thought so. Slipping into her role here had been easy, natural, like coming home. And now it was all threatened somehow. That silly man. If only that silly man hadn't come here everything would have been fine.

Oona Gorey was packing to leave. Well, she was packing in case they ever got the chance to leave. Surely they couldn't be held here at the abbey forever. The police could suspect whatever they liked, and she could tell that DCI Cotton suspected plenty. Just like one of those policemen on the BBC-America television shows she and Clement loved to watch.

But unlike on those shows, they couldn't prove a thing—not in one hour of drama, not in a whole season's worth of drama. With or without a break for commercials, they couldn't prove a thing.

She smoothed out one of the black travel garments she had washed in the sink and hung to dry last night, folding it in precise thirds. It amused her to think of how she really lived in comparison with the expectations people had of how people like her and Clement must live. To Oona, self-sacrifice and simple living were the keys to their success. She had an almost superstitious dread of losing it all should she suddenly start flashing her money around.

She dropped a rosary into her purse, soothed by the soft rattle of the small wooden beads. She'd tried to pray last night, alone in her room, uneasy, after waking to find Clement gone. She'd tiptoed to his room and, getting no reply, opened the door. She always worried he would find him dead one day. He didn't take care of himself, and that dreadful man Lislelivet had upset him.

Clement had told her the next day he'd simply needed fresh air. He didn't have to ask her to tell no one that he'd been gone. Their marriage was that close he didn't need to. The police would read all sorts of things into his taking a walk, when in fact he often took walks at night.

She heaved a great sigh. When she thought of the trouble they'd had with these nuns! Honestly! There must be better places to donate the Gorey millions. But Clement had his heart set on being buried here, inside the church. This is what came of being an art history major—all that trekking around the cathedrals of Europe had formed in him a burning desire to create a monument for the ages to the Gorey family name. To show his worthless father how far his son had risen, thought Oona, although, being loyal to the core, she would never voice such an opinion aloud to her husband or to anyone. But his funerary plans were part of the deal he'd worked out with the abbess. He'd even hired a sculptor to sketch a design for the tomb. Oona had to admit, it was a nice idea—once one got over the word "internment." So much nicer than any of their options back home, where they best place on offer was a late-nineteenth-century church, and a badly designed, wooden one at that. Oona, too, had been an art history major.

Oona had spent much of the morning trying to persuade her husband to call the American Embassy to get them bailed out of here. But he was strangely reluctant to do that. You'd almost think he wanted to tempt fate. After all, being involved in something this unsavory was bad for the corporate image. It was time for some damage control. Or so she had tried to persuade him. At the very least, he had to find some way to get in touch with his P.R. department at the company back home. He was strangely reluctant to do that, either. There was such a thing as bad publicity and his involvement in this mess, and hers, had its embarrassing aspects. Especially for a man whose reputation rested on his business acumen. He'd been had by these nuns, good and proper.

She paused in her packing long enough to press her curly hair against her scalp. The humidity here made her hair expand, precisely like a mushroom cloud, and all the products she had brought with her were useless against the English weather. She tied a scarf around her head, tying it under her chin, the way she'd seen in photos of the Queen. That for Oona was the Holy Grail—a meeting with the Queen. Dinner with the Queen— why not? That it hadn't happened yet was a sore spot with Clement. One of many sore spots—he felt that despite pouring money into British institutions, he had been soundly snubbed. Only the nuns had welcomed him with open arms.

Those nuns had more marketing savvy in their little fingers than . . . well, than all the Queen's horses, thought Oona.

Dear God, don't let this be a complete disaster.

Thus prayed Dame Sibil Papelwyk, the cellaress of Monkbury Abbey. Just when things were going so well. Just when I had things under control. Such great plans.

Man proposes but God disposes.

Ain't it the truth.

Had she but known it, her thoughts about the finding of Lord Lisle-livet's body strangely tracked the abbess's own. Such a silly man, to have come here. To have brought this disaster on us, trailing his messy life into ours. It was hardly a Christian train of thought but the cellaress's innate honesty wouldn't admit of any phony sentiment. The abbess had led them all in a special prayer this morning for the soul of the man, and that was that. In chapter, she had warned them not to discuss a single facet of the case amongst themselves. They could speak to the police, but only when asked and only under strictly controlled conditions. They could speak to Father Max, but only when the conversation had been cleared with her, the abbess, first. So firm was this injunction, they all completely understood that to defy this order would mean expulsion from the nunnery—a fate worse than death for many of them, who, after all, had nowhere to go. Not after this long time, not after being out of the job market so long, not with so many of their families long dead or estranged from them, baffled by the austerity of the life they had chosen for themselves.

Dame Sibil could not recall a time when such an edict had been handed down in chapter. Well, they'd had the food thief once. But that fell under the category of dormitory prank or one of the milder forms of mental illness. This was serious. Dead serious.

The cellaress looked at the stacks of invoices and bills on her desk, normally the fun part of her day—she loved making all the columns add up, when she could, and finding little economies or money-making opportunities for Monkbury, when she could not. In her heart, Dame Sibil was a *hausfrau* of the old school, a home economist, and folk who didn't understand what it took to run a house, especially one the size of Monkbury, were sadly underestimating both her and her sisters. It was a big position, the equivalent of today's CFO and COO positions rolled into one.

Big mistake, thought Dame Sibil, to do that. To underestimate the nuns. They didn't call her "The Owl" for nothing, and it had as much to do with her acumen as her looks. She happened to think owls were beautiful, those wise creatures, but she knew she herself had just missed being homely. Since childhood, her perfectly round face and eyes and small beaked nose were a source of amusement to others, and she had long accepted that it was so. It was how God had made her, and God loved all his creations.

Now she was in a position of authority, and somehow the demise of Lord Lislelivet made her feel, perhaps irrationally, that it was all slipping away. Her place of safety, slipping away.

"For we brought nothing into this world, and it is certain we can carry nothing out," she reminded herself. Dame Sibil's mind tended to be a repository of useful quotations, some in direct contradiction to one another. Still, she would rather all her hard work not come crashing around her head like a—well, like a ton of bricks in an earthquake.

She picked up a bill for the guesthouse insurance—the premiums had gone up again, although they'd never filed a claim. There were numerous bills for repairs and upgrades—that never seemed to end. But those repairmen from Temple Monkslip knew better than to overcharge the good sisters, for Dame Sibil was not above hinting that they might suffer eternal damnation if they tried to pull that one on her.

Many of the repairs had to do with the wall that had collapsed in the south transept of the church. It was not the sort of repair that could be patched up with a few bricks and a coat of paint. Oh, no, indeed. Thank God, thought Dame Sibil fervently, for Clement Gorey, who had guaranteed a seventy-five-thousand pound loan about that time, which had allowed reconstruction to begin immediately. This wall collapse was what had necessitated the various fund-raisers to retire the loan, most notably the one put together by Paloma Green and that ghastly gigolo of hers, that Piers What's-His-Name. God certainly worked in mysterious ways if the salvation of the nunnery had come in the form of this lot of unlikely saviors.

Still—and she shook her head, reproving herself—it is not for me to question why. It is but mine to do or die.

One of her sisters appeared just then at her door, her wimple askew. Dame Sibil crossed the office and, first asking her permission, straightened it for her. It was a little service they performed for each other several times a day. Life without mirrors was freeing but it could have some comic results.

The sister thanked her, and said, "Dame Cellaress, I am worried. May I talk with you?"

It was a violation of the Rule, this sort of sidebar conversation, which from her sister's expression could only be about the murder.

She knew it was forbidden, and Dame Sibil knew it was forbidden. Private conversations, special friendships, excluding others: they'd have to confess to the sin in the chapter meeting.

"Sure," said Dame Sibil. "Go ahead."

Chapter 24

...AND SUSPECTS

Idle hands are the devil's workshop.

—The Rule of the Order of the Handmaids of St. Lucy

Xanda Gorey felt she might just die if she couldn't get out of here. Die, die, curl up and *die*. Leaning over the fence, staring at the stupid cows, who stared stupidly back in that totally brain-dead way of theirs. She might have been a tree for all they knew. That moronic exchange was the highlight of her morning so far. Soon there would be lunch, which always involved lentils, some sort of vegetarian pâté, cheese, and salad. All of it homemade and fresh, but a greasy hamburger with fries would be so totally welcome right about now. The desserts were nice, though—Dame Fruitcake knew what she was doing.

The thought of Dame Fruitcake brought her up short. If anyone had killed Lord Lislelivet, Dame Ingrid Fruitcake had to be the main suspect. She was the right size for it, too. She looked like she had bodybuilder's arms under all those layers of cloth. And she had to have been the one who tried to poison him. Stood to reason.

Whatev. Xanda found she didn't care, so long as they wrapped up this investigation and let her *gooooo*.

After lunch began the long slide of the day toward dinner and then bed—bed at a time when she was usually just getting the night started.

No TV. No Twitter feed. No Facebook page to update. No Etsy or Pinterest—*total* shock to the system, that.

No one to talk to. *And* she was running out of nail polish. She'd read the one magazine she'd brought with her, like, a *thousand* times. It was no longer news, if it had ever been news, that Brad Pitt was hot, even if he was middle-aged and had all those kids hanging off him. The library was stuffed with books, but all of it was uplifting crap. She had tried to convince her mother to let her go into the village and she'd agreed, and then, *wham!* The police practically lock us all inside, just because that creepy perv finally went to his reward.

The investigation into his murder, which might at least have been diverting, was another closed door. They, the suspects, had all been told to stay out of the crime scene and to speak when spoken to. There were a lot of officious-looking people huffing about the place, taking samples of this and that, and dusting the already dusty place. Xanda had yet to be interviewed in any meaningful way except by a humorless young constable her own age, who offered zero romantic prospects.

All this because her father, in a throwback to the dark ages, wanted his soul prayed for. He also wanted to dictate the terms of the new guesthouse. It was just how he did business. Cash on the barrelhead. She wondered, and not for the first time, how he reconciled his religious leanings with all the people put out of jobs when he folded up their companies—the faceless people who were just, to her father, numbers on a spreadsheet.

Xanda made a face at the one cow who kept staring at her, pulling her lips wide in a clown mask. No reaction. Big duh.

In a distant field, one of the nuns was walking, maybe gathering something—probably nettles or weeds for another wholesome lunch. The cows ate better around here. No, wait, the nun seemed to be reading from that little black book they all carried with them. From the back Xanda couldn't see who it was. The nun walked with a swift unbroken movement, her legs and feet hidden by the long draperies of her woolen skirt, which dragged unheeded over the grass. She might have been on a conveyer belt, or a carved wooden figure gliding in and out of the face of a cuckoo clock. What a life.

Xanda realized, not for the first time, that they were sort of inter-
changeable figures, these nuns. They always walked with their heads
bowed, concealing their faces in church behind their cowl-like headdresses.
It must be like wearing blinders. They couldn't really see. They couldn't
really be seen.

Again, what a life. Not for her. She wanted—not children, that was
for sure, smelly, puking, clingy little things. But she wanted the freedom
to go where she wanted and certainly to dress as she pleased. Coming here
had been a mistake, and now here she was, good and stuck.

Xanda had enough self-knowledge to realize her predicament had
been brought down on her own head by her own self. She had come along
for this ride in the vain hope that Derek back home would notice her absence, a fact she had never shared with her parents. That continued a long
tradition of never sharing anything with them. After years of the religious thing at home, she had as a teenager become adept at finding escape
routes, and the easiest was pretending to go along with their hair-brained
religious beliefs.

As. *If.* The trick was to pretend to volunteer for some do-gooder thing
Mom would approve of, then ask to borrow the family car. For a few
months she had pretended to work serving meals at a homeless shelter.
This was less than satisfactory since the organizers of these meals tended
to be adults, and adults tended to talk with one another. The chances were
huge that some old dork would tell her mother how her daughter was leaving the soup kitchen almost as soon as she showed up to "work."

Then Xanda had stumbled upon the youth group meetings at the
local church, via a big poster at the church that was headed, no kidding,
"Jokes 'n' Jesus." It went on to describe how the church hall was given
over on Thursday nights to these naff events of an indescribable dullness,
aimed at keeping the teens off the street and out of trouble. They had no
idea. While all the *LOO*-sers congregated to pray and watch movies about
mission work—*gack!*—she and her friends would take the car for a smoke
and a whirl around town. It was harmless fun, but her mother would
never see it that way. All right, she had to lie to her mother about her
whereabouts, but lying was better than having no life at all whatso*e*ver. It

had set the course of their relationship for life, both of them sailing in diametrically opposed directions.

Oh, God. Here comes Paloma. What do you call that color she's wearing? Spoiled asparagus? At least she's not with Piers, as per usual, but with that librarian nun. The pretty one. What an odd couple they made.

Xanda jumped off the fence and scuttled into the forested area, hoping to avoid detection. The cow watched her go.

"That was Xanda just now, wasn't it?" said Dame Olive to her companion as they approached the spot Xanda had just vacated.

"Had to be. No one else within a hundred miles has hair like that," said Paloma.

"I need new glasses," said Dame Olive. "You spend all day staring at a computer screen and then one day you realize your distance vision is going, too, along with your reading vision."

"Try the laser surgery," said Paloma. "Worked for me."

Dame Olive was surprised, and realized she should not have been. Paloma's eyes would have been the only parts of her body that hadn't felt the surgeon's knife, from the look of her.

"I think it's just eyestrain," Dame Olive replied. "All the planning for the guesthouse took a lot of research. And then to see it all snarled up like this. Even before the questions about money arose, there were difficulties. Building in stone is no longer practical."

"I don't see why not," said Paloma. "These old walls have stood for centuries."

"I mean, it would be prohibitively expensive, even if you could find trained stonemasons, which you hardly can anymore. In Italy, maybe."

"Was there anything in particular you wanted to talk about?" Paloma asked her. Paloma, away from Piers, was edgy, wondering what he was up to. Even though they were in a nunnery, still . . . leave it to Piers to find the action wherever you plunked him down. It was the downside to having a lover so much younger than yourself. You always knew in your heart he'd leave you the first chance he got. You just didn't know when. She'd made the appointment with the plastic surgeon for next week, so it was really important they get out of here before then.

". . . think did it?" Dame Olive was saying. Her tone was conversational, but only someone as distracted as Paloma could miss the tension in her voice.

"Hmm?"

"Who do you think did it? Killed Lord Lislelivet?"

"Beats me. I just know it wasn't Piers," she said, protectively. "Or me," she added.

"How do you know that?"

"Because he was with me all night."

In flagrant disregard of the nunnery's rules, thought Dame Olive. Well, if I'm meant to be shocked, I'm not as green as I'm cabbage-looking. These two weren't the first, if the guest-mistress were any guide. Still, it was a good enough alibi—and it worked both ways, for both of them.

Dame Olive eyed her companion. Today it was animal-print tights worn with lace-up booties and a plunging neckline. At her neck was a necklace that looked like bottle caps sewn onto a crocheted doily. She wore a low-cut green shirt but had pinched a little black sweater across her outsized breasts—this in concession to Dame Tabby, who had had a word with Paloma about appropriately demur attire for a convent setting.

Dame Olive was tempted to warn Paloma about Piers—in fact, he was one reason she had invited Paloma on this walk. With police running about asking questions, this did not seem a good time for Paloma to be offering an alibi for Piers that perhaps was not true. Besides, in the nature of things, Paloma couldn't really provide an airtight alibi for him for the whole night. Unless one were to believe neither of them slept a moment.

And in the nature of things, thought Dame Olive, neither could Piers offer Paloma an airtight alibi.

She had nothing to go on but an inherent dislike of the man—of the type of man he so clearly was. She'd seen him trying to flirt with the postulant the other day—simply outrageous behavior. Dame Olive knew Piers would twist her instinctive dislike into a manifestation of some psychological failing of her own if she started issuing warnings with no proof to back them up.

But Piers was lying about something. That was as certain as the sun's coming up.

He was lying about *something*.

This was going to play havoc with his schedule, Dr. Barnard thought. Not that that was the first consideration, but he was champing at the bit to get back into routine now. And someone had to feed his dog. Surely the neighbor or his nurse would figure out he had been delayed.

As expected, the road had washed out with the rain. The nuns never seemed to understand that maintenance of the road at the bottom of the mountain rested with them, not with the government. More likely, they didn't care.

This morning he'd looked in on Dame Meredith, and that done, with no one else on the premises showing signs of illness, he had nothing else to do. The police might have used his help, but since he was, technically, a suspect, he supposed that wasn't going to happen. Nothing to stop him from having a few words with that DCI Cotton and bandying about a few theories he'd come up with, though.

He sighed, running his hands through his hair and straightening his tie in the mirror in his small, cramped room. How the nuns stood this confinement, he couldn't imagine. It was what he had liked about America—all those wide, open spaces, once you got out of New York. The endless horizons. How he missed it. Maybe once this was over . . .

It was taking a damnably long time for the police to get around to interviewing him. And Dr. Barnard was not a man who liked to wait.

Max was headed toward the crime scene. He had planned to spend the morning offering the Communion service before going over his notes, adding his impressions from his dinner with the abbess. He'd thought he might work on his weekly sermon in his little cell-like room as he waited for the nuns to finish their mandatory Chapter House assembly. All best-laid plans that now had gone awry, of course.

At dinner he had, however, asked and been given permission from Abbess Justina to speak with the women in her care, a need more urgent now that a murder had been committed. The abbess had seemed agreeable, even anxious, that her nuns be seen in their usual, day-to-day activities. Probably the sting of accusation from Lord Lislelivet still rankled, and she had felt it was in her best interest to eagerly cooperate with the bishop's emissary. Max wasn't going to treat the murder as a chance for her to withdraw her permission—quite the opposite.

Passing the kitchen of the guesthouse, he saw Piers Montague boiling a cup of Nescafe in the microwave. He decided to have a word.

He had seen both Paloma and Piers mooching about, hugging the walls of the monastery, he looking ever-so-trendy and ironic, she looking like a Vegas showgirl whose feathers were starting to droop. What, Max wondered, did they find to do here all day? Probably they would have left right about now, but of course DCI Cotton had forbidden it.

In truth Cotton would have to let them go sooner or later—today, tomorrow. Paloma could quite rightly say she had a business to run. He could claim—oh, who knew what? That the place was stifling his creative impulses.

"This is one for the books," said Piers to Max as he walked in. "But I'm being philosophical about it, for now."

"How is that?"

"Oh, just that there is inevitability about Lord Lislelivet's being taken out like this. It's like the sun's burning out. You know scientists predict it will happen, but there's nothing you can do. God is definitely running that show."

Max hadn't suspected the man of harboring this sort of long-view thinking. Let alone this sort of patience. He'd rather expected him to be on the phone to someone on high, complaining about mistreatment. Then Max realized that in all fairness, that was more the sort of pose Clement Gorey might be expected to adopt.

"Oh, I don't know," said Max. "My experience has been that the good, the bad, and the ugly often live to a ripe old age."

"I guess."

Today Piers wore blue jeans and a tweed jacket over a plain black T-shirt; his wavy dark hair curled nonchalantly over the jacket collar. He looked more the image of a trendy university professor than an artist. He might have been one of Rodrigo Borgia's sons teleported into the twenty-first century.

He was very tan, but only on one side of his face. Max commented on this, saying, "You must have been driving about a good deal lately."

"What a positively Sherlockian observation. What makes you say that?"

"Lorry drivers get that look. It is of course from sitting behind the wheel day after day. Only one side of your face catches the sun."

"Oh. Of course, yes, you are quite right. I have just returned from a two-week trip driving alone around Britain. Didn't I say? Scouting locations for a fashion shoot. Not my usual thing or, at least, not the thing I love doing the most. But it pays well."

Yes, thought Max. Hanging around gorgeous models all day must be such a trial. And to be forced to accept money for it. Darn. He smiled affably.

"I thought you were looking at building sites," said Max. But Piers might not have heard him.

"I will be allowed to go soon, won't I?" Piers asked him. "I'm pretty much booked solid this year and this delay will play havoc with my schedule."

Max heard him saying "I" and "my" but not "our." His friend Paloma was as inconvenienced as anyone. And certainly Lord Lislelivet was more inconvenienced than anyone. But not too surprisingly, Piers's concern seemed to be for himself alone.

"Early days," said Max. "And it is strictly up to DCI Cotton."

And to me, he added, silently. It will take me at least a day to gauge your true north, Mr. Montague.

Chapter 25

AT THE CAVALIER

The kitcheness may be said to have the most joyous of tasks, for
food is a sign of God's bounty and love, and its preparation is an
occasion for joy.

—The Rule of the Order of the Handmaids of St. Lucy

The Cavalier Tea Room and Garden back in Nether Monkslip was alight
with the news of Max's mission to the nunnery, news broken with customary efficiency and relish by Miss Pitchford, who had broken all land
records trying to get to the Cavalier the moment Elka hung out the OPEN
sign. To her chagrin, the usual suspects had already gathered.

"But I forgot my mobile back at the shop," Awena was saying. "I'll need
it in case Max tries to call. There's been an incident at Monkbury Abbey."

"Yes, I heard about it on the BBC," said Suzanna. "Max is there?"

"I'm afraid so."

"What a complete waste," said Suzanna, shaking her head in disgust.
"Max Tudor in a nunnery."

Suzanna could not get her head around the whole monastic ideal. To
give up the chance of a family life was just conceivable, she thought, if you
could pardon the pun. Here a significant glance at Awena, now close to
term. To give up sex, no. And shopping? What about the pure pleasure of
a white sale skirmish at Debenhams? Of a little refined scrapping over the

last set of four-hundred-ply sheets? For that matter, having to give up the indulgence of sleeping on four-hundred-ply sheets?

"I would say the same about DCI Cotton," said Elka. "He's in charge of the investigation, I hear."

"I would second that," said Suzanna. "He's also quite a dishy person."

Adam said, looking up from his crueler, "What do we really know about Cotton?"

"Really, not much," said Suzanna. "Wedded to his job, apparently. I do know his mother died after a long battle with hypochondria."

Elka, not really listening, said, "That's hereditary, is it?"

"I was joking. It was a joke, Elka. I meant that she complained all the time about her health."

Suzanna returned to her earlier line of thinking. Aloud she said, "What sort of life do those women at the abbey have? What trouble could they get up to in a convent?"

"Apart from the murder, you mean?" asked Awena.

"That surely has nothing to do with the nuns. Someone broke in, perhaps looking for silver chalices and things like that."

"Max would say the passing tramp theory of murder is passé. Certainly in literature it is. In fact . . ." Awena hesitated. "In fact I rather think he is starting to believe these cases he keeps getting involved in are related somehow. That they are not random."

"Why would he think that?" Suzanna pressed the tip of her index finger, its nail expertly painted in silvery pink, onto remaining pastry crumbs, and transferred the tidbit to her mouth. "Elka," she called across the room, "the blueberry scones—delicious."

"I'm not sure," said Awena. "Something the Bishop of Monkslip said to him, I think. And maybe something he has started to feel himself. Of course, don't we all know that nothing is random? That there is a great net connecting all of us in this life?"

"Hmm," said Suzanna neutrally. She was not always able to follow Awena down the more esoteric of her New Agey byways.

"Let's just hope," said Suzanna, "he returns in time for the next issue of the *Herald*. What a story he'll have to tell."

Chapter 26

DOSSIERS

Remember that it is commanded thou shalt neither steal nor even covet another's goods.

—The Rule of the Order of the Handmaids of St. Lucy

"I am just not getting it," said Cotton to Max. "I am starting to wonder if I'm the wrong man for the job."

He and Max had once again convened to discuss the case, this time in the room granted to Cotton for his use while he investigated the death of Lord Lislelivet. It was a room even more Spartan than Max's, but if the detective noticed it he said nothing. More likely he felt right at home, thought Max.

Cotton looked over at Max, sitting in the one "easy" chair in the room. Cotton, trying it out earlier, thought it might be stuffed with pinecones and nettles; he watched as Max shifted his weight uncomfortably before giving up and perching on the window ledge.

"I mean, I think it is a wise man who knows his limitations, don't you?" Cotton continued. "I'm not a religious person—at least, not in the sense people mean when they use that word."

Nondenominationally raised Cotton, whose mother belonged to the church of It's All About Me, found great comfort in Max's presence. There was old film footage of Cotton's mother dancing naked at a rock concert that still haunted him—occasionally it would show up on a

BBC documentary on flower power or free love or the peace movement. Cotton never knew quite what to make of his childhood, raised as he was by a largely absentee dancing mother, whether to curse it or be thankful. School had been a particular nightmare—his mother's antics had made him such an easy target. But it also had made him resilient, tough, resistant to intimidation, and hyperaware of his surroundings, giving him all the skills needed to be good at his job now.

Cotton didn't understand Max's religious beliefs, but the powerful impact of a man largely at peace with himself and the world was undeniable. For Max, it clearly was far more than a religion of "plaster saints."

Cotton knew about Max's past, of course. He knew that MI5 had asked more of Max than he could any longer give. But in putting that past behind him and choosing a new future for himself, it seemed to Cotton that Max had acquired a sheen and a polish that he may have lacked before, when he was at the mercy of fallible men. Belief in an infallible Deity must do something for one; Cotton only wished his skepticism didn't stand so firmly in the way. He'd nabbed too many con artists with their hands in the collection plate. There was also that old prayer of St. Augustine's: "Lord, Make me chaste, but not yet." Not that Cotton was a wild carouser—who had time for that, being on the police force, at everyone's beck and call?—but he wasn't sure he was up to the sort of personal sacrifices Max had made.

With a sigh, Cotton returned to the task at hand. Max was staring out the window, not a care in the world by the looks of him. Maybe he'd already solved the case and out of politeness was keeping the solution to himself until Cotton stumbled upon it.

Max turned from his reverie, eyeing Cotton with that calm regard.

Cotton busied himself pulling several files from his elegant leather briefcase.

"The background is trickling in," said Cotton. "You'll be surprised to know—or maybe not—that one of the good sisters has a somewhat notorious past. She killed someone with her car. She pled guilty to 'causing death by dangerous driving' and received rather a light sentence, but the whole thing reads more as an accident to me than anything."

"Which sister is it?"

"The one they call Dame Fruitcake. The kitcheness. Ingrid Castle."

"Ah," said Max. "That might explain the bad leg."

"Probably. She ran over someone who was drunk and staggering down the middle of the road. Ended up in the hospital herself when she overcorrected and the car flipped over."

"She spoke to me of an employer who drank. She didn't mention this part of her own history—but then, she was under no obligation to tell me. I suppose Abbess Justina knows about this?"

"Yes," said Cotton. "Dame Ingrid laid out the whole story on her application to the place. There was no hint that she herself was driving drunk, by the way. She'd had wine with dinner, but she wasn't legally over the limit. The puzzle is why she pled guilty, but I suppose that is how she felt."

"It suggests a rather complicated psychological history," observed Max.

"Is there any other kind?"

"No question that she left the scene—nothing like that?"

"No," said Cotton. "But having caused the death of another human being—it may have pushed her into following through on a decision she had already made, to come here."

"Hmm," said Max. "That more or less dovetails with what she did tell me. But leaving out some important bits."

"It is the Goreys who intrigue me," said Cotton. "That Horatio Alger, can-do attitude. I've always admired their spunk, the Americans." Cotton drew forth another sheaf of pages, clipped together and tagged with sticky notes. "He's more a middle-class, Midas touch sort of bloke, is Clement Gorey," said Cotton, reading from his notes. "He didn't come from nothing, that is to say, but his financial rise from where he began was meteoric. In 1993 he founded something called Excelsior Market Advisors. It's a hedge fund. Based in Omaha. That is somewhere in the midwestern United States."

"Yes, I know. I have been there. Omaha is in Nebraska."

"Oh." Cotton paused to scribble a note on his paper.

"You know," said Max, "I hear 'hedge fund' and my mind goes blank. I have never entirely understood what it is these people do for a living. I think it's the terms they use that baffle as much as anything. What is short selling when it's at home, for example?"

"You're asking me?" said Cotton. "I can barely keep track of what's left of my pension. Once in a while I take out an abacus and try to figure it out. That's how some of them get away with murder, if you will pardon the expression—they count on the ignorance of the man in the street. Even with wealthy tech gurus or organic farmers or fashion designers you know where you are, more or less. But with captains of finance? Nah. Anyway, the joke that goes around is that Clement gets his insider tips from God—he's that rich. Some think he's got a more mortal pipeline—it rather depends on whom you listen to. But the corporate culture of his company is religious to the extent the law will allow: Employees are practically required to be churchgoers, although it's not part of the official mission statement. The employee picnic must be a real knees-up. Anyway, he's estimated to be worth eight hundred million in U.S. dollars. That's about . . . let me see . . ."

"About five hundred fifty in Great British Pounds," said Max. "Wow."

"Too right, wow. Give or take a tax haven or two, that's a lot of private golf courses. Anyway, that kind of wealth is enough to throw the rumor mills into overdrive. But he claims to have made his fortune by hewing to a line of 'Morality First, Profits Second.' On paper it sounds terrific."

"In actuality?"

"Let's say the SEC—the American version of what we used to call the Financial Services Authority—would love to nail him. They just can't believe anyone could have that sort of good luck legally."

"That seems rather mean-spirited of them, when you think about it."

"I gather the SEC is not famous for its generosity and humor."

"Probably just as well. Every pool needs a lifeguard. What about Clement's wife?"

"Oona Gorey, born Oona Staunton of Omaha, Nebraska, is his first and only wife. They met at a church social. He likes to say he married her for her potato salad recipe, but in fact she came from money herself.

Nothing like the amount she enjoys today, but her father helped bankroll his son-in-law. He was something in cattle, the father-in-law."

"Your team has been busy."

"Actually, I think this was pretty easy information to dig up. Clement is an object of fascination to those who toil in media outlets. He's often been encouraged to write a book about his success. Think of him as a religious Donald Trump—people want to know how he did it, so they can go and do likewise. Oprah would probably see him as a big 'get.'"

"I did gather he has some of Trump's steeliness," said Max. "But would it be fair to say Oona is the proverbial woman behind the successful man?"

"Do you know, I can't get a handle on her, really. She's so behind him as to have no clear identity of her own. She agrees with whatever he wants to do and goes wherever he wants to go. Or maybe it's that *he* agrees with whatever she wants. Some couples are like that. You can't tell them apart, at the end of the day. Certainly she's no simpleton—just looking at her, one gets a sense of a strong personality."

Max thought of Awena. They weren't exactly inseparable, and on the surface they might appear to be poles apart in the ideas that divided many people, but he could not imagine life without her. In many ways they were becoming one another. He had no idea what a psychologist would make of it all. Max just knew that in his personal life, he was a most happy and lucky man. Perhaps Clement Gorey felt the same.

"Here is what I also don't get about this setup here," Cotton was saying. "And perhaps you can enlighten me. For a place that runs on a time schedule like a railroad, with certain hours for prayer, and certain hours for this and that, the puzzle is: How do they know what time it is? How do they know when it's time for Matins, say?"

"I asked about that. Time is hard to pinpoint since none of them wears a watch. Clocks, where they exist, are deliberately well hidden—obviously, they can tell the time using that computer of theirs, but somehow I don't think they do. That would be cheating, you see. In the old days, they used a water clock or astronomical observation. It was never precise to the second, of course, but close enough. Or they used candles that were marked to burn according to the hours of the day. I noticed one was always burning in the church."

Cotton looked at him. "You're joking, right?"

Max shook his head. "Welcome to the Middle Ages."

"How on earth could that sort of system be accurate? A stiff breeze blowing through an open door, a faulty candlewick . . ."

"I think after a while they just knew what time it was. There is always the body's own clock."

"Oh. Oh, really," Cotton fumed. "That's just great. Just try explaining to a judge and jury that the bells were rung more or less on time, when the nuns just *knew* in their hearts it was probably four a.m., give or take an hour. *If* we ever have a suspect and *if* this thing ever comes to trial, that is."

Max eyed him with that reticent smile, the smile that told Cotton he was overreacting.

"We'll figure it out," Max said. "We'll get there. We always do. Anyway, the system in the old days was that two nuns would stay awake in pairs, to make sure neither nodded off, then they would go wake up the abbess."

"And in the new days?"

"Same story."

"Let me be sure I've got this straight: rather than using an alarm clock, two nuns keep watch together all night and into the early morning hours, to make sure no one oversleeps. So who were the night owls the night Lord Lislelivet died?"

"The night of the murder, it fell to Sister Rose Tocketts, the novice, and Mary Benton, the postulant. Sister Rose also had early duty keeping watch at Dame Meredith's bedside. I gather it often did fall to these two—being low on the totem pole means you get the job no one else wants. They live in a constant state of exhaustion, these women."

"It's like a hazing ritual," said Cotton.

"I'm sure the nuns don't see it that way. They see it as discipline. And, yes, a bit of testing to make sure the newbie can withstand the rigors of the life." Max paused, thinking. "They say St. Francis was awakened by a falcon every night to say the Office."

"Yes. Well. St. Francis was a regular Dr. Dolittle," said Cotton. He fussed some more, muttering as he scribbled something into his notebook, bearing down hard with the pen. Finally subsiding, he said, "You've been here a little while. Any undercurrents you've noticed?"

Max replied, "Among the nuns, there is a bit of clinging to the past versus charging into the future. The lines are pretty clearly drawn among those with an opinion. Dame Sibil, the cellaress, seems to be all in favor of progress. So was Abbess Genevieve from the motherhouse in France, when I spoke with her. She sees great opportunity for partnership and expansion and, in her practical way, knows that the abbey is not going to survive without letting in a few rays of publicity and advertising. One or two of the other sisters, I got the impression, were not so happy with the way things were trending. They are content with doing things the way things have always been done."

"But they have mastered that whole obedience thing and are willing to go with the flow—once they figure out what the flow is," said Cotton.

Max agreed that was likely. "The disagreement among the nuns, if it rises to being a disagreement, probably is more over how to keep a balance between contemplation and charitable works. Income from their produce supports the poor and good works, and some of the sisters may want to do more of that. Become more socially engaged. The 'other' side may not want the world interfering too much with their original mission, which is to contemplate and worship the divine mysteries."

"If I had to guess, it's an age-related divide. The younger nuns want more social involvement. They are probably also the push behind the 'green' and 'organic' initiatives here."

Max thought about that, and then said slowly, "Not really. Dame Hephzibah seems quite proud of the gift shop and how well it does. But Dame Cellaress—that's Dame Sibil—while hardly a kid, is younger than many here. And with her business background, it is natural that she should think in terms of the bottom line. As far as the green and organic thing—that seems to be part of the fabric of the place. Young and old see the sense in conservation of resources, of leaving a small footprint and so on. They all probably see it as part of their mission to be good caretakers of the planet."

Max sighed in frustration. For all his upbeat talk, when he looked at this case all he saw was disparate threads that did not lend themselves to a pattern. Yes, they would get there in the end, he believed that, but it was going to take a lot of interviewing of suspects over days or weeks, and Max knew he couldn't afford the time away—and couldn't stand the thought of being away from Awena that long.

"What do we know about the man who brought us all here?" Max asked. "Lord Lislelivet? This poisoning business has turned into . . . I don't know what yet. More than we expected. More than *he* expected, that is certain. Certainly he seems to have been drawn by the treasure hunt aspect. I gather they all were, to some extent or another. But the misappropriated funds were the real draw for most of them." Max paused, thinking. "Had Lord Lislelivet donated money to the place?"

"A few thousand quid," replied Cotton. "Nowhere near the amounts the others were in for. But enough that I'm sure the idea of being ripped off was galling for him."

Max had met many such men as Lord Lislelivet in his time both as MI5 agent and priest. Men—and women—born to privilege and wealth. It gave some of them that aura of entitlement that made the working-class man or woman itch to reach for their knives. But in Max's experience many rich, well aware of the role luck had played in their birth, devoted much of their time and money to worthy causes helping others less fortunate.

He did not overwhelmingly feel Lord Lislelivet fit into that category.

"Wasn't there some old business of a kidnapping at that manor house of his?" Max asked Cotton.

"Yes. Many long years ago. It was quite the sensation at the time. It still is, since the crime remains unsolved. My team has pulled some photos from the file on the kidnapping." Again Cotton snapped open his leather briefcase and produced a sheaf of photocopied pages. Together they studied a black-and-white newspaper photo of the kidnap investigator. The caption beneath the photo informed them, "DCI Bodeau began to harbor suspicions when the silence deepened after the last ransom note." And there indeed was DCI Bodeau looking quite skeptical.

"I met him before he retired," said Cotton. "Sound man."

"Still around?"

"Alas no. He was killed during some sort of hostage situation."

Max, who had been involved in many such scenarios in his MI5 days, shook his head. He knew how quickly such a situation could go south. People with hair-trigger tempers and hair-trigger weapons did not mix.

"Lord Lislelivet at the time," Cotton was saying, "the father of the current lord, was rather an upstart who was always thought to have married for money. He had the title; the wife had the money. He was rather looked down on by his peers because of it. But I gather he was also disliked because he was a social-climbing, treacherous git."

"It doesn't sound as if the apple fell too far from the tree, in the case of his son. Can you get me some more of the clippings from that case?"

"Certainly I can. Whatever you need. But do you think there's a connection to the current situation?"

"I think that family has lived under what we can call a curse for a long time. It may be a coincidence. Maybe not. But I'd like to refresh my memory of events. I was too much a rookie at the time to be directly involved."

"That's right, MI5 became involved."

"Everybody became involved. Scotland Yard, MI5, even MI6 when the trail led overseas."

"They never found him, did they?"

"No, poor little tyke. It was assumed it was another case like that of the Lindbergh baby, but in this case, no trace of him alive or dead was ever found. I recall he had a birthmark . . ."

It had been, as Cotton had said, a media sensation, along the lines of the Lindbergh kidnapping or the disappearance of Lord Lucan. It was one of those stories that simply would not die, largely because it attracted conspiracy theorists from every corner of the globe, and on a slow news day the details and theories would be trotted out for a rehash in the tabloids.

"What," Max asked, "if anything, do you have on Piers Montague? He looks like a man with a past."

"Ah, yes. Piers Montague. All that shaggy charm of the midnight poet. 'Mad, bad, and dangerous to know.'"

"All that, yes," said Max. "True enough of Lord Byron."

"Byron wanted to be buried with his dog," said Cotton, "so I've always felt he couldn't have been a complete rotter."

"Did not know that," said Max. "Anyway, I'm not sure that's a tried-and-true measure of character. Well, what do we know of him? Piers, that is?"

"His parents ran a shop. Working class and proud of it. Hard workers—nothing to be said against them except that they may have lacked imagination."

"I remember he made a comment in passing that he dreamed of an academic career, but they held him back. Still, photography is hardly a secure profession, assuming that the quarrel with them was about his taking over the family business."

Cotton flipped through a few pages, finally stabbing one with his biro. "Piers's employment for a few years seems a bit vague. He hung around Parisian cafes, being artistic and drinking coffee and dating models. Nice work if you can get it. It's not clear how he made a living, but the rumor is he had, for want of a better word, sponsors. Wealthy women, generally older than he."

"Patrons of the arts, yes. I don't see why everyone has to go to Paris to be artistic, do you?" Max asked. "When London is a perfectly fine city with its own demi-monde."

"They've held the monopoly so long, no one questions it."

"Anything against the doctor? Barnard?" Max had asked Cotton to verify Barnard's credentials.

"No. He trained both here and in the U.S.—originally as an ophthalmologist in the U.S. His credentials are all above board and ship-shape. Why? Did you think he was a phony? An imposter?"

Max didn't answer at first. Then he said, slowly, "Not in the sense you mean."

Okay! So it's to be another round of "Stump the DCI," thought Cotton. Still, he knew if he gave Max his lead, Max could lead him to the proper suspect. So he said no more.

"You're thinking our suspect is a man?" Cotton asked instead.

"If the body was moved, it was probably a man doing the moving. You'd need the upper body strength to haul dead weight like that around, even given that Lord Lislelivet was not a large person. Although all the nuns are fit, from routine physical labor. Still, there would be limits on what they could drag or carry, particularly since the disposal of Lord Lislelivet involved hoisting the body over the ledge of the well, a height of about four feet, and pushing it down into the well. An awkward maneuver, at best. So the questions become, if the body was moved: when, why, and how was it moved?"

"'Why' is usually so the guilty party isn't immediately apparent. If the body were found in the abbess's front parlor, we'd certainly be looking at a narrower field of suspects."

Max thought it was like one of the nun's tapestries, the patterned cloth emerging slowly from the machine. The shades and textures, light and dark tightly woven. He turned to Cotton and said, "So this is what we have on the surface. Nine o'clock is Compline, preceded by a five-minute warning. Here, let's make it as a chart." And, taking a notebook from his inner pocket, he wrote:

  8:55 p.m.—Bell for Compline
  9:00 p.m.—Compline begins
  9:30 p.m.—Compline ends, Great Silence begins
  10:10 p.m.—Body of Lord Lislelivet discovered

"So far, so accurate. What is missing, of course, is the time of the murder and the name of the murderer."

"The coroner's preliminary assessment was that he was killed between eight and ten-oh-nine."

"That's cheating, that last bit. Of course we know the time he was found. Nothing scientific about it."

"I know. They always do that. But the man's watch had stopped—it was broken at some point in the violence surrounding his murder. And the time on the watch was nine-ten, an hour before he was found."

"Handy, that," said Max.

Cotton could tell by the distant look in his eyes that Max had moved on to examine another puzzle piece.

"What do we know about these people, really?" Max said at last. "No one talks of their past in this place. And as far as many of the nuns are concerned, they have no past, in a sense. Meaning, their past lives happened such a very long time ago as to be meaningless for investigative purposes. We can't even run a credit report on them—it would come up blank, wouldn't it? Not one of them has a credit card, owns property— nothing in the usual way of things. It's as if they don't really exist, isn't it?"

"Or that they ceased to exist when they joined the nunnery."

"Of course, that is the idea. To leave the past and all its encumbrances behind. It's going to make investigating rather a trial."

"A little thing like that won't stop us," said Cotton, with more optimism than he felt. "We're on it, going as far back as need be."

"We quickly learned about Dame Ingrid's past trouble in part because she admitted it on her application to Monkbury. Although the women have effectively disappeared behind these walls, we can't discount some sort of problem in their past lives catching up with them now."

"Not for a minute. But it will be a chore getting all the details."

"The devil this time," said Max, "really may be in the details."

Chapter 27

ON LEAVING THE ABBEY

No one may leave the abbey without the permission of the abbess, even on the shortest errand. Once outside the abbey, a sister shall be on guard against seeing or hearing any evil thing. No sister on her return shall relate what she saw or heard outside the walls of the abbey, for this causes great harm.

—*The Rule of the Order of the Handmaids of St. Lucy*

DCI Cotton left some minutes later to interview and in some cases reinterrogate various of the abbey's guests. The nuns had been collected to sit with a female sergeant in the Chapter House; Cotton had agreed to wait to talk to them himself until after whatever prayer session they held at mid-afternoon. Max had convinced Cotton to include Sergeant Essex on this case. She had been involved in previous investigations with him, and Max had the highest regard for her tenacity, discretion, and honesty.

"I don't know," Cotton had said. "She's got no rank, no clout. I can't just send her in there alone."

"Special-deputize her or something. You could force your way in and throw your weight around and flash your warrant card at the nuns, but it's much better to finesse the situation. This needs a woman's touch. Trust me on this."

Cotton, although scowling, agreed. Max had never let him down before.

It was agreed the nuns would come in pairs to the guesthouse living room for the interrogation, a concession Cotton had made given the general horror that had greeted any suggestion the male police use any of the cloistered areas for the interviews. It was bad enough that room-by-room searches were being conducted, and if the abbess could have seen a way around even that small indignity, she would have taken it.

The thing of it was, the obvious suspects were the nuns, who had easy access to all the areas of the cloister. But the other thing of it was, well, they were *nuns*. Difficult to get around that. Prosecution would be a nightmare. Cotton allowed himself a delicate little shudder.

He later ran into Max outside the guesthouse, just as Max was staring in frustration at his mobile phone, which stubbornly showed the "no service" signal at the top of its screen. Max told Cotton he didn't know why he had hoped things might be otherwise, but it seemed worth a try. The weather had lifted, lifting his hopes for better reception.

Cotton said, "You can pick up a satellite signal only at the end of the road, and then only when the moon is in Aries and Jupiter aligns with Venus—just as in Nether Monkslip. Your best bet is to go into the village of Temple Monkslip. There's an ancient pub called the Running Knight and Pilgrim—where Lord Lislelivet used to stay on his way to the abbey. Not too surprising, that. It's the only inn in town to speak of. It's on the High—you can't miss it. And they have free Wi-Fi."

Max's first thought was: I can call Awena.

"I know," he said. "I stopped there on my way out here." He paused, adding: "I think the place to start may be, as always, at the beginning. To see where and how Lord Lislelivet lived, to talk to his wife, and to try to get a handle on who Lord Lislelivet was when he was at home. And I need to call the bishop, given all that has happened. Oh, and Awena," he added casually, hoping it sounded like an afterthought. "I'll give her a call, too."

Cotton, who knew how far from being an afterthought Awena was in Max's mind, smiled and said, "Of course. And the manor house isn't all that far. You should be able to return from there this evening."

So Max went back to his room to collect his jacket and car keys, glad to escape the confines of the abbey if only for a little while and very much hoping Awena would be available when he called. For they still had much to decide.

He and Awena finally had agreed, after much discussion, to approach marriage in stages. The breakthrough conversation had occurred on May 1—Beltane, and a very big deal in Awena's calendar, halfway between the spring equinox and the summer solstice. It also happened to be the time of year to celebrate fertility, and looking at Awena then, he couldn't think of a more apt holiday. Carrying their child, she was literally blooming with health and happiness, more animated and happy than he'd ever seen her. And, if possible, more beautiful.

Max had reached out to touch her hair, pushing back the white strands at one temple. He wondered aloud if the baby would be born with that white streak.

"Well, that would be a bit weird. Mine didn't appear until I was twenty-one."

"Ah," he said.

"And besides, most babies are bald to begin with."

He thought now of the child on the way, wondering if it were peacefully awaiting its time, or kicking against confinement, heedlessly eager to join the dangerous and wide, wonderful world.

Every relationship in his MI5 days had been sabotaged by the secrecy of his life, by the lies told. What would marriage have been like then? Raising a child? How could you raise a child when you could never quite let on to that child who you really were?

Max thought of his own father, a caring and decent man if distant and distracted. Like every parent since the dawn of time, Max hoped to improve on his relationship with his own child.

I wanted his approval, thought Max; he wanted my love. Why were these goals at such polar opposites?

To ensure there would never be any doubt in anyone's mind how happily and surely this child, this child of starlight, was wanted by its father,

Max had agreed to go along with Awena's suggestion of having both a handfasting and a civil ceremony and did not push her on the church service. Handfasting was a recently resurrected tradition, begun in centuries past when people in small, remote villages had to wait weeks or months for a visiting clergyman to consecrate their marriages. Couples would meanwhile announce their commitment in a public declaration called a handfasting, considered to be a legal, valid union at the time.

Max's bishop had yet to be told any of this plan. Every time Max got near the subject, a murder got in the way.

Or so Max told himself. He wasn't sure which part of his news the bishop would react to more strongly: the baby on the way part or the no church service yet part.

Or the whole New Age shebang.

Surely the bishop would understand: Max couldn't force the issue. As it was, he was ecstatic about the ceremony as planned, overjoyed that he and Awena would legally be man and wife. As to the rest: baby steps.

The bishop simply *must* understand—this was a man who didn't balk overmuch at a priest in his charge being involved in murder investigations, after all. He'd learned to roll with it. But the bishop would have to be put into this particular picture before the ceremony itself, Max told himself sternly.

It was not as if Awena's religious beliefs encompassed a Galactic Confederacy, but whose beliefs could stand up to close scrutiny? The virgin birth alone was a hurdle too high for many.

The bishop would understand. He would have to.

Twenty minutes later, Max began the drive to Temple Monkslip. Mentally he added fifteen minutes to his trip, having been warned by Cotton that some of the road had been washed out and he'd have to detour round. Luckily the Rover usually could manage it.

His plan was to stop in Temple Monkslip to use his mobile and then continue on to Nashbury Feathers via Monkslip Worthy to interview Lady Lislelivet. He had not made a clean getaway from the abbey, however. Xanda Gorey, still teeming with ennui, saw him leaving, car keys dangling from one hand, and reminded him of his earlier "promise" to take her into town.

"If nothing else," she pleaded, "I need a change from all the orphanage food they serve here." She said this in the despondent tone of someone who has nothing more to lose. Max first cleared it with both Cotton and with her mother (her father, as was often the case, was nowhere to be found). "Besides, I need to pick up some fags. And some hair product."

Orphanage food, thought Max. Like Xanda would know anything of orphanage food, child of privilege that she was.

"You can come on condition you forget about the cigarettes," he told her.

"I'm quitting! I'm quitting. Honest. Soon."

"Today would be a good day," he said. But they set off, Xanda riding shotgun in leopard-print high heels.

The dye in her hair must have been temporary, because today the ends were colored sky blue and had been dipped in bronze sparkles, probably affixed with a shot of hair spray. The effect, Max thought, was strangely charming, like she'd been sprinkled with pixie dust. Perhaps it was a look to be outgrown one day but appealing for now. He wondered that two ultra-conservative types as her parents had managed to produce such a sprite as Xanda, but that was often the way the genetic lottery played itself out.

She was rifling through his CDs in the console between the seats.

"What, no Taylor Swift? Not even? And this—what is this?" She picked up his copy of Trio Medieval's album, which happened to be a gift from Awena, giving it a shake as if mothballs might fall out of the plastic casing.

"That," he said, "is wonderful. Put it in the player. You'll see."

She reeled back as if he'd asked her to spray hot sauce in her eyes.

"Oh, all right," she said at last. "If that's all you've got."

"It is."

They drove awhile without speaking, as the downward descent from the top of the hill was best not taken at full speed. He could see why trying to navigate it on a rainy night would be unwise. It was bad enough in daylight.

Max was a great believer in listening to the younger generation. They so often had a perspective that might have escaped him. So: "Now, tell me," he said to Xanda. "You must have some thoughts about this murder. A theory or two."

Xanda paused, deep in thought, then shook her head. It was as if this were the first time she'd paused to consider the meaning of the recent events. "I've got nothing. He wasn't anyone's choice for Mr. Congeniality, but I don't see why anyone would kill him. Or anyone, for that matter. There are always better ways to solve a problem."

"You think he was a problem for someone?"

She adjusted the dial on the CD player, turning up the volume. "Don't know, do I?"

She was a poor dissembler. Max decided not to press it, but he knew she was lying. Protecting her father? Her mother? Or herself?

He asked: "Did you ever see him—oh, I don't know. Doing anything suspicious? Snooping around?"

Actually, it was Xanda he suspected of snooping around. As bored as she was, she had to find something to do. Of course, he suspected all of the guests of the same thing—her father and mother, Paloma Green and Piers Montague.

"He was always skulking about the church," she told him. "Pretending an interest in the artwork. Once I saw him feeling along the walls."

"What?"

"Like he was looking for hidden panels or springs."

"The walls are made of stone and brick. That is most unlikely."

"He was kind of an idiot, if you ask me. He'd probably read too many boys' adventure stories."

Once they reached the village of Temple Monkslip, he dropped her off, having already explained that he needed to go his own way for a while. Their understanding had been that she would catch a taxicab back to Monkbury Abbey, or resign herself to finding something to do in the village while Max pursued his inquiries further afield. If all else failed, he had arranged for Mr. or Mrs. Gorey to come and collect their daughter, should she not reappear at the nunnery by six that evening.

Xanda spotted a café that promised American-style burgers and confidently sprinted off on the high heels, turning heads as she went.

Max had parked in front of the public house, the Running Knight and Pilgrim, grateful for the FREE WI-FI promised by the sign in its window. The sign reminded him of that old joke—who was Wi-Fi, and who was holding him captive?

Above the entrance, which opened directly onto the street, were three carved panels, each bearing a coat of arms—he recognized the arms of Monkbury Abbey. A further sign near the door identified it as a Grade I listed building dating from the thirteenth century.

Max knew that in those days English villages were often closely tied to their monasteries—that in fact, the dissolution had been the ruin of many a village that depended for its economic livelihood on the jobs created by the sisters and brothers. Domestic servants, tradesmen and craftsmen, attorneys, doctors, masons, and bricklayers—when the monasteries fell, the jobs went with them. Abbeys often had acted as landlords to entire villages, a lucrative and generally mutually beneficial situation. Particularly if an abbey attracted pilgrims to view its relics, those pilgrims needed lodging, food, and all the rest of it. As a system it had worked well, although it had greatly enriched the monasteries, leading to greed, leading to envy, and leading to all the rest of it. Their success—and in some cases, their arrogance—had led to their downfall.

Temple Monkslip undoubtedly had grown out of such a symbiotic relationship with Monkbury Abbey. From the looks of the Running Knight and Pilgrim, things had quieted down a lot in the intervening centuries. Max had the place nearly to himself.

Today the pub's landlord was working the bar. He had not been there when Max had taken his pub meal. The publican was a large, fleshy man with a high forehead and the sort of patchy red beard that made Max's fingers itch for a razor, as he suspected it covered up—or tried to—quite a nice face. As the man stretched out his right arm to serve Max a pint, Max could read the inscription tattooed along its length: "Stand Fast, Craig Elachie!"

"Thank you, Mr. Grant," he said.

"You recognize the motto?" the man said, pleased. He stuck out his hand, saying, "It's just plain Grant. Rufus Grant, at your service."

Max asked him for directions to Nashbury Feathers.

"Oh, you'll be wanting to talk with the grieving widow, is that it? Do you know, Lord Lislelivet was standing just where you are now, not that long ago. Chatting up some local blokes for information about the nunnery. They worked there, you see."

Max hazarded a guess. "Repairwork?"

"Precisely. Plumbing and masonry and such like. They were grousing because they and their pals had been promised a big job working on the new guesthouse for the sisters, you see. And then all that had ground to a halt. No money, the nuns said. No one really believed them. Monkbury Abbey's always had money; since the dawn of time they've had money."

"I see. And Lord Lislelivet wanted to know more about this?" Max was having a difficult time picturing Lord Lislelivet rolling up his sleeves and tossing back a few brews with "the lads." But then he realized, that was precisely the nature of a born politician. And that is exactly how Lord Lislelivet would have gone about collecting information.

Lord Lislelivet's claim of being driven to visit the nuns in a burst of religious conversion was looking even less likely than before.

The publican hesitated, looked thoughtful, and finally said, "It wasn't a casual conversation they were having. It was more intense, you know?"

"Like Lord Lislelivet was demanding answers to specific questions? Sort of grilling them, do you think?"

Rufus turned and replaced the glass he had been polishing on the shelf behind him. Max thought he knew the problem: it was bad business to badmouth the local lord and the local nunnery, when so much of the health of the village depended on both. But throwing caution to the wind, Rufus allowed, "He was. He wanted to know the layout of the place. He was asking about diagrams and plans and suchlike. And he said something like, 'I've looked high and low, I tell you. There's nothing there.' Then they saw that I could plainly hear the conversation and took themselves elsewhere."

Max ordered a pint from Grant, then took himself off to a corner where he couldn't be overheard and where he wouldn't be a nuisance to other patrons as he chatted on the mobile. As he went, he noticed several people sitting in that prayerful posture, heads bent, that meant they were reading the screens of their mobiles. As he powered up, he saw with gratitude that he had automatically joined the Running Knight and Pilgrim network and that he had a steady three bars to work with.

Awena answered on the second ring. They exchanged rapturous greetings, interrupting each other with questions about the other's health and well-being and generally reveling in the sound of one another's voices, nearly heedless of what was actually said. Max felt it as a balm to the soul to hear the lilting notes of her speech.

"I've been following the news from here," said Awena. "You may not be surprised to learn the BBC has shown an avid interest. As have all the other news outlets."

Max groaned. If it was news in Nether Monkslip it was news everywhere. He had passed a broadcast van with its large satellite dish on top on the way out to the village. Too much to hope it hadn't been heading for Monkbury Abbey. At least the abbess could confine them to peering up from the bottom of the mountain to the abbey walls. It was private property, and she would be within her rights to bar them from the place. An enterprising reporter would set up shop here at the Running Knight and Pilgrim and see what news could be uncovered or invented in the face of the nuns' silence.

"I think the situation can be contained, media-wise. But it would help very much to wrap this up quickly—help it to go away. What we don't want is a lingering mystery. Speaking of which: you are not going to believe this, but I want you to look up something for me in Frank's book."

"*Wherefore Nether Monkslip?*" she asked, her voice betraying her astonishment. "Is there something in particular you're looking for? Please don't make me read the whole thing again."

"I would not be so cruel."

"All the Holy Grail and King Arthur legend—he makes it sound so crackpot," said Awena. "I don't think it is, at all. There is always some truth in a legend that just won't die."

"Doesn't he speculate that the grail was made of gold and fantastically valuable? Set with rubies and emeralds?"

"He said the value was in the eye of the beholder. That I do remember."

"That may be so, but I think this current gold rush to the abbey is down to him."

"But he also says—I think—that it could be a holy relic. That it became an object of veneration that drew people by the hundreds."

"Right," said Max. "That is how many monasteries became wealthy."

"But he also says whatever it was disappeared. And then along came the Reformation, and that was the end of the pilgrimages to Monkbury Abbey."

"You seem to remember quite a lot of it."

"Frank brought the book in its various stages of creation to the Writers' Square meetings at The Onlie Begetter bookshop. I was forced to listen to it. Over and over and over. I came to believe it *is* possible to die of boredom."

Max asked a few further questions about Frank Cuthbert's book, which had inspired the more rampant speculation about Monkbury Abbey, ending with, "I was thinking I should get hold of another copy of the thing from him. Actually read it this time."

"Oh!" she said. "Frank is on rather a grand book tour in the U.S. He's been sent there by his publisher."

Max sighed. "Of course; I'd forgotten. Our famous author is difficult to reach these days."

"Yes. Lucie says he was awfully excited. Where exactly is Des Moines?"

"It's in Iowa."

"Lucie says Frank has been Skype-ing into book clubs and libraries."

"Is that anything like parachuting?"

"He would if he could figure out a way, I'm sure. I hear he's working on a sequel now."

Max couldn't stop the sharp intake of breath. No. *No!* What more was there to be said on the subject?

"Are you all right?" she asked him.

"At least," he said slowly, "it solves the problem of what to buy people for Christmas next year."

"I thought you liked your relatives."

"I do, I do. Actually, my mother claims to love Frank's stuff. Her book club read him." Max thought a moment. "I guess I could call him, but I'm not sure what precisely I want to ask him. I don't suppose you could put his book in the mail to me, could you? Use one of the express services?"

"Of course I will . . . if you think it will help." Awena sounded doubtful. Max didn't blame her.

"Monkbury Abbey and Temple Monkslip are mentioned in his book, am I right?"

"From what I can recall," she said. "Along with Glastonbury, of course. Not in any coherent way, though."

"Yes, Frank's style is his very own. His last performance at the St. Edworld's Night of Prayer and Poetry will not soon be forgotten."

"Nor forgiven by Miss Pitchford."

"Please. Yes. Don't remind me." Max felt Frank's "Ode on the Birth of a Hedgehog," complete with video footage, might stay with him forever.

"So, tell me," said Awena. "How is convent life?"

"Like being surrounded at all times by wise and highly competent women. Not all that different from living in Nether Monkslip, actually."

She laughed. "That makes me think of the old joke about the Three Wise Women following the star to Bethlehem. They didn't get lost on the way, because they stopped at an oasis to ask for directions. They brought appropriate gifts, like casseroles. They cleaned the stable and fed the animals. And they also brought peace on earth."

"That sounds exactly right," said Max, adding: "It's the eeriest place, is Monkbury."

"A thin place," said Awena. "Yes, after all these years, it would be."

"'Thin place'?"

"Mmm. There are places where the physical world and the spiritual world collide or intersect rather than running alongside each other as they normally do. It's the thin place where we can hear the voice of the Creator. Usually it is somewhere deep within a forest or near a body of water. Someplace where we stop the incessant yammering in our heads and just listen and wait for the Goddess to speak to us."

"'That's how the light gets in,'" mused Max.

"What?"

"Nothing. A poem by Leonard Cohen. Lyrics."

"How pretty. And yes, that's exactly it. The light gets in through the thin places," she said in her earnest way.

Awena. How he missed her! Awena with her eyes as clear as the waters of the Sargasso Sea. He asked a few more questions about her health and the baby's and was told the doctor was delighted with her progress. Max scrounged a few more excuses to keep her on the phone, until finally she said in her gentle way, "I have to go and help Tara with a delivery of herbs."

"What's for dinner?" Max asked idly. While the food at the abbey was splendid, it wasn't a patch on Awena's cooking.

"I'm making pesto from fresh basil. Then I thought I'd stop into Lucie Cuthbert's shop for some freshly grated parmesan and pine nuts. Will you be coming home soon? Please?"

Would he be home soon? What an excellent question it was. He had no idea. The investigation, such as it was, was just getting started. And he had appointments and projects of his own piling up back in Nether Monkslip.

"I will," he told her. "I promise. Save some pesto sauce for me."

Awena said, "You mustn't worry. It's bad for your blood pressure. Have some oregano tea. Or tea made from wild rosemary. Do they have herbal teas at the nunnery?"

Max laughed. "If there is a place on earth outside of your shop that's bound to have herbal teas, it's Monkbury Abbey. You would love talking with the herbalist here. Dame Petronilla. Dame Pet, they call her." Max briefly repeated the contents of his conversation with Dame Pet, the conversation concerning berries—the toxic and the merely irritating ones. Awena, naturally, knew all about the different properties of varying plants and their uses, so Max asked a few specific questions and they chatted awhile longer. Mostly, Max wanted to confirm the time frame of growth for the berry-producing plants that had been found in the fruitcake, which time frame he had heard from Dame Pet, and Awena was able to confirm what had been said. The fall was almost certainly the time when the fruitcake had been tampered with and given to Lord Lislelivet.

The yew tree, Awena told him, had great symbolic value to the pagans. "Because of its longevity, really. The Christians simply adopted it, as they did so many things, to get the populace to go along with the new religion. Oh, and if you're looking at poisons, monkshood would be a very fitting one, given where you are. They call it the Queen of Poisons. If you saw it—it's obvious how it got its name."

Suddenly Max felt that in coming to Monkbury Abbey he had stumbled into a veritable cauldron of poisons. A few more cheerful tips on what to watch out for ("Deadly nightshade you can easily recognize by its bell-shaped purple flowers. Also called atropine—doctors use it to dilate the eyes before surgery. It's in bloom right about now. Fifteen berries can kill you.") and then Awena said, "Max, I have to run. Once I've helped Tara I'm expected over at the church. My turn on the flower rota, you know."

Awena, it seemed, was always on the church flower rota because the other women claimed the flowers lasted longer when she was involved. Max, like nearly everyone else, somehow had come to accept these quasi-paranormal attributes of Awena's as quite normal and only to be expected.

"And then tomorrow there's the Ra Ma Da Sa healing meditation followed by a birthing class in Monkslip-super-Mare. Don't worry," she rushed on, forestalling his apologies, "this particular class is not something you'd need to attend, anyway. Plenty of chances for that when you get home."

Max had approached each birthing class session so far with a near-debilitating dread and apprehension while the sessions only seemed to increase Awena's otherworldly calm. The "natal facilitator," as she liked to be called, was a sweet, grandmotherly woman given to wearing lavender twinsets and fond of using "pain management" slideshows of a stultifying dullness, alternating these with videos of a graphic carnage that held Max, used as he was to scenes of massacre and bloodbath, spellbound in hushed, bug-eyed alarm. How in God's name was anyone brought into the world healthy and alive and whole, given what it took to get here? The fathers-only birthing class he had attended most recently had ended in a wild, boisterous, hours-long session in a nearby pub, which to all the fathers-to-be seemed the only rational response to their looming individual crises.

"But please, do hurry home," Awena said. "And again, don't worry. You always get to the bottom of these mysteries. You haven't failed yet."

There is always, thought Max, a first time.

"And do take care," she added. "Remember Robin Hood."

"Why should I?"

"He was bled to death by a wicked prioress."

Max laughed. "I love you," he said. He got her promise that she would drive safely to Monkslip-super-Mare and would look both ways crossing the street, having got plenty of sleep, and so on.

And finally, having run out of excuses, he rang off.

And called his bishop.

"You said it was a formal visitation," he was telling his mobile a few minutes later. The bishop's secretary, rather ominously, had put Max's call right through, rather than let him cool his heels or wait for the bishop's callback. "So it was part of a routine visit, planned well in advance?" Max asked his superior.

"Well, it was not a surprise visit," said the Bishop of Monkslip. "They were given a heads-up by my secretary, but it was not, say, a thrice yearly, scheduled thing. I prefer a little spontaneity so I get a sense for what is really going on. Especially . . ."

"Especially?" prompted Max, as the pause went on a beat too long.

The bishop sighed. "Especially in the case of the Handmaids of St. Lucy of Monkbury Abbey. It's not as if I was trying to catch them red-handed at anything dishonest—nothing like that. It was just . . . well. As I mentioned earlier, they tend to drift toward the conservative side of things. Even, one could say, the ultra-conservative. Or there were factions wanting to lean that way. I felt it was a situation worth keeping an eye on. I would hope I've created an atmosphere where it is possible to come to me with any topic, however unpleasant, and I would help them get it sorted. But they were used to running their own affairs, you see. Perhaps I should have been firmer with them. Interfered more."

He sounded exactly like a worried parent watching his teenaged daughter rebel over her curfew.

"I am not sure," said Max, "how much there is to worry about. As you say, they have their own minds and very strong wills, and may just have found asking for your guidance . . . difficult."

"They take vows of obedience, Max," the bishop reminded him.

Max, schooled in keeping secrets as he was, wondered if the nuns didn't have a few secrets of their own. The routine, the order—might they not chafe after awhile? That lack of variety, with every day divided into hours assigned to the sacred offices. That lack of *possibility* of variety, to the grave. And then, on top of it all, constantly being supervised and corrected.

In chapter, the abbess would hold her staff of authority, and the cellaress would wear her ornamental keys, and the nuns would inform on one another for the most minor of transgressions: taking the last slice of bread without asking, not stopping work at the very second the bells rang for prayer.

Everyone had to answer to someone at the end of the day. But this was extreme. Might it drive a person to keep a few secrets, to keep something back, to rebel?

Might it perhaps drive someone, unstable to begin with, off the deep end into murder?

"Was there any problem in the past that could account for the current situation, do you think?" Max asked.

"In what way do you mean?"

"I'm not certain, really. How, for example, did the abbess come to be the abbess? Was she a popular choice?"

"Her predecessor died. Abbess Iris."

"Yes. And she had suggested Abbess Justina as her successor?"

"No, now that you mention it. The cellaress is usually next in line. Rather an unspoken thing, you know: a custom. They all vote for whomever they want, but it is generally the current cellaress who is elected. Rather like in the U.S., where it is expected their vice-president will always run for president once the president has finished two four-year terms. It's because the cellaress knows so much about how the place operates. The only other rival for the position would be the sacrist, for similar reasons, but that was truer in the days when being in charge of altar valuables and sacred relicts and keeping jostling pilgrims in line was a much bigger job."

"So why didn't they choose Dame Meredith? She would have been cellaress at the time, right?"

"I'm not certain. I think she may have been felt to be too conservative. Dame Sibil was mentioned also, but there was a faction that felt she was too progressive, *too* modern. Abbess Justina was chosen as the safer, middle road. I must say I was relieved by their choice. Dame Sibil might have been a disruptive influence, pushing too hard for profits, you know, at the expense of the spiritual side."

"But now she is cellaress."

"And held in check to a large extent by Abbess Justina."

Max wondered fleetingly whether, if anything happened to the abbess, Dame Sibil might finally get free run of the place. Could the poisoning have been about that—about discrediting the abbess and pushing her from her throne of office?

"The politics are rather surprising," he said. But then, whenever two or more are gathered, there are bound to be two opinions on some things, aren't there? And quiet, behind-the-scenes jostling for position.

Max said as much about the jostling, and the bishop replied, "Quite. There is never anything overt—it's just human nature to have favorites, and somehow Dame Justina became the dark horse favorite. But of course, special friendships are forbidden."

"Special . . . ?"

"Oh, I don't mean that sort of thing. *No!* No. Not at all. I meant that any hint of favoritism, of excluding others, is poisonous to communal life. It happens, and when it does it has to be stamped out immediately. A too-close friendship, private conversations—all the same sort of thing as you see outside the walls of a nunnery gets magnified in a closed community with so few inhabitants. The slightest hint of that spells disaster. Even among those committed to the ideals of peace and forgiveness and generally getting along."

Max could see how easily, without a strong leader in charge, the whole thing could dissolve into petty feuds and taking of sides. Maintaining her distance from the fray did appear to be Abbess Justina's strength— that and the Teflon quality of the born politician.

"I will need to step in at some point and instigate better controls," the bishop was saying. "They need security cameras around the place, I suppose—I never thought I'd see the day. Their reputation is hanging on this, Max. Monasteries used to hold valuables for people, rather like a bank with safe deposit boxes. Because they were known to be honest, that they could be trusted."

"I know," said Max.

"We can't have them lose what matters most. Their reputations for fair dealing and integrity."

"Yes," said Max. The whole conversation was forcefully reminding him of what he had not yet told the bishop. Talk about a lack of integrity.

"There's something I must t—" began Max.

"I have to run now," said the bishop. "A cab is waiting to take me to the airport. I'm attending a conference where I'm the keynote. 'The Role of the Church of England in the Twenty-First Century'—you know the sort of thing. I do hope they don't notice I'm starting to repeat myself."

"I really n—"

"Talk with you soon, Max—when you've resolved all this at the abbey. I just know you'll get to the bottom of it."

And the bishop rang off.

Chapter 28

AT NASHBURY FEATHERS

Beware the sins of the flesh.

—The Rule of the Order of the Handmaids of St. Lucy

Soon afterward Max left the Running Knight and Pilgrim, setting off on the fifty-mile journey to Nashbury Feathers, the weekend home of Lady Lislelivet and former weekend home of Lord Lislelivet, deceased.

Max supposed she was the Dowager Lislelivet if she had a married son to take over the title from his father. Cotton hadn't mentioned other family but Max recalled some news story or other about the son of Lord Lislelivet's who, being somewhat of a rake, had been sent to spend his days raking in warmer climates.

DCI Cotton had related to Max something of his conversations with the dowager, for Cotton had stopped by Nashbury Feathers on his way to the nunnery. Of course the attempted poisoning had brought the matter to Cotton's attention initially, but now it had all landed squarely back on his desk.

"The wife," Cotton had told Max, "is concerned about what the coroner may find."

"That's only natural."

"But again, she seems mostly to be concerned because of the insurance angle. It can't be death from a heart attack, from where she stands. Or she would prefer it not be."

"Yes, more money for her if it's murder or accident, as the policy is written. What's her theory on what drew him to the nunnery?"

"Lord Lislelivet had had a very public religious conversion," Cotton said, "about which his wife is highly derisory. She thinks he knew a scandal was coming and was trying to do prewash publicity. She—" Cotton interrupted himself. "I don't want to put preconceived notions in your head. But I think she knew her husband very well." Cotton had then sort of squinted at Max and added, "You'll be lucky to get out alive."

"What do you mean?"

But Cotton, grinning, had just shook his head. "You'll see."

And so Max had driven up the long, tree-lined drive to Nashbury Feathers and found himself admitted to the fine old manor house by a housemaid wearing jeans and a T-shirt that advertised her support for the Monkslip Badgers. He had been announced—actually, he had just heard his name being bellowed outside, followed by some sort of hushed admonition—and then she had come back into the hallway to lead him into the Presence.

The interview took place on a wide terrace stretching across the back of the house, with a view over rolling green hills to the sea, a view interrupted only by the strip of blue water in the swimming pool. Max sat beside the bereaved wife, pulling a lawn chair near her chaise lounge but downwind of the cigarette she held in one hand. The Dowager Lislelivet was of middle years—to all appearances, frozen there in time by the skillful wielding of a plastic surgeon's knife—and wore a bikini that left nothing to the viewer's imagination. Her hair was of an artificial champagne-blond shade and of a texture usually found on a child's doll, with dark fake eyelashes adding to the largely plastic illusion. Max in his clerical collar felt as if he had stumbled into a bad French farce. It was an impression compounded when he was asked if he'd like the maid to bring him a martini.

Cotton had recounted how Lady Lislelivet had saved the remaining fruitcake brought from the nunnery by her husband, observing that "you could live off the stuff for years, really." But she had been planning, she told Cotton, to foist it onto the maid when her husband wasn't looking, or failing that, quietly tip it into the rubbish bin. The remainder had been analyzed at the instigation of Lord Lislelivet, as Max knew, and the tainted berries found.

After refusing the martini and exchanging some preliminary pleasantries and expressions of condolence, Max asked her, "How was your husband in recent days? Did anything unusual happen that could be behind this unfortunate incident?"

Max's choice of words seemed to remind her that she was supposed to be in mourning. She pulled a little sad face but just as quickly wiped it away, perhaps thinking outward signs of mourning might cause wrinkles. Or perhaps already tiring of the pretence.

"Nothing, really," she said. "That blond DCI asked me that, too. Ralph was about the same. Irritable and difficult to live with. Staggeringly full of himself. The usual."

"And before? Around the time when he visited the nunnery in the fall?"

"He was up to something, but I don't know what. Preoccupied."

"Worried?"

"Maybe. And that wasn't like him. Ralph tended to just bowl through obstacles in his life. He was a 'doer,' is how he put it. That's shorthand for 'bully.'"

"And he came back from that visit with the fruitcake."

"Right. We had it as our pudding one night for dinner not long after his return."

"What did he eat besides that?"

"A pork roast and vegetables. Nothing different from what I ate. Except that ruddy fruitcake he'd brought back from the abbey."

"You didn't have any?"

"I don't like fruitcake. I don't know a living soul who does, do you? I gave mine to Scooter, the dog, who thankfully didn't much like it either. Ralph did, though. Part of his general contrariness, to like what most people can't stand, if you ask me."

"And this incident encouraged him to revisit the abbey?"

"Um-hmm." She reached for a bottle of suntan lotion and began anointing her bronzed arms and shoulders. "Keeping up with a tan is hard work. God, I miss Rome."

"Lovely city," agreed Max. "Did you not think it strange he'd return? To the abbey, I mean."

"Yes. He said something about repair work and money, and then he decided he needed to 'explore his spiritual side.' It was enough to make a cat laugh. I didn't really listen. Whatever it is he was up to, I can tell you this: it'll make the Profumo scandal look like a vicarage tea party." She smiled winningly and added, "No offense. I'm sure you throw lovely parties at your vicarage."

"So you think visiting his aunt was just a pretext?"

"There is no question about it. He didn't care a toss about her, and going to see her was just an excuse. But for what, I don't know. The nuns aren't allowed visitors except on set occasions or in an emergency, but for years he didn't visit. Couldn't be bothered."

This reference to Dame Meredith made Max slightly uncomfortable. He had not visited his own aunt very often. It was a duty, a chore, an obligation, rather than something undertaken with joy, as it should have been.

"You have to understand: my husband was always *on*," the Dowager Lislelivet said. "Always putting on a performance, you know? Except when he was around me, of course. For me he didn't bother. Hadn't bothered in ages."

Max did see. As with most marriages, he supposed, the spouse saw the whole picture: the good *and* the bad. Max was still searching for Lord Lislelivet's good side. He had to have had one, Max reasoned. Didn't he?

"His publicity people had gone into overdrive to broadcast that he was at the abbey seeking spiritual renewal. What a load of bollocks. Trust me," she added, "if he was there for spiritual cleansing it was because a scandal was about to break and he was doing some preemptive image enhancement. 'Spiritual cleansing'—hah! He actually used those words, thinking I would swallow that. He must have thought I was as gullible as the reading public. Believe me, I know him too well." She corrected herself, first trying on and quickly abandoning her grieving widow expression. "Knew him."

"There is no question in your mind this was murder." It was not a question.

Suddenly a cagey look came into her heavily made-up eyes. She retrieved a pair of sunglasses from the small table that held her cigarettes, suntan lotion, and a beach read paperback: *Torrid Tuscany*. "I wouldn't know, would I? I wasn't there. But I also don't believe he just dropped dead of a heart attack and hit his head on the way down a well. Ralph would never be that considerate, for one thing. For another, he had just received a clean bill of health from his doctor."

"I do apologize for having to ask," said Max. "But do you believe he would be engaged in any activity that was . . . uhm . . . sexual in nature?"

At this she let out a loud bray of laughter. It was quite a contagious laugh. If I were casting an actress to play a Wild West brothel madam, thought Max, I would pick Lady Lislelivet for the role. "My stars, Vicar. That was nicely put. But in a nunnery?"

Max smiled, seeing how he might better have phrased the question. "I was speaking generally," said Max. "How he comported himself generally."

"The answer is yes. If I were a betting woman, which I am, I would give you even odds he was unfaithful, although I would also bet he confined that sort of activity to London." She paused, thinking. "But he could have been up to anything, really. I'd also offer even odds on financial malfeasance, bribery, arms trading—oh, you name it. He might draw the line at human trafficking but only with the greatest reluctance, and even then he'd first ask about the size of the profit margin."

That broad answer seemed so oddly definitive Max could think of nothing further to ask. But it was becoming clearer that Lord Lislelivet's visits to the nunnery were completely out of character and might indeed be what his wife believed them to be—attempts to divert the attention of the media or to polish his image in advance of some unsavory revelation or other he knew was about to burst forth. There was always the possibility of character change of a bolt-from-the-blue variety, but from what his wife was saying, Lord Lislelivet seemed to have reverted straight to type in between his visits to the monastery.

No, an ulterior motive for his stays was looking more and more likely. St. Paul may have been converted on the road to Damascus, but as much as Max disliked dismissing the possibility of miraculous conversions—they would, after all, make his job so much easier—Lord Lislelivet almost certainly had not had the benefit of such an experience.

"He had been reading that book," she said, screwing the cap back on the lotion bottle before wiping her hands on a towel. "And that may have had something to do with his sudden interest in the place. He read that book in one go, which was not like him."

That book. "That would be *Wherefore Nether Monkslip*?"

"That's right. He was highlighting pages and so on. Really, totally unlike him. He barely read a newspaper except to see if he was mentioned. And then there was the letter."

"The letter?"

"Ralph got some letter from the nunnery. I saw the seal on the envelope—that woman with a crown thing. He opened it and you should have seen his expression. I swear all the blood drained from his face."

Max, instantly on alert, leaned further in toward her, straight into the fumes of coconut oil and cigarette smoke. Cotton had said nothing about a letter. And Cotton would have said if he'd known. "Did you see what the letter said? Or whom it was from?"

"No. But that is why I remember what happened so clearly. He threw it in the fire and then pretended it was nothing. He said it was some sort of fund-raising appeal letter. He was an accomplished liar—just ask his constituents—and quick with a cover-up tale, but over the years I could generally spot when he was lying. Generally. After a while I didn't care. I developed . . . outside interests." Again she smiled, perhaps assessing Max for inclusion in her list of interests.

"Did he ever mention Piers Montague or Paloma Green in connection with fund-raising for the abbey?"

"No," she said. But she said it too quickly, dropping her eyes. Reluctantly, she added, "Piers is a distant relation to Ralph. A third cousin thrice removed or something." She perked up. "And a very dishy morsel is he."

"Could the letter have been from his aunt? Wouldn't that be the most logical person to be in touch with him?"

"I asked him that. He sort of went from snotty to outraged in an instant—he was good at that—and he was adamant that it was not from his aunt. He repeated that it was a fund-raiser, and he said it loudly, because he hated repeating himself. Once he started bellowing about anything I knew it was time to keep my head way down and drop the subject. Are you certain I can't have the maid get you a drink, Vicar?"

Max shook his head. "And it was after this he paid his first visit to Monkbury Abbey—his first visit in many years, at any rate?"

"That's right. And that is when he came back with the fruitcake."

"It seems like some sort of warning, doesn't it, that fruitcake?"

"That's what I thought, too."

"But instead of heeding the warning, he returned to the nunnery. You don't find that odd?"

She adjusted her sunglasses, shaking her head. "No, I don't. Ralph thought he was invincible. There was something at Monkbury he wanted and apart from taking a few precautions as to what he ate while he was there, he wasn't going to stay home quivering over some mishap with the fruitcake."

She blew a smoke ring. It hovered over her head like a halo before dissolving in the air.

"I can tell you this for free," she said. "He was snooping around there. He told me himself he looked at printouts of their financials."

"How did he get hold of such a thing?"

"He waited until the cellaress's back was turned, then took a peek."

"What did he find?"

"He *said* it all looked balanced. They were doing very well, he said. Everything in order."

So Lord Lislelivet, unsurprisingly, had no compunction about prying where he had no business prying. Max wondered if Lord Lislelivet had seen a more current—or accurate—statement somehow, on this most recent visit.

The visit that had led to his murder.

Chapter 29

IN OLDEN DAYS

No sister may neglect the times appointed for reading, or engage in idle talk during those times, as this would bring harm to herself and distraction to others.

—*The Rule of the Order of the Handmaids of St. Lucy*

Leaving Nashbury Feathers, trailed by longing looks from the newly minted dowager, Max was struck by a thought. Wasn't it likely Dame Olive would have obtained a copy of Frank's book for the Monkbury archives, dealing as it did with the history—or rather, the legends—of the abbey?

So on his arrival back at Monkbury Abbey Guesthouse, he went to seek out the librarian, Dame Olive, before the bell could call her to her meal or to Vespers.

He found her at her desk, so completely focused on whatever she was reading she didn't look up until he had cleared his throat to get her attention. She abruptly closed the book; much to his astonishment, Max saw it was a copy of Frank Cuthbert's *Wherefore Nether Monkslip*. Dame Olive blushed. There was nothing salacious in Frank's book, so far as Max could recall. But for anyone with any aspirations to serious historic scholarship, he supposed, it wasn't exactly like being caught reading Robert Graves.

As if echoing his thoughts, Dame Olive said, "It is a guilty pleasure, reading this thing. Of course, I could claim that since it mentions the abbey, even in passing, it is my duty to read it. But I find myself captivated by the . . . by the somewhat swashbuckling narrative style. The author has quite an imagination. It's transporting. Did you have something you wished to discuss, Father Max?"

Max, who was still adjusting to this new view of Frank Cuthbert and his book as anything other than a huge village embarrassment, took a moment before he said, "I don't suppose you could lend the book to me?"

Her reluctance was palpable.

"I'm not quite finished," she began. "I'm just getting to rather a good part."

There's a good part? "I promise I'll return it quickly. I'm only interested in the bits about Monkbury Abbey. The sections on Glastonbury and King Arthur's grave and so on probably aren't relevant."

"Ah, but you see, it all ties together in a rich tapestry; it's all woven together so beautifully . . ."

My, she *was* a fan. "I promise," said Max. "I will skip over anything not directly relevant."

"Your interest isn't connected to the murder, is it? I mean, how could it be? Just a silly little book, after all," she said.

Interesting, thought Max. She went rather quickly from "rich tapestry" to "silly little book."

"It's one thread I'm following up on," Max told her.

"I see." Still, she hesitated. "He's rather a mystery writer, is your Frank Cuthbert. He leaves many unanswered questions, some having to do with old crimes."

"Well, it's a mystery to many what he's writing about. That much is certain. And he's only 'mine' in the sense that we share a village."

She laughed, a light trilling sound. Max thought she probably had a lovely singing voice.

"What?" he asked her.

"Oh, just . . . what you said about mystery writers. I'm reminded of something I read recently. That the Bible authors were the original mystery writers."

Max smiled. He had a nagging suspicion she knew more than she was telling him but that she would dance round the topic until the next bell rang. Thinking that drawing out her knowledge of the abbey's history might put her more at ease, he asked lightly, conversationally, "Did Monkbury Abbey play a key role in the Crusades?"

She paused, considering the question. "That depends on what you mean by 'key.' Monkbury Abbey was always pivotal to the life of Temple Monkslip, which was rather a crusader magnet, and the residents of Nashbury Feathers were major patrons, too. You can see the tombs of some of them in the church—they were killed while on crusade and brought back here for burial. Time has not been kind to some of them; the brass nose of the fifth earl of Lislelivet has quite worn away. At one time, rubbing his effigy was thought to be lucky, you see."

The fifth earl. When would that have been? Fourteenth century? Fifteenth? He asked her to describe what the place might have been like back then.

"Smelly," she said succinctly. "Even though monasteries were models of cleanliness for the age, the stench must have been unbearable at times. They burned liquefied animal fat in lanterns, for example. And bathing was infrequent."

She folded her small hands atop Frank's ghastly book.

"The nuns did have running water; they diverted water from the river into a sort of trough outside the refectory, so they could wash their hands before meals. There was some basic understanding of sanitation, although the hand washing may simply have been a religious ritual involving no particular bow to hygiene. Of course, the infirmary was built over the river, so the worst effluvia could simply be dumped untreated."

Max smiled. "I saw a bumper sticker recently that said, 'We all live downriver.'"

"Isn't that the truth? As to diet—you really had to like fish—fish caught upstream of the infirmary, one hopes. Records show a ton of salted and dried fish being served with mustard sauce. As a special treat, they might have raisins or nuts.

"But they weren't as isolated as we are today. Men and women from Temple Monkslip would come to work the farm and help with the laundry and to work in the kitchen and the bakehouse. They were often paid in cloth."

Max imagined cash may have been more welcome, but who knew? It was a different time.

A bell rang just then. Half expecting her to jump up from behind her desk and run off, Max rose from his chair.

"It's a bell announcing visitors," she told him. "Poor Dame Hephzibah has been run off her feet with all the fuss about Lord Lislelivet's accident." She added a perfunctory, "May he rest in peace." Max nodded, thinking: So 'accident' was to be the official explanation for now, was it? He wondered if that idea had come from the abbess.

"But earlier someone left a trail of water in the corridor leading to the infirmary," Dame Olive was saying. "It often happens when the vases for the flower arrangements are overfilled. Dame Hephzibah got stuck with mopping it up, and she's got too much to handle already."

It had sounded like any other bell to him, but clearly they had a system to help them differentiate. Throughout his time at Monkbury Abbey, bells had punctuated the silence. The women lived all their lives in a Pavlovian way, responding to the ringing of a bell. Dropping whatever they were doing, on the instant, in anticipation of future reward.

Or punishment.

"You don't have any particular theories as to why Lord Lislelivet met his end here, in this place? Who may have been responsible?"

"None whatsoever," Dame Olive replied firmly. "And we have been forbidden to speculate."

Max did not really believe her. The nuns might insist, as he had heard them do, that they didn't know each other well. That they were forbidden or reluctant to talk about their pasts. But he didn't for one minute believe you could live in a fishbowl like Monkbury and not develop a sense for the personalities surrounding you.

"Did anything—anything at all—strike you as out of the ordinary that night?"

She shook her head firmly. "Everything was as usual. Lentils for dinner. Dame Petronilla drying her herbs—she was using coriander to treat
poor Dame Meredith. The warm weather brought us all outside more into
the cloister garden, and I have wondered—"

She caught herself up short with the forbidden speculation.

"I'll have to own that in chapter," she said, displeased.

Max gazed over her head, as if innocently perusing the shelves of books
and folders, as if thoughts of murder were as far from his mind as could
be. He wondered what Lord Lislelivet had found so fascinating about
Frank's book, but was afraid she'd end the conversation if he approached
the subject too directly.

"The Vikings," he murmured, as if struck by a sudden thought. "Did
they venture this far north?"

"Ah!" she cried, as though this very topic were never far from her
thoughts. "Those were dark days. The Vikings were no gentlemen, and
it was always feared they might attack. The nuns became rather clever in
dealing with the threat."

"How so?"

"They learned to hide the gold and silver valuables from the altar,
things like that. They replaced the communion chalice with one of wood
for as long as the danger lasted. And they were told to lie if need be—yes,
they received a special dispensation for that from their abbess. She must
have been a practical soul." She laughed lightly. The small hands in their
accustomed gesture flew to shift the oversize glasses. "We lived to see it
all: the Norman conquest, the Crusades."

By which time, Max thought, the nuns might really have mastered hiding places. Might they have become skilled in telling white
lies where needed, too? For he was beginning to wonder how much of
Frank's nonsense was nonsense. Was there treasure buried here somewhere?

"Not to mention fire and earthquake," she went on. "Now, Father, if
there is nothing more?"

There was a lot more, but Max could not formulate the questions that
might tease out the truth. And he had the oddest feeling that she would

only answer openly if he asked targeted and specific questions. She wasn't going to offer up abbey secrets on a plate.

Again he tacked the little wooden ship of conversation on which they sailed toward less dangerous waters.

"You have visited Glastonbury?" he asked her. He didn't know what made him ask. The famous landmark's physical resemblance to the mountain on which they sat, he supposed. Monkbury was like a large Glastonbury Tor, with foliage.

And hadn't Awena said something about Glastonbury, in summarizing Frank's book?

"Long ago," Dame Olive replied. "And yes, I've heard the rumors. So, apparently, has your friend Mr. Cuthbert."

Once again, Max's first urge was to deny this close affinity with author Frank Cuthbert. To deny, if need be, that he had ever met Frank Cuthbert. Instead he said, "Rumors?"

"That the Holy Grail of legend found its way from Glastonbury to here. Utter rubbish. Now, if you will forgive me, Father Tudor, I really must . . . erm . . . file these returned books. And some mice have found their way into some of the archives again. I can't bear to kill the poor things and it takes me most of the day to catch and release them."

She hesitated, eyeing him warily. "You may borrow the Cuthbert book if you wish, Father. Just be sure to return it before you leave."

Chapter 30

THE CELLARESS

The Cellaress shall be a wise, sober, and stable person, not given
to excess in food or drink or given to squandering resources. In
her important task of caring for the abbey, she must never become puffed up with pride. She is in the final reckoning answer-
able to the abbess.

—The Rule of the Order of the Handmaids of St. Lucy

Before he had another go at Frank's book, Max decided to interview the
cellaress, the financial pillar of Monkbury.

He retraced his steps of yesterday and followed a sign pointing to the
cellaress's office. He paused at the open door of one of the workshops
where a nun was working with terra-cotta. The clay was of a deep red—he
remembered from a label he'd seen in the gift shop that they were using a
clay from Devon—and the nun was surrounded by shelves holding little
pots and mugs and coffee cups with glazes of white and green and blue.
He watched as she deftly avoided catching up her long skirts and apron as
she went about her messy task. He could almost feel the weight of all that
fabric dragging down his shoulders, and he thought how unbearable all
those folds of cloth would be come August, if England were to endure
another round of the heat waves that had become so commonplace. He
and Awena had planned their ceremony for August, and while he would

walk through fire to be with her, he rather hoped that metaphor wouldn't be too apt come the day.

He thought this must be the Dame Potter the bishop had mentioned. She looked up from her work with a gentle smile but said nothing, and he was content to watch her for a moment, deciding that his favorite hue for the slip glaze was the white, an off-white shade the color of parchment. He was consumed by a sudden, somewhat irrational desire to take up pottery making, to feel the clay between the palms of his hands—irrational only in that he had no artistic ability of which he was aware. But watching her he felt something of her contentment in this simple, ancient act of creating something both useful and beautiful from an element so ordinary as terra-cotta.

He moved on, down the flagstone hallway, and in the workshop next to the pottery he found a nun at work with a floor loom, her dark hands rhythmically guiding the threads, her veil pinned back out of harm's way. As before, he didn't attempt to interrupt but watched mesmerized as the patterned cloth emerged slowly from the machine. He knew from the gift shop that the nuns made scarves and throws and blankets and placemats in complex, mathematically precise textile designs. The colors here were muted, soft heathers and shades found in nature, tans and pale greens, the designs interlocking as with ferns and leaves.

There hung from a drying rack in one corner several altar cloths and vestments in various stages of embroidery. They put him in mind of something William Morris might have designed. Or of something Awena, with her love of colorful, intricately woven and embroidered clothing, might wear. He had a fleeting image of her, back home in Nether Monkslip, knitting some infinitesimal garment for the baby, a jumper with sleeves not much bigger than his thumb. The child would still be tiny in January, when even Nether Monkslip felt the blast of winter.

The nunnery was like a microcosm of Nether Monkslip in its population of industrious, resourceful, and talented inmates, plying homey trades that had never gone out of fashion and that were only recently gaining new recognition. Unfortunately, as in Nether Monkslip, murder had invaded this sanctuary of peace.

•   •   •

Not really expecting her to be there, he tapped lightly on the door labeled CELLARESS. "All praise be to God," trilled a high, authoritative voice from inside.

The lights of a twinkling modem greeted him, and for a moment Max was transported back to the Bishop of Monkslip's spaceshippy office. But this setup was primitive by comparison. The cellaress had a printer that was a mate to Max's own unruly destroyer of paper and ink.

Dame Sibil looked up at him. She had large eyes and an intelligent countenance, her face flat, white and heart-shaped, like a barn owl's, and with the same alert stare. Round eyeglasses added to the effect. She followed his own gaze to the gadget on her desk and said, "It's not fast, but it often works. The telephone and cable companies want nothing to do with us—we're far too remote for them to bother with. Well, if we paid their exorbitant fees to install the infrastructure they'd be interested. But we won't. You, of course, are Father Max Tudor. The abbess told me to expect a visit from you. I must say I am surprised to see you here still."

"Surprised, how?" Max asked her, smiling.

"Well, I rather thought your role might be, erm, reconsidered. I understand the presence of poison was confirmed, and now that someone has succeeded in killing the man, surely it's a matter for the police."

Succeeded in killing? Max wondered at the choice of words. She seemed well-informed about the poison, but then, Max reminded himself, she was actually second in command of the place and was probably more in touch with the day-to-day happenings than was the abbess.

"Of course," Dame Sibil continued, "I understand how difficult you must find it to leave Monkbury. Those of us who live here would never dream of leaving. It is a choice we gladly embrace. Most of us." The owlish eyes closed complacently for a moment behind the round glasses.

"Most of us?"

"It is a calling like any other."

Max found he was losing patience with her indirect mode of answering. Hers and everyone's at Monkbury, for that matter. He reminded himself he was here on sufferance, and no one owed him an explanation for anything. No one owed him the time of day. But still he believed Cotton's, and the bishop's, thinking was correct—the nuns might talk to Max at some point about whatever might weigh on their consciences, but they would clam up in an instant in talking with the police. The reasons for that might be to protect themselves, but more to protect the integrity and reputation of the abbey. The outer world must not be allowed to intrude on the holy and tranquil space the women had created for themselves.

"Do you have someone in particular in mind, Dame Sibil?"

"Oh, no," she said quickly. Too quickly.

He let it pass, hoping she'd let down her guard with a change of subject . "I see you have Internet access," he said conversationally. "Making it easier to keep up."

"I'm not really interested in keeping up, Father. Just skimming the headlines brings me down. My eyesight is vastly improved lately, but the headlines strain the soul." She added, "Still, the satellite is indispensable to sales—although didn't I have a job on my hands, convincing the abbess? With a modem and a satellite dish, we are part of the world of commerce, as we need to be."

"I've seen the gift shop," Max told her. "Most impressive."

She nodded. "We are blessed. The response to our products is most gratifying."

"They generate a lot of income?" Max ventured.

"A lot," she agreed.

"The sort of wealth that brings its own problems?" he ventured.

"Not on my watch," she said, rather sharply. "No indeed. But yes, corruption and bad management and nepotism can creep in, if one is not vigilant."

"Nepotism? Surely not."

"With the sort of abbess who might exploit the abbey to enrich her own relatives—we had more than one of those. In the past, of course."

They were all so eager to assign their problems to the past, ignoring the chaos swirling around them. "There are controls in place to prevent that now?"

"Of course!" She seemed genuinely shocked at the question. She reached out a hand, putting the computer to sleep, and turned her full attention to him for the first time. "Everything we do is agreed upon," she told him. "The abbess monitors the finances closely, and has the final say. And the bishop of course keeps an eye out." Not really, thought Max. A situation likely to change now. "But whenever possible the majority rules," she added.

He was reminded of something Dame Olive had said yesterday in the library, something that hinted the majority might as easily be ignored as not.

"It sounds idyllic," said Max mildly. "Like a utopian ideal of harmony and cooperation."

"Doesn't it just," she said. "The abbess resisted the idea at first for some of our enterprises. She said, 'The lesson of Mary and Martha was that we should focus on God, and not just be busy, busy all the time.' But she has come around."

Hearing the triumph in her tone, Max pressed her: "There must be issues where the group is split down the middle?" He let his voice rise at the end of the sentence, a gentle hint for her to spill.

She shook her head. "The Rule is beautifully designed to deal with discord and human failings. Anyway, this group is most companionable. There are so few of us, and perhaps that helps."

"You know you can't afford an open breach," said Max.

"Precisely."

"And if there were one?"

"It is not unknown that a sister has been asked to leave. It is gently suggested that the communal life might not be best for her."

Max wondered if Dame Sibil realized she had just contradicted herself. First they all got along just fine, then it is clear there has been enough tension in the past that someone had been asked to leave. Max decided to change tack for now. He said, "I find it incredible that you manage all this with such a small staff. Admirable, and incredible."

She nodded, taking the compliment as her due. Easily he could see her in "civilian" life, on a telephone placing trade orders, or chairing a board meeting, the only sane person in a crazy room. "Basically," she said, "I run the physical side of things so the abbess can attend to the spiritual life of the nunnery."

Again the contradiction. A moment ago the abbess had her finger on the pulse of things, to avoid inroads of corruption. Now the abbess was living on a higher, otherworldly plane.

"You order food and other provisions?" he asked.

"Everything, down to the salt for the table. 'An Army marches on its stomach,' you know."

"This would include ordering all the ingredients for making the fruitcake?"

If she knew what he was driving at, which she must do, she wasn't going to give anything away.

"Yes," she said. "Everything. I told you." He waited for her to say that ordering berries was generally not part of her job, but she did not rush into that denial. His admiration for her went up a further notch.

"And how are most of these goods obtained?" he asked her.

"We have a standing order with Messrs. Black and Standford in Temple Monkslip."

"And you find them reliable?"

"I find them honest and reliable, or I would not deal with them."

"What is your background, if I may ask?"

"I was in the corporate world," she replied.

"In a management position, I'd wager."

"Yes."

He knew from her file she had been rather a big noise in London, but he saw little point in pressing her for specifics. The habit of not looking back was probably so entrenched she could hardly remember the time when she had "been somebody." She had given up a great deal monetarily to join the nunnery, that was certain. He made a mental note to ask Cotton to look further into her reputation for fair dealing—or not—in the City.

"If there's nothing else, Father?" she asked with pointed emphasis and a slight turn of her plump middle toward the computer screen.

"There is. Just bear with me a moment," he said. "Of all the people here, I would respect your judgment and opinion as to character and so forth, you having seen so much of the world outside. Yours no less than Abbess Justina's."

This blatant flattery seemed to work, even on someone as savvy as Dame Sibil. She sat up a little in her chair and fussed a bit, straightening the hem of her veil. But then as if recalling herself, she raised a sardonic eyebrow and said, "Of course, I'll not be carrying tales."

Dame Fruitcake had said as much, too. "No, of course I wouldn't ask you to."

Of course he would ask, given half a chance, but she was not to know that. Softly, softly, then.

"Out with it please, Father."

"I suppose . . ." he began. How to approach this? "What precisely are the requirements for joining the nunnery here at Monkbury?"

She paused to consider, and said, "We take everyone on a case-by-case basis. One size does not fit all. Generally, the applicant has to be thirty-five or younger, although we have admitted a few older women. Widows, mostly. The process starts when a woman writes a letter to the abbess, explaining what brought her to think she had a vocation. If the person seems reasonable from the letter, we invite her to stay for a week with the community. If neither side is frightened off at that point we ask for a formal application that includes health and financial history. No one is admitted without a doctor's certificate of a clean bill of health."

"I suppose recruitment is an ongoing concern."

"Yes, and no. We no longer have to actively limit enrollment, as in the past; we are a dying breed. That is not to say we have to take on just anyone who comes along."

Did Max imagine it, or was there was a particular notion behind her words, a certain unusual emphasis? He remembered her saying earlier: "It is a choice we gladly embrace. Most of us."

She continued: "The fall in the number of solid vocations is a temporary condition merely; religious vocations will come roaring back with a
vengeance one day. Until then, we keep the faith. Literally. We who have
chosen the religious life are not finished yet! I see a spiritual revival taking hold out there. Young people want, as young people have always
wanted, to do something relevant with their lives. Isn't that the word they
use? Relevant?"

Max acknowledged that it was.

"And authentic," he said, "Authentic is the word I hear most often
from the young. They want to lead lives that make a difference. I'm afraid
they've seen their parents chase the brass ring for too many years, and
they've seen how unhappy it's made them."

"There. You see?"

Later Max was to wonder at her certainty. Religious vocations were
so thin on the ground. What made her think that trend would be re-
versed?

"Now, back in the days of the Templars," she continued, "we could
pick and choose. A trend that, as I say, I see enjoying a renaissance. We
have had no end of guests trekking through the church after that silly
book was published. Day-trippers looking for the Holy Grail. Not that I
mind. Our revenues from the gift shop have positively soared."

Max sighed. "You don't mean *Wherefore Nether Monkslip*?"

She blew out her cheeks in a show of disgust.

"That's the one. What a load of hooey."

"Is it?" Max, while privately having the same view of Frank Cuthbert's book, wanted to be sure he wasn't just prejudiced by too many close
encounters with it. "Dame Sibil, what makes you say that?"

"Well, there was a fact here or there, but it was fact stuffed with the
straw of fiction, if you follow. It is true, we are very near Temple Monkslip.
And it is true, villages with the word 'Temple' in them have some sort of
historical association with the Knights Templar. However, there we reach
the end of what we can say with certainty about the relationship. That
didn't stop the author from writing the most appalling nonsense, and
making the most outlandish leaps of logic."

"No," said Max, who felt who knew this particular author intimately. "No, that wouldn't stop Frank Cuthbert."

"That was his name! So you know him?"

"Yes, I know him rather well. He and his wife live in my village, you see. His wife, quite a practical soul, runs a shop selling French food and wine and other imported items. Frank—well, Frank writes. As you know."

"Is that what you call it? Well, I mean no disrespect, but if he would like to verify his facts he need only come and see me. One way and another I know quite a lot about the history of this area."

Somehow Max didn't feel Frank would want to be encumbered by more veracity than was absolutely necessary.

"So, what do you think *is* fact, Dame Sibil?"

"Well, there's the rub, isn't it? With the Templars and the Holy Grail and all, we have a story so treasured and so often repeated round the English hearth, we may never know on what truth the story is based."

"Fiction does have a way of hardening into fact."

"The history of the Templars—well, it's like an Aesop fable or a fairy tale. A tale for children. And have you ever noticed that children will insist on the same story being told in *exactly* the same way each time? My nieces and nephews used to reprimand me quite sternly if I deviated from the received text of *Goodnight Moon* or *Runaway Bunny*. 'No, no!' They would say. 'It's a *young* mouse, not a *little* mouse.' And they would make me start over reading from the beginning. Children, like adults, are *quite* particular about their stories. Also, children are quite clever—they will do anything to avoid having to go to sleep."

There was a wistful look in her large eyes as she said this. He imagined she didn't see these youngsters often, if at all, since entering the convent.

"So it is with legends of the Templars, and the Holy Grail, and King Arthur—all those stories," said Dame Sibil. "If a tale is told in the same way often enough through the centuries, it must therefore be true. Anyway, when it comes to the Holy Grail, those who believe that Christ rose from the dead have a much simpler time accepting that there would be miraculous and verifiable evidence of his resurrection. Quite obviously, belief is a precondition."

"You say verifiable evidence."

"Of course. Science and religion are headed toward a meeting place. Any day now, miracles will be confirmed scientifically. Absolutely, I believe that."

"And not that science will disprove the miracles?"

That earned him a "What kind of priest are you?" look.

But she simply said, "How could they disprove a truth, Father?"

He was just asking her if she had noticed anything unusual the night of Lord Lislelivet's death when a bell rang from somewhere deep inside the cloister. With a nod in his direction she stood and walked past him, called to her choir stall in the church.

The look of relief on her face at getting out of the conversation was unmistakable.

Max followed her out, left with the certain feeling that the interruption by the bell had been welcome and that she knew more about the goings on at Monkbury Abbey than she let on.

And that not all of what she knew was a children's tale.

Chapter 31

IN OLDEN DAYS II

It is as valuable to read uplifting topics as it is to pray. Both honor the Creator.

—*The Rule of the Order of the Handmaids of St. Lucy*

Returning to his room, Max opened the copy of Frank's book that Dame Olive had so grudgingly provided him, noting that the copy was well-worn. Also that it fell open to the passages regarding Monkbury Abbey and Temple Monkslip.

The book was, as Max remembered it, the most exasperating blend of boy's adventure fantasy and utter hogwash passing as reasoned scientific inquiry. No legend or rumor was too small not to be breathlessly repeated as established fact or extrapolated into certainty by recourse to the "research" of delusional and ill-informed "experts" who seemed to live and work somewhere on Planet Mars.

Frank's literary influences were difficult to pinpoint. Lewis Carroll meets Tolkien in *The Crystal Cave*? Max took a moment to admire Frank's photo on the back of the book, in which the author was portrayed, one arm draped over a tree branch and his eyes gazing heavenward, as if it were from there alone he drew his inspiration.

As Max began to read he wondered if there were any way to actively prevent Frank from writing any more books. He didn't suppose hiding his pens and pencils would help. When last seen, Frank had upgraded to a very thin, very expensive laptop, which he worked on at the Witches Brew coffee shop, ostentatiously channeling Ernest Hemingway or another of the Great Authors.

Flipping through the pages (and there were many), Max was reminded how right his first impressions of the book had been. It was the strangest mash-up of Mary Stewart and Thomas Mallory. Like Awena, Max loved the Arthurian legends and held them to be somewhat sacrosanct, perhaps because his mother's people came from the region of Cornwall near Tintagel where Arthur was said to have been born.

Was said. Now he sounded like Frank, spouting wishful beliefs, sprouting whispy tendrils of history.

Max continued reading. He had brought a cup of coffee with him from the guesthouse kitchen, and it rested on the small desk, near his pen and notebook. Max grew fascinated despite himself as Frank's narrative made one of its dog-legged leaps of logic from Arthurian legend to speculation about the real, hidden purpose of the Templars, centuries later.

At one point Frank's story digressed into a discussion of a comparatively recent find, during World War II, at nearby Templecombe in Somerset. Known as the Templecombe Face, it was a painted depiction on oaken wood of a Christ-like visage, originally done in bright blues and reds, the head surrounded by golden stars. The painting had been deliberately concealed in, of all places, an outhouse—tied into the roof by wire and hidden by plaster. Hidden from whom and when and for what reason was not clear. Scientific analysis of the wood showed that it could be dated to the years when the Templars roamed the earth.

Leaving that topic for the moment, author Frank jumped back to the Holy Grail. Could this, he breathlessly asked the reader, be the sought-after Grail itself, an image of the living Christ's face?—thereby ignoring his own report that the image probably dated from the late thirteenth century.

From here Frank led the reader to Glastonbury—and why not? There were few spots in England as shrouded in legend, and much of the legend did have to do with King Arthur and his queen, Guinevere. Glastonbury Tor, near Glastonbury Abbey, Frank asserted without hesitation or a shred of proof, was the site where the Holy Grail, a bejeweled drinking chalice in this telling, had been buried. Along with many others, Frank held that the chalice originally had been carried to Britain by Joseph of Arimathea—and that it was the chalice used at the Last Supper.

Max had visited much of the world but generally had been assisted by the vast technology it now took to move one human from one end of the globe to the other. He marveled still to think of the wide-ranging travels of the largely underfunded apostles: James to Egypt, Thomas to India, Andrew clear up to Russia. He was also inclined toward the school of belief that Jesus had traveled widely during his "lost years." The ancients were anything but stay-at-homes. So to Max the idea of Joseph of Arimathea's traveling to England was anything but outlandish. What or whom he brought with him, who could say?

But Frank stated categorically that Joseph had come to Glastonbury carrying with him the chalice that had ended up (leaping a few more centuries) in the care of the monks at Glastonbury. It had disappeared at the time of the dissolution of the monasteries, along with anything else that could be melted down after first being stripped of its valuable stones, when Thomas Cromwell had sent men to denude the church at Glastonbury. The abbot had been hanged, drawn, and quartered as a traitor.

Frank also held, on no basis whatsoever, that in addition to the chalice the monks had been in charge of the Shroud of Turin—that this relict, much more so than the chalice, had been the reason for the abbot's fatal resistance to the plundering by Henry's men.

Hurtling across continents and centuries, Frank declared that until it was finally whisked to safety, the Shroud of Turin had found a home not in Italy but in England.

Finally bringing Monkbury Abbey into the tale, Frank stated without equivocation that "sources in the know" had assured him an exact copy of a contemporaneous image of Christ in death was in the care of the Order of the Handmaids of St. Lucy. An order whose sole purpose was "to keep the secret of their Sacred Charge until it was safe to reveal it to a desperate world of non-believers" (*Wherefore Nether Monkslip*, Third Edition, p. 546).

In Frank's telling, the Knights Templar, frequent visitors to the abbey, had been in on the secret. When they were persecuted out of existence, one of them had escaped with the Shroud to Turin. The escaping knight had left behind a copy of the Face, as it was called, which had become such a draw for pilgrims that the abbey would have been financially ruined had the running knight taken it with him.

At least Frank had explained, to his own satisfaction, the odd name of the inn at Temple Monkslip.

With the dissolution of the monasteries, the Face disappeared for good. But Author Frank maintained that to this day the nuns knew exactly where it was. And as part of their initiation ceremony, they vowed never to reveal the secret.

Shades of the Masonic rites, thought Max. The story had everything but sacred oaths written in blood. It was all very "made for Hollywood," and Max was certain it would end up there.

He read grimly on, skipping back and forth between the pages, as it seemed to make no difference where one alighted in Frank's narrative. "Rumors have abounded for years," he read, "that in or around Temple Monkslip could be found a relic related to the famous Turin Shroud—a relic long held to have miraculous curative powers, particularly the power of restoring sight. Pilgrims were said to have traveled from all over Europe to be cured by the famous relict.

"But the Face disappeared around the time of the Reformation, denounced as a fraud, as the worst sort of emblem of a corrupt Papacy. A swindle designed to separate the gullible from their coins. Of course, the fact that these coins went into Church coffers, and not into the coffers of the State, did not go unnoticed by the cash-strapped secular authorities of the time."

Max sat back at his desk, the small chair creaking as he resettled his weight, recalling what he knew as fact about the Crusades.

The First Crusade had been launched in 1095, when Pope Urban II put out the call. If you had no aptitude for the monastic life but were trained in warfare, here was your action-hero alternative. You could be a holy Christian warrior, your killing sanctioned and your bravery rewarded in heaven. Judging by today's headlines, thought Max, it was a case of everything old being new again. He thought of the League of the Righteous and their lethal agenda, so recently in the news.

And so the Crusaders had swarmed toward Jerusalem, where their erratic behavior had spawned conspiracy theories ever since. It was said—and there were a lot of "it was saids" in the retelling, Frank's and others'—that the Knights Templar took the opportunity to seize the folded burial shroud of Christ and carry it off with them during the chaos of the sack of Constantinople in 1204. And that they then had proceeded to worship this most holy of holy relics.

This worship had brought about their ruin—to be precise, it became the pretext for bringing about their ruin, used to justify their roundup and extermination.

The Templars were accused of, among other things, worshipping a head. It had been speculated that the "head" they worshipped was actually a face—the part of the cloth that showed when the burial shroud of Jesus was folded into a square.

Claims and counterclaims swirled about the famous Shroud of Turin, of course. What was convincing to many was the realism of the image—no early medieval artist painted in such a precise and realistic way. They simply didn't know how. Nor was any medieval artist acquainted with photographic images—for the body image on the cloth is undoubtedly a photographic negative, or a rendering of one. The cloth had been variously dated, with some claiming that parts of it dated to the time of Jesus's life.

The Templecombe Face, however, was of a different order. The painted face on wood, found hidden in an outhouse. Roughly if reverently drawn, amateurish. Was it a copy? Perhaps a copy made from memory?

Which begged the question, copy of what?

The bearded Face in St. Mary's Church in Templecombe, no great distance from the nunnery where Max sat now, was thought by some to be a poor copy of what the Templars had worshipped. For that matter, the image in Templecombe with its bearded man bore some resemblance to . . .

No, no, no. It couldn't be. Max had not admitted the connection before now, but the image that kept appearing on the wall of St. Edwold's Church, despite repeated whitewashings, bore a strong resemblance to the . . .

No. Max shook his head. It could not be. It was the stuff of legends, distorted by retelling after retelling through the ages. The stuff that amateur historians and nincompoops like Frank Cuthbert wrote about, embroidering the few facts into fanciful fiction presented as history. No one took any of Frank's nonsense seriously. No one.

Besides, Max thought, somewhat irrelevantly: the face on the wall at St. Edwold's realistically depicted a bearded man with his eyes closed. The amateurish Templecombe painting was of a man with his eyes open.

What connection could there possibly be?

Maybe, thought Max, it was time to join the others in the treasure hunt. And the church seemed the best place to start.

Chapter 32

SPIRAL

Look always for the miracle in small things.

—*The Rule of the Order of the Handmaids of St. Lucy*

Light filtered by stained glass threw abstract rainbow stripes down the crisp linen of the altar cloth before fanning out across the pitted stone floor. Max was reminded of his own St. Edwold's where the scene, on a doll's-house scale, would be similar at this time of day. Radiant, like a rare jewel, "like jasper, clear as crystal" with the glory of God.

The church cat, Luther, oblivious to all the glory, would be napping on the altar right about now, a habit of which no amount of scolding could cure him.

Max glanced at his watch. The St. Edwold's choir would be assembling soon for tryouts for the fall services. He decided now to just let anyone who wanted to, participate. What earthly difference did it make? Maybe they'd all improve with practice.

This coming Sunday, when please God he would be back standing in the pulpit in his church, little Tom Hooser would perch on the pew back until his sister Tildy Ann yanked him back into his seat. Their mother, Mrs. Hooser, would remain oblivious. Max often wondered what went on behind the bland mask she presented to the world. Judging by the results of her housekeeping efforts at the vicarage, she might be entertaining scenes of plunder and destruction, but more likely she was wondering if she'd left the Fairy washing-up liquid in the refrigerator again. Max was always finding misfiled oddments like that around the place. It made him wonder how Mrs. Hooser got through the day-to-day, how the children were being brought up, although thus far they were showing an amazing resilience, probably in response to their mother's vagueness.

Max slumped down in one of the pews, studying the play of light on cloth and stone as it shifted with the passing clouds outside and wondering: what was there here that had drawn Lord Lislelivet? The church was beautiful, a model of construction for its time and age, but nothing here of financial value was transportable. Still Max clung to the notion that Lord Lislelivet's interest in the place was financial. No heaven-sent flash of insight, no conversion for such as Lord Lislelivet.

Max dredged his memory for the Bible passages surrounding Paul's stunning conversion on the road to Damascus. At last he took a copy of the Book of Common Prayer from the back of the pew before him and flipped through until he found the story in Acts 9:9: "And he was three dayes without sight, and neither did eate, nor drinke."

A fine and compelling conversion story it was, particularly as it came from a former professional persecutor of Christians. But it had nothing to do with this case. It was interesting, though, how many references to light there had been here in the place of women who had devoted their lives to emulating Lucy, the patron saint of the blind. Max read on to the part of the story where Paul had been cured of his blindness by a man named Ananias: "And immediatly there fell from his eyes as it had bene scales, and he receiued sight forthwith, and arose, and was baptized."

And that was Paul's story, debated to this day. He had heard the voice of Jesus and had literally been blinded by the light until Ananias had cured him. The scales had fallen from his eyes. Had Paul had a seizure, some sort of psychotic breakdown? Was he simply exhausted and delusional? Or had he been blessed by a miracle?

Whatever had happened, Paul himself had fully believed it had been miraculous, to the extent he had given up all hope of an easy life and likely had died a martyr to his new faith. He may have died in Rome during the reign of Nero—a "killer in high places" if ever there were one. As Dame Olive's Leonard Cohen put it, the world collapses,

> *"While the killers in high places*
> *say their prayers out loud."*

But not much given to prayer had Nero been.

Wishing fervently that the scales might fall from his own eyes, Max replaced the Bible and rose from the pew. He turned round. It would soon be time for the next round of prayers in the abbey's daily cycle of offices, and he wanted to take advantage of the nuns' absence to prowl around on his own. Before the light gave out.

There it was again. That drift of phrase, set to music. "How the light gets in."

How the light gets in.

Again, the line threaded its way across his mind.

The date was June 21, the day of the summer solstice.

Light and day.

To the medieval mind, there was no guarantee of sunrise, no promise the now unstinting sun would return—all that was left to God's will.

Light flooded in from the window; the sky outside was cloudless, with nothing to block the sun. Max, walking toward the choir with its cartoon-like wooden carvings of St. Lucy's life, noticed that a cushion on one of the pew-seats was askew. It was not something he would normally have noticed, except for the light aiming straight at the seat like an arrow. Bending to straighten the cushion, he saw there was a hinge in the pew. Probably extra hymnal storage, he thought. Out of curiosity he lifted the lid to peer inside.

And saw, much to his surprise, that he had exposed a spiral staircase, coiling tightly down and undoubtedly leading to the crypt beneath the church.

His eyes drifted heavenward. Really, he thought, it was as if God were up there with a pea shooter sometimes, trying to get his attention by sending little hints and bits of information for Max to stitch together. Max offered up a silent word of thanks before turning his attention to the stairs. He supposed it would be too much to ask God to just tell him who the killer was, so he set his mind to examining the find revealed by the light of the summer solstice.

He had read about a similar staircase, discovered on St. Michael's Mount, just off the coast of Cornwall. He felt the natural reluctance of the living to venture into a musty old space, intended for burials and no doubt filled with cobwebs. He thought again of the abbess's tale of the old anchorite. But he was surprised that the expected fusty smell, familiar to him from his explorations of the crypt at St. Edwold's, was not what emerged from the opening. Instead, there was the voluptuous perfume of fresh flowers, along with the same clean scent of detergent and polish that permeated the rest of the convent. There was also the scent of candles and a stronger one of recently burned incense. This was no fusty mausoleum but a recently used space. The smell of the flowers was quite powerful. He was no gardener but he thought it might be gardenia.

What on earth?

Treading carefully, he made his way down the staircase to the vaulted crypt below. All was silence. He supposed someone might be down there cleaning or organizing the sweet-smelling flowers, but the silence was complete, and nothing stirred the air to indicate human occupation.

He crept along, feeling his way. There were no handrails, and what scant light there was poured in through the open lid of the seat in the choir stall. Wall sconces that long ago would have held torches had been modified to hold candles—the source of the flickering light he'd seen through the trapdoor beneath the belfry. He saw a box of matches on a nearby ledge and used them to light one of the candles.

The steps reached a platform, where they widened into a cascading sweep of stairs to the room below. These had recently been extensively repaired or replaced—they were too new and polished to be the originals. Max was starting to see where the money from people like the Goreys, and money intended for the guesthouse, had actually been spent.

The room was framed on two sides by rows of marble-faced columns surmounted by arches supporting the floor above. Max looked at the scripture quotation from Matthew, in illuminated text over the archway nearest him:

~ If thou wilt be perfect, goe and sell that thou hast,
and giue to the poore, and thou shalt haue treasure in heauen ~

And under another archway to his right:

~ Dominus illuminatio mea ~

Max translated: The Lord is my light. It was from one of the psalms. It also happened to be the motto of the University of Oxford. He recalled that Frank's preposterous book mentioned some Oxford connection to the abbey, as had Dame Olive. Could there be nuggets of fact in Frank's fantastic tale?

And here there was yet another statue of St. Lucy. He stood looking at the painted plaster statue of the woman known as Santa Lucia in her home country. It was a depiction of a lovely young woman with curly fair hair and a faraway look in her blue eyes, a look that only the truly gifted artist could portray well. This artist had not been so blessed, but had managed nonetheless to avoid the cloying, simpering, or even demented look of most representations of saints. Max recalled now more of the detail of her legend: Lucy had indeed refused to marry a pagan man, who out of spite had turned her over to the authorities for her Christian faith. If she'd ever needed confirmation that her instincts about the guy as marriage material were correct, that had probably sealed it. She had reportedly been blinded as part of her martyrdom, and thus became the patron saint of the blind. Fortunately, the artist had chosen to forgo depicting Lucy with her eyes on a tray—a once-popular representation for an age even more ghoulish than today's.

And the quote carved under statue of St. Lucy was in English:

And Jesus said unto him, Receive thy sight, thy faith hath saved thee.

Of course, what it actually said was:

And Iesus said vnto him, Receiue thy sight, thy faith hath saued thee.

It was the King James Version of the text, and so dating after 1611. Long after the dissolution and King Henry's do-over of all things spiritual.

Another arch, another carving, all quite fresh and new, or newly refurbished:

Sanctae Luciae sanitates credentis.

St. Lucy cures the believer.

But all of this was designed to lead the eye toward the altar, behind which was a stone stairway, which from its location, Max reasoned, had to lead up to the cloistered area of Monkbury Abbey.

The crypt, which undoubtedly predated the present church, held at one end a plain altar with a simple wooden prie-dieu before it, the kneeler covered in a brightly colored needlepoint pillow. Wooden chairs were arranged in rows on either side. Enough chairs, Max gauged, for all the nuns in the small nunnery. A statue, another quite ancient representation of St. Lucy, was nearby, tucked into a side altar behind one of the vaulted arches.

This explained what the mystery person had been doing down here the day he'd had his look around the belfry. They'd been praying, or possibly the sacrist, Dame Olive, had been tidying up after a service. It was a bit unusual that in an abbey named for St. Lucy, there would be this small, hidden area of worship clearly intended in her honor. Especially since the eyesight-restoring miracle worker was well represented in the main part of the church.

But then his eye was drawn to the centerpiece of the room, the clear reason for the room's existence. It was an image in a frame, the frame suspended by a chain from the ceiling of the crypt so that it hung directly behind and above the free-standing altar.

It was a carving done in a shallow bas-relief, and it was an almost modern depiction in stone of a face. The man's eyes were closed, his face bearded. The skill of the carver allowed one to know the eyes were closed in death. The whole was set into the thick wooden frame ornamented with gold leaf and precious and semiprecious stones.

Of course, this was the treasure. Not carved in solid gold. But such men as Clement Gorey had enough gold. Clement would understand the historic value. He would also prize it for the religious value, which was incalculable.

It looked, Max realized, exactly like the face that kept reappearing on the wall of St. Edwold's. The face like that on the Shroud of Turin. The face first spotted by little Tom Hooser.

Not *almost* like. Exactly like.

And if confirmation were needed, hanging suspended by two golden chains from the bottom of the frame was a map, similarly carved in stone in bas-relief. It was a representation of the area in which he stood—that much Max could decipher, even though the names of some places were greatly altered and the topography was crude at best.

Nether Monkslip was on this map, indicated by a star.

The hair on the back of Max's neck stood on end. Nether Monkslip was miles from the Monkbury Abbey, in a part of the world dotted with dozens of little villages. Hundreds. Why would his own Nether Monkslip appear on what clearly resembled a sort of treasure map? "X" marks the spot. Or in this case, a star does. Spot for what, though?

Then he saw the labeling beneath the map that explained it all for him—or rather, added to his puzzlement.

"The Church of St. Edwold's," it read. "The Place of Miracles."

His eyes closed in somber reflection, his head bowed.

And when he opened his eyes, he saw that at the foot of the altar were traces of what looked suspiciously like blood.

Chapter 33

THE ORDERS OF
THE ABBESS

The orders of the Abbess or of those appointed to act in her stead
are to be followed without question.

—*The Rule of the Order of the Handmaids of St. Lucy*

"What exactly is going on down there in the crypt?"

Following his discovery, Max had walked straight over to the abbess's lodge. The postulant, Mary Benton, let him in, the smile disappearing from her face as she correctly read that he was in no mood to be asked to cool his heels.

As the abbess walked into the lodge's reception area, he asked the question uppermost in his mind. The blood, if it were blood, put a whole new spin on the case.

The abbess lost not one whit of her composure, but the heightened blush of her English rose complexion, darkening from pink to red, was the chink in her armor.

"You may recall, Father, that I told you the story of our nun found dead in the crypt?"

"Yes," he said shortly. "I remember you telling me a story."

"The starving nun that I told you about, who was the voluntary guardian of the crypt?"

"What precisely was she guarding?" demanded Max.

"I think you know, Father. She was guarding our greatest relic, over the centuries the source of our fame, of our prosperity. She was guarding the Face."

"Tell me," said Max. "Tell me the whole story."

"I was just having some tea, Father. Please won't you join me?"

Used to being obeyed, like a queen she swept away into the lodge's dining hall, calling an order to the waiting postulant.

"The Handmaids of St. Lucy routinely hid 'The Face,' as they called it," Abbess Justina was saying, moments later. "As we call it still."

She and Max sat at the same rough-hewn wooden table where they so recently had dined, swapping pleasantries and histories in a getting-to-know-you fashion. But Max realized that in fact, the more Abbess Justina had told him, the less she had said. The strains of the song "Smooth Operator" flitted through his mind.

"In years gone by," she continued, "the abbess and her cellaress were often the only ones who knew about the Face. Each abbess would inherit a key to unlock a casket where the Face was kept hidden, when it needed to be hidden. They were sworn never to tell anyone, under pain of expulsion. So I didn't tell DCI Cotton."

"Of course not," said Max. "Why bother the police with this."

At least she caught the sarcasm. "How could it have anything to do with murder?"

Max ignored that bit of disingenuousness for now. "They hid it whenever danger approached Monkbury Abbey, which, according to Dame Olive, it did routinely," he prompted. "Vikings, raiders, soldiers of fortune."

"Yes." She took a sip of her herbal tea, calmly setting the cup back in its saucer. It was, he noted, a cup of fine china. Chipped and well-used, to be sure, but not the common pottery the nuns used for their refectory meals. "If you want a quiet life," she added, giving him the full wattage of her charming smile, "don't ever join a monastery. It's been one thing after another here at Monkbury Abbey, through the centuries."

"With most of the commotion centered around the Face. The push and pull of commerce, for one thing," he said. "Yes, I do see."

"That's right," she said, not in the least offended. "The Face came to us in the time of the Crusades, and it saved a small struggling house, turning it into one of the magnificent showplace abbeys of its day. It was deposited here for safekeeping by a member of the Knights Templar—a son of the manor house at Nashbury Feathers."

"An ancestor of Lord Lislelivet's, then. I see. Go on." Could that be the connection? The reason for Lord Lislelivet's interest in the place? He might have viewed it as his property—even have sought to lay claim to it.

"It seldom was kept on open display," she went on. "Even though it was known to have miraculous healing properties. That would have been far too dangerous. Crowd control was the biggest job of Dame Sacrist at one time. Only the prescreened were allowed to see it. Security reasons, of course."

"Of course." Only the wealthy would have been given access—never the rabble. It made a certain sense, but only if one believed the wealthy were honest and the poor dishonest. Or that only the rich required miracle cures. Still, there had been riots throughout the ages when rumors got started of a miraculous site or relic—a finger bone that cured cancer, a rib that cured gout, a scrap of cloth that aided women in childbirth.

"According to the archives, the leper chapel is where they hid the Face most often," she told him. "Knowing no one would have the courage to go near such a place. The nuns were inured to dealing with the sorriest of the sore-afflicted, men and women both—to comforting those without hope. Leprosy is not highly contagious, but no one knew that then, and the women who volunteered for this service were heroines, pure and simple. Saints, they were. It was rumored to be haunted, that sad little chapel where lepers would drag themselves to pray. The nuns repeated the ghost rumors to keep people out, to keep them from searching.

"Anyway, once the danger had passed—whatever that danger was: fire, earthquake, marauders, Vikings, Normans, busybody pilgrims, thieves—the nuns would move the Face to the church, where it long remained an object of veneration."

"Until it disappeared for good. Or so people thought."

She nodded. "More tea, Father? No?" She settled back in her chair. "No doubt Dame Olive mentioned the fire to you. The Great Fire, as it came to be known, for there were many such disasters in the years when fire was in constant use for cooking and warmth.

"During the Great Fire, the Face was rescued and the nuns, now realizing the danger, realizing what had nearly been lost, decided a permanent place had to be found for it. There was little sense of fire-proofing in those days but they did understand metal and stone had a better chance of survival.

"Of course, this was early days, and they couldn't foresee the wholesale destruction to be wrought by Henry the Eighth on the monasteries, but they had had the not dissimilar experience of Viking raids. And so they built a special hiding place for it, in the crypt. The abbey was prosperous enough that routine visits by pilgrims were no longer encouraged or needed. They might bring it out when funds were needed, put it on display for a time."

"Like a special exhibit of a Michelangelo or a da Vinci at an art gallery. Understood. Then following the recent earthquake . . ." began Max.

"Yes. Following the earthquake. The earthquake brings us up almost to the present day in our history. Until then it had all been long forgotten or passed off as legend. Lost to history. The written sources as to its existence were cryptic, to say the least—please forgive the pun. And then of course there was no nunnery here at all for decade after decade. Just a pile of stones, the beating heart of the place gone when the women were driven underground—temporarily."

"The earthquake revealed the bones of the anchoress."

"That is correct. A crack opened up in the floor of the church. We got out an electric torch and peered inside. Some of the wall down there had collapsed, probably ages ago. We saw her bones, first."

"And the earthquake, it also revealed the Face that she was guarding."

"That also is correct."

That's how the light gets in.

"And the funds for the new guesthouse got diverted to repair the crypt. Actually, from what I saw, it was more than repair work and shoring up. There's been extensive decorating and enhancement to the crypt, to create a setting for the Face."

The English rose complexion kicked up a notch. At least she had the grace to look abashed, if momentarily.

"None of the money went missing," she told him. "It's all there. Just . . . redistributed a bit."

"False pretenses," he said.

"No. There were no false pretenses. The fund-raising was officially to benefit the abbey. Full stop. But speaking of fund-raising, according to the cellaress, it appears likely that not all the money intended for us actually reached us. Palmona Green could tell you more about that. I'll say no more."

She was a born politician, all right. When all else fails, point the finger of blame. "Abbess Justina, how many people knew about this? About the crypt?" He just missed saying, "The Secret of the Crypt," which if it were not the title of a Hardy Boy's or Nancy Drew mystery, should have been. Frank could use it as a title in an expanded and revised version of *Wherefore Nether Monkslip*. There was sure to be one, once word of this got out.

"Apart from my sisters, you mean? My nuns?"

So they all knew, the nuns. And no doubt were sworn to secrecy. An oath of loyalty, probably sworn when they took their final vows. He should have known.

. . . how the light gets in . . .

"And who else?" he demanded. "Who else knows about the crypt?"

"Father Tudor, that is of course *precisely* what I have been asking myself all this time."

Chapter 34
ALL THE KING'S HORSES

It is written, that our treasure is to be found in heaven, where thieves cannot break through to steal. Remember: *"Ye cannot serve God and mammon."*

—*The Rule of the Order of the Handmaids of St. Lucy*

Max found Cotton helping supervise a team near the well in the cloister garden. One of the SOCO people, a woman of perhaps sixty with a halo of dandelion hair, was kneeling a few feet from the well, scrutinizing something that had caught her eye. She took a photo and then, using tweezers, extracted whatever it was—perhaps a thread?—from a blade of grass, sealing it in a bag. The sight of the small metal pinchers in her hand sent a little ping of recognition through Max's memory, one of those sudden bulletins the brain issues without reason or further explanation, and Max could not for the moment imagine the relevance. He continued to watch the woman for a moment and she looked up, giving him a small wave of recognition, for Max Tudor was becoming a familiar sight on these occasions of mayhem. Max returned the wave and went to tell Cotton his tale of the crypt, including the stain he thought might be blood. Cotton's team now had a whole new area to search.

Max explained where the entrance could be found in the choir. "The crypt technically is part of the church," he told Cotton, "not the cloistered

302 G. M. MALLIET

nun's area, so I think you needn't worry too much about inconveniencing anyone. Although it is evident the crypt connects directly to the cloistered area, via yet another stairway behind the altar down there. The entrance at the bell tower is probably sealed from within the crypt: I'm not sure about that. But it is clear that entrance hasn't been used in ages."

"And Abbes Justina said nothing of this to us. Which makes me think their little conspiracy of silence spreads even further up the ladder."

Max shook his head firmly. "The bishop knew nothing of this. Of that I am certain. The abbess admitted that she 'took full responsibility' for diverting the funds that were to go to build the guesthouse, using them instead not just to make repairs caused by the earthquake—an understandable emergency, after all—but to enhance the crypt itself. To make a fitting setting for the precious icon that the earthquake had uncovered.

"The abbess further told me that after the bishop announced his impending visitation to Monkbury, she called the sisters together and basically said that the matter was an internal one that he need not be bothered with. Remember, her word is law. She was buying time. Revealing the existence of the Face would unleash a deluge of publicity. Dame Sibil, now the cellaress, was all in favor of the publicity, and she had her supporters in that. Dame Meredith, cellaress at the time of this discovery, was opposed, by the way. She thought the place would become another EuroDisney, and many agreed with her. They came here, you have to remember, to escape the preoccupations of the world outside. Anyway, Abbess Justina became concerned that if the bishop knew, the decision would be taken out of her hands, and she did not want that. So she swore the others to secrecy about the find. As happened at Legbourne."

"Legbourne?"

"Yes. A famous old monastery where things similarly were hidden from the higher-ups and handled internally. Sexual transgressions, most likely. The reasoning went: how much better to fix the problem at a lower level than to kick it upstairs, where the reputation of the entire place might be put at risk once the scandal became common knowledge. It was thought to be a little local matter, and thus it should remain. The fear was that the establishment might even be closed if the transgressions reported were serious enough.

"That wasn't going to happen here—it wasn't as if someone was going to accuse the nuns of idol worship or something like that. No, the concern they had, Abbess Justina in particular, was of losing financial control—the hard-won financial say over how Monkbury Abbey was run. It was a power struggle, really. The nuns have done exceedingly well for themselves without the need to be supervised and told what to do by the bishop. This particular bishop, by the way, seems to have been respectful of their autonomy. He's been very hands-off in dealing with them, he told me, only occasionally becoming alarmed by their hewing so closely to tradition. Although once he hears of this . . ."

"He will lower the boom?"

"Probably. He won't be happy, that's for certain, and no doubt he will be paying much closer attention to everything they get up to from now on." A fleeting image of his upcoming union with a very pregnant Awena Owen flitted through Max's mind, a celebration of which the bishop, of course, remained blissfully unaware. It was an exaggeratedly bacchanalian image that came into Max's mind, and one quickly banished: he would have to worry about that when—if—this case was solved. Which might put the bishop in a better mood.

Although a still-breathing Lord Lislelivet might have kept him in a better mood.

"The problem is, and the abbess knows this well, keeping such a find secret from the bishop was wrong of her. Diverting funds that had been raised for one purpose—to build a new guesthouse—to this new 'secret' project made it doubly wrong. She claims, quite insincerely, that the money is not exactly missing. It's just that there will be 'a little delay' in breaking new ground on the guesthouse."

"I take it that means she floated cash toward the crypt repairs and was hoping to cover the difference via one of the abbey's different income-producing streams."

"Right. Her behavior was unprofessional, to say the least. Faithless or disloyal, as the bishop will see it: so much for vows of obedience. It is very possible he will remove her from her post and initiate proceedings for the election of a new abbess."

"And so much for avoiding scandal."

"Yes, between the murder and the out-of-control abbess, I'd say the bishop's equanimity will be completely shattered this week."

Max sighed. Probably not the best time to invite him to the hand-fasting ceremony.

Max was struck by a sudden, visceral longing to be standing in the garden of his lopsided little vicarage or sitting at his desk before the window, working on his sermon, his dog, Thea, at his side or asleep before the hearth.

He missed it. He missed everything about St. Edwold's. He missed going for a stroll and a morning coffee in Elka Garth's Cavalier Tea Room. He missed the church mouser, Luther, with his preternatural stare. He missed two-year-old Amy McIntosh, who if you took your eyes off her for a moment would draw on the pew seats with her crayons. He missed the church's dour, ghoulish sexton, with his thundering proclamations of impending doom. In a clear sign of his distraction, he even missed the tryouts for the choir rehearsals and the caterwauling shrieks that generally made the hair on the back of his neck stand on end.

Most of all he didn't see how he'd get through the next twenty-four hours without seeing Awena. What if something went wrong with her or the baby, and they both needed him? God forbid it. He didn't dare dwell on it . . .

"So," said Max, bringing his attention back to the crime he was anxious to solve quickly. "We find still more layers to this case. I have to wonder whether Lord Lislelivet used his aunt, Dame Meredith, as an excuse to visit or if she was the *reason* for his sudden visits."

"You think he was trying to cajole the information out of her?"

"Cajole or pressure it out of her. She once had been the cellaress, a person in the know. Would you be surprised to hear he applied some pressure? Even as ill as she was?"

He and Cotton agreed to meet in one hour. Max wanted a moment to clear his head, and think through what he knew of the case and the suspects. He set off for the stone bench he had seen along the side of the hill, overlooking the river. On his way he passed Dame Hephzibah, who seemed to be trying to avoid him, although she moved so slowly it was a near impossibility. He pretended not to see her, not wanting to add to her distress. This whole mess was surely not how she planned to live out her golden years, the only home she knew being overrun by the authorities, everything turned over, her routine disrupted as suspicion spread through the monastery hallways like a vine growing in time-lapse photography.

Dame Petronilla emerged from the infirmary. She was talking with the postulant, Mary Benton, both of them looking perturbed.

He hung back in the shadows, unseen by either of them, and unabashedly listened in to the conversation.

"How many times?" Dame Petronilla was saying. "You are *never* to leave her side."

The beautifully arched eyebrows over the dark eyes pulled into a frown. "But she told me it was all right," said Mary.

"I know some days it seems as if she is on the mend, but she's not as strong as she thinks she is. Letting her do what she wants will tax her strength, strength she does not really have. The doctor was very clear on this. And lights out means lights out, by the way. She—Oh, there you are, Father," said Dame Petronilla brightly. "Dame Meredith is asking if she can see you later today."

"I'll make a point of it."

"Please get back to your work," Dame Petronilla said to the postulant, who quickly scuttled off to the infirmary. Max stood back to let her pass. He was still keeping an eye on Dame Hephzibah as she walked toward the gatehouse. He waited until she was out of earshot before he spoke. Even though she was deaf, so that "out of earshot" was quite a relative concept, it was a very long time before Dame Hephzibah had hobbled her way out of what he judged to be hearing range.

"How old is she?" Max asked.

Dame Petronilla looked startled. "Do you know, I'm not quite certain. She's simply always been here, like the stone carvings. May we expect you in the infirmary around four, then, Father?"

The bell rang for prayer. Immediately she left without waiting for his answer.

Max came to the bench carved into the side of the hill, its center worn by the posteriors of who knew how many generations of nuns and visitors to the nunnery. The bench was in the shade of an overhanging tree, and today afforded a splendid view over the scurrying river below, the fields beyond, and the distant hills. The outline of another tor, its ancient purpose unknown, could clearly be seen as the sun drew shadows on the hill, highlighting concentric terraces.

He could hear the sound of bleating sheep coming from the pasture, acting as a counterpoint to the chanting of the nuns, the sweet sounds mingling as they were carried faintly to him on a breeze. Both songs were mournful today, strident and anxious. What was known was changing. What the future held was unknowable. He thought sadly of the rubble that was all that was left of Nether Monkslip's own abbey. Of how nearly Monkbury Abbey had missed the same fate. Noah of Noah's Ark Antiques lived now in the only building that had been spared, the abbot's lodge. Noah had turned it into a showcase.

Everything changing, and the future unknowable. The folly of man was in thinking he could know the future, could account for every unforeseen event, never taking the cataclysmic into account.

Max reviewed what he'd learned, turning it over in his mind, deciding how best to approach the matter, knowing what he now knew. For there was no question that he had been dealing with two different-colored threads here. The treasure in the crypt: the nun's secret. The attempted poisoning and now death of Lord Lislelivet.

Surely the two things were connected. Surely?

For sure.

His eyes rested on the tor in the distance. Just visible along the top were the faint edges of the ruins of a monastery, twin to the nunnery. Tors were an early example of public works projects: the ancients seemed to like hauling earth and stone about. Probably the tor he now sat atop was a burial mound for some forgotten king or wealthy family. The secrets of all these places in England—archeologists were just now scratching the surface, literally, of what the ancients had left behind. The nunnery was not far away from the Cerne Abbas Giant, a hillside chalk drawing of a naked man, another mystifying project of the always-busy ancients. Was it their idea of a joke—a sort of early graffiti? A fertility symbol? A marker for something or someone buried beneath?

The black and white sheep, as if in some unspoken agreement, began to shamble in his direction. Max thought again of the ewe who had taken on another's lamb as her own. He smiled at the recollection, then paused. His mind struggled to make a connection—his mind leaping from Cerne Abbas to the lost little sheep. Sheep, lambs—black and white. Nuns . . . robed in black and white. Except the nuns of Monkbury had added the splash of purple to their ensemble.

Cerne Abbas.

What? It was something the novice had told him, that sad story of the lamb's panic.

He sat quietly, trying to still his mind. Awena was of course a devotee of meditation, of cultivating, as it were, the art of doing nothing. He supposed it was a matter of finding that "thin place" she had described. It seemed to him it was all another name for what he had done all his life: when he couldn't see the solution, he would sometimes put it aside, sleep on it, or work on something mindless and repetitive, as removed from thought as he could get. Let his unconscious mind reveal the connections his racing mind could not stop to see.

But his mind would not cooperate. His eyes, refusing to stay shut, roved across the faces of the black-faced sheep, and his mind was soon making a game out of noticing their differences. They had ceased their desperate baa-ing for the most part, and having determined that Max was neither a source of food nor entertainment, they drifted to the further end of the field.

Max stood and stretched. It would soon be time for his meeting with Cotton. As he walked back up the hill and past the small forest glen, he saw the novice, Rose Tocketts, in the herb garden, near the rows of berry bushes. She was humming a tune as she worked—a chant he recognized from one of the Divine Offices. She looked up as he approached.

She stood and wiping her gloved hands said, "Well, I guess this is providential. I was wondering whether to tell you. And here you are."

She reached in one of the deep pockets of her skirts and pulled out an object. The keen young eyes in the square face looked at him apprehensively.

"What do you make of this, Father?"

A few minutes later, Max sat beside her on a wooden bench that ran along one side of the tool shed in the garden.

"It is my turn this week to act as chambress," she said, pulling off her canvas garden gloves to reveal tanned, work-hardened hands. "To some degree we have all taken over the function of the chambress, a full-time position which has been eliminated until the number of new recruits to the abbey increases. Which may, of course, be never. The nuns take turns, under the loose supervision of the cellaress, in taking care of the nuns' cells. Beyond simple day-to-day making of the beds and so on, each sister is responsible for daily maintenance of her own room—and the guest-mistress is responsible for taking care of the guest rooms."

She hesitated, until he said, "Go on."

"You see, it's just that . . . more and more, the nuns have to take care of their own things, as I say. But there are certain items of clothing that are collected by whoever is acting as chambress. Aprons, things like that. It makes much more sense to just chuck them all together and wash them as one batch."

"Okay. And you found this in an apron?"

"In a pocket. It's a lucky thing I search the pockets or we'd have had smelly wash water staining everything."

Max leaned toward her. Because this was of course the crux of the matter.

"Is there any way to tell whose apron it was?"

"Not really. They are one-size-fits-all things, and they tend to get used by whomever. It is forbidden to start thinking of any object as 'mine,' anyway. We own nothing. That's the deal. It is never 'my' apron or 'her' apron but an apron belong to the nunnery."

"So it is difficult to say who was wearing it last?

"That's right." She was wringing the garden gloves in her hands, twisting them back and forth. This was as far from the sturdy, practical young woman he had met previously as could be. She was frightened, agitated. "I shouldn't be telling you this," she said. "I should have cleared it with the abbess."

"But you didn't." He looked at the object she had found, which he held in the palm of his hand. It was a cigarette butt, a filtered iteration of a popular brand. "Where did you find the apron?"

"Hanging on a peg with several others. There is a hallway just outside the infirmary."

Meaning, someone who was not a nun had found their way into the cloistered area beyond the infirmary. Unless he was to believe one of the sisters had taken up smoking? Not entirely impossible, he guessed, although it begged the question of from where she had got hold of the packet of cigarettes. He played out the different scenarios in his mind. Someone offering a nun a cigarette? A nun walking into a shop and buying a packet? It was nonsense. Much more likely that someone had gained access to the cloister from outside. And that would be one of the guests in the guesthouse, none of whom he had seen holding a cigarette.

That didn't mean none of them did. It only meant he hadn't seen them doing it.

And of course there was Xanda, with the habit he'd encouraged her to quit.

It was weird. Definitely, it was weird.

"Why *didn't* you ask the abbess about this?" he asked. Her face flushed a bright red, and he had his answer. "You were not sure who to trust in the abbey, not anymore, were you? Even Abbess Justina."

"Yes!" she cried out, in what was nearly a wail. "And I'm sure it's too wrong of me to be thinking that way. The abbess, after all! But I don't know what to think any more—what to think, or who to believe. I've just been dithering, back and forth—what to do? And since you came here 'new,' so to speak, and couldn't have had anything to do with these goings on, it just seemed best to talk to someone about it who was completely neutral. You do see?"

"Of course I do. Calm yourself, Sister Rose. I think you acted quite correctly, under what are unusual circumstances." Given the parameters under which she lived, her every waking moment mapped out by one rule or another, Max thought it little short of a miracle that she retained the ability to think for herself, listening to her own instincts. How many others in the monastery would have done the same, thoroughly indoctrinated as they were after following the Rule for years?

Max looked at the cigarette butt. In and of itself, it didn't mean a lot. And there was also the possibility it had found its way into the pocket by innocent means. That someone had handed it to a sister, and she had pocketed it. That she had found it lying about, and picked it up.

Or even, that someone had planted it in the pocket to incriminate, thought Max. A much darker and more sinister explanation, that. The thought of a betrayer dwelling among these innocents was disturbing.

"Thank you, Sister Rose," he said. "You were right to tell me."

"There's more, though! The night of the murder, I had the night watch. To wake the others for prayer, you know. I went for a walk by myself, trying to stay awake—I'd fallen asleep earlier and was terrified of doing it again. And I saw someone running. A nun. Running through the cloister garden."

"And? Yes?"

"We don't run. We're forbidden to run."

"I see." And Max did begin to see. "Running away from the well?"

She nodded. "And there was one other occasion. It was just odd, that time . . . outside the church. *Out*side."

"What?"

Reluctantly she told him, adding, "I must tell the abbess all this."

"I would much rather you didn't."

He got a look much like the look Eve might have given the devil as he held out a delicious red apple for her inspection. Tempting as it was, Eve just wasn't *quite* sure . . .

"You obviously don't understand," she said at last. "I'm on probation here, and I'm the worst case they've seen in years. Well, me, and maybe one other. But I'm nearly always the last to get to the choir for the canonical hours. I'm nearly always late to chapter meetings. I burned the bread the other day—three entire loaves." Her lip trembled. "I've been punished for these things, countless times. And still I screw up."

"Punished how?"

She bent her head and shrugged, not able to look at him. "Made to eat my meals alone. Excluded from sitting in the warming room as the others sit having their tea and embroidering. That sort of thing." She hesitated, murmuring: "It gets lonely. But the more I try to do better, the worse I seem to get."

Today we would call it bullying, he thought. Cutting someone out of the herd—in this case, to "correct" their misbehavior. But whatever the reason, the end result was to make a person feel small, and isolated, and alone. It was a glimpse into the way of life he had not really seen before and did not much like.

What would Jesus do? Certainly not this.

"I must tell." She rose and started to walk away from him. But turning, she added, "Tomorrow morning, in chapter. I must tell. It would be a serious fault to hide this from the abbess or my sisters. Good day, Father. I hope you catch whoever did this."

He felt as if he had been given a deadline.

But sometimes, he realized, a deadline, inexorably closing in, focuses the mind in a wonderful way.

He rose and walked back to the guesthouse, now late for his meeting with Cotton. But the delay had been worth it.

"Among the last things you'd expect to find in a nunnery, isn't it?"

Max sat with Cotton in the guesthouse's living area, case notes spread before them on a low coffee table. They were alone, the guests having been banished to the kitchen. Max had made one further stop on the way, to look in on Dame Meredith.

He had handed the cigarette end over to Cotton.

"That or a spliff," Cotton had replied.

"Xanda smokes," Max told him. "For what it's worth, so does Lady Lislelivet."

"Forensics should be able to help with a DNA analysis," Cotton said, before sending it off with one of his constables for examination.

They sat now, looking at the forensic evidence to date.

"Whoever it was left no traces," Cotton was saying. "Probably wore gloves. Although with this type of killing—no knife or weapon—traces are thin on the ground. There were signs of a scuffle at the top of the stairs leading from the cloistered area to the crypt. We may get something there, but we expect to find the victim's traces, not the killer's. The doorway to the stairs is hidden, by the way, in the back of a utility closet. No one was meant to find that crypt in the normal way of things."

"Rather interesting, that." He paused, and Cotton waited in hope that Max would tell him what he found so interesting about it. But he waited in vain.

"Do you remember the timetable I drew up?" Max asked him. "I've made a few additions and changes that I think may interest you."

Cotton took the sheet of paper. He studied it for a long while, his eyebrows inching up and up as he read. He handed it back.

"That *is* interesting," he said. "One for the books, in fact. But—you're sure?"

"Quite. It's the only thing that makes sense."

"I must say, your powers of deduction are remarkable."

"Undoubtedly," said Max, smiling. "It also helps that I have a signed confession."

"A confession to the murder?"

"Not that. That would be too much to hope for. But I do know the motive."

Cotton stared at him.

"I think we will have to be content with that and deduce the rest," said Max.

"I don't suppose you could give me a hint?"

"I can give you several," replied Max evenly. "One question I began to ask myself was why such an obscure place as Monkbury Abbey attracted so many rich donors. There are many worthy causes fighting over a dwindling number of dollars and pounds sterling, and yet two rich Americans and a wealthy lord swan in and start writing cheques the moment it is announced funds are needed for an extension to the guesthouse. They start staying in the existing guesthouse—which everyone agrees is completely out of character in the case of Lord Lislelivet. One could argue the nuns are a worthy and attractive cause, yes. And the guesthouse needed work, yes. But was there an additional reason? A motivating factor—a factor especially motivating for people both of a religious persuasion and with a keen sense of how to exploit an opportunity?

"We know these people had caught wind of the rumors swirling around the place—the ludicrous rumors reignited by the sudden popularity of an obscure book by an even more obscure man named Frank Cuthbert of Nether Monkslip. But these were hardheaded people of business and sound financial judgment, both the Goreys and Lord Lislelivet. They were not the types to throw a lot of money around based on mawkish sentiment. No, they would want—what? A payoff. Proof.

"But proof of what, I wondered?

"And then, in doing a little quiet snooping about, I found in the crypt the very thing that had drawn them to this place.

"I found The Face.

"So, while the wealthy donors at first were—and continued to pretend to be—bent out of shape over the disappearance of their money, they were in fact on a treasure hunt. Somehow they learned what the earthquake had revealed—probably workmen in the village, while sworn to secrecy, had been unable to resist claiming that *they* had seen proof of what that crackpot book was claiming. The abbess should have known it was human nature not to be able to keep this 'knowledge,' this wild speculation, quiet for long.

"I think that when Lord Lislelivet stayed at the inn in Temple Monkslip, he heard something. The place was the hub of village life, as such places are. And what were the chances some of the same workmen who had come to work on repairing the crypt were later to be found drinking in their local? I'd say the chances were very good indeed.

"The inn is in fact the only gathering spot of its kind in the village, and the bar is the sort of snug little place frequented by all sorts of people from all walks of life. And having a pint in that bar, Lord Lislelivet undoubtedly heard whatever rumors were flying about. He prided himself on being a man of the people, able to talk to people high and low. Whether the lowly always appreciated his condescension may well be another matter. But over a pint he perhaps overheard the workmen talking about the crypt at Monkbury Abbey. About what they'd found there. What they'd seen. What the abbess had in fact begged them to keep to themselves. She was used to obedience, and these men were used to doing as they pleased, especially after a round or two."

"Lady Lislelivet said something of this when I spoke with her," said Cotton. "Her husband had mentioned running into two men who had been involved in the repair work in the church. Her husband had said no more than that, and otherwise couched his visit here in terms of his sudden need to restore his soul or whatever. And then, of course, she never saw him again."

"And his probing into the matter, we assume, led to his death? Now, why would it? It makes no real sense."

Cotton replied, "Because one of the nuns is so unhinged she doesn't want the secret to come out?"

"That was possible. A monastery, like any closed group, can be a breeding ground for that sort of instability. But was it credible? No." Max shook his head. "No, he was murdered for a simple reason, for a straightforward reason. He was murdered because he was recognized."

"Certainly that's to be expected. He was a well-known man."

"Not to a group of women who haven't seen a newspaper in decades. Nor to an American, I daresay." Max clapped his hands together. "Okay. Let's gather the suspects. Right here in the guest living room should do fine."

"Oh, please tell me we're not doing the Poirot thing again? The suspects in the library with the candlestick or whatever?"

Max looked at him. "Fruitcake, in this case. And what would you prefer? A car chase? It's the most efficient way to flush out a killer, as Dame Agatha Christie well knew."

"All right. Whatever you want. Just the guests?"

"The nuns, too. Meeting here, we don't invade the sanctity of their cloister any further than it's already been invaded."

"*All* of them?" Cotton looked around him. "We're going to need a bigger boat."

"Not of all them will be needed." Max rattled off a handful of names, ending with Sister Rose Tocketts, the novice.

"They're all suspects?" said Cotton, incredulous.

"They're all involved in some way, as we know. But only one of them holds a key that can help me solve a murder."

PART VII

Compline

Chapter 35

MAX AND THE CORRECTION OF MINOR FAULTS

A sister found guilty of constant relapse into a minor fault shall be excluded from meals and from the oratory. No one shall converse with her, and she shall work and live alone. She shall not be blessed by anyone, nor shall her food be blessed, until her fault be corrected.

—*The Rule of the Order of the Handmaids of St. Lucy*

There had been the expected protest from Abbess Justina to the effect that this was an outrage and a sacrilege, but she had been convinced that dragging her nuns down to headquarters one by one was a far worse alternative. Cotton himself requested that she gather "her people" together and sent Sergeant Essex to collect the guests.

Everyone was told to appear at a time nicely chosen by Max not to interfere with the nuns' cycle of prayer.

And so they assembled, in pairs and singles. The guesthouse inhabitants in the forms of the three Goreys, Paloma Green and Piers Montague, and Dr. Barnard. The nuns in the forms of the elderly portress, the guest-mistress, the kitcheness, the librarian, the infirmaress, the cellaress, the novice, and the postulant. Dame Meredith was excused from attending—she had taken yet another turn, and Dr. Barnard had decreed she must be spared this sort of ordeal. Max had agreed.

They all, thought DCI Cotton, were looking as nervous as pigs at a luau: thrilled to be invited but suspecting a trap. That one nun couldn't stop fiddling with the linen thing around her face. The wimple. And the pretty librarian nun kept polishing her glasses.

"Let's start," said Max, "where it all began. With the poisoning of Lord Lislelivet. He came here to visit his dying aunt—so he said. And, having found religion, to answer the call of God to pray for his own soul. But we suspected that he was drawn here by tales of the vast wealth hidden somewhere inside the abbey. He left instead with the 'gift' of a poisoned fruitcake. Yet he came back to the nunnery, instead of staying away like a sensible man would do. Why?"

"I can answer that," said Clement Gorey. "He would have felt it was entirely worth the risk. An antiquity possessing miraculous powers would fetch untold sums at auction. Particularly with all the free publicity being generated by that recent bestselling book. It's not just a curiosity. It's the *Holy Grail*. The actual Holy Grail! Sotheby's would have to turn billionaires away at the door if it came up for auction."

Yes, thought Max. What Xanda called the mandolin. The Mandylion, or the face of Christ. The Face, a contemporaneous representation of arguably the most famous man ever to live.

How many people had been lured by that promise of miracle and wealth and secret solving, all rolled into one great quest, Max wondered? Frank Cuthbert's book had spawned speculation similar to that surrounding *The Da Vinci Code*, a similar frenzy to get to the truth.

"You expressed concern," Max said to the Goreys, "that your dollars from the fund-raising were being wasted or misspent somehow and not used for the new building. And you sensed you were being given the stall and the runaround by Abbess Justina—you, such an important benefactor."

"That is correct," said Clement.

"Abbess Justina was not forthright about that, to be sure. And the abbess knew she should tell the bishop but was dragging her feet on that, as well. Why? Because she didn't want the place suddenly turned into a shrine, attracting pilgrims and sensation seekers."

"Who could bring in much-needed revenue," said the ever-practical cellaress, Dame Sibil. But for that she got a sharp reproof from the abbess and backed down immediately. That call to obey, thought Max, was very strong.

"Yes," said Max to Clement Gorey, "you wanted to know where the money went, but that wasn't the only thing that brought you and your wife here. You'd read about a 'gold icon,' or Mandylion, and you wanted to look for it. You were often to be found in the church, where you believed, rightly, that it was hidden. You are a deeply religious man, yes, but one on a treasure hunt. Had you found the treasure, I wonder?"

"You don't understand. It's not just any icon. It's the *Grail*," insisted Clement.

"Yes," said Max, astonished at his gullibility, this hardheaded man of business. Miraculous powers, indeed. "Indeed," he said aloud. "And if it fell into dishonest, unscrupulous hands, there would still be a buyer found somewhere for it. It might even just disappear into a billionaire's home, maybe into his private chapel, never to be seen again. At least not during his lifetime. Even a man with serious means might not want to run the risk of losing this coveted treasure to some other billionaire at auction. You business types tend to be competitive. Isn't that right, Mr. Gorey? Mrs. Gorey?"

"I say," said Oona Gorey. "How dare you imply—we'll sue for libel."

"Slander," said Max calmly. "Please go right ahead if you feel you must. My point is, this kind of treasure blinds people to all common sense. Isn't that right, Ms. Green?"

Paloma Green exchanged worried looks with her companion, Piers.

"What are you talking about?"

"I'm talking about some questions that have come up with regard to your art gallery and some previous fund-raisers held on the premises. Something in the dossier DCI Cotton compiled about allegations that all the money you helped raise didn't necessarily make it into the coffers of the worthy cause. Oh, and something else about forgeries. What was it, DCI Cotton?"

"Forged documentation for some of the work sold out of your shop." Cotton replied. "Manufactured provenances. The usual art fraud sort of thing."

"How dare you!" Paloma said. "There are operating expenses involved in putting on such an event. And if someone landed me with a painting that they claimed was genuine, well . . . how was I to know differently?" Twisting around in her seat, she invoked the others. "You're all witnesses to what he said. I'll sue, too!"

"By all means, join the queue," said Max. "Your worthy causes don't seem to have been made aware in advance of your operating expenses. Apparently the cellaress had begun to suspect some of the funds you had raised for the abbey had not actually reached the abbey."

"I can explain," said Paloma. "I told her . . . it's complicated." She turned to Piers for backup, but Piers seemed to have discovered a cuticle that needed his immediate attention. "I—"

"I would bet it is getting complicated. And that your complaining customers are becoming more numerous than the stars. If you're going to run an art gallery, Ms. Green, you might want to bone up on how to tell a forgery from the real thing. Just a suggestion. But let us leave the intoxicating environs of the art world for a moment and return to the murder of Lord Lislelivet, shall we?

"And perhaps we should focus for the moment on the *how*, before turning to the *who*. Sister Rose Tocketts has been invaluable in regard to the 'how.'"

She beamed at Max. Her sisters turned toward her at once, a flock of seagulls spotting a breadcrumb.

"If a murder happens in a nunnery," said Max, "which thankfully does not often happen, the obvious first thing to look at is the habit. At the fact that everyone, with the exception of the novices and postulants, looks basically the same from a distance. And since the Handmaids of St. Lucy also have a cowl or hood to cover their heads—well, the solution to the 'how' is obvious.

"At least, part of the solution."

Max, speaking quietly now, said, "The choir is divided into individual stalls for the sisters. The divisions are designed to provide a little privacy if one leans one's head back in the stall. But what really affords privacy is the hood pulled over one's head, obscuring the profile.

"The hood or cowl is only worn ceremonially in the choir or in winter for warmth and is not otherwise used—certainly not in summer. Which is why Sister Rose wondered at seeing a hooded figure in the passageway. She was being punished for some minor transgression, and so was free to wander about on her own, witnessing things that others missed.

"By tradition, the hood was not to be pulled up over the head until the nun entered the church proper. It is possible someone forgot—one of those tiny infractions of the Rule. There were so many rules it was easy to forget. But Sister Rose noted it, wondered who it was, and assumed it was Dame Hephzibah, who was often forgetful."

"Who's forgetful?" demanded Dame Hephzibah, sitting up from what looked to have been a light doze. "My mind is as sharp as ever it was twenty years ago."

Some of them might have been thinking that twenty years ago she was already ancient, but no one said so.

"But that is not all," resumed Max. "What Sister Rose saw later on that was even more curious, was someone running. An infraction of the rules of which she was generally guilty, or of which the postulant, Mary Benton, was guilty. The other nuns knew better. They did not run, and they most certainly did not run about at night during the Great Silence. It would be an exceptional circumstance for a nun to break conditioning like that."

Sister Rose looked at Abbess Justina, by a gesture to her lips asking permission to respond. Abbess Justina nodded, her face with its fine high coloring now pale, the pouches beneath her eyes betraying a sleepless night. Hers was a face made for wimple and veil, her bloodless skin as one with the soft marble-like folds of white linen.

"But even more so," said Sister Rose, "I wondered that she moved so fast. It was most unusual. She was running at full tilt. Generally only a postulant or novice in training does that, when she first comes here. One of the first things we learn is that we are on God's time, not mankind's— there is no great hurry once one realizes that."

She looked to Abbess Justina for confirmation or approval that she was learning her lessons, this bright young woman who was yet so afraid to question or defy authority. But Abbess Justina only continued to gaze stonily at Max.

Max said, musingly, "I had often noticed while I was here how well long, heavy skirts reaching nearly to the ground can conceal a person's gait. I thought at one point how Dame Hephzibah looked like one of those figurines attached to a clock that glided out on the hour."

"They all do. I thought the same thing. But this nun was running," Xanda reminded him.

"Yes," said Max. "So clearly, at the time of the murder, we have a nun breaking all protocol. Or we have someone disguised as a nun, running about."

"I don't see how this gets you any closer to the truth, if you don't mind my saying so," said Piers Montague.

"No," said Max vaguely. "I don't mind at all. I thought at first, you see, it had something to do with the sheep. With the black-and-white sheep, you see."

Heads turned in confusion. "Hmm?" said several voices at once.

"I kept thinking of something else Sister Rose had told me, when she was talking of the sheep and their lambs: that the lambs often didn't rec-ognize their own mothers once the mothers' coats had been shorn, and how sometimes the mothers didn't care about their missing lambs. Per-haps this basic bond of mother and offspring, being disrupted, couldn't always be repaired. Mother and offspring didn't recognize each other once the relationship was severed."

"You're losing me," said Xanda.

"Me, too," said Dr. Barnard.

"Am I? I also remembered, being reminded as I was of the sheep by their constant bleating, that a ewe can be tricked after giving birth into accepting the offspring of another sheep as her own. She will nourish it, treating it as hers. Perhaps, we might like to imagine, not caring that it isn't hers."

"And this has to do with the nun's habit—how?" Xanda asked.

Max returned to them with a visible effort, his mind wandering a landscape many years in the past.

"That part is simple. If you want to impersonate a nun, you borrow a habit. A novice or postulant would have to borrow such a disguise, as would one of the guests in the guesthouse.

"Of course, if you are already a nun, you simply pull the cowl over your head to disguise your face.

"But I believe someone borrowed a habit.

"The only question to be explained on that subject is: when?"

"Well, telling us *who* did it might be nice. You know, save us all some time." This was Xanda, who today was looking as if she had not washed her hair for weeks, more likely the result of using "hair product," Max felt, than a sudden lapse in hygiene.

"Getting to that," Max said. "You really need to quit smoking, you know, Xanda. Do it now, while your lungs are still able to recover."

"*Smoking?*" said her parents together.

"Thanks, Rev," said Xanda. "Just, thanks a bunch. I'll never hear the end of it."

"No, you won't," said her mother.

"Smoking nearly got you into some serious trouble," said Max. "Some evidence was found that may have mislead the investigators. Take it as a heaven-sent warning and quit.

"As to the imposter," he continued, "actually there were two. Let's take them one at a time, shall we?"

He swung back around and pointing at one suddenly wary, alarmed face, demanded, "Who are you, really? And why are you here?"

Chapter 36

MAX AND THE CORRECTION OF SERIOUS FAULTS

If after repeated attempts a fault be not corrected, the erring sister shall be asked to leave the nunnery.

—*The Rule of the Order of the Handmaids of St. Lucy*

Max let his eyes roam over the faces of the group. Only one face continued to show any signs of apprehension.

Interesting, thought Max.

He said: "You all know that song, I am sure, from *The Sound of Music*. 'How Do You Solve a Problem Like Maria?' Without fail, whenever I saw Mary Benton about the grounds, she was doing something absolutely marginal, something out of line for a postulant in a religious order. It was not mere incompetence or nervousness. It was a sort of fretting, of fighting and struggling against the many restrictions of the life.

"It was not just her actions, but her appearance that struck me as all wrong. Up to and including her perfectly groomed eyebrows."

They had all of course by this point turned to stare at the face with the offending eyebrows. Various glances were exchanged.

The abbess was nodding as if to say, "Of course!" She said aloud, "I simply could not put my finger on what the problem was. Of course . . ."

Max said, "I should think that grooming one's eyebrows is nearly impossible to do without a mirror," he said. "And having a mirror is a violation of the Rule of St. Lucy. Of course, she might have used the polished bottom of a copper pot or her reflection in a window.

"And so what if she did? I asked myself. Perhaps she was simply guilty of the sin of vanity. This attention to her appearance didn't make her a killer; it simply made her not fit in. I found it curious, definitely odd—an anomaly to be explained away. Where, after all, would she get tweezers? It wasn't until I recalled observing Dame Petronilla in the infirmary, using tweezers to pluck the thread from an old pillowcase she was restitching, that that mystery was solved. A personal grooming item like that in her cell might have been discovered, so here and there Mary must have borrowed the tweezers. All right, we were still in the area of minor infractions, of a forgivable vanity, an inability to readily let go of habits from 'civilian' life. That must plague most postulants to an extent.

"But then . . . then it also led me to the next step—to wonder if she was making herself attractive *for* someone, in order to please someone else. Why else, really, would she worry about a detail so minor, so frivolous? And that led me to wonder which person around here she would want to impress with her good looks. If we looked at young and attractive men it would likely be Piers. If we spread the net to include somewhat older men it might be Dr. Barnard or Lord Lislelivet himself. Forgive me, Mr. Gorey, but you did not strike me as a candidate for this young lady's affections."

"I should think not," Clement said, ardently seizing his wife's hand. "I'm a happily married man."

Mrs. Gorey's perpetual glower made Max wonder anew at the mysteries of married love, but it was undeniably true that he could not picture Gorey being unfaithful, certainly not with a girl not much older than his daughter. Clement's affection for Mrs. Gorey was apparently genuine. Nor could Max see Mary Benton being irresistibly drawn to Clement, no matter how hard he tried or how wealthy he was.

"And *I'm* not involved with Miss Benton," cut in Dr. Barnard.

"Of course not," said Max. "You heart's desire is elsewhere."

Dr. Barnard's gaze drifted to the floor. He looked, thought Max, suitably abashed.

Paloma suddenly could not seem to take her eyes off Piers's profile, willing him to look at her.

"There was one further oddity I couldn't fit into this scheme," said Max. "I saw a flash that seemed to come from a shiny object like a mirror. The flash came from one of the windows of the nun's dormitory. It was as if someone were signaling to someone outside, but to be honest I didn't put that construction on it at the time. I simply observed. I think now it might have been you, Mary, with your mirror, signaling to your accomplice, using some prearranged code."

Vehemently, Mary shook her head. "You're wrong," she said.

"Of course, it could have been someone else," agreed Max. "But it was definitely a signal."

"So, Mary Benton is the killer?" Xanda asked.

"No," said Max. "No, she's not. Mary is here as a plant. A spy. She is the red herring in this case. What was needed was someone attached in some way to the nunnery, someone who could be here day and night to hunt for the treasure.

"She was not here to kill, but to assist the man I believe is her lover."

"What?" This came from various voices around the circle.

"You, Mary, came here several months ago. I commented, you may recall, on your lingering tan. You said you had finished your art history course in Italy last winter and come here following a holiday. I think you went on one last holiday with your lover, before you took up your place here at the nunnery." *Not all widows are grieving*, thought Max, reminded of Lady Lislelivet.

"But, why? Why would I?"

"For the millions the icon was reputed to be worth—that would make the deception worthwhile. For the small sacrifice of a few months of your life, you could live like a queen forever afterward.

"Someone was needed who could wander about freely in a nunnery—someone female, of course—someone whose presence would not be questioned. However, the rules about lights out and so on—that constantly got in your way, didn't it? As did your instantly recognizable postulant's habit, with its short skirt and veil. That is why you borrowed Dame Meredith's habit whenever you could, a habit which was left folded on a chair in her infirmary room, near her bed."

"Oh, my," said Dame Petronilla. "I wondered why it was always folded wrong. The habit is a blessed garment and should not have been refolded any which way. But several times I noticed it folded wrong. Once it was even inside out. I wondered if it kept falling onto the floor by accident, or if Dame Meredith kept knocking it over and Mary or Sister Rose were refolding it wrong."

"And so *you* kept refolding it, in the prescribed way."

"Yes," she said.

"As for you, Mary," continued Max, "by using this ruse you were freer to roam about. Even if seen coming or going during the Great Silence, with the cowl over your head you'd be far safer from detection than if wearing that immediately identifiable short outfit. Wearing the long habit, you could have been any of a dozen sisters on a legitimate errand."

"Besides," interjected the abbess, "a postulant is not allowed to walk about after Compline but must go straight to her cell for quiet reflection."

"Somehow," said Max, "I don't think taking time out for quiet reflection has ever been an overriding priority for Mary Benton."

"Bugger this," Mary Benton said, reaching up to remove the short veil and headdress that bound her hair back from her face, and shaking loose a cascade of auburn curls. "The damn thing itches and it scratches my scalp, and it's ruddy boiling hot, especially in the great bloody outdoors, where they always seem to be sending me to pick lettuce or to milk the sodding goats or some feudal, forelock-tugging activity like that. I don't know how the rest of you lot can stand wearing that whole kit in summer. And for God's sake, do yourselves a favor and buy a frigging tractor."

She unbuttoned and rolled up her sleeves next, completely unselfconscious, ignoring the stares of her amazed audience. She had, Max noted, a brightly colored tattoo of a seahorse near the elbow of one forearm.

"The infractions of the Rule were without end in your case," said

Max sternly. But inwardly he was smiling. The ruse was so ridiculous, so poorly planned and executed. And it had failed in its objective, after all. The icon—the Face that had caused so much scrambling, so much disruption of the placid lives of these good women—remained hidden, safe and undisturbed. How long that situation might have lasted was anyone's guess. Mary would have been allowed into the secret when she took her vows, but would she have lasted that long?

"You were always doing something that just didn't fit: dropping things, creating a commotion, talking during the Great Silence, and—most of all—wandering around after lights out. I overheard you being scolded over this by Dame Petronilla. However, if caught in your postulant's clothing, you would pretend you didn't realize what time it was but of course you knew exactly. You had to wait, you and your compatriot, for everyone else to be asleep so you could carry out your search of the grounds. Or so you could meet up. This explains why you were always so sleepy and yawning. You and your friend."

The friend in question was squirming under the attention, mostly under the attention of Paloma. The light was dawning in her brain, and she looked stricken by the betrayal, as well she might.

"Tell me. How did you come to hear of the treasure? For you've been here since before Frank Cuthbert's book made such a splash."

"There was an American girl here for a while as a postulant."

"That's right," said Dame Fruitcake to Max. "Remember, I told you about her? Very chatty and overfriendly, like a big puppy? Liked to 'share.'"

"Yes. I wondered if she weren't a mole of some kind. Sent by someone to scope things out. And when her garrulousness became apparent, the nuns, trying to keep their secret, might have told her she wasn't suited to the life. But DCI Cotton's people looked into that. She did indeed attach herself to a missionary order when she left here. An order better suited to her temperament."

"Right," said Mary. "I met her while I was traveling around myself, killing time waiting for a plane. She 'shared' with me that she knew of this fabulous, secret treasure."

"Which you told Piers about straightaway. And you and Piers put your heads together and came up with this plan to infiltrate the convent from the inside. Clever of you: it almost worked."

"I found nothing, though," she said disconsolately.

"That's too bad. I didn't pay enough attention to Xanda's declarations that she could hear people moving about the guesthouse at night, for I assumed as she did that was Paloma and Piers meeting up after hours. Nor did I quite register the importance of the fact that Xanda heard the bolt to the guesthouse door slide open at night—something that could not be done from inside the guesthouse, but only from the outside, by someone in the cloister itself. It is a safety precaution, of course, meant to separate the nuns at night from the guests, who, after all, are not vetted in any way. There could be a serial killer asking to stay here and the nuns would welcome him or her, because their rule says that they must welcome anyone seeking refuge, a place to stay, a place of safety."

Max looked at Piers's Hollywood-handsome face—the face tanned more deeply on the left side of his face than his right. For Piers's earlier claim to have just returned from a 'two-week trip driving alone around Britain' could not be true unless he spent half the time in a tanning bed with his face turned to one side. Which was just possible, but unlikely. What was more likely was that he'd been driving around a sunny country, a country other than England with its right-side driving gear. For if he'd been driving in England, he wouldn't have such a deep tan, and what tan he had would be on the other side of his face. Why, Max had wondered, did he lie?

The answer had been easy once he came to think about it. Piers was lying to conceal an affair from Paloma. It had little to do with the case, but he'd been at the wheel of a vehicle with controls on the left-hand side. He might have been somewhere sunny driving about, but most certainly he had not been in England.

Max studied Piers's expression as he pointed out this fact to him and to the others. From Piers's guilty glance at Paloma, Max's suspicion was confirmed: Piers had been having a dalliance with Mary Benton, somewhere out of Paloma's sight. A last fling before they came to the abbey to look for the treasure, she in disguise.

And if Lady Lislelivet's hints were to be believed, Piers might be having an affair with her, too, or at least be in her sights. Perhaps Piers had been the reason for her own Roman holiday, which Mary Benton might be very unhappy to hear of. Tempting as it was, Max saw no reason to chuck Piers completely into it with all these ladies. Let them get it sorted later, amongst themselves.

Besides, thought Max, it was nothing to do with the case. Just one of those annoying details that needed to be slotted into place.

"So which one is the killer?" asked Dr. Barnard. "Piers or Mary?"

"Neither," said Max. "I have quite another person in mind for that role."

Chapter 37

NONE SO BLIND

May the scales fall from your eyes that you may see the Truth.

—*The Rule of the Order of the Handmaids of St. Lucy*

"We began by looking for a poisoner, and it's still someone with knowledge of herbs and poisons that we seek," Max told the group. "Someone who knows, for example, that certain plant poisons do not show up on a routine toxicology screen."

Several of the nuns, Max noticed, stared ahead in a way that told him they were desperately trying not to let their eyes slide in the direction of one of their sisters.

"Putting aside the poisoning of Lord Lislelivet's fruitcake, for the moment—what if the goal was not to kill someone, but to discredit someone? To cause someone to hallucinate, perhaps? Or to impair their vision, so their testimony was worthless?

"What if we were looking for someone who knew all the ins and outs of belladonna, for instance?

"Belladonna means 'beautiful woman,' something I rather forgot when talking with Dame Petronilla, the infirmaress, about ingested poisons—poisonous berries and so forth. Belladonna is poisonous if eaten—again, those black berries to watch out for! They look harmless and children are attracted to something that looks so sweet and edible—but belladonna got its beautiful name because it dilates the pupils, and this was thought, to make a woman attractive to men. Such a dangerous practice: at a minimum, it can cause blurred vision and sensitivity to light. If you've ever had an eye exam that required dilation of the pupils, you will know what I mean. You can't see your hand in front of your face, and to walk outside into the sunlight without sunglasses is nearly painful.

"Outside of an eye exam, it is difficult to see the use of it, unless you wanted to temporarily blind someone. And why, I ask, would anyone want to do that?" He left a significant pause. Most waited expectantly for his answer. In one case, the answer was known and written plain in the expression on the face.

"I'll tell you what I think. I think you would do that, temporarily blind someone, so that if they were a potential witness to something or someone, they couldn't see well. This potential witness, let us say, if she had poor eyesight to begin with . . . well. Putting a solution of belladonna into her eyes would certainly make it hard for the witness to recognize, say, the contours of a face shrouded by a coif and wimple, a veil and hood. Without the usual identifying features of hair color and style, the habit does what it was designed to do: make all nuns look as alike as possible. If one has difficulty seeing—if one is elderly, say—this would nullify their ability to witness anything.

"Of course, the same goes for someone wearing a hat, a scarf, an enveloping cloak of some kind."

Abbess Justina looked over at Dame Hephzibah, an expression of kind concern on her face. Dame Hephzibah seemed not to think anyone could be speaking about her in the context of failing eyesight.

"All clues pointed to a poisoner with a better-than-working knowledge of plants, and poisonous plants in particular. And that could only mean Dame Pet, the infirmaress, with her knowledge of medicinal herbs was involved.

"*Or* it could simply mean that she was being set up to absorb all suspicion.

"The only other person with some knowledge of plant life was the

novice, Sister Rose, who was studying the properties of plants with Dame
Pet, and who seemed to have a natural affinity for dealing with the plant
and animal worlds here at the abbey. It was also just possible that Dame
Ingrid, in creating her fruitcake recipe, had a better than working knowledge of which berry-producing plants were poisonous or had medicinal
properties.

"But once I remembered how belladonna got its name, and the use of
belladonna to dilate the eyes, I realized there was one other sort of person
who would be fully familiar with its properties. And that person would be
a trained ophthalmologist."

His own eyes flashed with anger as he turned with deliberation and
pointed across the room.

"That person would be Dr. Barnard. In the U.S., an ophthalmologist
is a trained M.D. Somewhat different from the requirements here in
the U.K."

The doctor shifted uncomfortably under the spotlight of the priest's
regard.

"Isn't that a fact, Dr. Barnard? That atropine, from deadly nightshade
or belladonna, is used by doctors to dilate their patients' pupils before eye
surgery?" This was one of the little facts he had picked up from Awena.

"Yes, of course it's true. And anyone would know that, or be able to
look it up. So what? What are you implying?"

What indeed. Max, knowing he was right, also knew he'd have to
approach from a slightly different direction in order to prove it. But then,
Dr. Barnard made it easy for him by saying, "And how am I supposed to
have gotten here?" he scoffed. "Climbed the hill, then climbed over the
walls? You forget I arrived after Lord Lislelivet was killed."

"No, although it is just possible. A skilled climber could have managed it."

"Well, how then?" He glanced down at his slight paunch. "I am no
'skilled climber' and there is no other way into the abbey. The place was
designed to keep men out, remember."

"You arrived by boat," said Max simply. That stopped Dr. Barnard cold. The effort it took not to swivel his eyes over to meet his accomplice's was palpable; instead he fixed his stare for too long a beat on Max's face, clearly trying to think his way out of the dilemma.

Max, sensing his advantage, began to hit his stride.

"You waited until you knew the nuns would be at Vespers, reducing the already slim chance you would be observed. You dressed in some sort of concealing garment like a hooded fisherman's coat or slicker. You must have looked like a yellow monk—and this is what Dame Hephzibah saw when everyone thought her delirious. You rowed up to the black door over the river that at one time was used for dumping refuse. Sister Rose mentioned in passing to me the terrible problems there once had been with sanitation. There had to be somewhere an opening into the river that made this dumping possible. St. John's College in Cambridge has just such a door. Interestingly, it is said to be the site of a murder, but that was a murder for another day and age. This is a modern tale. A tale of greed.

"Alongside another tale, and that is a tale of revenge.

"You rowed up to this door, conveniently left unlocked for you, thus bypassing the need to get in through the gatehouse—the only other means of entry to a place that, as you say, was designed to keep out the world of men. You moored the boat on the rusted old pins driven into the wall. And in that place you waited for your accomplice.

"The steps of your plan were so carefully worked out, as in sequence dancing. One wrong footfall would put everything out of alignment. Your partner had to keep in perfect step with you."

"Partner?"

"Yes. Of course, you had a partner.

"Now, the poisoning of Lord Lislelivet had all the hallmarks of an impulsive act, perhaps immediately regretted. A seeking of petty revenge. But for what?

"Was it done by someone defending the abbey? Someone trying to drive people or a certain person away?

"Monkbury Abbey recently has become the focus of media interest, because of the rather silly book that has captured the public's imagination. It is said that an icon of special value to the faithful has been hidden here for centuries. The Face, as it has come to be known. Its value might be intrinsic, or it might be an object of pure gold. It might even be a golden chalice—the Holy Grail of legend.

"So it seemed obvious from the outset that the overriding motive here was greed. Greed motivates nearly every visitor in the guesthouse."

"Not me," Xanda told the room. "I don't give a rat's. I just want out of here."

"Me, too," said Piers.

Max ignored them both. "When a wall collapsed during an earthquake, exposing the Face, the nuns were thrilled, but they didn't want—most of them—the notoriety, the crush of visitors stirred up by Frank Cuthbert's book. Finding the Face just confirmed Frank's crackpot speculation, but the nuns—again, most of them—didn't want anything to do with it. They didn't want sightseers with treasure maps, the way Paris and London and, in particular, Rosslyn Chapel became overrun with visitors when Dan Brown published his book.

"The nuns wanted, actually, to keep this miraculous and lovely find to themselves, at least for the time being, while they figured out what to do. But first, repairs must take place, the walls must be shored up, or the shrine honoring the Face would be destroyed.

"This is where creative accounting came into play. The nuns couldn't ask for money for such a secret project, and so money intended for the new guesthouse was diverted to refurbish the crypt. To create an altar for private worship of the icon, a project of which the bishop almost certainly would not approve, and to shore up the crumbling masonry. Wall coverings, pews, kneelers, and so on were needed. And after a while, people like the Goreys, who after all had contributed in good faith to the guesthouse renovations, began to ask where the money went. The abbess began to stall them. The pressure was on, because the abbess's desire to keep this quiet was not universally embraced, was it?"

The abbess said nothing, but she shook her head either in disagreement or remorse.

"Once I saw the Face for myself, I wondered whether Dame Sibil, the cellaress, might be all in favor of revealing it and inviting in the tourists. For in talking with her I was struck by her calm certainty that the ranks of applicants to the nunnery would one day swell. What made her so sure? Was it the certainty of the fanatic, or the certainty of someone with a marketing tool up her sleeve? The marketing tool being a relic that would draw not just sightseers and the curious, but religious converts?"

"I knew for myself that the Face was miraculous," said Dame Sibil. "It saved my failing eyesight. Would you expect me—would you expect anyone?—to keep that knowledge hidden from the world? Marketing—call it that if you will, but I am no snake-oil saleswoman. The Face is *real*. It is a miracle, one entrusted to our care. The world had to know of it."

Max smiled his benign and patient smile. "Belief is a miracle worker, no question about it. The placebo effect is always quite real."

"It is real *in and of itself*," insisted Dame Sibil. Obviously taking up a cudgel that had been used many times before, she turned to the abbess and said, "And it is wrong of us to hide it."

"Sisters, we must leave that for another day," said Max. "Only indirectly does it have anything to do with the murder. Now, where was I? Yes: renovations and groundbreaking on the new guesthouse are delayed, while the abbess pretends there is resistance among the nuns and among the villagers to the modern plans for the building. While the abbess and Dame Sibil, in particular, debate what to do about the find. How much to tell the world, if anything."

Abbess Justina looked suitably abashed at her part in this cover-up, as well she might. She was not the first nor the last person, thought Max, to overstep her authority, telling herself she was acting for the greater good. No doubt she felt she was protecting the integrity of the nunnery, of its great standing in the history of the region. No doubt she was. And no doubt she was concealing the truth not only from donors, but from the bishop—definitely forbidden.

"Then of course," said Max, "to add to this mix, we had Lord Lisle-

livet's sudden interest in all things holy, an interest that given his character we assumed could only be finance-based. He joined a crowd of other
people whose real interest in the abbey lay not in its holiness.

"Paloma Green was here to protect her involvement in the fund-
raising scheme that entangled the Goreys and others: a significant amount
of the money raised at her fancy fund-raiser appears to be missing. Paloma
had suffered a scandal recently in which the provenance of one of her acquisitions was questioned—an old religious icon from Russia. It turned
out to have been stolen years before from a church. So she couldn't have
another scandal following so soon on the heels of the last, and the donors
who bought paintings and photographs from her shop were starting to
ask awkward questions. Like the Goreys, Paloma wanted to know where
the money went.

"Piers Montague was here for much the same reason—it was his donated photos that were auctioned off and he wanted to know that the
money went where he was told it would go. Beyond that, he was here on a
treasure hunt with Mary Benton.

"This case had more than a few layers of greed. There was a monetary
motive in connection with the Goreys, the Americans." As Clement
Gorey looked set to protest, Max held up a forestalling hand. "But it was
not greed so much in their case. It was more of an honest bafflement
about where their money had gone, if not into the new guesthouse. And
an interest in the Face, to be sure.

"Again, in the case of Paloma Green, it was not greed so much as the
fact her gallery's reputation was on the line."

"Thanks very much," she said. "And too right, too. As I told you already, I organized the fund-raiser. Piers and I both had a lot at stake."

"Your gallery couldn't take another blow right now," Max nodded.
"And Piers had even more at stake than you knew."

Piers shrugged noncommittally, but he turned his full attention to
Max now, hanging on his words as if to memorize them.

"Was it a sort of lust for the icon that brought Lord Lislelivet here?"
Max went on. "He said it was to see his aunt, but he was always snooping

around the place, so we assume, knowing something of his nature, that the desire to own—to steal—this most rare artifact brought him here.

"But what if that weren't the whole story? Even more to the point: what if he were telling the truth for once, or part of the truth—that he was here to see Dame Meredith?"

They all exchanged puzzled glances.

"I have told you this was a tale with themes of greed and revenge.

"But there was yet a third motive—the most powerful motive in the world.

"And that motive was love.

"Lord Lislelivet came here to see Dame Meredith, to be sure. He was summoned here, in a letter she wrote him. But Dame Meredith was not his aunt."

"So, who was she?" Paloma asked.

Max turned to a certain face in the audience.

And looked across the room, to a second face.

"She was his mother."

There was rather a shocked recoil at this. Max gave them a moment to absorb the implications.

"Lord Lislelivet was the natural son of Dame Meredith. And Dame Meredith, knowing she hadn't long to live, wanted to tell the truth at the last, to clear her conscience. She was set to 'spill the beans' to Lord Lislelivet about his true provenance—how he came to be in this world. How she was his mother.

"Worse, from his point of view, she wanted to tell everyone affected by his birth the truth. To set things right, before she went to meet her maker. She had a tremendous need to unburden herself, having carried this secret too long.

"But what she didn't know was that the person she 'confessed' to initially in order to 'do the right thing'—her own son, a man who was her own flesh and blood, mind—was an avaricious, unfeeling monster. She had summoned him to her bedside, and he had arrived knowing full well what the subject of their discussion would be. He knew this because his own father had told him the truth and had sworn him to secrecy. And Lord Lislelivet, being the sort of man he was, had come prepared to make sure Dame Meredith wouldn't—or couldn't—tell the truth to ease her conscience. Because the truth would mean he was not the legitimate heir to his father's estate and fortune. According to a formula used by the family since the dawn of time, only males of the legitimate bloodline could inherit. Illegitimate children, and I gather there were dozens of those over the years, could not inherit. Female heirs were always left out in the cold. Funny how no one had a problem with that except, presumably, the females concerned. The true motive for Lord Lislelivet was less about the icon than about covering up the fact that Dame Meredith—his aunt—was in fact his mother. And that he was the product of an illicit liaison between his biological father and the woman who had been Meredith Fitzwilliam in her former life, before she became a nun."

There were several shocked intakes of breath at this, several hands that flew to cover mouths fallen open in amazement. Even nuns long schooled in serenity and calm were too shaken by this revelation not to let it show. This was their own quiet Dame Meredith who had dwelt with many of them for years, for decades. This would take some getting used to.

Max went on. "Meredith Fitzwilliam was the younger of the two Fitzwilliam sisters. Her sister married but it seemed she could not have children. The terrible irony was that Meredith's affair with her sister's husband produced a son. The longed-for son to inherit the title. But the problem of course was that it was an illegitimate child.

"So after much anxiety and unhappiness on the part of the father, he hits upon a scheme: since the child is his own, and he sees no reason why it shouldn't inherit, he persuades Meredith not to give the child up for open adoption, but to allow himself and his wife to raise the child as their own. There is one catch, and that is that Meredith must never name him as the father. Of course, to protect her sister, she agrees to keep this secret. She has many a chance to regret it, but keep her promise she does.

"She doesn't agree because there is money riding on it, but because she knows how much her sister wants a child. Guilt no doubt played a huge role here. And so she went abroad somewhere, and when she had given birth, her sister and brother-in-law—"

"Adopted it." Xanda cut into his narrative. "Adopted the baby. Wow. It's like something out of Dickens."

"Not adopted, no," said Max. "Not in the legal sense you mean. To the world, the child is presented as the natural child of Lord and Lady Lislelivet. Not the *adopted* child, but the natural one."

"But how—?"

"Lady Lislelivet, the sister of Meredith, simply went away with her husband on a long tour of Europe and the Middle East. She returned with a child. No one questioned it. Why would they?

"Had the woman who raised Lord Lislelivet been duped—or had she chosen to believe what she wanted to believe, as people so often do? That her husband was guilty of such a monstrous fraud would have been difficult to accept, perhaps especially when a much-wanted child was offered to fill what she felt was a void in her life.

"The thin ice of a marriage such as theirs might require a suspension of disbelief—a refusal to look down, knowing how fatal that look might be.

"Apart from the longing of Lady Lislelivet for a child, the question has to be why the elaborate deception was needed. And the answer is the child's grandfather. He had been despondent at not having an heir, and this seemed like a godsend. He was not, of course, to be made aware that the child was not legitimate.

"Meredith takes the veil soon afterward, and her sister—who doesn't know the awful truth, that her husband is the father of the child—thinks only that Meredith got in trouble and she, Lady Lislelivet, is helping her out.

"Time passes. And the more it passes, the more Dame Meredith wants to spill the beans on this setup. Not just because of her guilt at the part she played—deceiving her sister, denying her own child—but because of the way this son was turning out. She saw when he visited over the years, as a child, and a young man, how he had become corrupted by this wealth. She came to see the money as evil, even as a sort of punishment. She had sinned with the child's father and here standing before her was the sorry result. Might he have been a more worthwhile human being had she raised him herself? These were the kinds of questions with which she tormented herself."

"What would have happened to the estate if the ruse had been discovered?" asked Oona Gorey.

"That is a very good question, for it cuts to the heart of the matter. The estate would pass to an heir of the Montague family.

"To Piers Montague, to be precise."

"You are *joking*," said Piers. "You must be joking."

Max shook his head. "This subterfuge took place for the silliest of reasons—the Montague family was considered 'common' and decadent, and they did not want Piers, the only viable candidate, the nearest legitimate, blood heir, to inherit the stately home and all that went with it. It was thought he would never amount to anything and would waste the inheritance."

Max turned to a dumbstruck Piers. The hand that had been poised to smooth back his hair had stopped midair, and he seemed not to realize it. "I am sorry at the way this sounds," said Max. "I am only describing how Lord Lislelivet—father and son—thought about the situation.

"So Ralph Perceval succeeds in due course to the title and the estate, becoming the fifteenth earl of Lislelivet. But that is just the beginning. I know many of you remember the famous kidnapping case out of Nashbury Feathers."

"Of course," said Clement Gorey. "It was tabloid fodder for ages. Dozens of books have been written about it."

Max nodded. "The baby who was the only legitimate heir to the title—although no one apart from his father realized it at the time—was kidnapped. The younger brother who was a late and unexpected arrival when Ralph (let's call him Ralph, for clarity)—when Ralph was twenty. Ralph had this baby kidnapped. Ralph knew the sort of people who would do that for the price of a meal, let alone for a handsome fee."

"How can you possibly know about this?" demanded Piers.

"Stay with me," said Max, resuming his narrative: "Why the kidnapping? Again, the title and attendant properties had to go to legitimate offspring only. The remaining *legitimate* heir would be Piers, a distant relative—a cousin thrice removed or something of that sort. And Meredith, dying, knows this, and summons Piers to the nunnery."

Paloma looked at Piers. "You didn't tell me?"

"Frankly, I thought she was batty. She didn't say anything about any inheritance. She just sent a message, asking me if I would come and see her 'to discuss a matter to my advantage.' It was a tremendously old-fashioned summons, and I was intrigued."

Max pictured the dying nun, drugged on a dozen medications, penning the fatal, melodramatic summons. How was she to know it would lead to murder?

He said, "Ralph comes to hear of the cryptic summons via the letter Dame Meredith sent *him*, knows full well what it is about, and races to Monkbury Abbey, despite the poisoning attempt—to do whatever it takes to keep Piers in the dark about his inheritance. Kill Piers or kill Meredith. Or both. Ralph may even, in a state of heightened paranoia, have associated the poisoning attempt with an effort to get him out of the picture so Piers could inherit."

"How do you know all this?" demanded Abbess Justina.

Max reached inside his jacket and pulled out a thin sheaf of onionskin paper, covered from side to side in small, spidery handwriting.

"This is the handwritten testimony of Dame Meredith Fitzwilliam. It is what she herself calls her dying confession. She wanted the truth to come out, before the entire world. In this document she tells of the events that brought her here. Of the guilt that tormented her, making her conscience work overtime. Her 'sin' was nothing new: that of conceiving a child out of wedlock and giving it over to be raised by her own sister. That her sister had no idea the child was her husband's—that was what Dame Meredith could not forgive herself for.

"The cover-up was not that unusual, either: many grand families have gone to great lengths to keep their estates and bloodlines intact. What was unusual was the level of deception. That is what Dame Meredith berates herself for the most: that she betrayed her own sister with this illicit liaison and then compounded the error with this monstrous substitution and all the lies that attended on it."

"And Dame Pet?" asked the abbess now, more softly. "How does Dame Pet and the poison fit into this story? Or, does it?"

"Dame Petronilla. Yes. For that story we also have to reach back into the past, to a time when Dame Petronilla was Miss Petronilla Falcon, a young nanny in the charge of a small baby born at Nashbury Feathers, ancestral home of the Lislelivet family. The baby named Fontaine Perceval."

"The baby who was kidnapped?" This was Clement Gorey. He looked to his wife for confirmation. She nodded. "When was it this happened? Fifteen years ago or more, right?"

"Closer to eighteen," Max answered him. "It was a case often compared with the 1930s kidnapping of Charles Lindbergh, Jr., the son of aviator Charles Lindbergh and Anne Morrow Lindbergh. The tragic difference being that while the Lindbergh baby's little body finally was discovered, two months after the ransom had been paid, there was no such closure, no such small, cold comfort, for the Perceval family—Lord Lislelivet and his wife. The ransom was paid as demanded, but after detectives had been led on a wild chase over the countryside, the baby never was found, dead or alive.

"As is often the case, the blame for this tragedy spread quickly, and many innocent people suffered. The nanny, for instance, was accused of neglecting her duty, being otherwise occupied with her fiancé, when she should have been watching the baby. A charge, I hasten to add, that was baseless, but a charge that was trumpeted repeatedly by Ralph Perceval, the heir to the family's fortune. The engulfing investigation burned everything in its path, and when it was over—when the media had found new stories to cover—it had changed many lives. Many of the people who worked for the family suddenly found themselves let go, and then found themselves unemployable. No one was willing to take a chance on them, you see. Probably most particularly in the case of a nanny. The 'what ifs?'

loomed too large. What if the accusations were true? The same was the case with her fiancé, who was studying to be a doctor, a pediatrician, in fact, and who was suspected—and cleared—of being in collusion with the nanny. The child had been ailing with a mild cold, and the doctor-in-training had looked in on him once or twice. The innuendo in this sort of case is always enough to destroy lives, particularly in the case of a nanny and pediatrician— what parent would ever entrust either of them with the care of a child?

"His career was derailed as much by the ruin to his reputation as by the emotional wear and tear of the repeated dunning by the press, who blithely and irresponsibly repeated Ralph's accusations, working the sensational story for all it was worth. Imagine opening each day's news to find vile, baseless allegations printed against oneself?

"The implication was that the young, attractive nanny had been too busy cavorting with her fiancé to attend to her duties. But the baby was asleep—it was nighttime—and she told investigators no sound came through the baby monitor.

"So what she was expected to do other than what she did do is a mystery. Still this all got twisted into a seedy story of a licentious woman abandoning her responsibilities to a helpless child. The voice of reason, as so often happens, got shouted down. It was so ugly a story it is perhaps no wonder she chose entering a nunnery as the only way to prove she was the person she always had been: diligent, hardworking, smart, loyal—and deeply religious.

"The truth is the nanny loved the child, stolen as she slept. But the truth was no match for Ralph Perceval, the victim's brother. He kept saying the kidnappers entered the house while she was 'otherwise engaged.' The words were neatly strung together to imply, without actually saying, that she was busy entertaining her fiancé. But denials were fruitless. Otherwise, there was no juicy story to run repeatedly in the morning and evening news. Ralph Perceval even tried to claim she had left the window unlocked so her lover could enter, and that is how the kidnappers got in afterwards. Ridiculous. But it was necessary to make everything sound demeaning, and tawdry."

Dame Petronilla looked up from studying her tightly clenched hands. "I couldn't afford a solicitor on the wages he paid," she said. "So I just took the abuse. I never should have done that. But I thought it would all go away, it was so ridiculous. Accusations not worth responding to. Until you're there, you've no idea how insidious that kind of lie and suspicion can be."

Max paused, as if she might go on, but from her expression, she had retreated back into the memories of those life-altering days. After a few moments, he continued: "When first we spoke, you mentioned that you had some training as a nurse, not that you had been a nanny."

"I know," she acknowledged. "The glib lie. How easy it is to fall into the custom of eliding over the entire truth. I was hoping, of course, that no one would make the connection between me and Nashbury Feathers. Then when Lord Lislelivet was killed . . ."

"It was inevitable it would come out," Max finished her thought. Resuming his tale, he said, "So after a time of what I think we can rightly call persecution, you joined the nearby nunnery. And your fiancé, broken by the whole thing, left for the United States to finish his training, in a different area of specialization.

"But he couldn't stay away long. When he had completed his studies he returned and set up shop in the village of Temple Monkslip, to be near the woman he could not forget. Perhaps he carried with him the misguided hope they could reignite the old flame. He had given up a promising Harley Street career—been forced to give it up, actually, because of the taint of scandal that followed him everywhere. And so he became a G.P. in a small village and called himself content, although he was hardly that. He never married, still carrying this torch for Petronilla Falcon, the woman he had loved. He would come to the nunnery on occasion, eventually becoming the official doctor for the place. But his former fiancée avoided him and begged him to stay away from her. Loving her still, he did as she asked."

By this point in Max's narrative, all eyes had swiveled toward Dr. Barnard, who kept his own gaze straight ahead, his face revealing nothing.

"Then one day, Dr. Barnard heard of Lord Lislelivet's interest in the nunnery. There is one watering hole in Temple Monkslip, the Running Knight and Pilgrim, and Lord Lislelivet's staying there was news in a small village where nothing much happens. Every word of Lord Lislelivet's conversation got repeated, particularly the fact that he seemed as fascinated by the icon—the Face—as anyone else. One of the men who worked on the wall repairs had a story to tell, and tell it he would, to any and all comers, for the price of a pint. For the price of several pints, he would talk of vast golden treasure, precious beyond counting.

"He was making it up as he went, of course. The nuns would never have allowed him to set eyes on the Face. During the repairs, they found another, temporary hiding place.

"Anyway, the next thing you know, Lord Lislelivet is staying at Monkbury Abbey on what he calls a religious retreat. The doctor knows Lord Lislelivet well enough, as does the whole English-speaking world, to know he must be up to something. The doctor, making the logical leap, thinks he is probably after the icon.

"Lady Lislelivet doesn't know what her husband was up to, but she reaches the same conclusion. Lord Lislelivet got awfully keen on a return visit to the abbey, despite the apparent danger to himself.

"But in fact, and Dr. Barnard was not to know this at first, Lord Lislelivet had a more sinister motive.

"Still, whatever he was up to, it is enough to alarm the doctor, to have Lord Lislelivet in such close proximity to the doctor's beloved Petronilla. It doesn't mean she's in danger, necessarily. It is probably more in his mind that he can't stand the thought of this man anywhere near someone as innocent and unspoiled as he knew his old love to be.

"And perhaps . . . perhaps the good doctor thinks he has a chance to set things right, to undo history. To win her back by slaying the dragon—this time. To do the thing he had, in his own mind, singularly failed to do when he had the chance years before."

There was a slight, almost imperceptible nod of the doctor's head.

"I still don't get it," said Xanda. "What does this have to do with the kidnapping?"

"When it comes to the topic of greed, Xanda, I'm afraid it has everything to do with it. Greed on a monstrous scale, surpassing any sort of passing interest Lord Lislelivet may have had in the icon. For this greed involved the betrayal of innocents, the destruction of the family that raised and nurtured him. The greed of the viper in the nest."

"I still don't—" began Xanda.

"The inheritance," said Max simply. "The inheritance that, in the mind of the man who organized the scheme, was worth any amount of betrayal of those who had cherished and sustained him. An inheritance worth killing for, to his twisted way of thinking. Not only were money and land attached to the inheritance, but prestige. Perhaps above all—prestige. There was a title belonging to one of the most noble of ancient families in Great Britain. And having carried the title so long, Lord Lislelivet, as we will continue to call him for now, was not about to relinquish it. Not when just one woman of no consequence to him stood in his way.

"Even if that person was the woman who had given him life."

"You mean, Dame *Meredith*?"

"Yes. Of course. Sadly—of course.

"Dame Petronilla, now the infirmaress, was a nanny at the time of the famous kidnapping, when the nearly newborn son of the fourteenth earl was taken from his crib. The accusations flew, and a close rereading of the news stories of the time shows that behind every accusation and innuendo stood the young Ralph Percival. His father, the fourteenth earl, still being alive, Ralph, then aged twenty, was the heir presumptive. He was a spendthrift, an alcoholic, and a drug user; a liar, a thief, and a complete wastrel, but he was the heir, and unless he became completely unable to function in any capacity, he would remain the heir. The Lislelivets were not the first nor the last family of noble blood to have to deal with a black sheep, of course. The dissolute heir has been a staple of some of England's livelier spots of history.

"But these accusations, as I say, all from the same source, were so unrelenting the nanny and the doctor came to suspect what I know from Dame Meredith was the truth. They suspected young Ralph, the heir presumptive, of masterminding the kidnapping, enlisting and paying off some of his connections in the London drug trade. The few thousand pounds he spent were as nothing stacked against what he was going to lose."

"But—why would he do that?" Xanda asked. "And how did Dame Meredith know Lord Lislelivet was behind the kidnapping?"

"It may be hard for you or anyone normal to understand, but Ralph was livid when the child was born. There was probably a lot of plain old jealousy behind this reaction. His mother—meaning, the woman who had raised him, the then Lady Lislelivet—had been barren all her adult life and was thought to be well past her childbearing years. I am certain it never entered Ralph's mind there might one day be competition for him, the only child of this couple. That he might be given a brother, when suddenly new medical techniques allowed this baby to come along with the potential to snatch away the title from twenty-year-old Ralph. For the woman who had raised Ralph believed he bore no trace of the Lislelivet bloodline, and his father knew of course that the boy he had raised as his son was illegitimate. The parents' joy at this new arrival—the legitimate heir, mind—must have been enormous. Like Elizabeth in the Bible, who thought she was barren and who greeted her miraculous pregnancy with such happiness.

"But then . . . the parents both started to think in terms of how they were locked into this deception, a deception that was no longer necessary. Remember, she had only pretended to have given birth to Ralph. A real heir existed now. A real fifteenth earl of Lislelivet. Could they legally undo what had been done?

"This idea Ralph Percival could not bear. What if his parents went so far as to tell the truth, at least so far as Lady Lislelivet knew it—that the woman who had raised him had not given birth to him. Then under the terms of the estate he would be ousted, and his newborn brother inherit. Of course his parents wouldn't toss Ralph out on the street, nothing so melodramatic as that. In fact, Ralph would continue to live in what to most of the world was unthought-of splendor, riding his horse around the rolling green hills of the estate. But he wouldn't inherit the title, and he wouldn't be able to pass it on to his heirs. He wouldn't be able to enjoy the pomp and ceremony, the bowing and scraping, to which he was entitled as the fifteenth earl.

"So he did what any lunatic would do. Cold-bloodedly, cold-heartedly, but probably also in a mindless fit of jealousy and pique, he arranged to have the baby kidnapped. I don't think he knew or cared what happened to the child—it may have been spirited out of the country and put up for adoption somewhere where few questions would be asked. Once the baby was legally declared dead, Ralph could reign unchallenged—he remained the fifteenth earl of Lislelivet in place of his brother. His mother, the woman who raised him, died shortly afterwards, preceded in death by her husband, the fourteenth earl. The only living witness to the entire scheme, and the only person who suspected Ralph of complicity in his brother's too-convenient disappearance, was his birth mother, Dame Meredith, who years before had taken the veil. But even she could not really grasp that her own son was capable of such an evil deed. Certainly she had no sense of danger when she asked him to come and visit her. She was dying anyway—who would harm her? A sick woman with weeks to live, at best?

"Unfortunately the answer was her own son would try to harm her. Her very own flesh and blood. The boy she had dotingly treated as her nephew, never telling him the truth, telling herself that she had secured his fortune with this deception. But the deception and the fact she had evaded scandal—had evaded ownership of the wrong she had done to her own sister—that weighted more heavily with every passing year.

"Were the lies surrounding his birth made manifest in the man he grew to be?

"She saw less and less of him as the years passed. And perhaps she told herself everything would be all right. But then came his sudden devotion, his intense interest in his dying 'aunt.' Maybe she also believed he was mostly after the 'gold treasure' buried in the crypt, for that would have been in keeping with what she had grown to know of him.

"Then when he began pressing her—Had she told anyone? Whom had she told? Had she confessed? Was there any record of her confession?—I think she realized. In fact I know she suspected him. And she wrote out her confession to the affair, to the illegitimate birth, and to her suspicions about Ralph.

"He came here to kill her," continued Max, "never knowing that she had outwitted him."

"I am very glad at least for that. She saw through him."

Max paused and looked around the room, at all the waiting faces. Some puzzled, some concerned, and two with the look in their eyes of something very old that had caught up with them at last. The expression in those eyes was of sorrow, and relief.

Xanda again was the one who voiced the question in most of their minds.

"And his mother never knew?—I mean, Lady Lislelivet, the woman who raised him?"

"No. The woman who raised him as his mother never realized she was raising her husband's child. His hair and eye coloring were dark—like his father's, in fact—and she never looked beyond that vaguely Hispanic surface appearance. She was too elated at having a child at last to ask too many questions. Sometimes, one just does not want to face the truth. There was a family resemblance that I think she willfully ignored. A suspicion of her husband's infidelity with another woman was one thing. The sure knowledge of his infidelity? And with her own sister? *That* her mind would refuse to accept, even had such an idea occurred to her.

"And so the years passed, and one day she found herself, to her great joy and amazement, pregnant with her own child. The joy was short-lived, because that child was kidnapped—a crime that exhausted the resources of the police and of MI5. I remember the case well—as a young man I wanted so much to be a part of the investigation and was frustrated to be assigned to a different department at the time. It was *the* case every man and woman in law enforcement wanted to solve."

"And the baby was never found? That poor woman. The poor father!" This from Oona, who seemed genuinely distressed. A mother's heart, imagining what that worry would have been like, what the loss of this small and much-longed-for child would have been like. Max warmed to Oona for the first time.

Max thought of his own unborn child, his and Awena's, and the anguish he would feel in similar circumstances, and he thanked God the child would never be a vulnerable target the way Lord and Lady Lislelivet's child had been a target. He or she would be an ordinary child—at least in the eyes of the world, ordinary—never to be exposed to vultures as this young innocent had been.

He shook his head. "Not a trace was ever found, no. The kidnappers were thugs like the Lindbergh kidnappers, but they had probably learned from the mistakes of the original kidnappers, too. The ransom money was picked up, but the baby was never returned. The chances were great that the child was already dead, as is nearly always the case, sadly. And its father and mother, after weeks of worry and anguish, just collapsed from grief."

"The father had a stroke and lingered a short while," said Dr. Barnard. "The mother died of a heart attack. But there was not a doctor in the world who would not blame their breakdown on grief."

Max nodded, locking eyes with the doctor. "However, they did not die before everyone associated with that house was dispersed, in a spurt of fury by the fourteenth earl. The gardener, the maids, the cooks—and of course, the nanny. Everyone leaving under a cloud of suspicion. He couldn't stand to have any one of them around. You can sort of see his point. The man was driven to the edge.

"But the saddest story of all was the butler. After repeated questioning by the authorities, who became convinced he had deliberately left a window unlocked to aid the kidnappers, the poor man shot himself. There is to this day no evidence he had anything to do with it, or even that he was the one who left the window unlocked. But he cracked under the strain, and the certain knowledge his career, in which he took immense pride, was over.

"So, there you have it. Is it a coincidence the nanny would end up in the same convent as the birth mother of Lord Lislelivet? Not at all.

Consider the fame of this nunnery, and its proximity and long historical ties to the manor house where all these sad events took place."

He looked at Dame Petronilla as he said this. She shut her eyes tightly as if the dim light in the room were too harsh, and he thought he saw a nearly imperceptible nod. So many years of carrying that burden of grief and guilt, thought Max. How wrong, wrong, *wrong* it all was.

"So who killed Lord Lislelivet?" said Oona. "Was it some sort of conspiracy?"

Max answered obliquely. "Dame Meredith could easily have drugged him to render him weak and helpless—she had access, there in the infirmary, and knowledge. All the nuns have some knowledge of 'nature's remedies.'

"But I think it was Dame Petronilla, the real expert on plant poisons, who had a hand in this." He made the statement and waited. She would not meet his eyes, so he said, gently, "When the motive is love, there is no force stronger. How far would you go to protect a loved one? To avenge the harm done to them?"

"But, why?" asked Xanda.

But Dame Petronilla answered, "Because, child, I loved him once. I love him still."

"Pet, don't—"

"No," she said to Dr. Barnard. "It's over."

Chapter 38

TIES THAT BIND

Detachment is all.

—*The Rule of the Order of the Handmaids of St. Lucy*

"I saw Lord Lislelivet by chance when he visited the monastery," began Dame Petronilla. "Normally my duties keep me in the infirmary, separate from the main compound. And in choir, our view of visitors is deliberately cut off by the screen. So I don't see the guests as a rule, even at meals—they are seated apart, as you know, and more often than not when I have a patient I take my meals privately in the infirmary.

"But on this day, I was free. Dame Meredith was in hospital receiving treatment and, God be praised, all the other sisters were in good health. So I had all day to work in the herb garden. I was in heaven.

"And then he came wandering by. While I knew *someone* from the peerage was staying with us, for the abbess announces the weekend's visitors in the chapter meeting, I never expected Lord Lislelivet—the man I knew as plain old Ralph Perceval. Of course, he was the sort of man to use his title from the moment he came into it, and on every occasion. But on seeing him, I recognized who it was right away.

"He, of course, did not recognize me, had no need to, for I wasn't important then or now. I was the hired help. He never visited the nursery and never set eyes on me except in a grainy, long-shot newspaper photograph or two from the time. And in any event the years and the habit and the lack of makeup made me, I daresay, unrecognizable from the woman I was back then. I had been a redhead then. But when I saw him I quickly pulled the cowl over my head and moved away before he could see me plainly."

"Everything about your persona had changed with the years, I daresay," said Max.

She nodded. "We leave everything about our old lives behind. Or we try to. We try very hard . . ."

"So you called Dr. Barnard. And you told him that by some unthought-of, unlooked-for chance, Lord Lislelivet—Ralph Perceval—was at Monkbury Abbey. The man who had falsely accused not only you but many others, derailing careers and causing a suicide, a man who for the most purely evil motives had altered the course of all your lives."

She nodded. "Perhaps . . . perhaps if you had known the butler—his name was Phil Jamison—if you had known him you would have known what a tragedy atop a tragedy his death was. He was simply the nicest man. Leroy—Dr. Barnard—and I were just devastated when he killed himself. We both came undone. He was going to be best man at our wedding. He was so dear, so excited about it—do you remember?" She turned toward the doctor, her eyes welling with tears as they sought his. Her voice caught as she tried to continue; they all waited quietly. The only sound to be heard, coming from the open window, was the lazy droning of the bees, cruising from flower to flower. "On top of everything else," she said, "it was too much to bear. And when he died, the press was so cruel. 'The Butler Did It!'—that was too easy a joke for simple minds not to make a play on it."

Max prompted her, "So you called Dr. Barnard."

"Yes. I called him from the cellaress's office."

"And you told him to get out to Monkbury Abbey as soon as he could, on whatever pretext."

"Yes. I simply—" She turned to the abbess, her handsome face now haggard, the picture of distress. "I know how utterly and completely wrong I was in all of this, Abbess. I have broken so many rules. I, who was committed to comfort and healing—that I should have stooped to this. I am deeply, deeply sorry. For all of it." Max knew she must be reliving the disgrace of those days, the shame she had been made to feel by unthinking persecutors who told themselves they were simply doing their jobs. And he was sorry for it.

"Tell us everything you know, Dame Pet," said Abbess Justina. Relief showed on the infirmaress's face at the use of the nickname, at the compassion and implied forgiveness. "We will worry about what to do about all of it later. Right now it is more important that the whole truth come out."

Max, picking up the thread of her story, said, "The phone call brought the doctor out here. Of course, he would move heaven and earth for you, wouldn't he? But maybe you only wanted to talk, perhaps to have your sighting confirmed, to speculate on what could have brought your mutual, mortal enemy, the former Ralph Perceval, here. He could, after all, have come looking for you, for some obscure reason of his own.

"But Dr. Barnard thought he knew what brought him here. And that gave him an idea."

The pair exchanged glances.

"Or was it you, Dame Petronilla, who had the idea? I think perhaps it was, since you knew about the icon. That it was real. And you told the doctor. And no doubt like you, Dr. Barnard saw a way to get what he had long wanted more than anything in this life: a confession—even an apology. Ridiculous hope, that, but it seemed a heaven-sent situation. Dr. Barnard would promise his enemy secret access to the icon, dangling this precious artifact before the eyes of Lord Lislelivet in exchange for the truth of what had happened to that poor child that fateful night. He wanted above anything the admission of the elder brother's participation in that nefarious scheme. I am perhaps giving you too much the benefit of the doubt, but isn't that what you had in mind, Dr. Barnard? To extract the truth from him, promising your silence, in exchange for your revelation of where the icon was hidden?"

Dr. Barnard, staring at his folded hands with their white knuckles, would not answer.

"I prefer to believe that is how it happened," said Max softly. "At least, at first, wasn't that the plan? Of course, you could not know that the icon was not really uppermost in his mind. You could not know his real and deeply wicked reason for being at Monkbury Abbey."

Dr. Barnard would not look up, perhaps unwilling just yet to seize the lifeline Max was trying to throw his way.

"He must have laughed at you. I would imagine that is what he would do. You had it all so wrong. And it was such a hopeless idea, idealistic in the extreme, to try to make a pact with a demon like Lord Lislelivet. But perhaps the chance to bargain, to use this one bargaining chip you had, blinded you to the fact that you were dealing with a man so dishonest that he would never allow you to walk away, knowing the truth. Perhaps you struggled, and in the struggle he was killed?"

"No," Dr. Barnard said simply.

"Is that what happened, Dr. Barnard?" Max persisted. "Because otherwise, I have to believe you came here to murder cold-bloodedly the man who had ruined your life and the life of your beloved. The man who had in fact taken away the blissful union you had planned to have together. The children you might have had, the house and home. Not to mention the career that had been derailed by this man who dared put himself above all the rest of us. Who had achieved the pinnacle of respectable society by having had kidnapped, and possibly having had killed, his own half-brother."

"You must leave her out of this," said Dr. Barnard, his voice ragged with urgency.

"Would that I could," said Max. "Once she had tipped you off that Lord Lislelivet was here, how could thoughts of revenge not inevitably follow? You'd be less than human had such thoughts not flitted through your mind. Perhaps she begged you to do nothing. But she did agree to admit you to the grounds by leaving the black door over the river unlocked or by admitting you yourself. I might believe you if you said you told her only that you had a plan to expose Lord Lislelivet, to wring a confession from him, but that was only to gain her cooperation in this scheme. You wanted most of all to be sure no blame would attach to Dame Petronilla."

"I—" she began.

"No," the doctor interrupted. "Say nothing. Please, say nothing more."

"How could you not know what was in his heart?" Max asked her.

She did not reply, studying her tightly folded hands. Max had the impression she did not herself know the answer.

Barnard said, "She knew nothing of my plans, I tell you."

Max waited, looking patiently to her for an answer. Finally she turned to Max and said, "I thought we could expose him for the horrible fraud he was. I knew Lord Lislelivet had some financial motive or other in being here—he worshipped no god but mammon. It was also certain that whatever light of publicity he chose to shine on the abbey, it would be to the detriment of our peace here and to the advancement of his own career. I didn't think he was above stealing the Mandylion if he thought it was worth a lot. Fortunately, the rumors of its being pure gold were false. The value was in its antiquity, its—its very mysteriousness and rarity. Its possible holiness. And its newfound 'celebrity,' if I may use the term, brought about by that silly book."

How poor Frank Cuthbert, Author, would despair at hearing his book thus characterized, thought Max. The wonder of it was how much that "silly" book had played into the tangle of events at Monkbury Abbey.

"But I never thought beyond setting Lord Lislelivet up for a fall."

"Dame Petronilla, please. You surely—"

"I swear it. It was wrong of me to want revenge of any kind, I know that. I know that was where I took the first wrong turning. But I never wanted this—to take a life."

"It was an accident," began Dr. Barnard. "It had to have been an accident."

Max decided to relent. "I will say I don't think it was either of you who killed him, as much as you may have wanted to. No. That was another person entirely.

"Here is how I reconstruct what happened. In chapter, Abbess Justina announced the guesthouse was hosting an important visitor. And when you got a close look, Dame Petronilla, you knew exactly who he was. Older, more polished and urbane, rounder and balding—not the twenty-year-old kid you'd rarely set eyes on eighteen years ago. But back then he was Ralph Perceval. In the intervening years, you've had no access to the newspapers or broadcasts. I would imagine that after your experience with the media, part of the peace accorded you by the abbey was that you could avoid the daily news. So if Lord Lislelivet had appeared on television at any time in the past eighteen years promoting some bill or position or cutting a ribbon or riding to hounds or whatever he was doing, you wouldn't have known about it.

"But, on closer inspection, his face with its superior expression? That strutting walk? Oh, yes. You recognized him as the self-important little man whose false accusations had led to the guilty party's making a clean escape, while suspicion ruined so many lives."

Max turned to Dr. Barnard, watching him closely. "Dr. Barnard has lived in the U.S. all these years, and, unlike people living in the U.K., he has been spared the sight of Lord Lislelivet on television. But once he was pointed out by Dame Pet—oh, yes.

"She told the doctor of this unprecedented interest in the nunnery by Lord Lislelivet. They talked, coming to no resolution then as to what to do, but the seeds were planted in the doctor's mind. And when Lord Lislelivet scheduled a return visit, well . . ."

"If he'd not come back he'd still be alive," said Dame Petronilla.

"Was the poisoning a warning, then?" Max asked. But she did not reply.

"Soon the pair of you began to speak of a way to force the truth from Lord Lislelivet," Max continued. "Of a way to establish an alibi for yourselves.

"And as you spoke, you were overheard."

The pair exchanged startled glances.

"You were overheard by Dame Meredith.

"It was a simple plan, really. The first step was to neutralize any witnesses. The novice was given a drink before her watch began. There was nothing easier than to add a sleeping draught to her tea.

"Dame Hephzibah, now . . . she was more of a problem. You had to nullify her ability to witness. She had complained that her failing eyesight made her eyes tired and sore, so you gave her some eye drops. But what was in those eye drops was belladonna. That way, her eyesight, always bad, would be terribly blurry. She might also suffer confusion from the drug—a common side effect. That is how desperate you were that your scheme work. I don't think poisoning an elderly woman was in the usual repertoire for either of you. To take any chances with an elderly woman's health."

"No!" Dame Petronilla said, stung by the accusation. "It was an accident. She got it on her hands somehow and rubbed her eyes."

"Hush!" commanded Dr. Barnard

But the fight seemed to have gone out of Dame Petronilla. She could accept being an accessory to the murder of Lord Lislelivet, but not a poisoner of helpless old Dame Hephzibah. As strange a distinction as it was, Max could somehow see the logic.

"She rubbed her eyes . . . her eyes were always were dry, you see—she complained they bothered her. Old age, you know. If I'd known . . . if I'd realized . . . but I didn't."

"And this is why she couldn't see?" said Max. "I don't buy it. I think she ingested some of it, too. Her symptoms were severe, even taking her age into account. Her confusion was extreme."

Dame Pet turned to Dr. Barnard accusingly. "Did you—?"

"Hush," he repeated, this time in a soothing voice. "It will be all right."

Max went on, relentless now he was so close to the truth. "To be honest, I don't think she was completely hallucinating that night. She just couldn't see clearly what she *did* see, because of the drops in her eyes. She said she saw a 'yellow monk.' We thought she might mean a Buddhist monk or nun. I apologize, Dame Hephzibah, for doubting you."

She looked around at the others, an "I told you so" expression on her face.

"She did see someone that with her compromised eyesight looked like a figure wearing a yellow monk's robe with a hood. And she said she saw a "white nun," too, at which point her testimony was completely discounted. What she meant of course was that she saw either the novice Sister Rose in her white novice's habit or Dame Pet in her white nursing habit.

"I am now inclined to take her at her word. She could see—not well—but she was not having hallucinations."

"But . . . Dame Pet was in the choir," said the abbess. "We all saw her. She wouldn't have had time to commit the crime."

"There!" said the doctor, rallying. "You can't get around that, can you? She was in the choir. Her presence vouched for—by a group of nuns, no less."

"Yes, it all does seem very airtight, doesn't it?" said Max mildly. "But no. It was not airtight at all." He turned around, gathering their attention to him. They were all preternaturally still. The nuns, especially, looked perplexed and anxious, and he was sorry for it. He began to speak:

"What we are dealing with here is an elaborate double bluff. Seeing the nuns in their all-enveloping habits every day, it is easy to see how a woman or a man could impersonate a nun. It would be the easiest thing in the world to do. But what if this particular plan took things one step further? What if a person dressed in a nun's habit to act as a decoy, providing an alibi for the nun? And what if, simultaneously, a nun dressed in 'street clothes,' for the same reason—to provide an alibi for her partner?"

"O-k-a-ay," piped Xanda, thinking it through. "I can see that possibility. But how? How exactly did they do it? And why?"

"The time of the murder had to be carefully established so the alibis would hold. Lord Lislelivet's death was surrounded by such a lot of deliberate hubbub that no question could be raised about the apparent time of his murder.

"Once I began to think of the timing as being very deliberate and specific, very much of the essence, as it were, I began to wonder why. If it weren't done in such a way as to clear all those nuns in the choir, one in particular. There they were, all lined up and accounted for. There are so few of them these days that one missing nun would immediately be noticed."

Abbess Justina was nodding her head as he spoke. "It was always evident that my sisters were innocent of involvement this."

"It was evident as far as the eye could see," said Max. "But was that in fact the case? *Were* all the nuns in choir for Compline?"

She nodded emphatically. "All thirty-one. We always sit in our assigned places. An empty place would be obvious, I tell you. Like a missing tooth."

"Ah," repeated Max. "An empty place would be obvious, yes."

"So . . ." This was Xanda.

"So there were thirty-one bodies in the choir stalls at the service. But not all of them were nuns. One of them was an imposter dressed in a white nun's habit."

He turned quietly.

"Which can only mean . . ."

Xanda's kohl-lined eyes widened as she took in the implications.

Max said, "It was in fact Dr. Barnard who had taken Dame Petronilla's place. Because she was recovering from a cold, or so she said, no one noticed that her low voice was just a whisper that night."

"Dr. Barnard?" Several of them spoke at once, heads swiveling, looking for confirmation of the impossible.

Dame Olive spoke up excitedly. "My stall is next to hers in choir, and while I know this sounds odd, I thought she had a slightly different, well, *odor* about her that night. At first I imagined it was tobacco, but since that was impossible I discounted the idea. But she was always working with different herbs, so it could have been anything, really. If she were in a hurry she'd dry herbs in the infirmary oven. Lately she often smelled of coriander. She'd been giving it to Dame Meredith for her upset stomach caused by the chemo, poor thing. She'd also use it as a massage oil to help with Dame Hephzibah's arthritis."

"But if any of us had kitchen duty—well, you never knew what you were getting. I can always tell when Dame Petronilla on my left or Dame Agatha on my right had had kitchen duty because they would smell of whatever we would soon be eating or had just eaten. Fish days were often rather unpleasant. Or I might get the scent of flowers if it was someone's day to place fresh flowers on the altar or in the refectory."

"Thank you, Dame Olive. I am certain your perceptions are correct."

But she was not quite finished. "That night, I had the idea Dame Pet had been working in the cloister garden with its fruit trees. It was that smell of coriander, but mixed with a stronger scent of citrus. Rather a woody, spicy smell, it was. Coriander is quite popular in aphrodisiac blends." She added: "Or so I am told."

"Thank you, Dame Olive," said Max again. "Probably you were picking up the scent of Dr. Barnard's cologne mixed with the odor of tobacco.

"Here is what I think the plan must have been." He returned his gaze to Leroy Barnard's face. "You, Dr. Barnard, arrived at Monkbury sometime after the Vespers service, which begins at six, and before Compline, which begins at nine. You arrived not on foot or by car but by boat, and you were met at the black door—the door beneath the infirmary, opening onto the river—by Dame Petronilla. There was a trail of water leading down the short corridor to the infirmary—perhaps it was not water from an overflowing flower arrangement as Dame Olive thought, but water dripping from your yellow rain slicker. In any event, that is the 'yellow monk' Dame Hephzibah saw.

"You followed Dame Pet to the examination room in the infirmary, where you exchanged your outer garments for her robes—probably staying behind the screen in the examination room in case anyone walked in. You put on her white nursing habit, and she put on the clothing you wore beneath the rain slicker: your raincoat and trilby hat and neck scarf. She even put on your Wellies, so she was covered from head to toe. Even her shorn hair peeking from under the hat would be a match for yours. Your patient Dame Meredith appeared to be asleep, and so was the the novice assigned to watch her. Dame Hephzibah in her gatehouse had been blinded by the belladonna, so there was no one else to see. Even if there

had been, from a distance, the impersonation was close enough no one
would suspect.

"Then you, Dr. Barnard, in disguise, walked to the church for Compline, and Dame Petronilla, dressed as you, sat at the beside of Dame
Meredith. No doubt you had given Dame Meredith something to make
her sleep, too, although she did not take it. She needed her wits about her.

"Why all the subterfuge? To establish that Dame Petronilla could
not have been murdering Lord Lislelivet. Your main concern, doctor, was
to provide the woman you love with an alibi. Just as you were her main
concern.

"Again, timing was all, and the system of bells helped. When the bell
rang at five minutes to nine, Dame Pet—rather, her impersonator—had
to stop what she was doing and leave. This allowed just enough time to
keep a prearranged rendezvous with Lord Lislelivet. Dame Pet had
promised to meet him in the crypt and show him where the treasure was
hidden. He was to wait there for her, which of course he could be counted
on to do. I think your secret plan, Dr. Barnard, was to kill him immediately, and to set his enormous Rolex ahead, smashing it to jam the works,
pinpointing the time of his death as occurring during the service of Compline. You then would continue on to take Dame Pet's place in the choir
stall.

"That is what happened—almost. Because when you got to the crypt,
Dr. Barnard, in your disguise, Lord Lislelivet was already dead, wasn't he?"

"Yes. I—I don't know that I could have gone through with it. Please
believe that. I *wanted* to. But as you say—he was dead already. His watch
was broken, with the time set ahead. Everything as you said. Everything
as I had planned. But I didn't do it. And neither did she—I know it!"

"But you suspected she had," Max said, "for whatever reasons of her
own. And this is why you didn't raise the alarm. How could you, anyway,
dressed as you were? How could you ever explain the charade? So you
carried on into the church for services, wondering the while who had
saved you the trouble of killing your worst enemy."

The doctor allowed himself a sigh of relief, his rigid shoulders dropping as if a yoke had been removed. "That is it exactly. I couldn't believe my luck, if I can call it that. At the same time, I couldn't figure out who had killed him 'for' me, so to speak. So I just carried on, as you say. In the choir, I kept my voice low, almost inaudible—Dame Pet had already established that she had a cold and could not fully participate. As soon as Compline was over, the Great Silence started for the night, of course, which made everything easier—no one was going to stop me to look me in the face and start chatting about anything. I returned to the infirmary, where I told Dame Pet what had happened—although I wasn't sure she believed me."

"But, wait a minute," said Xanda. "Sister Rose knew the doctor—or someone dressed as him—had been there with her since before Compline, at nine. Why couldn't he have nipped out and done the killing and come back?"

"If she woke, she'd have no way of knowing what time it was, or so the reasoning went. None of them are allowed to own a timepiece. As it happens, she slept through most of it. It wasn't just chamomile in the tea given her by Dame Pet, but something more potent, added by the doctor from his bag. I believe she also received a third dose."

"Third dose?" asked the abbess.

"Of Dame Meredith's sleeping draught, yes. Sister Rose, dozing off and on, had no idea what time it was. It's a wonder the pair of you, trying so desperately to cover up for the other, didn't actually harm her or Dame Hephzibah, with this cocktail of drugs to which you subjected them. Of course, you had no way of knowing Dame Meredith was also trying to put Sister Rose temporarily out of commission."

Dame Petronilla, for the first time, looked completely stricken. Lord Lislelivet's death was one thing, but something happening to Sister Rose or old Dame Hephzibah was another matter.

Sister Rose looked stunned, just realizing her narrow escape. Her dark eyes narrowed in a kind of anguish. Possibly, thought Max, she had thought to be safe here and was just realizing there was no such place, no place of safety out of the line of fire.

DCI Cotton was wishing Max had shared some of these little inves-tigative insights with him ahead of time. But, *noo-o-o*. Max, ever the Lone Ranger.

"So who killed Lord Lislelivet?" demanded Xanda.

"I think it must have been his mother, don't you?"

"What?" This time they all, without exception, looked mystified.

"His mother, Dame Meredith."

Chapter 39

THE DEVIL YOU SAY

Verily it is said, give the devil his due.

—*The Rule of the Order of the Handmaids of St. Lucy*

"Why don't you start with the fruitcake, Dame Petronilla?" Max suggested.

Dame Petronilla heaved a great sigh, exchanging a glance with Dr. Barnard. And turning to Max she began to speak.

"Yes. It was months ago, on his first visit—his first visit in years. I took one of Dame Fruitcake's baking pans that she had left sitting out, full of batter, ready to go in the oven. We have a kitchenette over at the infirmary that has a small oven. I—I mixed the berries into the fruitcake batter, baked it, and wrapped it and left it for Lord Lislelivet as a 'gift.'" She paused, blushing. "I know how petty and small that sounds. How petty and small it *was*. I could not myself believe that someone such as I, someone whose sole interest was in caring for others, could become so filled with hatred that I . . . that I did this to him."

"With the intent to poison him? To kill him?"

"*No*, never—I swear it, Father. I just was so outside of myself. Filled with rage, *consumed* by it, I didn't really know what I was doing, but my aim never was to kill or seriously injure him or anyone. His wife or a guest could have died, and that was never, ever my intent. I easily could have killed him if I'd wanted to. I had the knowledge and the resources to do it. But I never wanted . . ." She turned and looked at Dr. Barnard. "I never wanted this. I may have wished him dead a hundred thousand times, but I could never kill him, or anyone. With my bare hands?" She turned up her palms and looked at them. "Never," she repeated. "I was trained to heal, not to harm."

And Dr. Barnard had sworn to be a healer when he took the Hippocratic Oath, thought Max. It didn't appear to have stopped him. Max looked at her, at this woman whose life had been dedicated to love and forgiveness. And he thought how difficult those concepts were in practice.

He believed her. About the berries in the cake, at least, he believed her. He was not sure he believed her disclaimer that she did not know what the doctor might be planning. Did she just convince herself that what she suspected could not be true? She had loved the man once, and she said she loved him still. People in love did all manner of strange things and would believe all manner of stories that would shield them from the knowledge that their beloved was a killer. His mind flashed to his parishioner Chrissa with her abusive husband, a case of love gone wrong if ever there were one. How far would Chrissa's ego go to shield her from the knowledge she willingly had made a foolish, hideous, life-threatening mistake in marrying such a man?

Dame Petronilla had told Max she'd given up nursing because it was hard to watch people die. It must have been harder still to have the child in your care disappear into probable danger and you be blamed for it.

Aloud he said, "There is little doubt Lord Lislelivet came here to do away with Dame Meredith if he couldn't 'reason' with her. Even if she had promised to carry her secret to the grave, could he trust her to keep the promise? But she made no such promise, the woman who stood between him and a fortune. Instead she declared that she must tell the truth, for his sake as well as hers. They were at perfectly opposed purposes, this dying woman of religion and her unholy son.

"Dame Meredith was ill, but she was not completely bedridden. She was also highly motivated, needing to set things right before she passed. Here is how I reconstruct what happened. Obviously, I must estimate the times in certain instances." He took his revised timeline from his pocket and read aloud:

8:00 p.m. – Dame Petronilla goes to gatehouse and doses Dame Hephzibah with belladonna, then returns to the infirmary.

8:45 – Dame Meredith slips away from her bed to meet her son, Lord Lislelivet, in the church. She knows from eavesdropping that Dame Petronilla has lured him with the promise of showing him the crypt, so Dame Meredith arranges an earlier meeting. She has not taken the usual sleeping powder provided her by Dame Petronilla but has used it to sedate her minder, Sister Rose.

8:50 – Lord Lislelivet meets Dame Meredith at the top of the crypt stairs. They argue. According to her confession, he slips on the age-worn stone and falls down the spiral stairs to his death. His watch is broken and she adjusts it forward to 9:10, so she and her sisters are alibied. She returns to the infirmary.

8:50 – Meanwhile, Dr. Barnard, arriving by small boat, has already entered Monkbury Abbey via the black door on the water.

8:55 – Dr. Barnard, dressed as Dame Petronilla, entering the crypt from within the cloister, goes to keep the meeting with Lord Lislelivet, but finds him dead.

9:00 – Compline begins. Dr. Barnard goes through with the prearranged plan to take Dame Petronilla's place in her stall.

9:30 – Compline ends; the Great Silence begins. Dr. Barnard returns to the infirmary. He tells Dame Petronilla he has found Lord Lislelivet dead. Dame Petronilla, still disguised as Dr. Barnard, gets in the waiting boat and rows to Dr. Barnard's car, which is parked in the woods.

10 – Dame Petronilla drives up to the nunnery and obtains the key to a room in the guesthouse from the vision-impaired Dame Hephzibah. Meanwhile Dr. Barnard carries the body of Lord Lislelivet up the stairs and through the cloister garden, and pushes it down the well: the body must not be found within the off-limits cloistered area, which might implicate Dame Petronilla. She returns from the guesthouse to the infirmary. Just before 10:10, Dr. Barnard sets up a hue and cry—a terrified yell, as if Lord Lislelivet were just being murdered.

10:10 – Hidden by trees, Dr. Barnard returns to the infirmary. He and Dame Petronilla exchange clothing, and she hands him the key to his room in the guesthouse.

10:20 – Dame Petronilla wakens Sister Rose from her drugged state.

10:20 – Dr. Barnard loses himself within the abbey grounds, in the confusion of the discovery of the body.

"Good grief," said Xanda when he had finished. "Are you sure of all this?"

"As sure as I can be without confirmation from Dame Petronilla."

He looked at her, and she said, "That is more or less correct. I hid an extra habit in the guesthouse so I could change there. It reduced the risk of being caught out in disguise."

"So I am right in thinking the plan all along was to kill Lord Lislelivet? Because otherwise, such an elaborate ruse seems totally unnecessary. It's overkill, if you'll pardon the expression. Temporarily blinding Dame Hephzibah with eye drops was not just improvised. It was the first step in your plan."

"I didn't mean—" she began, but Max held up a hand to stay her. He had heard enough.

"And poor Sister Rose," he said. "She was expecting a major scolding from Dame Petronilla for having fallen asleep, but the scolding never came."

"I didn't understand myself why I would nod off so suddenly and completely," said Sister Rose, "even given the fact we rise early each day. Now I see . . ."

"On top of the early rising," said Max, "and all the manual labor under a hot sun, you were overdosed with a powerful drug meant to give

Dame Meredith several hours respite from her illness. It was enough to fell a horse."

Dame Petronilla had pulled out her rosary beads and, eyes downcast, was silently saying over her prayers. A series of thirty-three beads, one for each year of Christ's life, helped mark her progress. Max's eye drifted to the distinctive red-and-black beads. He could see that one of a group of seven beads was missing, just as Dame Petronilla seemed to realize that her count was off. She looked down at the strand in her hands, a puzzled look on her face.

"What is it, Dame Pet?" he asked her, suddenly alarmed.

"I'm not sure. But one bead is missing. Not to worry. They are quite safe, rosary peas. That is, unless the coating is broken."

"And what happens if it is?"

"Why, if it gets in the bloodstream it is a deadly poison."

This woman must be barking.

Max turned to DCI Cotton. "Get the medical examiner over to the infirmary—*now*. Say it's a suspected poisoning. Self-inflicted."

"Dame Meredith," said Cotton.

It was not a question.

EPILOGUE

Max had learned immediately on his return to Nether Monkslip that Chrissa Baker, the woman he'd gone to see in hospital before leaving for Monkbury Abbey, had upon her release returned to her husband, ignoring the temporary safe house Max had arranged for her use until she could find her feet. All the resources of the village would have been at her disposal.

People who knew Chrissa loved her. No one understood it.

Max's heart sank at the news—there was literally a dropping sensation, as if his heart had plunged from a great height. How could she? How *could* she? And most of all: *why*? When he had thrown her a lifeline. Why?

He thought of another Cohen lyric, where Leonard spoke of finally hanging it up—hanging up his robes on a peg at the Buddhist monastery on Mount Baldy and driving down from that particular mountain after five long years:

> *"I finally understood*
> *I had no gift*
> *for Spiritual Matters."*

It had been at that moment exactly how Max had felt. What did *he* know of anything? What ability did he have to absorb, let alone impart wisdom—he who couldn't even a talk a woman into saving her own life?

Into running from the man who was breaking both her body and her spirit?

At that moment Awena had entered the room. He opened his arms to welcome her.

"You've heard about Chrissa then, have you?" she said, lifting her face to his. She always seemed to know—when he was happy, or when he was distracted, or when he was bereft, as now. He gathered her body to his, holding her tightly, as though his heart really would fall and shatter without her there.

"Some people have no center to them, Max. And no sense that our time here on earth is short. They cling to any passing branch in the river, never noticing that it's carrying them straight over a waterfall. I don't think there is much else you can do for her except to let her know you're still here."

"Until he kills her one day."

"He may very well do that. We've both known it to happen."

"I don't understand. She's not a stupid woman."

"Of course she's not. She's one of the brightest people I know, and the most loving. I will go and see her. But I won't waste my breath trying to talk her into anything. Just knowing you have people who care can make you stronger. Things may change. We'll have to wait her out."

They sat then on the sofa by the fire and began to knit together their days by talking of many things. The upcoming handfasting ceremony consumed them both, not to mention trying to come up with a name for the baby on the way. They had had little chance to talk about the events at Monkbury Abbey, and Max, still thinking it through, had not been inclined to talk about it.

"Of course," Awena said. "Rosary peas. They were originally from Indonesia, but now they grow almost anywhere with a tropical climate."

"The nuns got in a shipment of rosaries to the gift shop, made from these rosary peas," said Max. "The rosaries were made by missionary sisters. Only Dame Petronilla recognized the red-and-black beads for what they were when they arrived. She pulled them from the shop, confiscated and destroyed them, just to be on the safe side, but she kept one set of beads for herself because they were so pretty and unusual. They weren't dangerous unless they were broken open and ingested, which she had no intention of doing.

"As I say, only Dame Petronilla recognized the rosary pea for what it was. For the fact is each pea contains a poison even more deadly than ricin. And when Dame Meredith saw them being used by Dame Petronilla, and commented on the pretty beads, Dame Pet told her what they were, never imagining . . ."

"And Dame Meredith stole the one when Dame Pet wasn't looking. Broke it off the chain."

"That's right. Effectively unleashing its poison. They are safe enough left alone, but once the coating is broken . . . I suspect her idea was to keep it close by—just in case. In case things got to looking too bad. In case the treatments got to be too horrid—or hopeless—for her to endure any more. Or in case she saw everything in her life, past and present, closing in on her. Which is exactly what did happen."

"What a completely sad ending to a sad story."

He agreed. "It is terribly sad. And they doubt she'll regain consciousness. A waste of a good person, over a mistake so old."

"So, it was really about that horrible old crime that came back to haunt them all?" Awena said.

"Nearly twenty years on, yes. But we will never know what happened to that small child. That is the one question I wish I could answer, for everyone's sake, including mine."

"And Dr. Barnard and Dame Petronilla—well, we can't call her that anymore, can we? But—it seems right that they would be together at last. I guess we'll get used to calling her plain old Petronilla Falcon, now that she has left the order."

"Leaving really was the only thing, the best thing she could do. Her vocation, as she now sees it, was not so much one of choice, but of fleeing the world. The nuns talked of that a lot—how a true vocation was a running toward God, not away from man, or words to that effect. I would say running away from yourself fits in there somewhere, too, as not leading to a true calling for the life."

"Is that what Dame Meredith was doing, too? Running away?"

"I suppose. But I like to think she found some contentment. Until . . . well, anything like contentment was blown apart when Lord Lislelivet came along, desperate to save his title and his money."

"Poor woman," said Awena. "How desperate she must have been."

"I think we have to take it as given that she was not herself. She had been writing a letter to leave behind, addressed to the abbess and the community as a whole. If she'd been guilty of murder, I think she would have admitted it—and I for one don't think she was capable of that. But she admitted to all the old scandal and subterfuge—to the fact that she was Lord Lislelivet's natural mother and how she had conspired to hide his true origins from her own sister. To the fact that she had betrayed that sister in the first place and then indulged in a cover-up that went on for decades. It must be said: Lord Lislelivet, unpleasant a man as he was, had a right to know who he was. But his father's telling him, in this case, was a very big mistake."

"Just think how the truth all those years ago, as disagreeable as it may have been, would have spared everyone years down the line."

Max said, "Dame Meredith was mostly guilty of being naïve. Perhaps it is a trait that overtakes someone in the life there or that was always part of a trusting nature. She actually thought she could convince her son to give up the blood money, as she thought of it—in her letter, she quoted the rich man and the camel passage from the Bible: how it is easier for a camel to pass through the eye of a needle than for a rich man to enter into heaven. Lord Lislelivet believed without a doubt she would give the game away if he didn't do something fast, for she had said as much in the letter she wrote to him—to his mind, she was absolutely unhinged to be talking the way she was. Give away money? Never! He tried 'coming clean' with her—at least his distorted idea of coming clean. He told her what he'd done to his baby brother and that he would surely go to prison for it if this all came out, thinking she would want to spare him. Well, that was all she needed to hear to be completely horrified. He overplayed his hand, forgetting that those maternal bonds had never really been forged between her and him. All she could think was of the nightmare her sister had gone through and how she, Dame Meredith, *must* make it right before her time ran out."

"I can see that. Everything in her training, in who she was, and who she was trying to be, cried out for the truth to be told. And the one thing a man like her son feared the most was the truth."

"Do you know," Max added musingly, "I even saw the family resemblance, but at first I wrote it off to the fact the son resembled his father in photographs I'd seen of them both. Dark hair and eyes, and olive-skinned. Both men had the same body type, with the massive chest over an otherwise small frame. Only much later in the case did I realize that what I was noticing also was Lord Lislelivet's resemblance to his *mother*. His facial resemblance, in particular, to Dame Meredith. They both had that rather aristocratic cast to their features—her face much thinner and more drawn because of her illness, of course.

"Without the distractions of hair color and style, what is left are the basics—the planes of the face, the angle of the nose, and the width of the brow. Even then, I missed it. I just had this tantalizing sense that I was seeing a familiar face when I visited Dame Meredith in the infirmary."

"There is no question she tried to commit suicide?"

"None, according to Cotton's medical examiner. It all just collapsed on her. All of her life. The despair and the weight of guilt overwhelmed her in the end. For there was one added element. During all the medical testing and treatment she had undergone, Dame Meredith learned she carried a gene for a progressively debilitating disease that had likely been passed along to her male child. This as much as anything made her want to have it all come out, to want to tell her son all of the truth. She felt so guilty, not about depriving him of an inheritance—what did a nun care about that, after all?—but of maybe having handed along this disease that amounted to a death sentence. So she thought, 'I must tell my son the truth; it is the least I can do for him now.' Unfortunately, she found him to be not grateful but more determined to keep what was 'his' at all costs. To keep the truth of his parentage hidden."

Awena said, "I wonder how alike the brothers might have been, had the younger one survived, that is. The thing with two siblings born that far apart is that, fully related or partly related, they have little in common from a generational standpoint—exacerbated by the fact they were practically raised by different parents."

"I don't follow," said Max.

"Parents in their twenties are different from parents in their forties. They are practically different people from their younger selves. Child-rearing techniques evolve like any other skill."

"I'm sure you're right. I can only hope *I'm* ready. I don't want to just practice on this little one. I want to be—I don't know. Perfect, I guess. Everything a child can look up to."

His eye caught on the crèche scene in his office, purchased from the abbey shop. He'd decided not to pack it away but to leave it on display year round. The little painted figures brightened his bookshelves, which otherwise mainly held the heavy religious tomes inherited from his predecessor.

"I nearly forgot," he said, and striding over to the desk he handed her a small package, wrapped in white cotton cloth and tied with a yellow bow. "As I was leaving the nunnery, Dame Hephzibah rushed out—well, for her it was rushing—and handed me this gift."

Awena unwrapped the present to reveal one of the tiny christening dresses Max had seen in the abbey gift shop.

"Oh, Max," breathed Awena. "I've never seen anything so beautiful. I'll have to write and thank her. What kindness."

Just then a little car trundled by, laden with flowers for the handfasting ceremony. The windows had been rolled down to allow the blossom heads to wave free. The white car with its burden of summer flowers—Max recognized the marigold, and cornflower, and pink roses, and daisies—was on its way to Awena's cottage, where the ceremony was to be held the next afternoon.

"I thought the day would never arrive," said Max. And resolutely, he tucked the case of Monkbury Abbey into the back of his mind. But the memory of Dame Meredith would be a constant in his prayers for years to come.

The handfasting ceremony of Maxen Tudor and Awena Owen was to become the stuff of legend, the sort of event destined to be woven into the lore of the village. The details were to be embellished and improved upon in the telling, although in truth, it was as perfect a day as it could be, from beginning to end.

The preparations for the handfasting had been under way for weeks; the heavens cooperated with nightly meteor showers in the clear skies over Nether Monkslip. Max and Awena would stand before the village and speak the vows they had written, promises that would seal their unity and affirm their greater strength as a couple. The service would invite Air, Fire, Water, and Earth to witness the healing power of their love. The celebrant, having poured cleansing water over Max and Awena's hands, would then lightly bind together their hands with a silken handkerchief as the words of blessing were spoken. The pair would promise to support each other through good and bad times and daily renew with word and deed the loving foundation of their lives.

The day itself continued a warm and languid trend, although the villagers under the somnolent clouds had been anything but idle. Indeed, all of Nether Monkslip had been in a fizz of activity. No one could recall a social occasion to match it since the owner of Totleigh Hall had brought home his bride many years before.

"But this," Elka Garth, in charge of organizing the food, told one and all, "will be even better."

And of course Elka herself had gone into overdrive, keeping the ovens at the Cavalier Tea Room and Garden going practically night and day to produce the magical baked goods for which she was known. There were summer berry tartlets, including almond tartlets made with raspberries and glazed with red currant jelly, each piped with tiny rosettes of whipped cream. And there were glazed figs. And melon cubes. And small squares of chocolate cheesecake. She had rented several tables to hold the food, and worried there would not be enough room for it all.

Elka, Suzanna Winship had decided, was often happiest when worried, in having something or someone to fuss about. This, thought Suzanna, would be her shining hour.

Even Elka's normally feckless son Clayton had pitched in, helping his mother with the washing up. And even though he chipped a few dishes in the process, it was generally agreed, his attempt at helpful participation was a miracle in and of itself.

Max, seeing the arriving delicacies—the red, black, and white currants on the pies, biscuits, and cakes, and the summer berries of every kind—had a sudden flashback to the doings at Monkbury Abbey, which he quickly erased from his mind. But Dame Ingrid had not forgotten him and had produced a specially decorated fruitcake, his name entwined in icing with Awena's. Enclosed was a note wishing them happiness and pointedly assuring them that this cake she had made herself.

Courtesy of the Grimaldi brothers of the White Bean restaurant, there were dozens of appetizers: bruschetta by the platterful, and artichoke hearts, mozzarella cheese, cherry tomatoes, and basil leaves speared together on sticks, the whole painted with pesto sauce.

In addition to the food there was a world of things to drink: cucumber water, lemonade, and of course wine. Lots and lots of wine, provided as a handfasting gift by Mme. Cuthbert of La Maison Bleue.

Then there were the marzipan creations for which Elka was most famous. Elka had thought long and hard about this, wanting to symbolize what many saw as a mystical union between two people operating on similar spiritual planes. In the end a fiery sun and half moon seemed to symbolize it best, each candy decorated differently and with exquisite precision.

Of course the pièce de résistance was her handfasting cake, a towering confection of white pastry and icing decorated with summer blossoms of every color. Small figures representing Max and Awena stood atop the cake, holding hands.

Elka, not quite believing she had pulled it off, took dozens of photos for her Web site. Orders from future brides and grooms already had started to pour in.

And then there was Awena, the bride herself, resplendent as all the meteors of heaven on a clear night, in a foamy ashes-of-roses dress she had made herself, a dress that shone and glittered with a million beaded and appliqued flowers in oranges, reds, and yellows, colors chosen to represent both the warmth of the summer sun and the approaching changes of the harvest season. Her dark hair with its streak of white at the temple had been braided through with vines and flowers.

The ceremony was held on Lammas Day, a day to celebrate the first wheat harvest of the year, and officiated by a woman from Awena's childhood in Wales, a woman of wide-ranging druidical beliefs who yet operated within the confines of the established church. Druidism, recognized in the United Kingdom as a religion, did not particularly speak to Awena's own beliefs but was flexible enough that a Universal Mind was acknowledged in the ceremony—a ceremony preceded by a brief civil union in Monkslip-super-Mare, to placate the authorities and Max, who had insisted on it.

Sitting in the congregation for the handfasting were Awena's sisters from Wales, Max's mother, and assorted cousins and nieces and nephews belonging to both bride and groom. DCI Cotton was there, of course, along with Sergeant Essex, to watch Max and Awena promise to live lives full of courage and love. Also in attendance were the Bishop of Monkslip and his wife, she in a fascinator hat and beige mother-of-the-bride type of linen suit. They both looked determinedly game if rather bewildered by the proceedings, and they may have stumbled a bit over the responses, but as the bishop had told Max on receiving the handfasting invitation: "I don't see how Awena can meet us halfway unless we try to do the same for her beliefs and customs. And I hope I'm not too old to learn new things." The generosity of the statement summed up everything Max loved and admired about the man, completely describing how the bishop had achieved the highest reaches of his calling.

Music was provided by the small, high voices of the Nether Monkslip Angel Choir singing *a cappella* and, for the after-festivities, by the St. Edwold's Rock of Ages band, which seemed to get better as the night wore on and the wine disappeared. As a special request from Max, they played "I'll Never Find Another You," by the Seekers. Max and Awena, laughing, held hands as they followed the age-old custom of jumping over an antique sword, to symbolize the cutting of old ties. The dancing and whooping and celebrating went on into the wee hours. There was no one to complain of the noise, for the entire village was there.

And for a little space of time, Max and Awena came to know that it was true, that happiness was not in the future, and never in the past, but right in the here and now.

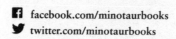